Daddy's Girl

Lin Stepp

Daddy's Girl

A SMOKY MOUNTAIN NOVEL

LIN STEPP

MOUNTAIN HILL PRESS

Daddy's Girl
Copyright © 2017 by Lin Stepp
Published by Mountain Hill Press
Email contact: steppcom@aol.com

This is a work of fiction. Although numerous elements of historical and geographic accuracy are utilized in this and other novels in the Smoky Mountain series, many other specific environs, place names, characters, and incidents are the product of the author's imagination or used fictitiously.

Scripture used in this book, whether quoted or paraphrased by the characters, is taken from the King James Version of the Bible.

Cover design: Katherine E. Stepp
Interior design: J. L. Stepp, Mountain Hill Press
Editor: Kim Peterson
Cover image and map design: Lin M. Stepp

Library of Congress Cataloging-in-Publication Data

Stepp, Lin
Daddy's Girl: A Smoky Mountain novel / Lin Stepp
          p. cm – (The Smoky Mountain series; bk. #10)
ISBN: 978-0-9985063-0-2
First Mountain Hill Press Trade Paperback Printing: April 2017

eISBN: 978-0-9985063-1-9
First Mountain Hill Press Electronic Edition: April 2017

1. Women—Southern States—Fiction   2. Mountain life—Great Smoky Mountains Region (NC and TN)—Fiction. 3. Contemporary Romance—Inspirational—Fiction. I. Title

Library of Congress Control Number: 2017901371

Printed in the United States of America

This book is dedicated to Pat McCarter of Broadway Flower Shop in Lenoir City, Tennessee, who offered fabulous consulting tips for my novel and let me spend a happy workday in her shop learning about the operations of a florist business. Thank you Pat!

ACKNOWLEDGMENTS

Acknowledgment and thanks goes to the charming city of Bryson City, North Carolina, where this book is set and to its wonderful citizens who graciously welcomed my husband and me into their lives and businesses while we researched this novel. Special appreciation goes to the Miller family, who own Deep Creek Store and Campground, and to Sue Miller for taking us on a tour of the area and sharing local stories with us. Thanks also to Gil Crouch of Gil's Bookstore, now O'Neill's Shop on the Corner, where I enjoyed happy book signings in past for my Smoky Mountain novels. Please note that one or two businesses mentioned in this novel have changed hands or closed since this book was written but I still wanted to celebrate them in memory. Any mistakes in Bryson City place names or facts are purely the author's fault.

Heartfelt thanks goes to my fine editor Kim Peterson, for her meticulous work and help in making this book the best it could be, and to my daughter and graphic arts designer Kate Stepp for the beautiful book cover design. The photo on the cover of *Daddy's Girl* was taken on the Deep Creek Trail in the Great Smoky Mountains National Park outside of Bryson City—one of our favorite hiking trails in the area.

Continuing gratitude in this and every book written goes to my husband and companion in my writing journey, J.L. Stepp, … and to the Lord for His generous inspiration and guidance in all I do.

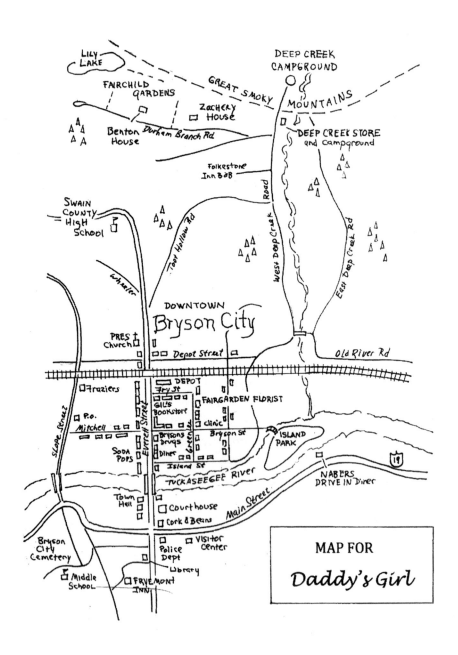

MAP FOR

Daddy's Girl

CHAPTER 1

Olivia pushed away an odd sense of unease she'd felt all day as she hurried down the main street of Bryson City, trying not to bump into the summer tourists. Spotting Bryson's Drugstore ahead she smiled and slowed her pace. Few old pharmacies existed like Bryson's anymore complete with an authentic fifties soda fountain, twirling stools, and vintage booths with red vinyl seats.

"Just another reason to love small town USA," she said, pushing open the door and activating the chime she'd heard a zillion times.

"You're late," Roberta Simmons called from their favorite booth by the front window.

"I know." Her eyes moved with fondness over her three long-time friends as she slipped into her spot beside Louise Riley Frazier. "I got tied up at the store."

Louise shot her a pixie grin, a cute match to her short dark hair and elfin face. "It's okay. I was late, too. I ordered a diet cola for you already." She pushed a frosty glass toward Olivia along with a menu. "Rob's meeting with the embalmer at the funeral home ran over schedule so I had to wait before I could leave Eva with him."

Roberta wrinkled her nose at Louise's words. "Eeew, Lulu. I can't believe you leave that child in a funeral home when you go out, even if Rob's family does own the place. The idea creeps me out."

Louise opened her mouth to reply but Roberta ignored her, snatching Olivia's menu out of her hand. "No egg or tuna salads today, Olivia Benton. We're throwing diets to the wind and ordering burgers and fries." She waved to the waitress walking toward their table and held up a finger. "Make that one more, Charlene."

"Actually I'd planned on ordering ..." Olivia started to protest and then shrugged.

"Roberta rules," Vickie Leigh said in a singsong voice before giggling. "You know it's useless to argue with her. In fact, it has *always* been useless to argue with her about anything."

Roberta examined a perfectly manicured nail. "You make me sound like an ogre, Vickie Leigh Derryberry."

Vickie shrugged, pulling up the top of a chartreuse tank top that had slipped to reveal a little too much cleavage. "Come on, Roberta. You *are* bossy and surely you can't deny being the undisputed leader in our group ever since middle school." She looked across the table. "The same way Olivia was always our fair beauty, Lulu the cute one, and me always the ...." Her voice trailed off as she searched for the right words.

"The easy one?" Roberta gave her a cat-like smile, her eyes drifting over Vickie's loose wavy hair, tight shirt and big dangling loop earrings.

"That is so *not* nice." Vickie colored.

"And not true, either." Olivia reached across the table to squeeze Vickie Leigh's hand. "You were always the *fun* one."

Vickie sent Olivia a grateful smile. "Thanks. You're nice as well as beautiful. Unlike *some* people I could name." She raised her eyebrows at Roberta. "And just because I got divorced, doesn't mean I..."

Roberta interrupted. "Divorced *twice*." She stirred her straw in her cola and looked out the window. "Both times before twenty-four."

"Why are you picking on me today?" Vickie kicked at her under the table.

"Simply bored, I guess." Roberta fingered a silver necklace around her neck in a distracted way. "Sorry."

"Well, I am *seriously* working on my self-esteem, so you tread carefully, Roberta Ray Simmons." Vickie tossed her head. "An article I read in *Cosmopolitan* magazine at the beauty salon said you need to challenge those who try to put you down and value yourself so others will, too."

"I read that same article." Louise's face lit. "The author said to focus on the positive about yourself and to not be distracted by criticism."

Roberta ignored them, leaning toward the window with sudden interest. "My, my, would you take a look at that, girls." She pointed with one finger. "A black Mercedes Benz SLS with a tall, sweet-looking man climbing out of it."

Diverted, Vickie Leigh turned toward the plate glass window by their table. "Oh, wow. Who *is* that? He certainly doesn't look like a Bryson City boy, that's for sure."

Louise peered through the glass, squinting in the July sun. "Hmmm. Sharp clothes. Movie-star sunglasses. Suit jacket even in July. And he's checking a smartphone. See him scrolling the screen with his finger?" She shook her head. "No. I don't think he's from around here. Wish I could see the license plates on his car."

Olivia glanced toward the stranger briefly and then back to the waitress bringing their lunch order. "Our food's here, girls. Let's eat." She helped Charlene pass the plates.

Vickie's mouth dropped open as she craned her neck around Roberta to see out the window again. "Oh, my gosh. I think he's coming across the street right toward us. Can you believe it?"

"Well, then quit staring." Olivia frowned.

Vickie tried to pull her gaze away from the window.

"Olivia's right." With reluctance, Louise turned her attention back to her food. "We probably shouldn't stare."

A slow smile curled Roberta's lips. "I don't think I'll quit staring—nice or not." She practically purred the words, her eyes still following the stranger. "I'm watching every single minute of this diverting little drama because this *particular* boy's no stranger at all."

The bell on the drugstore's door chimed and Roberta's deep laugh sounded after it. "Well, would you look at who the cat's dragged in?"

A deep voice replied. "I see the Scratch Cats are still hogging the front booth at the drug store window." The man laughed. "Haven't you girls found anything better to do since high school?"

Olivia, her back to the door, froze. She knew that voice.

"Well, Warner Zachery in the flesh." Vickie Leigh flipped her red hair flirtatiously. "Who would have thought you'd turn out so fine?"

Warner laughed while Louise kicked at her under the table. "Watch your tongue, Vickie Leigh."

Roberta smiled. "Oh, I'd say Warner knows he looks a little better than the last time we saw him. When was that, Warner? Ten years ago at least, I think."

He pulled off his sunglasses and slipped them into his jacket pocket. "You should know, Roberta, since you e-mailed me an announcement for our ten-year class reunion only a few weeks ago."

"So I did." She picked up a napkin to toy with it. "But you're a little early for that, aren't you? The reunion isn't until Swain High's Labor Day weekend game in September."

Olivia took a shaky breath. She could feel Warner's presence behind her, even smell a waft of some citrus musk cologne he wore, but she couldn't seem to collect herself. *Count to ten, Olivia. It's only Warner. Turn around with a polite smile and say hello before someone notices you're acting odd.*

She forced herself to pivot in the booth. "Hello, Warner. How nice to see you." She let her eyes drift past him to the pharmacy department further back in the store. "I'm sure your father will be glad to see you, and I think Vance is working today. I guess they know you're in town."

"Not yet. I just got here."

She sensed his eyes on her but couldn't bring herself to meet his gaze.

"How long are you staying, Warner?" Louise asked. "I know Rob would love to see you if you'll be in town for a while."

"I'd like to see Rob." Warner leaned against the side of the booth.

"I heard you two married."

"Yes. Five years ago this summer, and we have a little girl named Eva who turned two last month. I'm sure you remember Rob and I dated in high school, but you probably don't know we shared two years together at Western Carolina before Rob transferred to the College of Mortuary in Cincinnati. I really missed him, but it helped that Olivia went to Western with me during that time." Louise chatted away merrily as if absolutely nothing was wrong.

Olivia wanted to throttle her.

Roberta, watching Olivia's reaction with interest, said, "Why don't you pull up a chair, Warner, if you're going to chat a while?"

He paused, studying her—everyone suddenly quiet and waiting for his answer. "Perhaps I will," he said at last, pulling a chair over from a nearby table and then straddling it to prop an arm on its back.

His knee brushed against Olivia's and she thought she'd scream with the contact. *What was he doing here? Why hadn't she heard he was coming?*

Warner glanced around the table with a small smile. "So ... what have you She Cats been up to these years?"

Roberta leaned an elbow on the table and eyed him thoughtfully "Off to college like you. Then getting married. Coming back to settle down in Bryson."

"Not *all* of us are married." Vickie Leigh fluttered her eyelashes.

Warner ignored her remark, reaching to snatch one of Olivia's French fries and settling a smile on Louise. "Why don't you catch me up on everyone, Lulu."

Louise, sensing nothing amiss, brightened. "Well, let's see. You know Rob works at Frazier's, his family's funeral home." She paused. "Roberta went to Vanderbilt, where Russell Simmons went, too. They dated, then married while Russell finished dental school, and later came back home. Russell has a practice near the hospital and they have two little boys now, Conner three years old and Eddie one."

She hesitated, looking toward Vickie Leigh.

Vickie waved a hand. "Oh, I've experienced two unfortunate marriages. One impulsive one to a kayaker I met working at Nantahala my first summer out of high school after Logan and I broke up. When that relationship fizzled out, I linked up with a man in Sylva. He seemed real nice but turned out to be abusive and an alcoholic." She looked down at her hands. "That proved a real bad time for me but after our divorce he moved away—thank goodness. I'm making a whole new life now and working at the Swain County Visitor Center."

"She's going out with Logan Staley again, too," Louise chimed in.

"We've gone out on *three* dates. That's all." Vickie Leigh waved three fingers for emphasis. "That hardly means we're a couple, Louise. I'm takin' my time to be sure I find the *right* man this go around." She sent Warner a suggestive glance.

"And Olivia?" Warner turned blue eyes toward her then—familiar, Mediterranean blue eyes that the light could play over to change the hue.

Olivia swallowed, trying to find words in reply.

Vickie Leigh spoke up as she hesitated. "Oh, Olivia's turned down more good proposals than beads and bangles on my charm bracelet." She shook the silver bracelet on her wrist with a giggle. "Both Russell Simmons and Brody Hanks tried to get her to marry them right after high school." Her eyes shifted to Roberta. "Sorry, Roberta, but you *know* Russell bounced you two girls back and forth all through high school, and he *did* propose to Olivia once before you and Russell went off to college together."

"You can be sure I made Russell regret that momentary lapse in judgment, Vickie Leigh." Roberta's cool voice intervened.

Overlooking her remark, Vickie continued her story. "Two more boys at college chased after Olivia and proposed—Louise probably remembers their names, since she and Olivia went to Western together—and then after college Matthew Bradford dated Olivia and wanted to marry her. You remember Matthew; he graduated a couple of years ahead of us. He owns that chiropractic clinic on the highway now—makes good money. Then that handsome

Evan Parker pursued Olivia while she worked with Verlie McBride at The Flower Box. I never could understand why Olivia let Evan get away. He's vice president at the bank in Sylva now and *so* good-looking."

Olivia wanted to slide under the table.

Vickie sighed. "I swear, Olivia has such favor with men. Lucky thing. Now she's dating Brody Hanks *and* that nice doctor, Martin Reese, who works for her father at the clinic. Maybe with her florist business all set up, she'll pick one of them and finally settle down."

Fighting embarrassment, Olivia focused on her food.

Roberta sent her a smug look and then turned her eyes back to Warner. "I believe Olivia turned you down once, too, Warner—but maybe I don't remember that right."

Warner picked up another of Olivia's French fries. "A lot of gossip circulates in small towns. It's hard to know what's accurate and what's made up."

Olivia felt like smacking him.

"I also heard you lost your wife a year ago." Roberta picked at her necklace again. "We were sorry to learn that. It must have been terrible—a shooting or something wasn't it?"

"Yes."

Warner's face closed over. He glanced behind him toward the pharmacy area. "I see my dad's come back from lunch." He stood and pushed his chair back into place at the nearby table. "See you girls around."

He strolled toward the back of the store, and they could see a little of the warm greetings that ensued between Warner, his father, his brother Vance and his grandfather "Doc" Floyd. The Zacherys, a close-knit family group, had owned Bryson's Drugs for three generations.

Sensing Roberta watching her, Olivia slid out of the booth. "I need to go to the restroom." She angled across the store to the bathroom, eager for a few minutes of privacy to catch her breath.

She locked the door to the ladies room and leaned her head against it, trying to calm her heart and thoughts. Ten years had slipped by since she last saw Warner. Ten long years. She assumed she wouldn't feel anything anymore. That time would erase all the old feelings she'd once held for Warner Zachery. Obviously not.

Walking to the mirror over the sink, she studied her reflection. *Had any of her feelings shown?* Olivia hoped not because it was far too late for any future with Warner. It had been too late for a long time. They'd both moved on, made different lives.

"Perhaps he won't stay long." Olivia pulled a lipstick from her purse to busy her hands. "And even if he does, I probably won't see him much."

But, oh, how he's changed. Bolder, more confident, and sure of himself. So well dressed and easy in the way he walked and talked. Nothing like the Warner of the past, especially the Warner whenever others were around.

"That probably explains my feelings," she whispered. The shock of seeing how much he'd changed and that she didn't expect to see him today, the surprise alone would create a reaction.

Feeling better, she put away her lipstick, walked back through the drugstore, and scooted into the booth with her friends. When she glanced toward the pharmacy, Louise caught her gaze. "He's left already."

Vickie Leigh giggled. "And, goodness me, we enjoyed seeing him stroll across the street again. He looks as good from the back as from the front."

Louise sipped at the last of her cola. "Isn't it amazing how a person can change that much? I always remember Warner as sort of awkward and uncomfortable with himself, usually acting weird or odd in some way."

"Weird Warner." Roberta looked out the window to where his car had been parked. "He always followed his own drummer and never seemed to care what anyone thought much of the time. At other times you could tell he wished he could fit in. Belong more." She laughed. "Did you see his face when I asked him to pull up a chair?"

"That was almost mean." Louise made a face. "You only used to invite the most popular boys to pull up a chair to our booth. I don't think Warner knew what to do for a moment when you asked."

"Oh, I don't know." Roberta smoothed a hand down her silk blouse. "He seemed to handle himself very well with that little test."

"You were testing him?" Olivia blurted out the words.

"Well, sure." She shrugged. "He looked different. And we've all heard he found success after he moved to the city. He seemed suave and New York City from end to end, but I wanted to see if the change went past the surface. Obviously, it did."

Vickie Leigh finished the last bite of her hamburger and pushed her plate away. "He seemed real upset when we mentioned his wife, didn't he?"

"Well, sure. Who wouldn't be?" Louise straightened the headband holding back her short hair. "We all heard some crazy thief came into the neighborhood grocery store and shot up the place. Went nuts or something. Killed three people, including the cashier and Warner's wife."

"Probably someone on drugs or a wacko." Vickie fingered an earring. "I feel sorry for Warner. It must be awful to lose your wife in such a tragic way." She frowned. "Granted, sometimes I used to wish crazy Bob, my second husband, would get shot at the bar one night instead of coming home full of vinegar, but I never really wished him dead."

Roberta looked out the window once more. "Well, it's kind of nice to see how Warner has turned his life around. I always thought he'd stay weird and never make much of himself. Most everyone else thought so, too." She paused. "Remember when he first left for college in New York? He went on some sort of scholarship, of course—Warner always was smart—but he worked as a janitor somewhere in the city while in school. It seemed so typical. Then he worked in some other low skill job." She turned her eyes toward Olivia in question.

"I think his mother told me he worked cleaning and as a gofer for one of the big publishing companies—did odd jobs and ran errands." Olivia had kept in touch more than the rest of them, since Warner's family lived next door to hers.

Roberta brushed some loose crumbs off the table with her napkin. "Funny how Warner suddenly got that big crush on you toward the end of high school, Olivia—and actually asked you to the prom. Can you believe he dared to do that? As though you'd be caught dead going to the senior prom with Weird Warner." She laughed and Vickie Leigh joined in.

Louise wrinkled her nose. "Actually, I always thought Warner was really nice most of the time. I felt kind of sorry for him being so odd with both his older brothers sports stars and real popular in high school." Her eyes drifted around the drugstore. "It helped Warner being a Zachery, though. Everyone likes the Zachery family and the drugstore, so we never acted too mean to Warner."

"Who said we were *ever* mean?" Roberta asked.

Vickie Leigh flipped her hair. "Roberta honey, we were *all* Scratch Cats a lot of the time to the less popular kids. That's simply the way high school was. But we're older now. Times change."

Yes, thought Olivia. *Times do change.*

When she let herself in the door of Fairgarden Florist a short time later, Olivia's emotions still simmered in turmoil. After moving through the front display room, she tucked her purse on a shelf under the register and sat down on a stool to look through the mail.

"Hey, Patti, I'm back." She glanced to where Patti Headrick, her assistant manager and best designer, sat working on a lavish arrangement of flowers at her desk. "Has it been busy?"

"Not much." Patti angled a white spider mum into the glass vase. "Only a few customers and calls. I hope you had a nice lunch."

Olivia nodded.

"Did you hear the Mexican restaurant got hit by the vandal last night?" Patti paused on the lush arrangement, partially assembled. "We heard it from Mr. Bumgartner."

Wanda Baylor, Olivia's other full-time employee and floral designer, walked in from the workroom carrying a handful of bright, silk sunflowers. "Yeah, that daffy Mr. Bumgartner came in while you were gone. He said the vandal wrote stuff all over the restaurant windows."

"That's too bad." Olivia glanced toward Wanda. "Did Mr. Bumgartner place an order with us when he came in?"

"Yeah." Wanda rolled her eyes. "He wants another floral wreath to drape over his wife's grave. Daisies this time. Said she always loved daisies in summer." She settled on the stool at her workstation behind Patti's. "I told him I didn't know if we had enough Gerbera daisies in stock to do the whole monument wreath in daisies alone, but I said you had purple coneflowers blooming at the Fairchild Gardens you might bring in tomorrow for us to mix with the daisies. I told him coneflowers looked a lot like daisies and that I thought Lucille would like them."

She worked several big sunflowers into the grapevine wreath on her desktop and then held the wreath up to study its design. "Do you suppose he'll ever stop taking flowers to his wife's grave every season of the year? Lucille has been gone four years now."

"Sometimes it's hard to move on." Olivia sighed and shook her head. "Memories linger and then come back to haunt you. The past doesn't always stay tucked away in the past."

"Well, diddley-dee, that sounds way too serious for a sunny July afternoon." Wanda put a hand on one plump hip. "Are you all right, Olivia? You look a little pale even for you."

Patti scowled. "What does *that* remark mean, Wanda Baylor?"

"Oh, don't get all defensive. You know Olivia has the sort of pale, fragile complexion that makes it hard to notice if she whites out."

Olivia couldn't help laughing. She always found it hard to stay moody around Wanda. "I'm fine, Wanda, but thanks for worrying."

Wanda flashed a big smile. "Well, I'm glad everything is okay and I hope you enjoyed a nice time with your girlfriends." She stood to pull down a spool of yellow ribbon from a high shelf for her wreath.

"You'll never guess what we heard while you were gone." She

wound off a length of wired ribbon from the spool. "W. T. Zachery, that celebrity guy from Bryson City, is coming back to town. Patti's boy Rich told us. He saw a sign in Gil's Bookstore announcing a book signing at the store next weekend. Can you believe it? Right here in Bryson City—and him so famous for writing all those young people's books that the teens and kids are so crazy about." She looked toward Patti. "What are they called?"

Patti looked up from her arrangement and smiled. "The Geeky Gilmore books. Richard loves them. He's read every one of them multiple times and practically idolizes W. T. Zachery, the author. He's thrilled that he might get to meet him. He got so excited earlier I had to remind him three times where to deliver the birthday arrangement for the Hanson birthday luncheon."

Out of school for summer, Richard did occasional in-town deliveries to places where he could walk or bike. Patti rented a small house on the street behind Olivia's florist shop, so Richard could help on deliveries with little notice.

Olivia looked up from the mail she sifted through. "So Richard likes Warner's work?"

"Loves it. He's read those Geeky Gilmore books until they're practically threadbare." She tucked a sprig of purple statice into her growing arrangement of white roses, mums, and pink carnations.

"You've got such a gift with color and arrangement," Wanda commented, leaning over to watch Patti place several other branches of statice into the vase for balance and symmetry. "Did you learn all that with your grandparents?"

Patti ran her fingers through her short crop of black hair. "Yes. My Italian grandparents loved their florist shop, and I lived in an apartment above it with them, so I grew up around the business. I started arranging flowers as soon as I grew big enough to climb on a stool to reach a station." She chuckled. "I guess it was much the same for you, Olivia, growing up beside Fairchild Gardens and working in the gardens with your mother and your grandmother Lila Fairchild. You told me you started learning to make arrangements as a child, too."

Wanda began to twine the ivy into her wreath. "Well, I started later than both of you, working for Verlie at The Flower Box while in high school, but she made a fine teacher."

Olivia sent her a genuine smile. "Yes, she did, Wanda, and you're becoming a good floral designer in your own right. Verlie would feel really proud to see all you're doing now—and to know you earned your Accreditation in Floral Design."

"Thanks, Olivia." Wanda smiled, settling back to work on her wreath. A large, full-figured girl, Wanda possessed a smile and laugh that lit up a room, a big contrast to the quieter and petite Patti.

Olivia didn't know what she'd do without either of them at the florist.

"You know my Vern was so proud of me for gettin' that accreditation he took me to a fancy dinner at the Fryemont Inn when my certificate came in the mail." Wanda wiggled her eyebrows. "You girls are missing out on a lot of perks not being married."

Rich burst in the front door then, a tall, lanky boy of twelve with a mop of dark, black hair like his mother's and Italian brown eyes. "Guess what? I saw W. T. Zachery." Rich loped to the cash register to drop off the signed delivery slip from Pasqualinos. "I really did—no kidding—driving right down Everett Street in a big black car that looks like the Batmobile in the comics."

Olivia couldn't help laughing. "That black Benz *does* look like a Batmobile. I'll bet Warner chose it for exactly that reason. He always loved Batman and decided to go to Cooper Union in New York partly because that's where Bob Kane, the creator of Batman, went to college."

Rich turned to her, mouth dropping open. "Wow. I always forget you know W. T. Zachery, Miss Olivia. You're so lucky." He jumped on an empty stool by the counter, babbling on about how Warner looked, what he wore. "I can't believe he's going to do a book signing here next week. Man, I'm going to buy another copy of every one of his books and get him to sign them. Won't that be cool?"

The ongoing chatter proved too much for Olivia's nerves. She glanced at the big clock on the wall. "You know, since it's slow this afternoon, I think I'll go home early. I want to see if I have enough coneflowers in the garden for that monument wreath for Mr. Bumgartner." She tucked a pile of papers into the drawer and stood. "I'll cut the flowers in the morning before I come into the shop if I do. If there aren't enough coneflowers, I can bring dahlias or gaillardias to mix in. I'll let you do the wreath for Mr. Bumgartner, Wanda, since you took the order. He'd like that."

"Okay. I'll fix it up real nice for him." Wanda grinned.

After some final chitchat, Olivia walked to her office to retrieve her purse. As she left through the back door, Richard prattled on and on about the wonderful W. T. Zachery.

"Honestly," Olivia muttered as she started her car. "However did Weird Warner Zachery, with his clothes that never matched and his black glasses usually taped with a wad of duct tape on some broken spot, turn into the wonderful W. T. Zachery?" Her mind played over the mystery as she drove out West Deep Creek Road behind Bryson City toward home. As she drew closer to the Great Smoky Mountains National Park boundary, she turned left to follow several quieter side streets to Durham Branch Road.

She glanced at the Zachery family's rambling country home as she passed. *I wonder if Warner will stay here with his family or in town somewhere?* Slowing her car, she stopped at the mailbox in front of her house, a stately, white two-story with black shutters and a pillared porch. The Fairchild Gardens, hidden by tall brick walls, spread behind it.

As she let herself in the side sunroom door of the Benton house, she found her father scrounging through the refrigerator in the kitchen.

"Is that you, Olivia?" he called, closing the refrigerator door with one hand while balancing two plastic storage containers in the other.

She stopped in the kitchen doorway. "You're home early, Daddy.

Looking for something to eat?" Olivia eyed the food containers. "If you'll hold off, I can start supper in a few minutes."

"No. No." He sat the containers on the table next to a plate, a sleeve of crackers, and a spreading knife. "I've got a funeral to attend and thought I'd grab a snack to tide me over until after the service. Martha Bills, one of my patients, died."

Olivia sat her purse on the side counter and opened the refrigerator again to pull out a pitcher of tea. "Do you need me to go with you?" She dropped ice cubes into two glasses and poured tea for them both.

"No." Ray Benton settled into a kitchen chair. "You didn't know her. Helen did though. She's going to meet me at Frazier's for the visitation at five and then the service." He spread leftover dip, thick with spinach and water chestnuts, over a couple of crackers and then snagged a handful of purple grapes from the other container.

Remembering how little lunch she'd eaten, Olivia got a plate of her own and sat down to join him. "What time will you be home? I'll plan dinner around that time."

Between bites, he said, "I thought I'd take Helen to eat supper with me afterward since it may be late." He smiled across at her. "It'll give you a nice break from cooking for your old dad tonight."

She smiled back. "Daddy, you know I love cooking for you."

He studied her, frowning. "I know, I know. But it worries me sometimes that you don't get out more. See more young people your own age."

"Silly. I shared lunch with the girls today, and went to the theatre in Cherokee this weekend with Martin, your new doctor." She spread dip on a cracker. "The weekend before, I went to a cookout with my school friends after the annual Fourth of July festival downtown."

"Hmmph." He cleared his throat. "I suppose you stay busy enough, but you're still not married. Time's getting away and you're twenty-seven years old now, heading toward twenty-eight in September. I'd like to dangle a few grandchildren on my knees before they get too arthritic to support them."

She put down her cracker. "Daddy, are you okay?"

"What?" He looked up in surprise. "Oh, I'm fine, just fine."

She studied him thoughtfully while he spread another cracker with spinach dip, her eyes moving over his full, kindly face, his hair totally white now and a little thin on the top. Silver-rimmed glasses perched on his nose and, although a little overweight at fifty-nine, his shoulders remained broad and his posture straight.

"What's the verdict?" he asked, catching her eye and grinning.

"You look very fit to me and, in fact, very handsome and distinguished." She crossed her arms. "Except that I hope you'll change your shirt before going to the funeral. I see barbeque stains on the front."

He glanced down. "Yep, remnants of lunch from the Bar-B-Q Wagon. My lab coat covered the spots at work, but I'd better pitch the shirt in the hamper and put on a clean one before I leave."

Olivia poured him another glass of tea. "What did Martha Bills die from?"

Her dad shrugged. "Old age and a weak heart. I watched her go down in health and grow frailer after she turned ninety-six this last year. I wasn't surprised to hear about the heart attack. It's a blessing in some ways she died quietly at home without having to go into a nursing home. Her daughters had started looking at homes last month, worrying about her living way up the mountain by herself."

Olivia nodded, popping a grape into her mouth.

"I heard Warner Zachery was back in town." Ray Benton changed the subject. "About time, I'd say. He hasn't come home once to visit his family since he left ten years ago. That's disgraceful. I don't see why he couldn't have visited now and again, especially after making a little money with that writing work he does." He frowned. "That boy always did do his own thing without much regard for what was proper. Plane fare isn't that much from New York to Asheville. He could've flown in and rented a car to drive the sixty-fives miles to Bryson City."

Olivia suppressed a prickle of annoyance. "I remember no one thought Warner would amount to much of anything and everyone criticized him going so far away to New York City to study." She watched her father's face. "I guess he surprised people, turning out successful."

"Hmmph. Writing's not a very stable career choice. No regular income and subject to the whim of the public. Popular today and forgotten tomorrow—that's how that sort of work can go." He waved his spreading knife for emphasis.

Olivia had certainly heard this spiel before. "Maybe so, Daddy, but you have to admit Warner's done all right—with the Geeky Gilmore books becoming national best-sellers and then signing movie rights a few years ago."

Her father's eyes met hers. "He's been lucky. Most authors or illustrators don't make enough to live on from their work and they need to carry another job for their living. However, the boy might be all right now if he invests wisely. His father says some big money passed into his hands with that movie deal. I hope he doesn't fritter it away." He finished his tea. "The talk is he rolled into town today in a Mercedes—danged expensive car, those. Boy probably bought it just to make an impression. Always was a bit of a show-off. He once rode a skateboard down the courthouse steps. Almost got arrested, too. Remember that?"

Seeing no point in answering, Olivia stood to put the tea pitcher back in the refrigerator, popped the tops back on the plastic storage containers to put them away, and then sat back down. "It's nearly four, Daddy. If you want to shower and change, you'd better get started."

He glanced at the clock. "Yep. Do you have a good book or something to entertain yourself with tonight?"

She nodded. "Yes, and I plan to work in the garden until dark, maybe a little longer since you won't be home until late."

He got up and leaned over to place a kiss on her forehead. "Always eager to work in the garden, exactly like your blessed mother. I still miss her, even after fifteen years. Going to funerals always makes me remember more keenly." He sighed. "Helen says the same thing. She lost Bob three years ago, so her wound's even fresher."

"But Helen has her shop, and it's doing well. I heard she added some nice home accents very popular with the tourists."

"Hmmph. No shop or business keeps you warm at night." He gave her a pointed look.

Olivia shook her head. "Daddy, you don't want me to marry someone I don't love, do you—simply to be married?"

He considered this. "No. But love often grows from friendship and you tend to cut off your relationships about the time they're warming up. Give young Martin a chance since you're seeing him. He's a good man and a fine doctor." He looked away, his thoughts drifting. "I met your mother before I came to Bryson City to practice with her father. Never regretted a moment being married to her."

"I know." She stood to kiss her father's cheek before he left the room. "Martin is nice, Daddy. He's asked me out for dinner again this weekend—so I haven't chased him off yet."

"As though you could chase anyone off," he mumbled as he left the room. "Prettiest girl in town. Can't see any reason why someone hasn't snatched you up."

CHAPTER 2

W.T. Zachery experienced a thrill of pleasure and recognition as he crossed the bridge on Hwy 19 over the Tuckaseegee River. He was nearly home—or home to where he grew up. The city of New York, where he lived now, was a long way from Bryson City, North Carolina, a small town nestled on the southern side of the Great Smoky Mountains National Park.

He glanced with humor at the GPS navigational map on the dashboard. It would soon cease to chart his way along the backwoods roads around Bryson City. His cell phone probably wouldn't work, either, in the remote areas. Good. He'd come for a well-needed break—and perhaps more. New York no longer seemed the same since Nelle died. Warner often felt restless, tired and stressed, discontent with the city. When he walked the downtown streets there, he experienced no excitement and joy anymore. And his writing had fallen off.

His grandfather advised, "Go home for a while. Paint with your mother. Hike the hills and mountains. Spend time with your family. Do simple things again."

"A change will do you good." His grandmother agreed.

Warner had spent a lot of time with his Delacourt grandparents on Staten Island since Nelle died. Or more correctly, since Nelle was murdered. A big difference. Death made you sad, but murder made you angry and sad.

As he pulled into the Hot Spot for gas, people paused to stare at his car. A Mercedes was ritzy for Bryson City standards. An extravagance to cluck over. But he'd wanted to drive the car down to the mountains. New York wasn't a place for cars, and the Benz sat parked in a garage most of the year. He'd received it through some promotional deal his agent negotiated. Success had its perks.

Back on the highway, he turned onto Everett Street, the main street through Bryson City, passed the old courthouse with its gold dome and then crossed the bridge over the Tuckaseegee River. Flags still hung on many of the buildings from the big Fourth of July Freedom Fest held earlier in the month. He couldn't make it in time for the annual festival, still finishing the last of his book tour signings and all the media interviews his publisher had scheduled in selected cities on his route south. Worn out last night from his three final events scheduled in Asheville, he'd crashed in a motel room before heading out again this morning.

Seeing the prominent drug store sign for his family's business ahead on the right, W. T. cruised past, made a left at the next traffic light, and then headed back up Everett Street to snag an empty parking slot across from the store. Climbing out of the car, he pulled out his iPhone to make a call.

"Leonard," he said, after hearing his old friend's voice. "I just pulled into a parking slot across from Bryson's. I'm going to run in and see Dad and Grandpa—let them know I'm home—then I'll head to your office for lunch. Can you hang around until then?"

"Sure." His friend laughed. "I'll keep attacking this pile of paperwork on my desk. Take your time. We've got a nutty vandal in town with a new incident I need to write up, too."

W. T. clicked off the phone, dropped it into his pocket, then headed across the street between the traffic flow.

A throaty voice met him as he let himself in the door. "Well, would you look at who the cat's dragged in?"

He glanced toward the voice to see Roberta Ray Simmons seated in the front booth of the drugstore with Vicki Leigh Derryberry beside her. Across from them he could see Lulu Riley Frazier, turning to peer over the top of the booth, and beside her a familiar head of light blond hair.

W. T. sucked in a breath. He'd known he would see Olivia Benton eventually. Funny it would be here in the old drug store booth that the four elite girls of Swain County High School always claimed as their own. Wasn't that a déjà vu event?

Listening to Roberta's baiting, watching Vickie Leigh flirting and batting her eyes, and hearing Louise prattling away almost pulled him back in time. Except that he was different now. He could see their actions and ways like he couldn't before, even laughing at many of their comments. How ironic. He was hardly the awkward boy of those past days.

W.T might not have stopped to talk to them at all, if it hadn't been for Olivia. Already, he could smell the sweet floral scent of her, stirring old memories. He pulled off his sunglasses and slipped them into his jacket pocket, leaning nonchalantly against the side of the booth behind her and waiting for her to turn around, while bantering back and forth with Roberta. Was Olivia purposely ignoring him? Surely she wasn't still angry at him after ten years for daring to leave Bryson City. He stepped forward, more directly into her vision.

She spoke at last, saying hello, and he watched the effort it took. Her eyes didn't meet his directly but drifted instead toward the pharmacy at the back of the store, while she made some comment about his family.

He studied her as she talked, noticing that, if anything, she'd grown even more beautiful. The sun played over her white blond hair, making it shine, and her complexion glowed porcelain and peach. He could see her clear blue eyes looking toward the pharmacy counter, if not at him, and noted her figure still hourglass perfect. Olivia Benton had always been the prettiest girl in Bryson City. That certainly hadn't changed.

"How long are you staying, Warner?" Louise interrupted his thoughts, reminding him once more that, here in Bryson, he would simply be Warner again and not W. T. Zachery.

He lingered, making idle conversation with Lulu. She still had the cute, pixie looks he recalled, Vickie Leigh the strong sexual allure, and Roberta the arrogant beauty and confidence he remembered so well.

As the talk flowed back and forth, Olivia quietly ignored him. He clenched his fist in his lap, wishing he could shake her. He'd imagined many times what it would be like to see her again. But he'd hardly expected her to snub him in front of her friends, as she'd done so often in the past. He thought she might have grown up—changed from her old high school self. Obviously not.

Roberta interrupted his thoughts. "Why don't you pull up a chair, Warner, if you're going to chat a while?"

His eyes, wary, moved to rest on hers. It had always been a coveted privilege to be invited by Roberta Ray, now Roberta Simmons, to sit at her table. Noting the hushed breath of the others, Warner said at last, "Perhaps I will." He hadn't meant to visit longer but the invitation proved irresistible. He pulled up a chair from a nearby table and then straddled it to prop an arm on its back. It put him closer to Olivia, his left knee brushing hers. A familiar jolt of feeling flooded him.

He settled into conversation then, observing Olivia's obvious discomfort out of the side of his eye. *What was she feeling?* He'd noticed that little flush crawl up her neck, heard the small intake of breath he felt sure no one else heard but him.

Warner listened to Lulu catch him up on their lives, but still Olivia didn't enter into the conversation. Finally, he caught her eyes with his, asking her a question, trying to get her to speak to him.

As she hesitated, Vickie Leigh jumped in to answer for her, giving him a long litany of all the men Olivia had dated and who, according to Vickie, had proposed marriage. Warner kept count— six, ending with Evan Parker. And now she was dating Brody Hanks from their high school days and some young doctor at her father's clinic. Her father would certainly approve of the latter. He'd always wanted her to marry a doctor like himself.

Olivia tensed through Vickie's chatty recitation, a deep, pink flush rising up her cheeks. However, she still said nothing—not correcting or adding to Vickie Leigh's story.

Roberta gave him a cat-like smile, seeming to pick up on the tension thrumming between them. "You know, I think I heard Olivia turned you down once, too, Warner—but maybe I didn't hear that right."

Warner turned to her, no longer intimidated by this strong-natured woman. She'd developed a confident maturity so much sooner than the rest of them and always used it to her advantage—frequently to hurt others.

He sent her a calm, level look, responding easily, letting Roberta know she hadn't rattled him. He wished he'd been this wise at fifteen.

Absently, Roberta picked at her necklace, an old habit Warner remembered all too well. It usually meant she was thinking up her next mode of attack. "I also heard you lost your wife last year." She gave him an artificial half smile. "We were all sorry to learn that. It must have been terrible—a shooting or something wasn't it?"

"Yes." He'd had enough of her games. Glancing back at the pharmacy, he spotted his father heading in the back door from lunch.

Warner stood, excusing himself, pushing his chair into its place at the nearby table. Then he walked away without another backward glance, at either Roberta or Olivia. As usual, Olivia—like the other two in Roberta's select group—never said a word when Roberta probed painfully at his past, picked at a wound still sore. Evidently, Olivia hadn't changed one bit. Pity.

Soon caught in his father's embrace, and then his brother's and his grandfather's, Warner's mind moved with pleasure to the joy of seeing his family again. Their love and support was what he'd come home for after all. The love and unconditional support he'd always known with them—even when awkward and odd as a teenager, when he undoubtedly caused them embarrassment. To his family, he'd always simply been Warner, the beloved and youngest member of the Zachery brothers.

A little more than an hour later, he sat on the front porch of

Leonard Goldstein's log cabin high on a twisty mountain road behind Bryson City. They ate hot roast beef and Swiss cheese sandwiches, feet propped companionably on the rustic middle rail of the porch. Leonard, once pudgy with a hooked nose and hairy legs in their high school years, also had grown into a better-looking man.

Between bites, Warner said, "This place you bought is beautiful. You e-mailed me about it and sent photos, but it's better than the pictures." He pointed down the hillside. "I love the stream below the property and all these mountain ranges to enjoy. The only problem I see would be getting up your steep hill when there's ice and snow."

Leonard grinned. "That's why you followed me up the mountain driving my big, 4-wheel drive SUV." He laughed. "Besides, I can always stay with the parents in town if it's really bad."

"What does Imogene think about living up here on the mountain?" Warner asked, referring to Imogene Vogel, a professor at the community college in Sylva who Leonard had recently become engaged to.

"She loves it and she helped me decorate the cabin, but she's keeping her little apartment near the college, even after we get married, for when she teaches late or when the weather is a real bear and the streets ice over."

"I always liked Imogene." Warner polished off the last of his sandwich and washed it down with a canned cola.

"Yeah, she was one of us," Leonard said, referring to the brainy, non-conformist group he and Warner belonged to at Swain High.

Warner laughed. "Funny to think of Imogenius Vogel marrying Loser Leonard Goldstein. Who would have thought?"

Leonard punched him. "Imogenius is now Dr. Imogene Vogel, and I've bought three small local newspapers in the vicinity to add to the Bryson City newspaper I inherited. We've done all right." He caught Warner's eye. "So have you, Weird Warner. I read the other day that Daniel Radcliffe, the actor who played Harry Potter, remembered being different from all the other kids in his class as early as six years old. In an interview, he stated that he always thought there must be a reason for being so weird, a payoff at some point. You've had yours."

"I've been lucky." He shrugged.

"No." Leonard shook his head. "You were always gifted. We all saw it, in our kid-like way in high school, but none of us held the vision to see what you could do with your talents—or we'd have encouraged you more."

"I didn't encourage you much either."

"Yes, you did. You always kept telling me, when we did errands down at my dad's paper, that I'd own the newspaper one day and probably several more. It kept me balanced amid all that peer harassment." Finishing off his sandwich, Leonard picked up a bag of chocolate chip cookies to pass toward Warner. "Homemade cookies. Want one?"

"Yes. Thanks." Warner reached into the bag and shifted the subject. "I saw the Scratch Cats today."

Leonard's expression sharpened with interest. "Let me guess. At the drugstore. They still meet for lunch there about once a week in the same old booth. It knocks me right back into the past when I run into them. Imogene says it's why they still meet there—to continue perpetuating their high school status."

"The Elite Eight," said Warner, referring to the four girls and four guys who'd ruled the popularity ladder at Swain County High. "Do they all still live around here?"

"Yeah, more folks stay than leave in a small town. All the Eight went to college like we did, or at least to community college, but then they came back—Roberta with Russell, who she followed off to Vanderbilt to marry, Vickie Leigh to work at the visitor center after her last divorce, Rob to return to Frazier's after mortuary school and, of course, to marry Louise. That's hardly a surprise since they got engaged before Rob left for Cincinnati." He wolfed down a cookie. "And then Olivia, like Louise, never really left Bryson City at all, except to commute to Western. Then she opened her own florist shop when Verlie McBride died and The

Flower Box shut down."

He paused. "Logan and Brody came back, too, after playing football for colleges around the southeast. Logan owns a fitness center over on the highway. Appropriate with his sports background. That loud-mouthed Brody Hanks is working with his father. He's sniffing around Olivia Benton again, and Logan is seeing Vickie Leigh. The elite always dated each other. Still do. Since Olivia wouldn't marry Russell, maybe Brody hopes he can get a chance now."

Warner let the memories float over him. "We called Russell Simmons Mr. Everything and Brody Hanks Mr. Cool."

Leonard started on another cookie. "Russell was one of those charismatic guys with an easy, natural leadership. He and Olivia Benton seemed a perfect 'Barbie and Ken' couple—blond, good-looking, and always voted sweetheart roles together, like Prom King and Prom Queen senior year."

Warner certainly remembered that.

Leonard chuckled. "Brody's still playing Mr. Cool—lording it over all the peons who work for a pittance with no health insurance at his family's Paving and Construction Company. I never did like Brody's father, Hooter Hanks, a loud, smart-mouthed, arrogant man. Brody grows more like him every day, I think, but in a subtler way. Do you remember how he used to cut everyone down to make himself look better?"

"I remember." Warner looked out thoughtfully over the trees. "The Scratch Cats told me today that Russell proposed to Olivia after high school. Brody too. I didn't know that."

"A lot of guys went after Olivia." Leonard pushed his glasses up on his nose. "I doubt Olivia ever took Brody seriously, but Russell was a different matter. A classy guy and smart, and his folks could afford to send him to medical school at Vanderbilt. I heard not long after you left for New York they started dating again, but when Russell got accepted at Vanderbilt, Olivia didn't want to follow him to Nashville."

"Olivia didn't want to leave the garden or her Daddy."

Leonard turned to him with a questioning look. "You think that's really it? Or that Russell wasn't the right one?"

"I don't know." He stood up, brushing off his slacks. He didn't want to analyze Olivia Benton any more today. "I need to head out to the house now. Mom will be anxious to see me and annoyed I didn't go there first." He reached out a hand to his old friend. "Leonard, thanks for the lunch and for running an article in the paper about the signing at Gil's Bookstore next weekend."

"I like Gil, and you can look for my article in tomorrow's paper. Except for the report about the new vandal incident, it will be the biggest headline in Bryson City. 'Small-town boy comes home a big success' is always a reader favorite. Your name will sell papers." Leonard clapped a hand on Warner's back after shaking his hand. "It's good to have you back. Come do lunch again after you settle in."

"I will. You've given me some things to think about for the future. But I need to take it one day at a time."

He waved a final hand to Leonard as he drove down the mountain. He'd connected with one of his best friends today. He'd get together with the other tomorrow after visiting the family tonight. Undoubtedly his mother would plan a family gathering— even with no advance warning.

Warner didn't err with that assumption. The entire Zachery clan held a party to celebrate his homecoming. His mother baked two pans of homemade lasagna, his favorite, and both his brother's wives—Vance's wife Susan and Dean's wife Lisa—brought chilled bowls of crisp salad, hot garlic bread, and plates of gooey brownies and lemon squares. Afterward, the family played outdoors, another Zachery tradition—volleyball, badminton, and horseshoes. The three Zachery grandchildren, Vance's son Steven and Dean's Abigail and Kent, shrieked with fun while the goldens barked, running around everyone. The family had always owned golden retrievers, from Old Molly, the loving, gentle dog Warner remembered from his childhood to Biff and Annie, the family's current dogs.

It felt like entering a warm cocoon to be back, and Warner

enjoyed the evening—eating, playing, and catching up on all the family news. He listened to their happy banter—Vance and Susan expecting again, Dean promoted at the high school where he coached football and taught health and PE. His father talked about his mother's paintings selling more widely and displayed a copy of a recent article printed about her work in a major magazine. She pooh-poohed it all away, of course, but Warner could tell she seemed pleased.

"Did you have a good evening?" his mother asked later, leading him up the stairs to the apartment above the garage to open the door.

He nodded, yawning, even though he'd caught a nap in a lawn chair for a short time after dinner.

"You're tired." She patted his cheek before pushing the door wide. "I didn't get a chance to air out the apartment as much as I'd hoped to, but I cleaned it earlier knowing you'd arrive sometime this month. Your father and I decided you might enjoy your grandfather's old place and a little privacy while here. Granddad can't climb the stairs with ease anymore so he moved over with us a few months ago. I may not have mentioned it."

She ushered him in, setting a box on the kitchen table and gesturing toward the bedroom where he dumped his duffle bags, laptop, and other belongings. "I packed food, snacks, and drinks in this box." She gestured. "I didn't have time to bring it all over earlier. Come to the house for breakfast in the morning or sleep in. Whatever you want, Warner."

He looked around the apartment—familiar and yet unfamiliar with different furnishings and colors than he recalled.

His mother followed his glance. "There's a comfortable bed in the main bedroom, a nice TV here in the living area, and a big desk in the spare room. Your grandfather liked to do his paperwork there, and I thought you'd like it for your work. The window looks over the wall toward the gardens." She reached out to hug him. "It's good to have you back again, Son. Enjoy your time while visiting. Do things you want to do. See people you like. Create some good times. The last two years have been difficult for you."

She put a hand to his face again then turned to leave, pointing out a few more things about the apartment before shutting the door behind her.

Warner sagged onto the couch and closed his eyes for a moment, enjoying the peace. He wasn't used to the noise and activity of the Zachery clan anymore. He spent more of his time in quiet now—working, drawing, writing, cartooning—lost in his imaginary worlds. Creating characters and fictional worlds for others to enjoy.

Regretfully, he needed to check his e-mails. Preferring his computer to his iPhone when possible, he carried his laptop into the spare room, took it out of the leather case, set it up on the desk, and plugged it in. He couldn't take a total vacation while here, but he could take a partial one. The upcoming months would be lighter now after the blitz and tour for his latest book.

He worked for a short time, answering e-mails and needed correspondence, while glancing out the window now and again. At seven, twilight started to fall, casting a soft glow over everything. In winter, it would grow dark by now but, in July with the long summer days, darkness wouldn't fall until after eight.

A spot of color caught his eye. He leaned toward the window. Olivia was in the garden. A rush of old memories swamped him.

He hesitated only a minute before shutting down the computer and letting himself out the door to head down the stairs. His steps instinctively followed the worn path winding from the Zachery's back yard to one of the wrought-iron gates leading into the Fairchild Gardens.

The gardens spread to the side and back of the Benton's country property, tucked with skillful design behind the family's green lawn, white picket fences, and large two-storied colonial. Warner always thought the lush formal gardens looked like a British regency movie set dropped into the backwoods of the Appalachian Mountains. Not even visible from the street, the extensive gardens lay hidden behind tall brick walls draped in ivy, vines, and climbing roses. Inside the garden gates, a fairyland of pathways wove underneath rose-covered arches and along tidy gravel walkways—all amid a vast profusion of decorative shrubs, flowers of every kind, tinkling fountains, statuaries, and inviting benches.

Warner found Olivia standing on a ladder, reaching up to prune a vine heavy with purple blooms. The vine weighed down a lovely arched trellis that stretched across the garden path.

"Wisteria or clematis, I think." His eyes moved to the rich blooms. He knew she'd heard him open the gate, shut it, and walk down the path, even though she hadn't turned around.

"It's clematis, specifically *'Jackmanii Superba'*. It loves to climb, but like all wisteria needs to be pruned back or it will take over." She continued clipping. "You can tell the difference between clematis and wisteria by the flower. Wisteria blossoms drift down from the branches in clusters, like grapes, and bloom in the spring, not the summer. Clematis with its star-shaped blooms, like this variety, loves the summertime."

She turned to look down at him now, her face shaded by an old, floppy sun hat, her legs bare below faded denim shorts. A ratty pink T-shirt stopped about an inch below her midriff, offering him a glimpse of smooth, ivory skin. Even with grass stains on her legs and dirt on her clothes she looked beautiful.

"You're never more in your element than in the garden," he remarked.

She gave him a pointed look. "You mean I'm never more at a disadvantage. Gardening is dirty work."

He laughed. "You've always loved it."

She turned back to her pruning. "I heard your family partying earlier in the evening. I gather they hosted a homecoming get-together for the prodigal son."

"Am I prodigal—a wasteful spendthrift returning to a warm welcome I don't deserve?"

She paused. "Well, perhaps not a prodigal, but simply a wanderer returning home for a welcome after a long time away."

"Well, thanks for that, at least."

"You've changed." She handed him the bucket she'd collected

pruning scraps in and climbed down the ladder.

"You certainly haven't." Sarcasm laced his tone.

Her eyes widened. "Why do you say that?"

"You snubbed me as neatly as ever with your friends earlier today."

Her mouth dropped open. "That is not true. I was simply surprised to see you. I couldn't think what to say."

"Liar. You let Roberta jab at me and did nothing to stop her."

She put a hand on one hip, scowling at him. "It looked to me like Roberta openly flirted with you, Louise sucked up to you, and Vickie Leigh practically drooled over your august presence." She leaned over to snip irritably at several loose branches of a yellow butterfly bush pushing its way across the path.

Warner laughed. "Come to think about it, the atmosphere did seem a little different at the drugstore." He stooped over to retrieve a snipped piece from her plastic bucket, holding it to his nose. "I'd forgotten how wonderful this plant smells."

"It's a butterfly bush called Honeycomb. It's fragrant, but it doesn't attract many butterflies, like the lavender does." She pointed to another shrub across the path. "That lavender one, called Butterfly Heaven, really draws the butterflies when in bloom. However, the yellow draws honeybees, and that's good for pollination."

Warner looked around. "This section is called The Butterfly Garden, isn't it?"

She nodded, reaching with her pruning shears toward another plant.

Warner put a hand on her arm. "I've missed the garden, Olivia. Take me around and show me the changes. Let me see everything again."

She looked toward the west where the sun was falling rapidly. "There isn't a lot of time left before dark."

"Just a quick walk-through then," he urged. "You don't have to give me the full tour; we can end up in the White Garden."

She dropped her eyes at his last words. "All right," she said at last. "We'll go through the Formal Gardens behind the house, cut over to the Rose Garden and then back to the White Garden. There won't be time to do the Wildflower Walk behind the lake on the park boundary. It's more shaded and gets dark there earlier."

He nodded, glad for any concession.

"I need to put away these buckets and my tools first." She set off along the pathway toward the garden shed. Warner followed, easily remembering the way. He'd worked and played with her in these gardens since they were small.

Catching up, he took one of the buckets she carried and the long pruning shears she'd tucked under her arm. "We met in this garden when we were only four years old."

She smiled then—one of the first real smiles he'd seen, touching her eyes and making his heart skip a beat. A beautiful woman could make a man forget good sense.

Her words interrupted his thoughts. "Your family had just bought the house next door," she said. "We met when your dog ran into the garden and chased my cat."

"Do you still own a cat?" he asked, as they came to the shed.

She opened the door to put away the tools and buckets. "I still have Sybil." She latched the door back and turned, an amused smile touching her lips.

He grinned. "You mean that smoky gray kitten I gave you for Valentine's Day our senior year? The one allegedly labeled a purebred Russian Blue but without papers?"

"The same one, now a full grown cat. She's still arrogant and stubborn and thinks she owns the garden, too. She'll probably pop out before we finish the tour. I had to scold her earlier for chasing a finch, and she's irritated with me. She almost caught it before I intervened."

"Cats will be cats." He trailed her now as she headed behind the house, through the back yard, and into the floral-decked main archway leading into Fairchild Gardens. A familiar sign stood just inside the entrance. "*Walk into the garden. Draw nearer to God*," he read. Warner traced a hand over the sign. "Who was the writer?"

"My great grandmother," she said. "They're words from a poem she wrote." Olivia began to quote it: *"Come into the garden and walk with me; Down flower-lined paths 'neath draping trees. Hear the tinkle of fountains, the hum of bees; Catch the scent of roses upon the breeze."*

She paused before continuing. *"Come into the garden, a place unflawed; Taste of peace and draw nearer to God."*

She laid her hand on the sign then turned to look at Warner with a sweet smile. "It was my mother's favorite poem. She used to quote it to me every time we entered the garden through these gates so I'd learn all the words."

A lump formed in Warner's throat. He remembered Olivia's mother with fondness, had loved her, and grieved with Olivia when she died. Olivia had only been twelve. "It's beautiful," he said. "I don't think you ever quoted it to me before."

"No?" Her eyes caught his. "Perhaps I thought you'd think it silly."

"And now?"

She giggled. "Perhaps now I don't care. Or perhaps the twilight and this time of year makes me sentimental." She started into the garden, almost reaching out to take his hand. "Let's go or we'll lose our daylight before you even get to see a little of the garden."

CHAPTER 3

How foolish! Olivia started down the main path. She'd almost taken Warner's hand—as if still a child ready to race with him down the trellised pathway to the pond.

To cover the moment, she pointed overhead. "This is one of the best times of year in the garden. The arbor roses are in full bloom and the connecting arches overhead are draped with blooms. The red roses you see are Altissimo, vividly colored and with multiple petals. Mixed with them are white Sombreuil, a tea rose with a delicious fragrance."

She stopped to inhale and glanced back at Warner. He stood looking overhead in wonder. The roses, particularly prolific this summer, stole everyone's breath away on the entry path.

She let her eyes slide over him. He'd shed the suit jacket of earlier in the day but still wore the neat dark slacks and gray shirt. How she'd missed him! He was the only one she'd ever truly shared the garden with—besides her family and Verlie McBride who owned The Flower Box in town. Of course, the Leland family worked for them several days a week to keep the garden, but that hardly counted since they were paid. Only Warner had been her age.

He glanced toward her, seeming to pick up on her thoughts. "You once called me your best friend on Durham Branch Road and your only friend who really loved the garden. Do you remember?"

"We knew happy times as children," she answered, avoiding a direct answer to his question. "Here's the pond up ahead."

She stopped before a large rectangular pool at the center of the Formal Gardens. In the middle sat a serene white marble statue of a woman in a long dress, reading an open book, oblivious to the fountains burbling to either side of her. "I always thought this statue looked like my Grandmother Lila."

"Stern and disapproving and prim?"

"Oh, you." Olivia turned to punch him playfully on the arm. "Grandmother was also a beautiful person, and she loved the garden."

Warner made no comment.

His silence didn't surprise Olivia as her grandmother Lila Fairchild had always disapproved of Warner for some reason. Even when Warner was a child, her grandmother never liked him as her mother did, and as Warner grew older, her grandmother liked him even less. She called him "impulsive, reckless, and fanciful."

"That boy is dangerous," she used to say to Olivia. "It worries me that you spend so much time with him."

Looking back, Olivia knew her Grandmother Lila colored her father's thoughts, making him less fond of Warner, too. This seemed especially true after her mother died.

"Your grandmother never liked me," Warner stated, following her around the pond to stroll down one of the open pathways.

"But Mother liked you," Olivia said, deciding not to argue. The pebbled walkway led between carefully planned beds of annuals and perennials—all set amid flowering shrubs, lush groundcovers, colorful hostas and coleus. She paused, mentally counting the array of purple coneflowers tucked against the garden wall in front of a row of gladiolas.

"I thought coneflowers were always purpley-pink." Warner's gaze traveled to a cluster of red and yellow flowers nearby.

"Most still are." She gestured to the sweep of purple flowers against the wall. "But hybridizing has created a multitude of new colors of coneflowers, or Echinacea to be more specific. Now there are marvelous bright red ones like these called Tomato Soup." She gestured. "And the yellows to the right called Mac 'n' Cheese."

Warner chuckled. "Some guy must have felt hungry when he named them."

"Maybe so." She laughed. "I never thought before how many of the new varieties carry food-related names. The large pinks with the fat centers are called Raspberry Truffle and the ones beside them Tangerine Dream." She reached to snip an orange flower with a small pair of pruning shears she'd tucked in her back pocket, and held it out to him. "Take a sniff."

"Umm. Spicy." He raised an eyebrow. "Surprising aroma when you're expecting sweet."

Olivia smiled. It had always been like this with Warner. Other people grew bored with her talk about flowers, her recitation of botanical names and endless facts about every variety. But Warner always loved it.

"We used to make up names for the flowers." He propped a foot on a nearby wall. "Silly ones and elaborate botanical-sounding ones. I think they should have contacted us for more original ideas before naming these coneflowers after macaroni and cheese, soup, and tangerines."

She laughed again, enjoying his company.

He glanced toward the sweep of purple coneflowers. "Why were you mentally counting these when we stopped earlier?"

"Mr. Bumgartner wants a big wreath of daisies to put over his wife's gravestone. Wanda, one of my staff at the florist shop, wasn't sure we had enough Gerbera daisies in stock for the full grave wreath he wants, so she told him I might have coneflowers in bloom we could use."

"They do have a daisy look." He studied them. "I'd say they'd look good in a wreath with daisies. Do they hold well?"

"They make a great cut flower." Olivia turned to walk the path, hiding the emotions swamping her now. Blast him. He'd always been like this, so interested in every aspect of the garden and the flowers. That's why it made no sense that he condemned her when she didn't want to pack up and leave. Had it been so easy for him to simply walk away?

She opened the gate into the Rose Garden on the west side of Fairchild Gardens. Like the Butterfly Garden on the east, its paths wove in and out under covered archways, lined with varieties of roses rather than shrubs that attracted butterflies. Of course, other flowers and plants grew interspersed between the roses, so the gardens held attractions and color year-round.

"It's beginning to get dark." She glanced toward the last glow of sunlight sinking behind the trees. "You'll need to come back another day to see the Lily Lake, take the Wildflower Walk, and see the additions to the Pavilion we've made. It's nicer for events than before. I hosted twenty parties and wedding events at the Pavilion from April to June this year."

"Always an event-maid but never a bride," he teased.

A blush stole up her face. "Vickie Leigh shouldn't have prattled all that nonsense about my proposals."

He ignored her. "Let's go to the White Garden now. I want to see all the flowers glowing in the twilight before too much darkness falls." He snagged her hand and took the pathway to the gate leading back to the Formal Gardens.

His hand felt warm and firm, but Olivia pulled hers away, using it to reach back to latch the gate.

"Tell me about the White Garden again," he said. "How it started."

"My great-grandmother Olivia Fairchild, who I was named for and who built the gardens, visited the castles and estates in England for inspiration for her garden design. She got the idea for creating a White Garden from a lovely white garden at Sissinghurst Castle Garden, one of the most visited gardens in the world. She created our White Garden at the back of the formal gardens as a little oasis of white and quiet. I'm told she spent many hours there, reading and playing with the children."

They'd arrived at the arched entrance to the White Garden, its rounded trellis smothered in white roses, their heavenly scent spreading into the evening air to envelop them.

"What are these called?" Warner reached up to touch the blooms.

"They're a Noisette called Madame Alfred Carrière. The rose is a prolific climber, and hardy, with a good repeat bloom and a delicious fragrance." She cupped a blossom to smell it, before following Warner into the garden.

He stopped just inside the gate. "It's exactly like I remember." His voice grew soft as he looked across the garden, lovingly laid out around a large green lawn. A charming gazebo and cozy seating area nestled among flowering shrubs, while a delightful children's playhouse snuggled near a wrought iron fence smothered in ivy. "Even the little house that we played in is still here."

"Look around, Warner." She spoke the words in reverence, catching his mood. "So many of the flowers are holding the light and glowing in the twilight. See?" She began to name the flowers as she pointed them out. "Clematis with their starry blooms, snowy daylilies, milky evening stock, white hydrangea, and delicate four o'clocks." Olivia walked to a trellis covered with the latter. "These four o'clocks got their name because they never bloom until after four o'clock when the daylight begins to fade."

"This is truly a magic place." He turned around, looking in every direction. "Where are the moonflowers that open in the evening and bloom all night?"

"Here." She led him to where trumpet-shaped white moonflowers climbed in profusion over a wrought iron fence. "They look like morning glories but are exactly the opposite. They won't close until the sun comes out while the morning glories only bloom as the sun comes up." Without thinking she put a hand on his arm. "Do you remember why so many of the evening and night blooming flowers are white?"

He smiled down at her. "To attract the moths for pollination. Moths can see the white flowers better than other colors and Mother Nature seemed to know that—or God did in His infinite wisdom in creating the earth. Your mother, Margaret Fairchild Benton, taught us that." He took both her hands. "Your mother also taught us to laugh and dance in the garden."

On impulse, Warner swung Olivia around in whirling steps and turns she remembered instinctively from childhood until her head spun and laughter bubbled out of her. She fell against him at last, dizzy.

Warner's arms wrapped around her. His voice floated down, soft against her forehead where his lips touched so easily, so naturally. "This was the first place where I kissed you. Do you remember?"

She nodded, looking up at him, and then realized she probably shouldn't have. His lips lowered to hers like a whisper, moving softly back and forth over hers, so welcome and so sweet.

Feeling drugged, she swayed against Warner, opening to him as the kiss grew deeper, letting him press her body against his and unashamedly reaching her arms around his neck. Her fingers moved of their own accord to wander down his broad back and then over his arms. The citrusy musk smell of his cologne filled her nostrils along with his own familiar scent she knew so well.

How could he have left her?

Warner pulled away, cupping her face in one hand for a moment. "I probably shouldn't have done that." His breath, husky and soft, tickled her cheek. "But I knew you felt something earlier today, as I did, when we saw each other again."

His hands tightened on her arms then and his tone changed. "It made me angry that you denied your feelings, Olivia, avoided speaking to me, even looking at me. Even after all this time, you wouldn't let your friends know you had feelings for me, once cared for me—even loved me." His gaze burned into hers. "Although I hold many sweet memories of growing up with you, of discovering first love with you, I also carry painful memories of how you never acknowledged your feelings for me outside our garden world here."

Warner dropped her arms and stepped back. "I never understood that. Even now, after all this time, I still don't."

Hurt and wanting to strike back, Olivia hugged her arms tight against herself, feeling suddenly cold. "Well, I never understood how you could go away and leave me, marry another when you said you loved me."

He flashed an angry look at her. "You wouldn't go with me. You wouldn't believe in me. Nelle believed in me, Olivia. I loved her for that and many other things. She loved and cherished me even when I worked as a janitor pushing a trash can through the publishing house where she worked as an assistant editor. She never felt ashamed of me. She took me into her circle of friends when I was nothing and nobody, simply because she liked me. Do you have any idea how wonderful that felt to me after the life I lived here with you—kissing you in the garden but being shunned at school around your friends?"

Tears trickled down Olivia's face. "It was different at school. You were different there, too, Warner, having your own set of friends that didn't like me, either. You know I needed to be careful, too, because of Daddy and Grandmother Lila. They already had problems with you, and if they'd known I cared for you, they might have forbidden me to see you at all."

"That's a crock." He started toward the side gate to the garden. "That's what you *told* yourself and me, so you could have your cake and eat it, too. Be the popular, pretty, Miss Swain High cheerleader at school and the secretly loved and cherished Olivia Benton with me in the garden."

"That's mean, Warner." She wiped at her face. "That's not the way it was."

"Yes, it is, and what's sad is that you still won't acknowledge it or admit it." He paused, his eyes fiery and dark. "Do you know how much it hurt me to see you go to the senior prom with Russell Mays when I'd asked you first? When you'd already told me you loved me with a forever love? You'd let me hold you in my arms and kiss you. We shared our dreams and hearts with each other."

"But you know I couldn't go with you because—"

He interrupted her. "No, you *wouldn't* go with me. There's a big difference. I let you convince me of some poppycock story about why we shouldn't go together, but the truth is you weren't brave enough, Miss Conformity. You didn't want to risk the titters and whispers of your friends if you'd gone with me as your escort. So you went with Russell Mays, Mr. Everything." Warner clenched his fists and stepped back. "You wouldn't even dance with me at the prom. How do you think that made me feel?"

She sniffled, putting a hand over her mouth. "I never knew it hurt you."

"Well, you should have known." He turned, striding toward the garden gate. "And I should have told you long before how I really felt. But I felt terrified of losing you." He stopped, turning to look back at her. "Then, as it turned out, I lost you anyway because you wouldn't leave here with me, wouldn't believe in me, wouldn't even talk of going away to school where I needed to go or of getting engaged to me until I could make enough money to marry and support you. You stayed here instead to date and entertain proposals from a variety of other men. Six of them, if Vickie Leigh's report is right."

"It wasn't like that." She reeled over his harsh words. "You know it wasn't. We were practically children when you left. We had college ahead of us with no incomes. I had Daddy to think of. Grandmother Lila died right before we graduated. Daddy was alone again. How could I think of leaving him or of leaving the garden with Grandmother gone? Who would have cared for it? Or for Daddy?"

Cold eyes glared back. "Always Daddy's girl, right? Daddy's girl with the beautiful garden. I hope you've been happy with your choices. I grieved and hurt at the time, I admit, but I think life favored me afterward. I found new happiness and meaning, and I learned the world is a lot bigger place than this stagnant little pond in Bryson City. I'm not sure you've learned that yet."

With that, he simply turned and walked away, not giving her another chance to respond.

Olivia wanted to scream at him for what he'd said. It wasn't right. And it hadn't been the way things were. So many other factors entered in. He held blame, too, for many things that happened.

She wanted to run after him. Make him listen. But she stood by the arch to the White Garden instead, watching him disappear down the path.

Sybil, her cat, came walking up the opposite pathway on her long, elegant legs, meowing and looking toward the direction Warner had gone.

"Too late to see him," she told the cat, picking her up to head for the house. "He's judged and damned us and left already—forgetting completely that he could have stayed here to go to college if he'd cared so much."

She strode the pathway, under the rose arbor through the formal garden, the cat draped over her shoulder. "All the sacrifices didn't have to be on my part alone. My dreams lay here, Sybil. I didn't want to go to New York City to live in a pencil-sized apartment on a grimy, busy street with no flowers to enjoy except a geranium on my windowsill. I tried to tell Warner I couldn't imagine myself in a life there." She looked around with a sigh. "And, yes, the gardens here are a part of me. They're in my blood and in my soul. Who would care for them if I left? They're my legacy. Could I be happy without them? I don't know. I think they'd cry out to me wherever I went.

"Wretched man. Only he could tear me up like this, make me feel sad and miserable." She kicked at a stone wall as she walked by. "I hate it."

Olivia stomped through the house, Sybil trailing on long sleek legs, meowing for a snack in the kitchen. She fixed food for the cat and then fed herself, heating up homemade potato soup she'd made the night before. One of her Daddy's favorites.

The cat jumped into her kitchen basket, licking herself after her meal, watching Olivia as if expecting her to pick up the conversation.

"He talked to me like family weren't even important, Sybil—what Daddy or Grandmother thought, what their needs were. He forgot Daddy was grieving at that time and so was I, losing Grandmother. It wasn't a time to go away." Her voice grew choked. "And how can he criticize me so harshly when he waltzed off and left his family high and dry all these ten years without even coming home for a holiday or a visit? They had to load up and go to New York to visit him if they wanted to see him. Was that fair or loving of him?"

Olivia kicked at a table leg, angry now. "No, it wasn't. Personally, I can't see Warner Zachery going up for any saint award in my mind. He didn't even come home when his Grandfather fell and broke his hip. Just sent a gift basket. I know, because I was at the hospital with Grandmother Lila when it came. He didn't come home when his brothers' children were born either and he never came home for Thanksgiving or Christmas. It hurt his mother and father, I can tell you that. Maybe Daddy and Grandmother Lila were correct about Warner. Right now, Sybil, I'd certainly hate to think about being married to him after the things he said to me."

She stomped upstairs to her room after cleaning the kitchen, purposed to read the book she'd planned to start. However, after bathing and climbing into bed, she wept instead—despite her best intentions. In her mind, she could still feel Warner's kisses, feel his arms around her, smell his familiar scent. Even mad at him, and knowing him angry with her, she wanted him, wished she could hold him again. Wretched man.

Olivia's father came in, climbed the stairs, and stopped outside her door. "You gone to bed, Livvy?" he asked, using her old childhood name.

She faked a sleepy voice. "Yes, Daddy."

"Well, see you tomorrow. Sleep tight."

Olivia wept again as he walked down the hall to his room. Sweet man.

Despite his loving words, she doubted she'd sleep tight or well at all tonight. Or for many nights to come. Warner Zachery was back in town.

CHAPTER 4

Warner didn't sleep well after his encounter with Olivia and found work difficult the next morning. He fiddled away time eating breakfast with his parents and then came back to the apartment, hoping to complete the ongoing chapter on his new Gilmore book.

Carrying a second cup of coffee back to his desk, he stared moodily out the window toward the gardens instead. Irritated at his inattention, he prowled through the living room for a change of scene. His eyes wandered to the photo of Nelle he'd put on the end table by the sofa.

"I was unfaithful to your memory yesterday, Nelle. Not noble of me." Dropping into the deep, leather sofa, he picked up her photo to study it. "The old magic of the garden sucked me into its vortex. Then it sprinkled me like fairy dust with the silvery seduction of my childhood love, Olivia Benton. Maybe I made a mistake coming back here, Nelle. I avoided visiting all these years exactly for this reason."

Warner leaned his head back against the sofa. "Despite all that happened, I'm not sorry I finally told Olivia how I felt about things. I hated how she acted at the drugstore yesterday—awkward and odd like it embarrassed her having me around. It brought back too many painful memories."

He drummed his fingers on his leg and then stood, putting Nelle's picture back on the table. "I need to get out of here for a while." He found his cell phone and dialed Barry.

Thirty minutes later, he let himself in the door of Barry Jacobs's

Computer Shop on a side street in downtown Bryson City. Inside, an array of laptop and desktop computers, printers, and computer supplies filled the store. Barry sat behind a work desk toward the back of the shop scowling at the screen of a computer.

"Hey, Barry. Ready for lunch?"

"Almost." He reached across the counter to shake Warner's hand, his eyes barely moving from the computer screen. "I only need a few more minutes with this."

Warner grinned, leaning against the counter. Same ole Barry— nose stuck in a computer to the exclusion of all else. "What are you working on?"

"Transferring data from an old computer to this new one here." He gestured between the two and then tapped a device wired between them. "This snappy gadget zips the files from one to the other."

Warner walked closer to observe. "Couldn't a guy simply buy a USB cable and do the same thing at home?"

"Nah." Barry pushed wire-rimmed glasses up his nose. "Transferring data requires special software and user interface to do it right. You gotta copy the files from one computer to another and then use an eraser program to wipe the files from the hard drive by U.S. Defense Standards." He looked up with the lopsided grin Warner remembered so well. "That's why I make $50 to $80 an hour to do this."

Warner laughed then wandered the room while Barry finished. "Nice place, Barry." He stopped by a brand new Mac. "I see you sell both Macs and PCs."

Barry began disconnecting wires. "Yeah. Bryson's a small town. Not big enough for two sales stores—not even big enough for one, really. It's the repair business that pays the rent."

Warner studied a display of laptop cases and sleeves. "You're doing all right from what you told me last year when you visited New York."

"Yeah. Good break for both of us, that visit, and more enjoyable than the trip for Nelle's funeral the year before." He finished his work and dusted off his hands. "How are you doing about that now?"

"Better, but New York's lost its luster for me. It's one reason I'm down here."

"Well, it's good to have you—for however long you stay." He joined Warner at the display. "Have you seen Olivia yet?"

Typical Barry. Always direct, no game-playing or tiptoeing around the issues of life. Best friends since kindergarten, there was little Barry didn't know about Warner.

"I saw Olivia yesterday. Twice." Warner frowned out the window.

Barry's eyes lingered on him. "Let's close up shop and go to lunch. I'm hankering for a burger, with slaw-all-the-way, and a cherry-lemon Mountain Dew at Nabers." Barry swatted him on the shoulder. "Where else can you get a lunch like that except in Bryson City?"

Warner's dark mood lifted a level. "Do they still sell those good chili dogs and cherry milkshakes?"

"Yeah, some things never change, champ." Barry laughed. "Did you drive over in the Batmobile? I'm dying to ride in that car to Nabers." He snagged a "Closed for Lunch" sign to hang on the front door. "Besides, I'd need to clean the front seat of my truck before you could ride with me. Got an old computer and a pile of equipment in there I need to unload later."

Mimicking Batman actor Adam West's voice, Warner opened the shop door. "The Batmobile awaits, Robin."

Barry shot back a typical comeback of Batman's sidekick Robin as he followed Warner out to the curb. "Holy Kamoly, Batman, that's some car." He ran a hand reverently along the side of the sleek, black Mercedes. "Your agent and publicist sure negotiated a sweet deal for you getting this toy."

"Yeah. A couple of clever commercials and TV spots with a kid who looks like Geeky Gilmore—and I'm drivin' away in this fine machine."

"Success certainly includes some nice perks." Barry slid into the front seat and Warner coaxed the engine to life.

"Here's a little perk for you." Warner reached into the back seat to retrieve a Batman ball cap, which he tossed to Barry.

Barry studied the Batman symbol on the front. "Nice hat, Warner. Where'd you get it?"

"Ordered it off eBay. You can keep it; I have several more."

"Thanks." Barry tucked the cap on his head with a grin. He and Warner had always loved superheroes, especially Batman.

Crossing the city bridge and turning back toward the tourist town of Cherokee, Warner headed for Nabers, a drive-in restaurant by the Tuckaseegee River and an institution in Bryson City. Most longtime locals had some fond memory or story to tell about Nabers.

"There aren't many old drive-ins like Nabers anymore with carhop service," Warner said as he angled the Benz into a slot overlooking the river a short time later.

They studied the outside menu—complete with enticing illustrations—by their parking spot and ordered more food than probably either of them needed.

"When our food arrives, let's eat outside by the river." Barry pointed to an empty picnic table. "I couldn't enjoy myself eating in this spotless car." He leaned back against the leather seat. "While we wait, champ, you'd better fill me in on your meeting with Olivia. I could tell by that frown of yours things didn't go well."

Warner told him about encountering the Scratch Cats at the drugstore and about Olivia's reaction.

"Roberta always was a nasty piece of work." Barry scowled as Warner paused. "She still is—in that subtle way of hers. She brought a cute Acer laptop into the store one day wanting me to fix it. Said, 'I knew if anyone could fix this, it would be Brainy Barry.' "

Warner snorted at Barry's old nickname from high school days. "What did you say?"

"Nothing. What's the point?" He grinned. "But I added fifty bucks on her repair bill."

Warner sighed. "I thought all that name-calling and popularity nonsense would be finished after all this time. I'm surprised the

Cats didn't call me Weird Warner at the drugstore."

"Probably did after you left." Barry shook his head. "Nothing's really ever finished in a small town. In a bigger city, people scatter and move on. Here, life is slower; there isn't much going on. Everyone still hangs out with the same people, goes to the same old places, like Nabers, and shows up en masse for the football games at Swain High. Did you know Swain County High School has one of the most impressive stadiums for a small town in the southeast?"

"No. But it is impressive." The carhop arrived with their order and Warner pulled a twenty from his billfold, waving away Barry's contribution. "This one's on me, Barry."

Barry opened the door. "I'll take the food down to the table; you get the drinks."

Warner studied his old friend as they settled on a bench and spread out their lunch. Barry hadn't changed as much as he and Leonard, still a nondescript guy with short brown hair, wire-rimmed glasses, ears a little too large for his face, and a quirky smile.

Barry caught his glance. "I'm the same old guy in nearly every way. You're the one who's changed."

"Maybe."

"No maybe about it." He bit into a burger piled high with slaw. "Tell me the rest of the story with Olivia. You said back at the shop you saw her twice yesterday."

Warner shared a modified version of his encounter with Olivia in the garden, around wolfing down his lunch.

"Well. That's some story." Barry looked out over the river after polishing off his burger and fries.

Warner frowned. "Is that all you have to say? I kissed this woman, whom I don't even like, and I was unfaithful to Nelle."

Barry pushed down his glasses and looked at Warner over the top of them. "This is Barry you're talking to, Warner. Don't try to tell me you don't like Olivia Benton. What a crock. I think you stayed away from Bryson for ten years because deep down you knew you still carried a torch for her and didn't want to face it or deal with it."

Warner opened his mouth to protest. "I married Nelle—"

"Let me finish." Barry waved him quiet. "Remember I'm older than you."

"Only two months older." Warner grumbled.

"Still older." Barry continued. "And I mean no disrespect to Nelle's memory. I liked her. It's not impossible to love two people in a lifetime—even more than two—nor is it wrong. But Nelle's been gone more than two years now. She wouldn't want you to keep hugging her memory in a way that blocked you off from a future. You know that."

He stiffened. "Who says I want a future with Olivia Benton? I think I told you—"

"You told me you kissed her, and there was a sizzle."

"I didn't say that." His brows drew together.

"You didn't have to; your face said it." Barry shook his head.

Warner scowled as he looked out over the river, watching a group of summer tubers float by. "I hate how she treated me in high school."

"You hated how *everyone* treated you in high school. It always bothered you more than it did me or Leonard, or some of the others that you weren't in the popular group."

Warner turned on him. "I didn't want to be in their group."

"Yes, you did." Barry sipped on his drink "Even though you won't admit it. Did you know statistics show only ten percent of any class of students will be rated highly popular by their peers? That's two in a class of twenty, eight in a group about the size of our senior class. Yet, despite the odds, there's a side of us that always wishes to belong in that elite percent. Probably in the same way we all wish we could win the lottery, become a famous movie star, be the richest man in America or president of the United States. We're egoistic, all of us. We yearn to be the stars—and perhaps even to lord it over others when in that elite percentage."

He turned to study Warner. "I think you experienced a harder time with all that peer pressure than most of us because your brothers were jocks, leaders, and two of the most popular guys in school. Everyone, naturally, expected you to follow suit—including yourself. People compared you to your brothers rather than seeing your unique gifts and characteristics."

"What unique gifts and characteristics?" Warner slumped.

"You see?" Barry punched him companionably. "You're still dealing with it, despite the fact that you drove into town yesterday in a Benz everyone in Bryson City is talking about, wearing slick rich-boy clothes, looking like a million dollars, and smelling like fifty dollar cologne."

Warner grimaced. "And still getting razzed by the Scratch Cats."

Barry laughed. "Your perception of that and mine are different, Warner." He drained the last of his drink. "The Cats actually treated you with a new respect—saw you as a hottie. The real problem is that, although all of us have moved on with our lives in some way, you're just now coming back. So you're seeing things like they were when you left. You're still affected by people based on your experiences from the past. A little time will help that, Warner, as you see how things have changed here—even if less obviously."

Warner considered Barry's words. "So how does that impact what happened with Olivia and me?"

"I don't know." He shrugged. "But I do know this. Putting all the past behind and looking only at what happened last night, some major fireworks went off. You felt attracted, she felt attracted, and when you acted on those feelings the results were pretty spectacular, right?"

Warner avoided his glance.

"As for past grievances, you chewed her out like you'd always wanted to. Even made her cry and feel bad."

"You make me sound like a creep."

Barry raised an eyebrow.

Warner dropped his eyes. "Well, maybe I was a little rough."

Barry grinned, sliding off the bench to go dump their lunch remains in the trash. "What did your mama and mine teach us to do when we weren't polite to little girls and made them cry?"

"To make nice and apologize." Warner pulled a face.

"Well, there you have it." Barry looked at his watch. "I need to get back to the shop, no matter how great this time's been."

Warner stood, searching for his car keys in his pocket. "It's hardly been great for you, Barry, with me whining about my day yesterday."

"You're not heading back to New York any time soon, champ." Barry grinned. "I'll schedule my day to whine."

Warner dropped Barry at his shop a short time later. As Barry stepped out of the car, he paused. "Listen. I'm trying to build a relationship with the woman who works in Olivia's florist, Patti Headrick. Stop by and see what you think about her. If her kid's around, he'll go crazy to meet you. He's a big Gilmore fan." He wiggled his eyebrows at Warner. "You can offer Olivia an olive branch while you're there. Fairgarden Florist is just around the corner on Greenlee Street, not far from Olivia's father's clinic."

"I'll think about it," Warner replied, sending Barry a small salute before he drove away. He wasn't sure he was ready to see Olivia Benton again so soon.

CHAPTER 5

"Whew! It's been busy today for a Wednesday," Patti commented to Olivia as they settled back to work after a quick lunch. "Two funerals at Frazier's tonight right on the tail of the one for Mrs. Bills last night."

"Yes, and I still haven't found time to put the Fourth of July decorations back upstairs in storage." Olivia glanced toward the stack of boxes piled near their work area.

"Maybe Wanda can work on those later when she gets back from her deliveries, but she needs to finish the new FTD orders for the funerals first." Patti poked more larkspurs into the arrangement she assembled at her workstation. "Mrs. Harper insisted on larkspurs in her sister's order I'm working on since they're July's birthday flower."

"I'm glad we had enough larkspurs on hand for the arrangement." Olivia stopped to study the symmetry of the spray she worked on. "I had to order extra flowers, especially larkspurs, Gerberas, carnations, and mums, for all the standing sprays and casket covers we're doing for the funerals."

Patti chuckled as she formed a wired bow to add to her bouquet. "Mrs. Harper waxed on and on to me about the meaning of larkspur yesterday. To shut her up, I felt tempted to tell her the seeds of larkspur could kill lice in the hair."

"Patti. You didn't?" Olivia giggled.

"No. Don't worry; I kept my tongue. But I remember those old remedies concocted from flowers that my grandmother used to talk about. I often wonder how many of them really work."

Patti changed the subject. "You know, it worries me that vandals are running around town defacing property and leaving crazy messages behind. The newspaper said they wrote on the wall of the Swain County Recreation Center this time." She glanced down at the newspaper folded open by her work desk. "They spray painted the words: *The vandal strikes, you know not when.*"

"Probably a bunch of kids, bored for the summer." Olivia tucked another big mum into her arrangement. "Mostly it's been surface damage, writing on walls or windows. Defacing property. Nothing a little cleanup and paint can't fix."

Patti wrinkled her nose. "I guess it worries me because of Rich, in case there's a gang running around or something."

"Gangs happen more in big cities, Patti. Don't worry. Rich will be fine." She put a few final greens in her arrangement and stood up to stretch.

"I've almost finished this half-casket spray for the first funeral tonight." She rubbed her neck. "Patti, I want our focus for the arrangements for the first funeral to be pinks and purples unless call-in orders specify other colors. For the casket spray I used white chrysanthemums, pink stargazer lilies, purple lisianthus, and larkspur, mixed with green myrtle and eucalyptus for filler. When you and Wanda work on the standing sprays, use some of those same flowers to coordinate the colors, would you? People may attend both funerals tonight, and I want the main flowers for each to be different, especially since both funerals are at Frazier's."

"What colors are you focusing on for the second funeral?" Patti asked. "A warmer palette of yellows, golds, and russet? That would make a good contrast. We have a lot of those orange Asiatic lilies, yellow mums, and plum carnations that would work well."

"Good idea." Olivia studied her arrangement again. "I'm going to run back to the cooler to grab a few more flowers so I can finish this spray. Then I'll start on the full casket spray for the Whitlow funeral." She started toward the cooler. "Catch the phone for me if it rings."

In the back, Olivia checked the temperature gauge before letting herself inside the heavy cooler door. Forty-one degrees. The refrigerated room needed to be kept between thirty-nine to forty-two degrees. Inside, she gathered the greens and flowers she needed, enjoying the musky scent of flowers and plants while in the cool room.

Returning to her workstation, she finished the Bowling casket spray, and then carried it back to the large workroom. She stood it by the back entry beside four finished table arrangements and two other floral sprays on wire stands—all ready for delivery to Frazier's, the main funeral home in Bryson City.

Olivia actually appreciated a hectic day to keep her mind occupied after the fiasco with Warner in the garden last night. Fortunately, neither Patti nor Wanda grew up in Bryson City and neither knew of her past with Warner. In fact, Olivia had no close friend she could talk to about her problems with Warner since no one really knew they'd developed a relationship years ago. Olivia sighed. Warner had been right about that fact he'd thrown at her.

When the front door bell chimed, Olivia headed back into the store. Several tourists had filtered in from the depot area not far from her florist. A plus in Olivia's downtown location was its proximity to the Great Smoky Mountain Railroad depot with its popular vintage railroad excursions, the nearby train museum, and a side street of colorful shops. Olivia's floral and gift business sat within view of the depot behind a neat white picket fence. The florist's profusion of porch plants, garden art, and whimsical garden stakes often drew tourists to the renovated cottage.

Olivia walked into the storefront to greet the three tourists browsing the store. She was soon talking about her store items and answering questions about Bryson City.

"We're staying at the Folkestone Inn," one of the ladies said. "It is the most charming place."

"It is," agreed Olivia. "And their food is wonderful."

"Oh, look at this cute floral bag, Sylvia." Her friend snatched up a purse covered in stitched daisies she found hanging by a shelf of houseplants. "You know how I love daisies!"

Olivia smoothed a hand over a similar bag with a velvety design of tulips across it. "A woman who lives nearby in Whittier makes these. I loved the floral tapestry designs and decided to carry some in my shop."

Both ladies bought a purse before leaving, as well as hand-painted butterfly garden stakes they found clustered in a tall floor vase. The man in their group, who introduced himself as Bob, bought a stack of postcards and a garden stone that read: Life is Good.

As Olivia rang up their purchases, the front bell sounded again and Warner walked in. He lingered near a display of silk flower wreaths and dried arrangements by the doorway while she finished.

Gathering her courage before he started some sort of scene in front of Patti, she followed her customers to the door and then walked to stand near him. "I didn't expect to see you today."

He reached into a display rack to pick up a carved, wooden bluebird and ran his hand over it. "I thought I owed you a bit of an apology for last night."

She waited.

He sat the bluebird down carefully and picked up a second carving, a cardinal this time. His eyes studied it, avoiding hers.

"I like these birds," he said, at last.

"So do I." Her eyes skimmed his neat maroon shirt and trim, khaki shorts while he looked at the array of bird carvings. "Maurice Wendover carves these and lets me sell them in the shop. He lives on the mountain off Galbraith Creek above Ela. He also makes birdhouses and painted wooden chapels like the one you saw on the front porch. The chapels sell well not only to tourists but as funeral memorials."

Warner glanced around the store, a half smile playing over his lips. "Who would imagine, in a million years, that Flora Fair could do all of this?" He grinned at her.

She pushed him behind the display, out of Patti's sight. "Don't start with me, Warner. I'm working here." She glanced toward the register and the work area behind it, dropping her voice. "I thought you said you came to apologize."

"I did mention that."

She waited, watching him. If there was one thing her Grandmother Lila had taught her it was the power of silence at the right moment.

Warner shifted, uncomfortable, then sighed. "Olivia, I said things I hadn't planned to say last night and was out of line."

"I see." He seemed sincere. Olivia found her eyes shifting to his mouth then, remembering the kiss.

He followed her gaze, seeming to read her thoughts. "I haven't decided yet if I'm sorry about that." He grinned at her.

Irritating man.

She turned and started toward the register and her workstation. "I have work to do, Warner. Patti and I have flowers to finish for two funerals tonight at Frazier's plus our usual orders."

He trailed behind her toward the register. "I don't believe I've met Patti."

Surprised at his interest, she introduced Patti Headrick to Warner. He walked behind the register to shake her hand and talk to her—certainly more congenial than the Warner of the past.

Never neglecting work, Patti continued putting flowers into the FTD order on her table while she talked. "My son Richard is a big fan of yours. I wish he were here to meet you. He can hardly wait for the signing at Gil's next Saturday. He's using the delivery money he's saved from the past months to buy all five of your books, personally autographed."

Warner propped against her desk, watching with interest while she designed a lush floral bouquet of lilies and roses. "Gil's is offering a book special with multiple buys," he told her, "and the publisher is giving free Geeky Gilmore hats with three or more book purchases."

"Rich will be thrilled to hear that." She gave him a shy glance. "Would you mind if I snapped your picture for him while you're here? If it's an imposition, I'd understand ...."

Warner waved a hand. "It would be fine, Patti." He glanced Olivia's way while Patti dug a small digital camera out of her purse.

"You can take the photo of me and Olivia together if you'd like. Our families are neighbors and the two of us grew up together. I'll give you my e-mail address and you can send me a copy. Olivia might want one, too."

Olivia pasted on an appropriate smile.

About ten minutes later, as Patti finished snapping the last of several photos, the bell rang again, letting in Vickie Leigh Derryberry, Brody Hanks, and Logan Staley.

Logan's voice boomed across the store. "Well, well. If it isn't Weird Warner. I heard you were back in town."

Brody laughed. "And would you check out this scene, Logan. He's getting his picture taken just like a big celebrity." Brody strolled across the room in the loose walk so characteristic of him.

Vickie Leigh followed, pulling Logan along with her. "I told you Warner had come down to Bryson City." She sent a bright smile Warner's way. "I also told you he'd gotten better looking, too, didn't I?" She fluttered her eyelashes toward Warner, as if that compliment should thrill him.

Patti, looking annoyed, opened her mouth to comment, but Warner gave her a little shake of his head. He pulled a business card out of his pocket and laid it on her desk. "Patti, here's the e-mail address you'll need. You tell Rich I'll look forward to seeing him next Saturday."

Patti nodded. "Thank you. I look forward to seeing you again, too."

"Oh, yeah. The big book signing is coming up at Gil's Bookstore." Brody stopped by the register near Olivia. "I saw the big splash in the paper today. Guess it helps to know someone on the newspaper. I'm sure Loser Leonard felt tickled pink to write up a splashy article about his old school buddy."

Vickie Leigh crossed her arms. "Brody Hanks, you're being rude. I thought Leonard wrote a nice article about Warner and his little books."

Ignoring Vickie, Brody leaned toward Warner. "What are you doing back here in Bryson City, Warner?"

"In general, visiting my family and, in particular, stopping by to see an old friend today." He moved a step closer to Brody. "And what are you doing here?"

Brody bristled. "We came by to talk to Olivia about a class reunion meeting. We're all on the planning committee together." He turned his back on Warner to speak to Olivia. "The gang is getting together this Friday night at Roberta's and Russell's for another meeting. Roberta's mother is keeping the boys, so we're doing a pool party afterward, with everybody bringing something for dinner. Just the eight of us, like old times."

Brody rounded the counter to sidle up to Olivia, leaning over to plant a wet kiss on her mouth before she realized what he planned. Still keeping an arm around her waist, he sent a cocky look Warner's way. "I guess Olivia told you she and I are a number now?"

"I don't think she mentioned it." Warner moved past them, heading toward the door. He paused near the display at the front of the shop. "Olivia, you wrap up a selection of those carved birds for me. I know someone I want to send them to. I'll pick them up later when I'm down this way again."

The door's chime rang out its two notes as he let himself out.

Uncomfortable, Olivia shifted away from Brody, opening her calendar book near the register. "What time is this meeting on Friday?"

"It starts at six o'clock." Brody winked at her. "Is that good for you, sweetheart?"

Olivia ignored him, turning to Vickie Leigh. "What can I bring to help with dinner? Did Roberta plan what everyone should contribute?"

"You should know Roberta planned out *every* detail." Vicki giggled. "She told me to tell you to bring a dessert."

Olivia nodded, making a note in her desk calendar. "Well, I'm glad Roberta could host the first meeting. It's going to take a lot of work for the committee to create a good reunion by early September."

The phone rang, interrupting their discussion and bringing in yet another floral order for one of the funerals tonight. Olivia rolled her eyes. "I've got to get back to work," she told her friends, studying the new order in her hand. "We have two big funerals tonight, and Patti, Wanda, and I will probably be here until after hours finishing all the flowers."

"Okay. We'll see you Friday." Vickie Leigh wiggled her fingers in a wave as she herded the boys out the door.

Her mind turning to business, Olivia headed toward her workstation, pausing at Patti's desk. "That phone order I took came from Mr. and Mrs. Bratcher. They've been out of town and only learned this afternoon about Fannie Bowling dying. They want a sympathy arrangement sent. Mr. Bratcher said anything we could put together would be fine with them, ordering at the last minute."

She glanced at the clock. "If you'll make their arrangement, I'll start on that full casket cover for the Whitlow funeral. I think I'll use the workroom to spread out. Those cover arrangements are large. You can keep an eye on the storefront and then start on the standing sprays for the Whitlow family. Wanda should be back any minute to help."

No quick answer followed, but Patti finally spoke, her words measured. "I thought W. T. Zachery was your friend, Olivia. He mentioned you used to be neighbors and grew up together."

Olivia nodded.

Patti's hand tightened on the roll of florist tape she held. "Well, your friends acted insufferably rude to him." Two spots of color came into Patti's cheeks. "And so did you."

"What?" Olivia looked at Patti in surprise and then thought back. "Oh, ... Brody, Logan, and Vickie Leigh are always like that. Warner knows how they are; I'm sure he didn't think anything about it."

"I don't think that's true." Patti shook her head. "How could you condone their behavior so easily? They called him an ugly name, some nasty cut from the past. They belittled him as an author, made rude remarks about the write-up in the paper today, and insulted Leonard Goldstein who wrote the article and owns the newspaper."

She glared at Olivia, obviously upset. "Also, what brought on that public kiss Brody Hanks gave you—like some sort of in-your-face challenge to Warner? It's not like you to let someone kiss you in public. Gross." She wrinkled her nose in distaste. "Anyway, even if those three always act rude like that, why didn't you speak up for W. T.—make some defense for him? Even Vickie Leigh tried to chide Logan and Brody."

Olivia felt stunned. "You don't understand. Logan and Brody always act that way around Warner."

Patti's mouth dropped open. "And that makes it all right?"

Olivia didn't know what to say.

"Listen, perhaps I'm out of line here." Patti turned her eyes back to her work. "I know this is your business; I only work for you and I didn't grow up around here." She hesitated, obviously weighing her words. "But rude is rude, Olivia." Patti put a hand on one hip. "I felt hurt for W. T. I really did. It made me think of how mean some of the boys at school are to Richard. They behave like that with him."

"Richard?"

"Yes. Surely you've noticed. He's a little different from many of the other kids, and still relatively new in the area. He's experienced trouble making friends and fitting in."

"I didn't realize. Rich is a great kid."

"I know he is, and I think W. T. Zachery is a nice person, too." She snatched up a flower to stuff it in her arrangement. "A lot nicer than any of that group that just left. Honestly. I can't believe you didn't notice how awful they acted."

Before they could converse further, Wanda came in, bubbling over with conversation about her completed deliveries. "What a day! Reeva Richards hunted for twenty minutes trying to find her purse to pay me for her delivery. Then I ran into a wreck out on the highway. The traffic piled up for an age. I'm sorry I'm late. What do you need me to do?"

"Start on the Baker order you took earlier for the Bowling

funeral," Olivia answered.

"I'll get right on it." Wanda huffed back to her station.

Olivia glanced toward Patti, but she'd returned to her work, evidently reluctant to pursue their former topic in front of Wanda.

"Just as well," she thought. With so much work to do, they needed all their time and effort to complete their orders before their day ended.

CHAPTER 6

A week passed. Warner worked his way through his feelings by writing. His Gilmore books provided a good outlet for his anger and frustration. Actually, he felt disappointed more than anything. He'd convinced himself through the years that perhaps he viewed the actions of his high school peers through youthful eyes, partly imagined the ways they acted. Or even projected his own feelings onto them. Reality quickly slapped him out of that notion these first days back in Bryson City.

A little depressed by it all, Warner escaped, as he always did, into his art and his imaginary worlds. He had control there. Real life too often proved messy, painful, and disillusioning.

Traveling to Atlanta for a speaking engagement that his publisher had scheduled helped pull him out of his funk, too. It reminded him of who he was now—of his strengths, his better self never acknowledged or recognized in those high school years. The crowds and their enthusiastic appreciation and applause didn't hurt either.

Wanting to give back, and knowing that doing so always lifted any stint of depression, Warner stayed in Atlanta to speak at several schools and to visit a children's hospital. On the way back to Bryson City, he took a side trip into the Appalachian Mountains of northeast Alabama to the Kate Duncan Smith School at Gunter Mountain. His grandmother's DAR group sponsored a class there, and he visited her group's fifth grade classroom and spoke in a school assembly. The director graciously put him up in a guest cottage overnight and he hung out with the kids all evening, encouraging their dreams.

He felt more like himself again when he returned to Bryson City late Tuesday night. The following day, with his grandfather's car in the shop, Warner dropped his granddad off at the drugstore for work. Then on a whim, he cut over a few streets, parked his car at the end of Bryson Street and walked across the bridge to Island Park. Tucked on a pocket of land in the middle of the Tuckaseegee River, the park created a green oasis for a quiet walk or picnic.

As he strolled down the path along the riverbank, he remembered this had always been a favorite spot of his and Olivia's for lunch when downtown. He spotted her now sitting at a picnic table beside the river.

"Taking a break from the florist?" he asked, walking to her table under a deep shade tree.

She looked up, startled, her cheeks flushing, but then quickly collected herself—drawing on her years of Fairchild training in etiquette and poise drilled into her by her grandmother. Warner almost snorted with the thought. Lila Fairchild nearly schooled the spontaneity out of Olivia after her mother died.

"Hello, Warner." She gave him a practiced smile.

He sat beside her on the picnic bench, not asking if it was all right. "Nothing has changed much at the park."

"No." She looked out over the river. "But I'd like to see renewal and beautification started here, some more grass, maybe daffodils scattered along the riverside, a few flowering trees planted."

"You could organize that. Get one of the local civic organizations or scout groups to help. You've always been good at that sort of thing."

She looked at him in surprise. "Why, thank you. I may work on that this fall when it's the season to plant."

"Maybe, but it might be hard to find time with the class reunion committee consuming all your spare hours." The catty remark popped out before he could stop it.

Her eyes dropped. "Listen, Warner, about that."

"I shouldn't have popped off." He stood.

"No." She put a hand on his arm. "I think you had reason to. Brody and Logan were rough on you last week. So was Vickie Leigh, in her own way." She sighed. "Sit down again, Warner. I'll share my lunch with you."

He glanced at her lunch sack on the table.

"It's a Subway sandwich. It's a better deal buying a whole sandwich, so I usually get the whole thing and save half for another day. You can share the second half." She pulled the sandwich out of its bag. "I even bought cookies."

"Well then, if there are cookies." He moved closer to her, letting her put half the sandwich in front of him on a napkin.

They ate, watching the river drift by, the sunlight playing over its surface. It was quiet at Island Park, despite the town being so nearby, with only bird song and sounds of squirrels scampering among the trees to interrupt their thoughts.

Olivia cleared her throat. "Patti read me the riot act for how rude Brody, Logan, and Vickie Leigh acted to you at my shop. She fussed at me because I didn't stand up for you or intervene."

Warner watched her twist her hands, nervous about her words.

"I felt shocked by her criticism." She turned pale, sky blue eyes to him at last. "I'm so accustomed to how they act that I honestly didn't notice anything wrong in their behavior. It didn't seem improper or inappropriate to me because I'm so used to their ways."

She fidgeted with a loose strand of her hair, biting at her lip. "I've thought about it ever since—what Patti said and what you told me before in the garden."

Warner polished off his sandwich, waiting for her to finish her thoughts.

"Maybe I simply drifted along too much, like that fictional character in your Gilmore books, Flora Fair." She sighed and looked at him. "Was she based on me?"

He sent her a grin. "Ah, I see you've been reading my books."

Her eyes shifted away to watch a squirrel scamper down a tree. "I've read all your books, and not only the Gilmore titles."

"And you think you see yourself in Flora Fair?"

"Oh, honestly, Warner." She sent him a look of exasperation. "Anyone can see those Gilmore book characters bear resemblances to our crowd at Swain High."

He laughed. "Do you think so?"

"Fine, make a joke." Her cheeks flushed pink and she began to stuff lunch remains into her bag, preparing to leave.

"Settle down, Olivia." He pulled the bag out of her hands and put it back on the table. "I'm only laughing because you're the first person here besides Barry who seemed to notice any resemblance between my book characters and the people in Bryson City."

She crossed her arms. "Did you purposely base your characters on people here?"

He took a deep breath, thinking how he wanted to answer. "One of the big questions I'm often asked, in interviews and when I give author presentations," Warner said at last, "is whether I base my characters on people I know. I generally answer no, telling the audience with a grin that I possess an expansive and overly fertile imagination that constantly seethes with ideas for new characters, dramas, and funny stories. They laugh and I usually move on to other questions."

"Warner, that's not exactly an answer to my question." She fingered a pinecone that lay on the picnic table.

"Then perhaps I should tell you a little bit about how the Gilmore books came to be." He glanced at her. "Will you keep this information in confidence if I'm candid with you? I try to keep my private life out of the media."

She sat up primly. "Despite some criticisms you have of me, Warner Zachery, I think you might remember I always kept every confidence and secret you ever shared with me."

He considered her words. "That's true. I believe you did."

She waited.

Warner rubbed a hand over his neck, trying to decide how to begin. "After Nelle and I married and I started working on staff with Kite Publishing, that produces *Kite Magazine*, I came home one day to find her curled up on the sofa reading through a pile of spiral-bound notebooks I'd scribbled stories in during middle and high school days. She found them among a pile of my old books and papers while on a cleaning spree."

"And?" Olivia prompted when he hesitated.

" 'These are good,' she told me as she tapped a small stack of notebooks beside her. 'And don't get mad,' she added, grinning, 'but I hauled them over this week to an editor friend of mine who handles young adult titles at Whitehouse Press. He really likes them. I think Whitehouse may offer you a contract after we polish these up.' "

Warner paused to give Olivia an explanation. "Nelle was an editor at North Street Publishing. North Street doesn't handle young adult or children's titles, but Whitehouse does and Nell helped initiate that contact for me."

Olivia sipped on her cola, listening.

"I told Nelle the cartoon antics, character stories and sketches she'd read in my old notebooks, about Geeky Gilmore and his friends, were character takeoffs on peers I went to school with in middle and high school. I explained that I wrote them as a way to vent and that I felt uncomfortable about publishing them for that reason, good or not."

Warner ran a hand through his hair. "She laughed and said no one ever recognized themselves in fictional works like this. Especially with zany character names like the ones I created and with comical titles for the schools and the places I used. She claimed the fictional spoofs I'd penned hardly qualified as a *Peyton Place* exposé."

Changing position, Warner got up to sit on the picnic table, propping his feet on the bench. "Nelle was a pusher when it came to work. And she was convinced my chronicles about Geeky's struggles with his middle school peer group would score a hit, so she soon had me editing, revising, and rewriting the old stories in my notebooks into book format to get them ready for submission." He glanced at Olivia to gauge her reaction.

"So the characters were really based on people here." Olivia turned her eyes to his. "I think I can see who many of them represent."

He shrugged. "Most of it was made up. I created a peer world with an odd kid who had a hard time fitting in—a storyline exaggerated from the one I remembered."

Olivia caught his glance. "Geeky Gilmore is you."

"In some ways but in others Gilbert Gilmore, or Geeky, is a composite of all socially awkward kids in the middle school years."

"I think Nelle is right that few people would recognize themselves in your characters." She shook her head, smiling. "None of our group seem to realize how any of the Gilmore characters parrot them—but then not many have read your books. Actually, I think only someone who knew you very well would recognize the resemblances."

She glanced toward a kayaker on the river, thinking. "I believe the cheerleaders in the Gilmore books, Lina Lou Topps and Betty-Letty Leadbetter, are prototypes of Roberta and Vickie Leigh. Ross Boswell, who everyone calls Mr. Popular in the books, feels like a mix of Brody Hanks and Russell Simmons, while Biff Gridiron reminds me of Logan, our star quarterback." She fingered the pinecone again. "A lot of the others I don't recognize at all—like Gilda Gay Go-Along and Lester Leechman."

"Pretty sharp." Warner felt flattered Olivia knew his characters so well that she could reel off their names. "What about Beaner Stringer, Geeky's best friend?"

She giggled. "Oh, that has to be Barry, a lovable, awkward, brainy guy, and Owlie Olden seems a little like Leonard, smart, sensible, and intense." She pushed a strand of blond hair behind her ear. "Do Barry and Leonard recognize themselves and do they mind?"

"They don't mind. They think the whole thing is a hoot." He laughed. "Barry came to New York to visit me a couple of times. Once, I took him to a book signing with me, and he wore a Beaner Stringer T-shirt."

Her eyes widened. "There are T-shirts based on all the characters?"

"Yeah." He grinned. "T-shirts, hats, and a line of action figure toys coming out with the movie next year."

"Oh, my." She considered this revelation and then grinned. "I want a Flora Fair T-shirt and a hat."

Warner laughed. "I'll get you one if you promise not to wear them around town. I don't want trouble like that here."

"I can see how it could be a problem. I felt a little touchy about Flora Fair even though you painted her in a sweeter way in comparison to some of the other characters." She looked thoughtful again. "Was Nelda Nerdle or Ella Phant based on any of our friends?"

He frowned at her. "Not any of *your* personal friends, Olivia. I doubt you even noticed them except to snicker at them."

Olivia shot him a dark look, stiffening. "That's not kind, Warner. I wasn't cruel to anyone at school, even if I did get overly caught up in my own social set much of the time."

He didn't reply to her denial. "Ella Phant represents girls like Frances Rutherford, plain and overweight, with Nelda a type of Imogene Vogel, an intelligent girl, always reading, looking ahead to future dreams."

"I certainly remember Imogene." Olivia gave a disgusted snort. "We called her Imogenius. She made straight As on every paper she wrote and looked down her nose at any of us who cheered for sports teams as stupid." Olivia threaded a hand through her hair. "Did you know Imogene tried out for pom-pom squad the summer before freshman year in high school, made the team, and then quit after school started? She called it boring to sashay out on the football field grinning and waving pom-poms."

Warner doubled over laughing. "God bless her. I wish I'd heard her say that, and I wish I'd been that strong and sure of myself at fourteen."

Olivia's mouth dropped open. "Is that how you see it?" She turned questioning eyes to his. "Isn't it a form of reverse snobbery for Imogene to make fun of the pom-pom squad as stupid and boring and then to turn around and criticize girls on the cheerleading and pom-pom squad because they made fun of her? Everyone on the pom-pom squad and on the cheerleading team work hard to create their routines, support the school sports program, and represent their school at outside events."

His lips twitched. "Imogene worked on the school annual, the newspaper, and in other capacities."

Olivia tossed her head. "Well, all I'm saying is that the hostilities, if you want to call them that, between peer groups swung both ways, Warner Zachery. I know for a fact that Leonard, Barry, and you made fun of the jocks at school and poked fun at many of the popular boys in leadership positions. You often looked down your nose at the dumb guys from out in the country, too, the ones who could hardly string a coherent sentence together for English class or figure out a simple geometry problem."

"I don't remember that." He locked eyes with her.

"Well, I do." She refused to back down. "It's natural to remember how others discriminate against us in the past while seldom wanting to recall how we often did the same or more." She reached for her cola.

"What did you think about Flora Fair?" He decided to skirt the subject.

She twisted at a thin silver bracelet on her arm. "You painted her to be very beautiful and admired."

"She is beautiful and admired." Warner lowered his voice. "Surely she knows that?"

Olivia blushed self-consciously. "You also painted Flora as unsure of herself, often following after the crowd with Gilda Go-Along, sometimes looking and talking a little silly."

"But Flora had her dreams. She loved flowers and wanted to open a flower shop one day, but she feared telling anyone her dream."

She passed him her cola to finish it. "Why didn't you let her tell Geeky her dreams? I told you mine all through the years."

"In the Gilmore books, Geeky and Flora had little to do with each other. Geeky could only admire Flora from afar. Anything he learned about her he learned through others. That's why he secretly left flowers on her desk sometimes or in her locker."

She smiled. "You used to leave me flowers."

"I know." Warner felt a rush of desire again, seeing that misty look in her eyes. He pushed the empty cola cup into the lunch sack. "Let's take a walk around. Do you have time?"

She looked at her watch. "A little more time."

Warner watched her slide off the park bench. She wore striped summer slacks and a simple shirt in a rosy pink that enhanced her complexion and willowy blond beauty. Warner never remembered a time she hadn't attracted attention. "I'm glad you opened your florist and fulfilled your old dream."

Olivia walked along beside him on the dirt path twining around the island park. "I have to admit your character Flora inspired me, reminded me of my childhood dreams and yearnings. The first Gilmore books came out five years ago, before Verlie died. When I learned Verlie's shop would be closed and all the equipment and supplies sold off, I found myself thinking: What would Flora do?"

He smiled at her. "And so you bought her florist business."

"Not exactly, but I bought all the equipment and supplies and opened my own shop in Daddy's and Mother's old house near the clinic—the one they lived in when first married, before Grandfather Fairchild died. After his death, they moved out to live with Grandmother Lila."

"That's right. I forgot. Your dad rented out the house in town afterward."

"Yes, and the house sat empty several years, needing repairs, before I approached Daddy about it. Daddy didn't really want to update the house and rent it again, so he let me buy it." She leaned over to pick up a big maple leaf to study. "I used my own savings and the money Grandmother Lila left me to buy Verlie's equipment and supplies and to renovate the house into a florist shop."

"The location is perfect for a florist business, next to the depot area and downtown."

"I thought so."

They walked on, not talking, thinking their own thoughts.

"Warner, will you tell me more about Nelle?" Olivia asked,

hesitating over the words.

Surprised at her question, Warner stopped to look down at her. "Maybe. If you'll tell me about Brody and the doctor you're seeing."

"There's little to tell there." She wrinkled her nose.

He shot her a dark glance. "Evidently Brody doesn't think so."

She twirled the leaf in her hand. "All of us in our group dated each other for years. You know that. We went to ball games, parties, and dances together and exchanged a lot of kisses." She shrugged. "They don't mean anything. I tried to tell Patti that about Brody's kiss."

He lifted an eyebrow. "Oh, I believe Brody's kiss did mean something. He was staking a claim and letting me know I wasn't to poach."

She snorted. "Well, that's silly. We only go out now and then, both being single, and he knows I date other people, too. He knows I'm also dating Martin Reese, the new doctor who joined Daddy's practice." She folded the leaf in half so that its symmetrical sides matched. "Martin's a nice young man and new in town. I wanted to get to know him since he's working with Daddy."

Warner chuckled. "You don't need to date someone to get to know them."

She looked annoyed. "Well, if you don't date someone now and then, people start to think you're ...." She blushed. "Somewhat peculiar."

Warner laughed, kicking at a stick across the path. "So you're dating Martin and Brody because it's what proper people should do."

The flush in her cheeks deepened. "I'm very traditional."

"I remember," he said with a touch of sarcasm.

Olivia ignored his tone. "It's your turn now. You said you'd tell me more about Nelle."

"All right." Warner stopped to prop a foot on a bench by the river. "I started seeing Nelle Wyatt in New York while still in college at Cooper Union studying art. We soon shared confidences about ourselves as most dating couples begin to do. She quickly weaseled the truth from me as to why I worked as a janitor at the publishing company—that I wanted to illustrate and write comics or books and was trying to learn more about the publishing world by working at North Street."

As he paused, Olivia asked. "Was she pretty?"

"Yes, but not beautiful like you," he answered candidly. "Soft brown hair in a page-boy style below her ears, gray eyes the color of a cloudy sky, fair skin that burned too easily. She had an earnest face that could be stern or gentle, depending on her mood, and an incredible capacity for listening."

He let the memories roll into his mind. "Older than me, she'd finished college and was already an editor, used to reading and evaluating the worth of writers' submissions, her days filled with the ins and outs of the publishing world. North Street published a wide variety of works of different genre." His mind drifted back. "Nelle soon started reading works I had in progress, comics I'd created, like the little dog series, and a couple of young adult books I'd written and illustrated. Anything she liked she pressured me to finish and polish. She pushed me, got excited about my work and my possibilities. She painted pictures of success for me I'd never dared to dream before."

Warner sighed. "Whenever I doubted myself, she always said, 'Why not, Warner? Why not you?' Then she'd tell me some incredible motivational story of someone with less talent than me who'd succeeded beyond his wildest dreams. She constantly painted a picture of accomplishment before my eyes, pushed me to be my best."

He thought back. "She helped me get my first stories and cartoons published with Kite, that creates *Kite Magazine*, where I went to work after graduation, and then, as I mentioned before, she helped pitch my first Geeky Gilmore book to an editor friend of hers at Whitehouse Press. That was an incredible moment."

"And you married her."

"Yes, I did. I'd graduated by then, started to make a little money and had a good part-time job with Kite. She actually proposed to me." He shook his head with the memory. "I told her I needed to wait until I could properly provide for her, but she said I needed to let her provide for me so I'd have more time to write."

"She sounds remarkable," Olivia said.

"She was." He started back up the path again, and she fell into step.

CHAPTER 7

It hurt hearing about Nelle, but Olivia felt glad, even so, to learn what sort of woman stole Warner's heart. A smart one, obviously. And one who loved and believed in him.

The walking trail curled to circle back around the park now. Olivia pointed to an old tree ahead. "There's the oak we used to leave messages in. Do you remember?"

"Yes, I do." He walked over to look in the charred hole in the tree trunk. "We used to leave scribbled notes and little gifts to each other here inside an old mason jar." He leaned into the hole. "I don't find the jar, but maybe I'll stick another one in here one day and drop you off a surprise."

Olivia glanced at her watch with regret. "I really need to start back to the shop Warner. Wanda needs to leave for deliveries, and I can't leave Patti with all the work."

"I'll drive you. That will save time. I parked my car across the bridge."

"The Batmobile." She giggled.

"It's great, isn't it?" He headed up the path again. "I got it as a perk for doing television commercials."

She stopped, stunned. "You mean they gave it to you for free?"

He made a goofy face. "You didn't think I bought it?"

"Well, sure." She started walking again. "And how in the world can you get a car like that for free by doing television commercials?"

He grinned at her. "Amazing isn't it what television pays. Especially if you're a celebrity."

"I see." She pursed her lips.

"Just joking." He punched at her arm. "But I walked into a windfall of financial success with the publication of the Gilmore books. It knocks my socks off sometimes when I sit down to talk to my accountant."

"I'm happy for you. It's wonderful you've been so successful." She started across the railed bridge off the island. "I always believed you had a great talent."

He paused. "I know you believed in me, Olivia. You're the first one I ever verbalized my dreams to and the first one who ever encouraged me. I'll always remember that."

She felt glad he remembered her early encouragement, but regretted she didn't believe in him more later on, when he felt driven to go to Cooper Union in New York.

"You always knew where you wanted to go." She stopped by his car on the other side of the bridge. "As soon as you visited New York the summer you turned thirteen and saw Cooper Union College, near all the big New York publishing houses, you said you wanted to go there. After that summer visit, you worked hard to earn good grades in high school and to create the portfolio and accomplishments you needed to get in."

Warner opened the door for her before walking around to slide into his side of the car. "You're right. That summer did prove a turning point for me." He started the car. "It gave me a vision that helped me endure and get through the high school years to come."

She looked at him in surprise. "You saw high school as only something to endure and get through? You didn't enjoy it?"

"No, Olivia. I didn't enjoy it." His hand clenched on the steering wheel. "But I know you did. It was your time to shine and be a star. To walk down the hall in your cheerleader outfit, with every boy in school watching you and wishing he could date you. Waving and smiling from an open convertible in one parade after another, wearing whatever crown you'd won for yet another contest. Always knowing you were beautiful, admired, popular, and loved. Most of us didn't have that." He turned the corner, heading the car up

Greenlee Street. "High school isn't a time for most teens to shine, Olivia. It's a time to endure until you can get out."

She looked out the window as they drove the short distance to her shop. "My high school years were happy, and I enjoyed the years before and after them, too. I like my life here in Bryson City."

"I know." He smiled, pulling into a parking space beside the store.

As she let herself out of the car, he swung out, too. "I'll come in with you to pick up the carved birds you put back for me last week. They're for Grandmother and Grandfather Delacourt in Staten Island. They'll love them, and I owe them a lot for the help they gave me while I attended Cooper Union and then, afterward, as I started my writing and illustration work."

She headed up the sidewalk to the door of Fairgarden Florist. "You lived with your grandparents for a time, didn't you?"

"In summers and for a short season after college until I could save up for an apartment." He followed her into the shop. "Will you show me around? I didn't really get time to see your business the other time."

"Okay, if you'd like." Olivia tucked her purse under the desk by the register and waved at Patti, on the phone. Then she turned back to Warner. "You already know Fairgarden Florist is a converted house. The two old bedrooms upstairs are simply used as storage rooms, but downstairs the contractors gutted most of the interior to convert it into a business."

She walked toward the front of the store. "The old entry, living and dining rooms became the main storefront entry and display area." Olivia gestured around. "Against the wall is the big, refrigerated floral case where we keep fresh flowers made up and ready to go. Around the room are shelves and display cases with plants, gifts and seasonal arrangements."

She led him to the right. "Through this door is an outdoor garden room where the cottage's old sunroom used to be."

"I like the fountain." Warner pointed to an ornamental structure in the corner, with water bubbling over rocks into a pool below.

"Yes. Visitors always like this room with its tinkling fountains, outdoor items, garden décor, and cozy wicker furniture."

Moving back into the front entry, she led him across into the second display area. "This room behind the main area, once a bedroom, is filled with silk and artificial flowers, wreaths, and more gift items."

Warner picked up a pink ceramic baby shoe.

"I keep a lot of ceramic pieces made by a local craftswoman. People like them to mix in with floral arrangements and, like the baby shoe you're holding, many can be used as floral containers."

Warner glanced around. "The way all the areas open up, you can see every area from the front desk and register. And you put a chime on the front door."

"Yes. It helps to alert us to customers when we're busy with arrangements or on the phone." Olivia moved through a doorway by the desk, gesturing for Warner to follow. "This area, that used to be a hallway and part of the old kitchen, houses our workstations, with shelves and storage bins built from floor to ceiling." She laughed, rolling up a strand of ribbon trailing on the floor from a dowel rod loaded with other colored rolls of ribbon. "We try to keep the shop neat, but it's a challenge."

Patti, still on the phone, waved as they walked by her work area.

Olivia smiled at her as they passed. "Patti is my main floral designer and my assistant manager. She works full-time, while I work part-time since I also manage the Fairchild Gardens." She paused by the next workstation behind Patti's. "I set up our stations one behind the other, so we can all see the front of the store while we work. This is Wanda Baylor's area. She's my other full-time employee and floral designer. Behind her workstation is my area. When needed, we can create more design space in the workroom in back. During our busiest times, like at Valentine's, I bring in extra part-time help."

"Anyone I know?"

"Usually Dixie Cavett, who used to work with Verlie McBride at the Flower Box. You might remember her, with her cap of short white flyaway hair and twinkling brown eyes. She's in her seventies now, but still a fantastic floral designer. She likes to keep her hand in."

He chuckled. "Verlie used to call her Dixie Darling."

"She's a peach." Olivia grinned as she led Warner around the corner. "Here in the workroom, we load and unload deliveries from the back entrance, process the flowers that come in, wash floral buckets, vases, and equipment at the sinks, store finished sprays and arrangements ready to deliver, and create big orders that need more work area."

She looked around at the piles of boxes and at the buckets full of flowers and greenery from the morning's delivery. "Fortunately, the public doesn't ever see this area; it can be a mess sometimes. Wanda does the processing when the flowers arrive. She also does most of the deliveries."

"A versatile woman."

She smiled. "A fun woman, too. Wait 'til you meet her. She keeps us laughing around here."

Olivia gestured ahead. "Down this hallway is a large storage closet, packed with a little of everything, and a bathroom. A door at the end leads back into the front of the shop." She put her hand on a thick, heavy door with strong metal latches. "This is the cooler. The flowers and greenery are kept here. I converted the house's old garage to create this cold room plus a non-refrigerated storage area behind it."

She opened the cooler door to let Warner step inside. "It's always cold in here. You probably won't want to explore for long."

He pulled a flower from a big bucket of water inside the door. "This is a flower I don't know."

Olivia smiled. "It's alstroemeria, a lily from Peru. It's not a flower I grow in the gardens, but it's common in the floral business and very hardy. Clients love the alstroes because the cut life is so long. The blooms will last a week or more with only a little care."

He twirled the flower in his hand. "Are they always golden yellow like this?"

"No, they come in a multitude of colors—salmon, pink, red, orange, mauve, purple, and even bicolored varieties." She pointed to some in other containers.

He sniffed the flower in his hand. "Not fragrant, but pretty. Maybe you can make me a mixed vase of these to take to mother when I leave." He tucked the stem back in the bucket, stepping out of the cooler while Olivia shut the door.

She led him down the back hallway next and into a cozy office in the far corner of the building.

"This has to be your office." He grinned, pausing in the doorway. "It looks like you—peaches, pinks, and greens with floral prints on the walls and this deep floral rug you could sink your bare toes into."

She felt a small flush steal up her cheeks. "It is my office, and I like that it looks out on the patio and the shady yard in back."

"Nice wrought iron furniture outside," he said, glancing out the back window.

"It came with the old house, and I cleaned and painted it."

He looked around with admiration. "You did a fine job with everything. You have reason to be proud of yourself."

"Thank you." Feeling awkward, she wondered if she should ask him to sit down. Seeming to read her mind, he glanced at a green side chair in question.

She nodded, and he dropped into the chair, propping his feet on the matching ottoman. Olivia settled across from him in a smaller coral and green club chair.

He picked at the collar on his shirt. "Tell me about Patti Headrick."

"Why the interest?" she asked.

"Barry likes her."

Olivia grinned. "I thought I'd noticed that."

"Barry isn't making much progress with Patti. He says he doesn't think it's because she's interested in someone else."

"No." Olivia picked up a floral paperweight on the side table to toy with it. "Patti keeps very much to herself. Barry is the only man she's even gone to lunch with or spent any time with since she started to work for me. And I've noticed she keeps him at arm's length."

"What do you know about her?"

"Feeling protective?" she teased.

"No, only curious. This is the first woman I've known Barry to have more than a passing interest in."

Olivia considered her words. "Patti knocked on the door one day before I opened my shop and found me still unpacking boxes and putting stock on my new shelves. She said she was visiting the area, saw my florist sign, and wondered if I might be hiring." Olivia paused. "We talked at length, and I learned she'd grown up working in her grandparents' florist shop. She had experience in every aspect of running a floral business plus accreditation as a floral designer. I liked her immediately." Olivia sat the paperweight back down. "Hiring Patti turned out to be a godsend for me. In many ways she possesses more business sense, and certainly better accounting skills, than I do. We make a good work team."

Warner crossed an ankle over his knee. "She has a son so I assume she's been married."

"Yes, and she told me she took back her maiden name for herself—and for her son Rich—after her divorce."

"That's odd."

"Perhaps, but not if the marriage proved a very unhappy one, and I think that must be true. She never discusses her married years and she clams up about the subject if questions are asked. So does Rich." Olivia picked at a fingernail. "I decided, if Patti wants to keep her past personal, she should be allowed to do so."

Warner gave her a little smirk.

"Okay. I've probed often enough for more information but without any success." She grinned. "Heaven knows Wanda has probed and queried her often enough, too. But Patti keeps herself to herself."

"Maybe her past is making it hard for Barry to get to first base with her."

"You could be right." Olivia tapped her fingers on the chair arm. "He'll need to give her time. I've worked with Patti for three years and we're friends, of course, but not really close friends. I helped her and Rich find a small house to rent behind the shop and I got her involved in church and a few activities. I let Rich run downtown deliveries for me now that he's twelve and in middle school. Patti told me the other day Rich doesn't have many friends. I didn't know that before."

They heard a door open, and Wanda's hearty laugh and voice floated out to them.

"Wanda's back from deliveries." Olivia smiled at Warner as she stood. "Come meet her. I'll fix the arrangement for your mother and gift box the carved birds for your grandparents. After that, I need to work."

"Sure." Warner pushed up from his chair, but he caught her hand as she started by him. "I had a good time with you today, Flora Fair."

Olivia felt color flood her cheeks again.

He leaned closer, pressing a kiss on her forehead. "I still carry strong feelings for you. I keep thinking they'll lessen with time and more familiarity, but they don't. I admit it troubles me to feel so strongly about you. I haven't dated another woman since Nelle."

"Do you think she might have liked me?" Olivia found herself asking.

Warner smiled. "Yes, I think so. She would have loved the garden, too. I used to tell her about it."

"Did you?"

He nodded.

They stood, staring into each other's eyes like two starstruck teenagers. Olivia saw his eyes darken, caught a whiff of that citrusy scent again, and heard his breath hitch.

She broke the mood with some regret, glancing toward the door. "I need to go, Warner."

"I know." He winked at her like he used to do when they were kids then raised a thumb to touch hers. "Thumb to thumb. Remember?"

"Yes." Olivia laughed. "I loved that old joke between us—my green thumb of the garden to your black thumb of the bookish writer and illustrator. I guess some of our old dreams came true, didn't they?"

CHAPTER 8

Warner wanted intensely to kiss Olivia Benton, standing there in her cozy floral office, the space scattered with her intimate personal items and filled with her sweet lily-of-the-valley scent. But it wasn't the place or time. Instead, he followed her back through the hallway into the main store to meet Wanda Baylor and talk to Patti Headrick once again, while Olivia chose a vase for his mother's flowers and gift-wrapped the carved birds for his grandparents.

He was ready to leave when a gangly, dark-haired kid banged through the front door, carrying a skateboard under one arm. "Hey, Mom," he called. "Can I have a couple of dollars to go over to the soda shop? I want to get a chocolate shake and ...." His words fell off and his mouth dropped open.

"W. T. Zachery?" He croaked out the words.

Warner held out a hand. "You must be Rich Headrick. Your mother told me about you last week."

Rich stumbled over his feet to take Warner's hand, giving him a firm if somewhat overly enthusiastic handshake. "Wow, it's so cool to meet you. I have all your books and I put one of the pictures my Mom took of you and Olivia on my bulletin board by my computer." He gulped. "I can't believe you're really here in Bryson City."

Warner grinned. "I grew up here, Rich. My family lives near Deep Creek Campground and the back entrance to the Park. I'd say you're more a stranger to the backside of the Smokies than I am. You've only lived in Bryson City a few years." He paused.

"How do you like it here?"

The boy shrugged and his gaze dropped. "It's okay."

In the silence that ensued, Patti's voice chimed in. "Richard, I really need you to mow the grass at our house this afternoon instead of heading to the soda shop. Besides, I don't like you wandering around town too much on your own. You're only twelve."

Warner watched the boy's shoulders sag. "Hey, tell you what, Patti." Warner turned to her. "I need to stay in town until my Granddad gets off work at the drugstore. His car's in the shop. Why don't you let Rich hang out with me for a little while? He can mow the grass later ... and I've been wanting to visit Soda Pops myself. It's an institution in Bryson City, and Paul Crawley makes great old-time milkshakes."

Rich's head jerked up, his eyes flashing to Warner's in obvious excitement and then to his mother's for approval.

Patti sighed. "I could never live down saying no, W. T. Are you sure you want to take Rich on? He'll talk your ear off, I'm certain, and probably ask you a million questions."

"It'll be fun." He clapped the boy on the shoulder, his eyes moving to the skateboard Rich still held tucked against one leg. "Unless you have another of those skateboards I can ride, you better drop that one with your mother before we leave."

Rich darted across to Patti's station to leave the skateboard. She opened her purse to dig out some money for him.

"Nah, Patti, this one's on me." Warner waved a hand at her. "It's not every day I get to share sodas with a fan who's read every one of my books." He grinned at Rich. "And more than once from what I've heard. I may need him to give me some tips."

With Rich practically dancing to leave now, Warner turned to Olivia, who was finishing up the arrangement of alstroemerias for his mother. "Can you put those flowers in the cooler to stay fresh until I bring Rich back?"

"Sure." Olivia gave him a soft smile, obviously pleased at his interest in Rich. "And you tell Paul I said hello over at Soda Pops."

A few minutes later, Warner strolled down Fry Street past the train depot with Rich Headrick. As Patti warned, the boy talked non-stop about the Gilmore books and asked Warner a stream of questions.

At the corner of Everett Street, Rich pointed to the sign hanging in the window at Gil's Bookstore. "See? Gil's got a big poster up about the book signing and a display of your books in the window." He turned excited eyes to Warner. "Are you really going to give away hats and stuff on Saturday like Mom said?"

Warner nodded. "Yeah. The publisher sent hats, T-shirts, and other promotional items to give away because it's my hometown."

"Wow. I'm going to get there *really* early." Rich loped ahead across Everett Street to start down the sidewalk toward Soda Pops. Two boys came out from a shop and spotted him.

"Hey, it's Dickhead!" one called. "How come you're walking around town without your Mama."

"Yeah, where's your flowers, Flower Boy," the other added in a prissy voice. Laughing, the boys punched each other after their well-fired insults.

Rich's eyes dropped and his walk turned into a weary shuffle. He glanced back at Warner with embarrassment as the boys pushed by him, nearly bumping Rich off the curb.

"Nice guys," Warner said with a touch of sarcasm. "They always that nice?"

"Yeah," Rich said, not adding more. Scowling, he headed toward the striped awning and doorway of Soda Pops, shoving open the door.

Deciding to let the matter go for now, Warner followed, looking around with pleasure at the colorful shop, still filled with its forties and fifties décor and Coca-Cola® memorabilia he remembered so well. The two stopped at the ice cream counter to study the wall menu.

"Well, if it isn't Warner Zachery." Paul Crawley, the owner of Soda Pops, came out from the back wiping his hands on his apron. "I heard you were back in town. Long time no see." He reached across the counter to shake Warner's hand. "What can I get for you?"

"I'm trying to decide between a shake and one of the 'have-it-your-way' banana splits." Warner watched Rich's eyes light at the mention of banana splits. He turned to the boy. "Rich, do you think you could eat a whole banana split if I order one? I hate to sit and eat one of those by myself."

"Yeah, I could eat a whole one." Rich nodded, a little enthusiasm returning to his face.

Paul grinned, putting one hand on his hip. "Two custom splits it is. Tell me how you want yours, Rich." He obviously knew the boy.

Rich tapped his fingers on his chin, studying the menu intently. "Instead of the standard strawberry, vanilla, and chocolate ice cream, I want cookies and cream, raspberry cheesecake, and rocky road ice cream, with all the regular toppings, lots of whipped cream, and cashews scattered across the top." He paused. "And don't forget the cherries."

"Coming right up," Paul got out a banana split dish and started to dip ice cream into it. "What about you, Warner?"

"I think I'll get the same thing Rich ordered. It sounds great." Warner watched the boy's face split into a wide grin. "Plus we'll take two of those cherry limeades, too, that Soda Pops is famous for."

Five minutes later, the two sat at one of Soda Pops red and white Formica tables, spooning their way through two huge banana splits.

"Man, this is good." Rich popped a maraschino cherry into his mouth.

Warner finished an ample bite of ice cream drizzled with chocolate sauce before he answered. "It sure is."

After they wolfed down about half of their splits, Warner caught Rich's eye. "Those guys do that a lot, Rich?"

The boy's gaze dropped to the table—answer enough.

Warner stirred a straw in his limeade. "The guys in middle school used to call me Weird Warner."

Rich's eyes popped open.

"Yeah, I was a pretty big misfit back then. Awkward in sports, a little wimpy in appearance. I read and scribbled pictures all the time. Got ignored or made fun of by the more popular kids." Warner spooned out a scoop of rocky road ice cream and stopped to eat it. "It didn't help that my older brothers were big football and basketball stars in school. My older brother, Vance, led the debate team too—always president of something through his school years. My brother Dean wowed the whole town as star quarterback on the Swain County High team and then played pro ball after high school. He coaches now at Swain High, because he hurt his knee and needed to find a new career."

Warner sipped at his drink, thinking back. "I remember grade school as a better, happier time. I had friends there, felt okay about myself, but in middle school everything changed. The two elementary schools combined, and we started changing classes. You know. All the groups and cliques began forming, and I didn't seem to fit in well with any of them." He gave Rich an honest look. "I really hated some of the guys who made fun of me and kicked me around."

"I know." Rich's eyes blazed. "I hate it here in Bryson City now. A couple of the guys liked me in elementary but then in middle school none of them seemed to be in my classes anymore. Everyone seemed to settle into some sort of group all of a sudden, except me. Then kids started picking on me and making fun of me for stuff I liked or did." He hung his head. "They call me Dickhead from Richard, and they call me Flower Boy because I sometimes work for the florist shop."

A rush of memories washed over Warner at the pain and hurt in the boy's voice.

Rich fiddled with his napkin on the table. "I like computers, too, and I'm good with them, so they call me Geekhead and Computernerd for that."

Trying to shift the conversation a little, Warner asked, "What do you like to do with computers?"

Rich shrugged. "Mess around, play games, write stuff, but I don't like all that messaging and dumb shorthand stuff. LOL and BFN, you know. It's so stupid." He kicked at the bench under his feet. "I like to skateboard, and most people think that's dumb, too, but it's not. You need to practice hard to do good moves like an ollie or a kickflip."

Warner started to tell him he'd skateboarded down the courthouse steps one time but thought better of it. "I liked to skateboard at your age, too," he said instead. "Always wished for a skateboard park in Bryson City where I could practice."

"Yeah, sometimes people get mad and tell my mom when I skate somewhere they don't like." He scowled.

They forked into their banana splits again, intent on eating for a time.

"Did you ever figure out a way to get people to like you?" Rich asked at last. "I mean, you're all famous and everything now."

Warner thought about what to say. "I finally figured out how to get along better and be happier, but I don't want to make it sound easy." He ate a bite of cookies and cream ice cream drizzled with chocolate. "In school here, I never figured out a way to make some people like me."

"Bummer." Rich kicked at the bench again.

Warner studied the boy while he attacked the last of his banana split. He was on the skinny side, hair an unruly mop of black, ears too prominent, mouth too big, but he had bright, expressive eyes—dark chocolate in color. Although not much of a looker now, Warner knew he'd grow in time and come into his own, probably making a fine-looking man. He tried to think what he wished someone had told him at that age, what might have helped him.

After a few minutes he said, "The middle school years are the worst time in life for bullying and peer victimization."

"Peer what?" Rich wrinkled up his nose.

Warner smiled. "Peer victimization—it's a term for bullying, or verbal and nonverbal aggression, among youth. Being picked on is not something you alone experience. More than seventy percent of kids are bullied, particularly nonverbally, by the time they reach the ninth grade."

"Oh, yeah?" Anger crossed the boy's face. "So how come no one does anything about it if it's so prevalent? Teachers and adults don't care. They say 'that's just the way kids are' and stuff like that. They tell you to find a way to get along better with others if you complain. They won't do anything to help you when kids get you in the bathroom and do stuff to you, or call you names in the hall, or trip you and laugh at you."

"Have you talked to your mom?"

"Some, but I don't want to worry her." His eyes lifted to Warner's. "And don't you go telling her about those guys today. It was nothing."

Warner knew it more than "nothing," but he wisely finished his banana split, not arguing further. He didn't know this boy well enough to interfere too much in his life.

"You said you figured out some stuff to make it better," Rich said. "What did you do?" The boy's eyes assessed his chest and shoulders. "Did you beat them up?"

"I work out a little now, but I was never much of a fighter." Warner lifted a shoulder. "Besides, my protagonists always seemed to come at me in twos or threes with only one of me."

"Yeah." Rich stiffened. "Me, too."

Warner tried again to think what to say, not knowing if Rich had experienced physical as well as verbal bullying. "Mostly what I faced in school was relational aggression, like what happened with those guys on the sidewalk—name-calling, ridiculing, put-downs, kids saying things to make me feel stupid or not important."

"I hate that. It makes you feel like—" He stopped, avoiding the inappropriate word that almost slipped out.

"Like dirt." Warner gave him an alternative. "I remember."

Rich picked through the remains of his banana split, spooning out the cashews. "I wish we could move away and live somewhere else, but Mom is glad we found this place after ...." He hesitated. "She loves her job with Miss Olivia," he said instead. "She likes our little house, too, although it's nothing like our old ..." He checked himself again. "She says I need to try harder."

"Maybe." Warner replied, wondering about the pieces of Rich's past he held back. "What helped for me, rather than trying harder, was finding a vision for the future and working toward that. When I started doing that, I found some friends of my own—people I could like, people I enjoyed doing things with. I stopped worrying so much about what everyone else thought or said. I figured out after a while that some of the more popular kids were cliquish and would never like me." He grinned at Rich. "I also realized, in some ways, that I didn't really like them very much either. I didn't really want to hang out with them even if they suddenly started to like me."

A muscle in Rich's jaw bunched. "Figuring out people are never going to like you doesn't make it all right for them to treat you like dirt. It's still wrong."

The door of the shop opened before Warner could form an answer, and Barry Jacobs walked in. "Hey, Warner." He waved. "I thought I saw you as I walked by." He stopped by their table. "I see you've met Rich Headrick."

"Yeah, grab a seat, Barry." Warner scooted over in the booth. "Rich and I just finished two huge banana splits. You wanna order one?"

Barry sat down in the booth beside Warner. "Nah. I ate on my way back from a service call after fixing a computer at the library." He glanced at his watch. "Can't stay long and visit today. I need to get back to the shop."

He pulled a phone out of his pocket to check messages. "I stopped to ask if you wanted to come to my place after the book signing on Saturday for a cookout. Leonard, Imogene, and I want to host a little celebration party. Frances is coming, too. I know you remember her. She married Wesley Leland, a year older than us and in our scout troop. His family runs the Garden Center out on Deep Creek."

As Warner watched Rich's eyes light up, an idea popped into his mind. "Maybe Rich and his mom can come, too." He sent Barry a wink.

"Oh, wow, could we?" Rich leaned forward. "I've never seen your place, Mr. Jacobs. You live down on the river, don't you?"

"Sure, you and your mom can come. Let's walk over to the florist shop and ask her. We'll see if Olivia can come, too, her being Warner's old neighbor and all." Barry sent a catbird smile Warner's way. "We'll make a real party of it."

Warner kicked at Barry under the table, but then actually decided it might a good idea. They could always ask. But whether Olivia would come to a gathering with a group less socially approved, even with Patti and Rich present, would be interesting to see.

CHAPTER 9

Warner's signing at Gil's proved a grand success. Crowds turned out, with a line out the door and around the corner waiting to get books signed by W. T. Zachery.

Olivia attended earlier with Patti and Rich, and now sat at the dresser in her bedroom putting on makeup for the party at Barry Jacobs's place on the river. She glanced at the clock by her bed. Warner planned to pick her up. Just like a date.

Olivia told her father earlier in the week she planned to attend Barry's party.

He lifted an eyebrow in surprise. "Well, this is a new group for you to socialize with. Good for you."

His words surprised her.

"I like Barry Jacobs—solid kid, clever with computers. He's built a nice little business here in Bryson." He forked into the dinner of chicken and dumplings Olivia had prepared. "Who else is coming?"

"Patti and Rich, and old friends of Barry's and Warner's— Leonard Goldstein of the newspaper and his fiancée Imogene Vogel, Wesley Leland, who's Clyde and Ira Jean's boy, and Wesley's wife Frances."

He interrupted her. "Frances? The little Rutherford girl?"

She nodded.

"Used to be a plump little thing, Frances. Imogene Vogel, too. I remember both of them from church." He reached over to add more green beans to his plate. "Always smart girls, if somewhat homely back then. Shaped up to be right nice-looking women now, Imogene teaching over at the community college in Sylva and Frances running her own catering business here in Bryson." He stopped to eat a bite. "If I remember right, Frances caters a lot of the weddings you do the flowers for."

"I think so, Daddy."

He smiled at her. "It sounds like you might have a right nice time. I'm glad to see you branching out and socializing with more folks than only that same old group from high school."

She glanced across the table at him. Since when had her father not been fond of her friends? She'd actually worried he might criticize her going out with a new group tonight. Her Grandmother Lila certainly would have.

Spreading butter on a roll, her father rambled on, unaware of her discomfort. "Barry Jacobs lives outside of Bryson on the river if I remember right. You don't drive well at night. Your mother never did, either. Can you get a ride over and back?"

She looked down at her plate. "Warner is taking me."

"Good. That makes sense with him right next door." He bit into his roll. "Is he picking you up here?'

Again she nodded.

"Fine. Fine. I'll get a chance to say hello when he comes. Haven't seen him yet."

Thinking of those words now as she finished her makeup, Olivia decided to go downstairs ahead of Warner's scheduled arrival time. Who knew what her daddy might say with her not in the room?

Warner arrived promptly, wearing the navy slacks and blue shirt he'd worn to the signing earlier in the day, only missing the Geeky Gilmore ball cap and his suit jacket.

"Come in, come in." Olivia's father's voice boomed as he opened the door. "Did you grab dinner after the signing? If not, Olivia can heat you up a little chicken and dumplings."

"No, thank you, sir. I ate at home." Warner stepped into the door, following his host's gesture into the living room.

"Sit down, sit down." Ray Benton, ever the congenial host, soon had Warner settled and conversing with ease.

To Olivia's surprise, Warner talked comfortably with her father, even making him laugh about stories from the afternoon signing.

"Well, you've become quite the town celebrity." Her dad paused to give him one of those examining looks over his glasses. "Too bad you couldn't have come back sooner to see your family. What kept you away so long?"

Here we go, Olivia thought, groaning inwardly.

Warner smiled at her father. "I had an unrequited love here, Dr. Benton. You know how young people are about those things; I didn't want to face the girl again."

Ray Benton's eyes flew open, as did his daughter's. "I see," he said, noticing the spots of color Olivia could feel staining her cheeks. "But apparently you got over that youthful infatuation since you married in New York. I remember your father telling me about the wedding. Your parents liked your wife very much. I'm sorry, but I can't remember her name."

"Nelle," Warner offered.

Ray nodded. "My sincere condolences to you on losing her so young." He shook his head. "I lost my wife early, too, you know. It's hard."

"Yes, sir, it is." Warner crossed a foot over his knee. "I'll always carry fond memories of your wife, Margaret, sir; she was like a second mother to me. I truly loved her."

Her father's face softened. "Thank you. You know, while you avoided Bryson City over an unrequited love, I actually came here pursuing and hoping for love."

Olivia's mouth dropped open and her father chuckled at her expression. "I met your mother, Olivia, when her father brought her with him to a medical conference in Atlanta." Turning to Warner, he added, "I went to med school at Emory there."

He smiled, straightening his glasses before continuing his story. "Margaret came, not to sit in on any of the medical meetings, but to shop with her mother and go to the Swan House Gardens. I was a young whippersnapper at the time, finishing my residency, and Margaret's father suggested he might be seeking a young doctor to add to his practice. My own desires leaned more toward city living, perhaps a large practice in Atlanta, Birmingham, or Charlotte, but I decided on Bryson City."

"I never knew that." Olivia blinked in astonishment.

He regarded her with interest. "We don't always know all there is to know about those we love, even those we love best."

Warner cleared his throat. "I appreciate your hospitality, sir, but Barry and the others will be expecting us."

"Yes, yes. Of course." Ray rose, starting toward the door. "You two run along. I'll lock up after you."

"Daddy, there's some banana pudding left in the refrigerator if you want a snack later." Olivia kissed his cheek.

"Yes, Livvy." He smoothed her hair fondly. "I'll find it. You go and have a nice time."

Fortunately, Olivia found the evening less awkward than she'd thought. Barry lived in an interesting stone rancher outside Bryson City, set on a bend in the Tuckaseegee as the river twined west toward Fontana Dam. A large patio sprawled behind the house, a perfect spot for an outdoor gathering.

Barry also had invited his next-door neighbors, Reed and Cheryl DeMatteo and their young son Sam for the evening. Sam, twelve, and also a big fan of the Gilmore books provided Rich with a ready-made friend and companion for the evening. Probably exactly what Barry had in mind.

Olivia sat in a metal lawn chair now beside Patti, watching the two boys play on the dock by the riverside. "It's nice to see Rich enjoying such a good time. He and Sam seem to like each other."

Cheryl followed their eyes to the boys. "Yes, and I'm pleased to see Sam make a friend. He's an only child, we live far from town, and he doesn't always find friends with similar interests."

The group dynamics of the party had shifted several times throughout the evening. Olivia felt the most uncomfortable earlier when talking with Frances and Imogene. She'd never been close friends with either, even with all three of them in the same school grade and church. As her father mentioned earlier, Frances and

Imogene had improved in appearance since high school, although both were still full-figured and wore rather unconventional clothes to Olivia's way of thinking.

"I'm pleased to hear about your engagement, Imogene." Olivia smiled, making an effort at conversation.

"Thank you." Imogene straightened the colorful gypsy-length skirt she wore, adding no further comment.

A small silence ensued. Olivia studied Imogene's patterned skirt, keeping a cordial smile on her face. "Are you planning to marry in our church?" She tried again to initiate conversation.

"Yes, she is." Frances leaned forward with excitement. "And I am already planning the catering for the wedding." She turned to Imogene. "I have the most fantastic idea for a cake."

This brought a smile from Imogene at last.

"I'm visualizing four layers." Frances shaped the layers with her hands in the air. "With pearls around the layers and decorative sugar ribbons wrapping each layer." Propping her thick-soled boyish sandals onto a nearby chair, Frances pushed a clump of short, permed hair back behind her ear, while she talked.

"No lavish colors or fussy pastels, Frances." Imogene finally offered a comment. "Leonard and I are keeping it simple with only whites, ivory, and dark burgundy for the wedding colors."

The two friends exchanged ideas back and forth with enthusiasm, leaving Olivia slightly on the outside.

"I hope you're going to let me do the flowers." Olivia tried to reenter their talk. "Especially since you're getting married in our church."

The two women passed a look between them before Imogene threaded her fingers together to speak. "I contracted Ray's Florist in Sylva to do the flowers."

Olivia's mouth dropped open. "But Ray's is more than thirty minutes away while Fairgarden is five minutes from the church. Everyone will expect me to do the flowers, Imogene, since I'm a member of the church and because you and I went to school together."

Imogene and Frances exchanged a second look before Imogene finally spoke again. "I work in Sylva on faculty at Southwestern. I know a lot of people there, many of whom will come for the wedding." She hesitated. "I have a good friend who works at Ray's Florist." Her eyes met Olivia's. "People generally ask their friends to do their flowers, Olivia."

It took effort for Olivia to keep a smile on her face. Imogene's cut was as neat as any Roberta and Vickie Leigh ever sent Imogene or Frances's way, and Olivia felt stunned. "I'm sure your friend will do a lovely job," she said at last, as several others joined their group, helping to break the awkward moment.

Through the rest of the evening, Olivia found herself more aware of Imogene, noticing her poise and confidence, and admiring Frances's ease and ready wit. They certainly acted differently from the two awkward girls of high school she remembered.

To her further surprise, Patti and Cheryl gravitated to both of them, laughing and sharing stories, talking about their lives and work. Olivia, standing to the side watching them giggle and talk, felt a little awkward in their general company.

"Feeling left out?" Warner slipped up beside her, following her gaze.

She turned to him, lifting her chin. "Of course not. I was simply looking around, noticing what a lovely place Barry has."

Annoyed with the grin he shot her way, Olivia swished away to slip into a group discussing favorite songs of the past.

"Hey, Barry," Leonard called out a short time later. "You got any old 1980s music around—songs from back in the past?"

Barry laughed. "Coming right up, Leonard. I bought two of those multi CD sets—best hits of the seventies and eighties. I'll run inside and pop them in the CD player. We're wired out here on the patio for sound."

Old classics of the seventies and eighties soon floated into the evening air around them, taking them back to years past. Talk and laughter rose and fell around the Bee Gees, Stevie Wonder, Prince, Billy Ocean, The Pointer Sisters, and Olivia Newton-John.

To Olivia's surprise, when songs from the movie soundtrack of *Grease* came on, nearly all of Warner's friends—Barry, Leonard, Frances, and Imogene—jumped up impromptu to mimic a great rendition of "Born to Hand Jive", including comical moves and hand motions. Warner whooped, encouraging them, and then he joined them singing along and laughing to "You're the One That I Want."

"You have great friends," Patti said, clapping and joining in on the chorus.

Olivia smiled and nodded, not bothering to mention she'd never spent time with this group before tonight, her memories of them from high school years very different from the way they acted now.

As the evening grew late, the talk quieted. An old song, "I Go Crazy," from the 1970s wafted out from the speakers. Olivia shivered, recognizing the words as ones she and Warner used to sing to each other—dancing in the garden when they first realized a sweet attraction crackled between them. How old were they then? She tried to remember. Maybe Rich's and Sam's age—only kids, playing at kissing, discovering the opposite sex. Finding first love.

She felt Warner's eyes on hers, watching, even before she looked across the patio at him. A slow smile touched the edge of his mouth and he made a twirly sign with one finger.

Crazy. It stood for crazy. It had been an old joke between them, and they'd loved every song that came out afterward with the word "crazy" in it. They used to see who could name the most "crazy" songs.

He walked across the patio, propping himself against the wall beside her. "This song is 'I Go Crazy' by Paul Davis, in case you forgot. Here's another, 'Crazy' by Patsy Cline." He sent her a challenging look.

She tried to ignore him.

Warner pulled himself up to sit on the wall. "How about 'Let's Go Crazy' by Prince?" He cocked an eyebrow at her. "I'm three up."

Olivia sighed, unable to resist the challenge. " 'Crazy for You' by

Madonna and 'Crazy for Your Love' by the Bee Gees."

" 'Crazy Train' by Ozzy Osbourne." He grinned. "Four to two."

"This is silly," she said, noticing a few people turning, listening in, wondering what they were doing.

Barry grinned, walking over to drop into a chair near them. " 'Crazy Little Thing Called Love' by Queen," he added. "One for me."

"How about 'Crazy Crazy Nights' by Kiss," Leonard added, jumping into the game. He laughed. "Dang, I remember sitting around and doing this for hours at school." He flopped into another chair beside Barry. "Let's do songs with "Rock" in them."

Imogene walked over. "I know one, 'Rock and Roll Is Here to Stay', 1958, by Danny and the Juniors."

"Man." Leonard complained. "You always remember the dates, too."

"Not always." She leaned over to kiss him. "And I can't remember who sang 'Like a Rock.' Can you?"

"Bob Seger and The Silver Bullet Band," Patti came to join the group, smiling. "And I loved 'Rock and Roll Heaven' by The Righteous Brothers."

"I've got two more." Barry patted the seat beside him, gesturing for Patti to join them. " 'Jailhouse Rock' and 'Rock-A-Hula Baby' by the King himself."

Drawn by the laughter, the others in the party wandered over, soon joining in. When they ran out of "Rock" titles they started on song titles containing the word "Jump" and then "Moon."

Olivia watched their fun a little wistfully.

"What are you thinking?" Warner whispered, close beside her. "You're quiet."

She felt silly replying. "I guess I thought this was only our game."

He smiled at her. "It is our game. We invented it, but I taught it to the others later." He brushed a hand over hers out of sight of his friends. "But 'Crazy' will always be my word associated with you."

She giggled. "Well, I'm not sure that's flattering."

"Yes, it is. I never heard a song with 'Crazy' in it through all these years without thinking of you."

His gaze bore into hers and she turned her eyes back to the others, feeling that shiver again. Yet, even with her eyes averted, she could still feel him watching.

Several hours later, Warner walked her up to the front door at Benton House. She started digging for the door key in her purse, but Warner stopped her, taking her hands in his. "Do you know this is the first real date we've ever had?"

She tried to pull away. "It's hardly a date. Don't be silly. You simply drove me to Barry's party. You know I experience night blindness and can't see well to drive myself."

"Don't spoil it," he said, the words soft and seductive. "Pretend we've been on a date, shared a good time, and now we're standing on the porch nervous, knowing it's time to say good night, wondering if we should kiss."

Olivia wet her lips without thinking. "Why are you doing this?" she whispered.

His tone grew husky. "Because you still drive me crazy, Olivia Benton. When I look in your eyes like this I still go crazy."

A little trill of excitement rippled through her just before his mouth met hers, moving sweetly over her lips. Tense, remembering the last time he kissed her, Olivia found it hard to relax.

Warner kissed her eyes, pulling her closer. "Have you ever made love with anyone?"

It took a minute for his words to slip through the hum of desire swirling around them. "What?" She opened her eyes to look at him, shocked at his question.

"Ten years have passed ...." Warner let his words trail off.

Annoyed, Olivia pulled back, fumbling in her purse for her keys with shaky hands. "Just because you married and have been out in the world doesn't mean I slept around." She hugged her arms to herself. "Besides, it's unbelievably rude of you to ask."

He chuckled softly, making her even madder.

She pushed at him. "I was ready to tell you I had a really good time tonight, Warner Zachery. But now I've changed my mind about saying it."

"It doesn't matter if you say it or not." He traced a finger down her cheek. "I know you had a good time, and I know you didn't expect to. You thought an evening with the Swain High losers would be a massive bore. But we surprised you, didn't we? We turned out to be a fun and interesting bunch."

"That's a mean thing to say." She pushed at him again, trying to get her key in the door. "I really hate you sometimes, Warner Zachery."

"No, you don't hate me, but you definitely don't like me forcing you to look at things differently from how you've always looked at them in the past." He leaned against the doorframe, blocking the keyhole with his body. "I'll bet you ten dollars you had more fun with me and my friends tonight than with the Elite Eight at Roberta's last night."

She straightened her shoulders. "You don't know what sort of time I had at the planning meeting at Roberta and Russell's house."

"Don't I?" He smirked.

"No, you don't." Provoked now, she tried to reach around him to the door handle. "Go home, Warner."

"Okay, I'll go home. But I enjoyed our date. " He gave her a quick kiss, then headed off the porch and to his car—whistling no less.

Fuming, Olivia let herself in the house. She found the house dark, except for the light her father had left on in the entry before going to bed. Switching off the downstairs light, she made her way upstairs, tiptoeing past her father's room to avoid waking him. Inside her room, she sat on her dresser stool to begin taking off her jewelry. Glancing at herself in the mirror, she put her hands to her lips, remembering Warner's kiss and troubling over his words. In her bed later, she wept.

CHAPTER 10

Warner avoided Olivia Benton for several days, writing and working in the office apartment above the garage. He answered calls from his publicist and his agent and replied to the usual pileup of e-mails needing attention. The signing at Gil's renewed acquaintances with a number of friends, and Warner started receiving social invitations as well as requests to speak or visit at area civic organizations and groups.

After long hours at the computer, he often took a break and walked in the gardens. Olivia's cat Sybil frequently kept him company. He wondered if the cat remembered him from so many years ago. Warner also tromped up familiar hiking trails into the mountains, went tubing and kayaking with Barry and Leonard on the Nantahala River, and explored spots he remembered around the town and in nearby Cherokee.

Coming back from an afternoon walk in the garden, Warner saw the light shining in his mother's studio and realized he'd shared little one-on-one time with her since coming home. He made his way through the backyard to the outdoor room his mother had renovated from a small garage into an art studio. Around the joys of being a wife and mother, Rena Zachery had always been a working artist. She painted under her maiden name Rena Delacourt, and her work hung in many well-known galleries around the southeast.

Warner tapped on the French doors leading into her studio. His mother turned from her easel, paint brush in one hand, and motioned him in. Annie, one of the family's golden retrievers keeping his mother company today, got up to greet Warner, tail thumping.

"Is this a bad time to interrupt?" He reached down to pet Annie.

"No. I'm almost at a stopping point. Sit down." She motioned to a wooden bench, strewn with pillows, on the wall near her easel.

It felt familiar to settle onto the cushioned bench. He'd spent many childhood hours here, watching his mother paint.

"Do you have work of your own you want to do?" She glanced at him. "You know you're welcome."

"I know," he said, also remembering hours of working on his early drawings here and of his mother teaching him to draw and paint.

"You are my only child who had artistic leanings." She dabbed a dark shading of Alizarin Crimson onto a spill of flowers cascading from a windowsill pot in her painting. "Vance and Dean had other interests." She laughed. "And as you well know, neither could draw worth a twit."

"I remember." He laughed, settling a needlepoint cushion behind his back. "They used to pay me to do their school posters."

She pursed her lips in disapproval. "And no doubt to write some of their high school papers even if you were much younger."

He grinned. "I edited a lot and practically wrote a few."

"Hmmph." She squeezed out more of the red paint, darkening it with a dab of black before adding it to her painting.

Warner stood to walk around the room, studying some of her completed works. Her style, a mix of impressionism and realism, portrayed dreamy scenes of gardens, meadows, or sunny fields of flowers. He took his time studying several of her new works featuring shaded doorways, quaint cottages, quiet ponds, and bridges spanning lazy streams.

He turned to smile at her. "Your work is so relaxing in a tense and stressful world. No wonder people love it. They can escape into one of your paintings and unwind."

"How nicely put, Son." She turned to look at her paintings with new eyes. "I'd like to think I help people find peace and pleasure."

"You probably come by that honestly through your parents—Grandfather a psychiatrist and Grandmother an art therapist."

She laughed. "Oh, well. You know what they say about the apple never falling far from the tree."

He sat back down on the bench. "I'm not sure I had the maturity at thirteen to thank you for taking me to your parents that summer."

"You were losing your way." She changed brushes and added veining to the leaves behind her flowers. "I watched it start in middle school. Being artistic and independent didn't seem to matter in elementary school, but in middle school when the cliques began to form and conforming became critical, you started having problems. Your father and I tried to find other activities for you to get involved in …." Her voice drifted off, remembering.

"Like scouts and outdoor pursuits. Lessons in art over in Sylva. Summer camps and classes at John C. Campbell Folk School while you taught workshops." He propped a foot on a nearby chair. "I noticed those efforts, Mother. My problems didn't happen because you and Dad weren't good parents."

She paused, paintbrush in air. "Perhaps, but a parent feels responsible when their children aren't happy." Daubing at her painting again, she added, "I told your father the main problem was that you were a Delacourt through and through. Vance and Dean are Zacherys—so much like their father and grandfather, and like Millie Zachery, your father's mother. They all loved sports and business, made friends easily, rose naturally into leadership, and fit into any social set with ease."

Warner watched her stand to study her painting from several angles before sitting back down to paint again. "Has it been hard for you here in Bryson, Mother—being a Delacourt, even if a Zachery by marriage? Being an artist in a small town?"

"Well, of course." She turned to grin at him. "But, darling, I knew who I was before I married your father and moved here. That made a lot of difference. And you have to remember I grew up with your grandfather. A specialist in child psychology does tend to make one's life different as a child." She laughed. "All of us, my brothers Elton, Alex, and I, were encouraged to find ourselves and celebrate our individuality at an early age."

He frowned. "Are you unhappy here, Mother? I guess I never thought to consider it. You don't think about those things as a child."

"I have my work, my family, a few good friends." She began working playful shadows into the windowpanes of her painting. "And living next to the mountains and beside the Fairchild Gardens has given me constant inspiration for my work. The minute I saw this house, situated down a quiet drive with the Smoky Mountains at its back and those incredible and unexpected gardens on the property next door, I begged your father to buy it. I knew the old one-car garage behind the property would make a wonderful studio, too."

"I see many scenes of the gardens in your work. Like that one." Warner pointed to a painting of an arbor of roses hanging on the wall.

"Isn't the rose arbor leading into the gardens stunning this summer?" A smile lit her face. "I simply had to paint it."

She turned back to her painting and to her former topic. "Many of the people in Bryson City, because it is such a small rural city, don't really understand my work or my passion for it. People today, as in the past, don't always understand artists, Warner. We have peculiarities of action and thought other people don't possess. I think we're more intense about life in some ways. That makes for occasional discontent and unhappiness."

Warner considered this. "Grandfather helped me see some of that at thirteen and more along the way since. He also helped me find constructive ways to pull myself out of times of discontent and depression."

She smiled at him. "Having your work helps now, doesn't it? Then you only had young talent and vision."

He shook his head. "Before my summer in New York, I didn't even have vision, and I didn't recognize and celebrate my talent. My artistic gifts and temperament seemed only something people made fun of and called weird, rather than something I could value."

"I sometimes think life is wasted on the young." She chuckled at her joke. "The older we get the more we value life—living it, using it to the fullest, treasuring its sweet moments."

Annie came to lay a head on Warner's knee, wanting affection.

He scratched her neck. "I think Annie remembers me. Maybe Biff, too, even after so many years."

"Animals possess a long memory." Her mouth twitched. "That gray cat of Olivia's remembers you. I've watched it follow you around the garden. Perhaps it recalls you brought it home here first and kept it until time to gift it to Olivia. In a sense, you were its owner for a time."

Hearing Olivia's name reminded Warner of Olivia's father's remarks, chiding him for staying away for so long. "Mother, I'm sorry it's been so long since I came home."

"We understood. You had unpleasant memories here, things you weren't ready to face until now. You lived through your high school years dreaming of getting away and never coming back." She turned warm eyes to his. "It takes a while to realize the problems weren't all in the place and in the people; some were in you."

He shifted in discomfort. "You're as bad as Grandfather."

"Artists learn to be observant." She began mixing Thalo and Ultramarine to create a soft true blue, stirring the paint with a palette knife. "How are things going with Olivia?"

"Fine." He tried to sound nonchalant.

Her dark blue eyes shifted to his in a knowing gaze. "We tiptoed around this subject years ago. I don't think we need to do that anymore. You're a grown man. You've been married, you lost a wife, and—before Nelle—you dated other girls in New York." She daubed a ribbon of blue highlight into a morning glory in her painting. "I know Olivia was your first love and I know, to some degree, how difficult first love is. You wanted Olivia to go with you to New York."

"That was a long time ago." He got up to pace to the French doors, looking out over the lawn toward the back of the house.

"As you said, I moved on, married, grew past that young crush."

"Son, I saw your eyes when Olivia walked into the bookstore Saturday during your signing." She kept painting. "I watched you forget who you were supposed to sign a book for and forget everything around you."

"Olivia's a pretty woman." He frowned.

"Yes, a pretty woman you still care for."

Warner clenched his fists and turned to his mother. "Nelle got murdered not that long ago, Mother. I don't think this is an appropriate conversation or a respectful one to Nelle's memory."

She eyed the morning glory she'd finished and started another. "So you're going to snap at me and try to throw guilt into the picture because you still care for your first love, is that right?" Her eyes met his. "It makes me wonder how you're acting with Olivia. Mean and snarly? Making her feel guilty for once being seventeen and not knowing her own mind or what direction she should take with her life?"

"That's hardly the way it was," he said with a tight voice, annoyed with the direction of the conversation.

"Wasn't it? Olivia was an only child. She lost her mother at a young age, her care taken over by her grandmother—a rigid and demanding woman, critical and never easy to please, even on a good day." She shook her head. "I watched that child try so hard to be good, to give no trouble to her father and her grandmother, to be perfect and agreeable in school, a model child. I think she felt as determined in her way to meet up to every social expectation in high school as you did to defy them. The two of you made quite a pair. Like polar opposites."

Changing brushes, she drew a dark vein of blue into the morning glory on her canvas. "In senior year, I couldn't help seeing how the two of you looked at each other. Watched how many times you went to the garden, obviously to meet her. Then her Grandmother Lila died right before graduation. She and her father grieved again, facing another loss. And Olivia, being the good child she was, took on the responsibility of caring for her father, the house, and the gardens all at once. Just at a time when she should have been able to leave home and find her own way, attain some independence."

She paused in her work, her eyes searching Warner's. "Have you ever thought what it must have been like for her to see you leave when you did? To not only leave Bryson City to go away to college, but to go all the way to New York to start a new life? Nearly eight-hundred miles away. And to see you leave angry at her because she wouldn't pack a bag and follow after you? She hadn't applied to any colleges in New York, and I doubt her father would have supported her to move so far away. Or to a big city. Especially to chase after you. Surely you can look back and see how impossible the situation was for her?"

"I'm not enjoying this conversation, Mother." Warner turned his back to stare out the window again.

"Perhaps I'm not enjoying it, either. But I stayed here and watched a young girl shoulder a huge amount of responsibility with grace and dignity. I often saw that same girl weeping in the garden in the places where you and she used to play as children and meet later as young lovers."

"We were never lovers," Warner snapped. "It wasn't like that."

"Nor did I mean the term lovers in that way. I know your relationship was innocent." She turned back to her painting, irritating Warner that she could paint while throwing out all these harsh revelations.

Warner paced the room. "Don't we owe Nelle any respect here, Mother? You and Daddy liked Nelle."

She smiled gently at him. "Son, your father and I loved Nelle. She was a beautiful woman, a beautiful person. I regret with all my heart she was killed. But you know Nelle would be the last person to want you to continue grieving for her past a reasonable time. And she knew about Olivia. It wouldn't hurt Nelle to know that you still carry feelings for a girl you met before her. It shouldn't hurt you to acknowledge it, either."

"I thought I'd be past those feelings," he finally admitted. "It's made me angry to see them flare up again. A lot of things have made me angry, coming back."

"Then deal with it now as a grown man and as an adult—not as the young, vulnerable, unsure boy you were before."

"You sound like Grandfather again."

She shrugged and quoted a familiar Bible verse from Corinthians, *"When I was a child, I spake as a child, I understood as a child, I thought as a child: but when I became a man, I put away childish things."*

"I hate trying to argue with the Bible." He grinned at her, conceding defeat.

"Then maybe you shouldn't." She picked up a palette knife and worked the instrument around the window frame on her canvas, creating a roughened effect.

Warner glanced at his watch. "I came originally to tell you I planned to meet Mac Olsen, my old scout leader, for supper—that I wouldn't be home for dinner with the family."

She nodded.

"I envy that you can paint and work right on regardless of what is going on, regardless of the mess of feelings swirling around."

"Painting takes less mental energy in some ways than writing." She glanced up at him, concern on her face. "Are you having trouble settling in to your work here?"

"Some." He shrugged. "But it's better now than in the early months after Nelle's murder."

She reached out a hand for his. "Decide to be happy again, Son. A lot of whether you're happy in life lies in whether you want to be or not."

He squeezed her hand then turned toward the door, but paused with a final thought. "Did Olivia really cry for me in the garden?" Warner glanced back toward his mother in question.

"Yes, and she became a sweet friend to me in the years after you left. She visits with me when I sketch or paint in the garden and she comes to talk with me here." She pushed her short hair behind her ear.

"Did you and she talk about me?"

She shook her head. "Never directly, but Olivia's heart was often easy to read. Haven't you ever wondered why she never married, as beautiful as she is and as kind and loving?"

Warner scowled. "I'm only visiting here, Mother. Don't start matchmaking."

"I'm not the one keeping company with Olivia Benton, Son, or devising meetings with her." She smiled at him, glancing at the big clock on the wall. "I thought you said you needed to leave to meet Mac? I hope you'll tell him I said hello." She turned back to her painting.

"I'll do that," he said.

CHAPTER 11

"Well, Lordy dee. Those vandals defaced your friend Logan Stanley's fitness center last night." Wanda looked up from the newspaper to shake her head in disbelief. "This is getting to be a real problem around here. I hope they don't mess with our florist shop."

Patti frowned over the FTD order she worked on at her station. "I wonder why someone is doing all these random acts of vandalism—defacing property, breaking windows, setting fires in trash cans. It doesn't make sense."

"They always write messages they leave behind," Olivia said. "Maybe there's a clue in those." She paused in sorting through a pile of orders by the register as she entered into the conversation.

"Well, I don't see how." Wanda scanned down the lines of the article. "They only wrote: 'Be wary, a vandal lurks.' That doesn't tell much."

"It says *vandal*, not vandals," Patti commented. "Maybe it's not a gang at all, but only one person."

"Must be a very unhappy, disturbed person. What could all these different places have in common to upset someone so? The recreation center, the Mexican restaurant, the fitness center, even the jail ..." Wanda paused, scanning the newspaper page. "It doesn't make sense."

"What place did the vandal hit first?" Olivia asked.

"The Courthouse back in May," Wanda answered. "It says so here in the article. The message left there said: 'Be wary. A vandal stalks where no justice prevails.' "

"Hmmm. That has a vigilante sound," Olivia said, before a stream of customers poured into the front door, demanding her attention.

Later in the day, she felt a slight unease as she left the florist by herself to walk to the church for choir practice. The front porch of the shop held many pretty statues and plants she'd hate to see toppled over or defaced. She wouldn't want her picket fence spray painted or damaged, either.

Taking out her cell phone, she called her father. "Hi, Daddy," she said, leaving a message when he didn't answer. "I'm heading to choir practice; I just wanted to remind you. I know you're working late at the clinic, so I'll see you later at the house."

The walk to Bryson City Presbyterian Church took only a few minutes from Fairgarden Florist. The historic white building with its pretty bell tower stood on a clean, green lawn on the corner of Everett Street and Bryson Avenue. Olivia, like her mother and grandmother before her, grew up in the church, and every inch of the old building felt familiar to her. On Sundays, Olivia attended Sunday school and church with her father; she sang in the choir, attended the Thursday night women's circle, held office in the Presbyterian Women's Association, and took flowers to decorate the front of the church sanctuary every Sunday morning. It felt comfortable belonging to a church and its people as Olivia did.

The choir, like the church congregation, was small, but Olivia had developed sweet ties with all the choir members and their music director. Her soprano voice, decent if not solo quality, contributed to the group, and she could play the piano in accompaniment at choir practice, if needed. Eight years of piano lessons did come in handy every now and then.

"Isn't it exciting to have Warner Zachery back in town?" Mildred Claxton said, as they finished practice and switched off the lights in the choir room.

"It is," agreed Betty Olsen. "Mac and I both went to the signing on Saturday, and Mac is still wearing his Geeky Gilmore ball cap.

I hope Warner will come to church one Sunday with his family."

The three woman headed out the back door, locking up the church behind them. "Oh, there's Mac." Mildred waved.

Olivia looked ahead to see Mac Olsen coming around the corner of the church, Warner beside him.

"Well, Warner Zachery." Mildred stepped forward to wrap him in a warm hug. "We were just this minute talking about you."

Warner raised an eyebrow.

Betty laughed, giving Warner a hug herself. "It was all nice talk."

"Yes, and we're hoping you plan to come to church on Sunday with your family. You did grow up here at Bryson Presbyterian, you know. Those who couldn't come to the book signing on Saturday will want a chance to see you before you leave." Mildred patted Warner's arm fondly. "I remember you as a little boy with glasses and shaggy hair. You always asked more questions in Sunday school than any of my other children. Didn't he, Olivia?" Mildred turned to her with a smile.

"That was a few years back, Mildred." She tried to hide a smirk from Warner.

Mac clumped Warner on the back. "I dragged Warner over here to see my wife before he heads back to the house, and I've almost talked him into helping me with an upcoming Boy Scout meeting." He waved a warning finger at the ladies. "So don't you girls go scaring him off with too many old remembrances. We want to keep him around for a while if we can. Warner could have a real positive impact on some of my boys."

"Well, of course." Mildred started toward the parking lot. "Warner, you give your mother my best and tell her we're counting on her to donate another of her paintings for our Fall Fundraiser."

Warner said good-byes to Mildred Claxton and the Olsens then caught up to Olivia as she walked back toward the street. "Where is your car? I'll walk you to it."

"I left it over at the florist shop. You don't need to go out of your way."

"Actually, I parked on Greenlee since I met Mac at Anthony's for pizza." He moved to walk beside her. "We had a good time catching up. How was choir practice?"

"Good. Although our numbers always fall off in summer with everyone vacationing and traveling." She glanced toward Warner. "The recreation center where Mac works is one of the places where the vandal struck. Did he talk about it?"

"No, why?"

She shrugged. "I just had it on my mind since another incident occurred last night."

He grinned. "Probably because the vandal hit Logan's fitness center."

Her mouth tightened in disapproval. "No, because another incident happened again at all, and because the police have no clues about who is instigating them. I worry that my shop might be targeted. Or that someone might get hurt in the future."

"Leonard said incidents have occurred nearly every week since sometime in May."

"Yes." She turned the corner to start down Fry Street. "It worries me. Bryson City is usually a quiet place, without ongoing problems like these."

He glanced at his watch. "It's still early, Olivia. Come walk around town with me. We can poke up and down some of the streets and then walk to The Cork and Bean for coffee and a treat. It's open until nine."

She hesitated.

"Think of it as my way of apologizing for being sort of a pill the other night." He ran a hand through his hair. "Old habits seem to slip back on me down here. I forget to be my fresh, suave New York self."

She bit back a smile. "You look very New York tonight." Her eyes flitted over the khaki pants and neat shirt he wore, all obviously expensive. "It's not the old Warner look." Olivia's eyes lifted to his face. "Don't you wear glasses anymore?"

"Contacts," he answered, swinging along beside her. "Do you agree with Vickie Leigh that I turned out fine?"

"Don't fish for compliments." She straightened the purse over her shoulder. "You know you look better than you did in high school days."

"And you look more beautiful, as if that could be possible." His voice softened.

Olivia avoided his eyes. "Would you mind if I stop by the shop to lock my purse in the car? Then I won't need to carry it while we walk."

"I am sorry I picked on you the other night when I took you home," Warner said as they stopped to drop off her purse. "I know ten years have passed, but being away all those years, it seems like only yesterday to me sometimes. As if I'm still an odd kid, trying to fit in where I don't belong."

"Do you still feel you don't belong here?" Olivia stopped to look in the window of Nannie's Country Store. "None of us are kids anymore. We all grew up and changed."

"Maybe." He stopped beside her, propping his foot on a bench.

Olivia turned to him. "You know, Warner, you need to be fair and realize some of the problems you had in high school you brought on yourself."

He groaned. "I already heard that lecture today."

"From Mac?" Her eyes widened in surprise.

"No, from my mother, the resident shrink and chip off the old block." He walked on and Olivia fell into step beside him.

She giggled. "I almost forgot your Grandfather Delacourt was a psychiatrist and a specialist in child psychology, if I remember right."

"Yeah, and those psychiatrist types have a way of making you look at things in ways you don't really want to."

Olivia considered that. "You have that tendency, too."

"Well, it didn't help me much in earlier years, and sometimes I don't think it helps me much today."

She heard the bitterness in his voice. "Do you still have trouble making friends and fitting in?"

He rubbed a hand down her arm, giving her a shiver. "No. I have more friends than time to enjoy them now, but I still don't fit into certain situations well—especially those demanding any type of mindless conformity, going along for going-along's sake only. I still hate seeing individuality squelched and censured. And I don't like making nice."

Olivia laughed despite herself. "You never did. I remember so many times you said the worst possible thing in a situation, alienating almost everyone there."

He chuckled. "Not a very good team player, huh?"

She paused to pick dead flowers from an outdoor arrangement in front of a store. "You could be a good team player when you wanted to, with scouts, at summer camp, in situations you liked."

"Maybe." He took the dead flowers from her and dumped them into a nearby trashcan. As they walked on, he asked a question, "Did you never make new friends outside the Elite Eight from high school?"

She bristled at the implication. "There you go again, picking at me." She stopped to sit at an outside table, gesturing him into the other chair. "Lulu is my best friend since first grade, like Barry was yours. She's a wonderful person, a sweet wife, a good mother, and a fabulous friend. We met Roberta and Vickie Leigh when we went to middle school. We all tried out for cheerleader together and bonded."

Warner rolled his eyes.

"I saw that," Olivia said. "Since we're being honest, I want you to know I always hated how you made fun of me for being a cheerleader. I loved cheering. It was one place where I could holler, laugh, leap, jump, and not have to be so proper."

A regretful laugh escaped her lips. "Grandmother Lila was very restrictive over my life after mother died. I had to be so proper in every way. Through cheering I could break out of those restrictions. I found a new identity there, too. An admired one. I was good at cheering." She lifted her chin. "I still am. I work with the high school cheerleaders, advise and help them, judge the tryouts every year. It's meaningful to me, like working on the newspaper and creating those wonderful, witty cartoons was to you."

Warner drummed his fingers on the table. "It wasn't the fact that you cheered for school that I saw as a problem, but how you and your group of friends excluded and often put down others in school who weren't in your social set." His lips twitched. "Can't you look back and see how vicious those peer groups acted sometimes? How can you not remember some of the mean-spirited comments, snickering, and ostracizing that went on? You and your little group of friends often acted as if others simply chose not be as good-looking, confident, and popular as you. You brushed them off, avoided them, refused to speak to them."

"It wasn't that bad, Warner." She felt a blush steal up her face.

"No, sometimes it was worse." His brows drew down. "I remember the time you feigned being sick to avoid going to Imogene's birthday party. You went to church with her, belonged to the same Sunday school class, but you didn't want to go to her birthday party. Do you think she didn't know why you really didn't come?"

Olivia tried to remember back. "I think I had a cold that week and missed a day of school."

Warner shook his head. "But you didn't miss cheerleading practice the same day or a chance to stop by the drug store with your friends for a soda afterward."

"Perhaps I might have gone." She looked down at her hands.

"It's the hundreds of little decisions like that, conforming decisions, hurtful decisions that I hated, Olivia, and cheerleading seemed to nurture them. I watched you change in middle school in so many ways." He reached across to lift her chin. "And you changed toward me. As I failed to fit in readily with any of the more popular social groups, you began to pretend you barely knew me. Soon, you only acknowledged me as your friend when we were home, in the garden and on our quiet little street, when no one else was around. Did you ever think how that made me feel?"

"Maybe my world became too small and limited. Maybe I went along more than I should have." She looked up at him. "But you never helped anything by despising my friends, by sneering at the cheerleading squad and at sports, by having your own sarcastic names for social groups you didn't like and didn't participate in. You weren't always kind either. Your bad attitude and surly ways in middle school made everyone want to avoid you. I can tell you any number of times where you acted as rude to my friends as any of them ever did to you."

"When?" He challenged her.

She put her hands on her hips. "When you, Barry, and Leonard made those non-jock jackets to wear around school, ridiculing the sports award jackets the boys on the sports teams won. That was despicable. And you made little smart remarks when my cheerleading friends and I walked by sometimes, like rah-rah-rah, as though we didn't hear them. I felt so embarrassed." She stood and started to walk again. "You weren't perfect either, Warner Zachery."

He laughed, coming along beside her. "I'd forgotten that."

"See? You think it's funny when you remember what you did that showed peer group exclusion, but you think it's mean when you remember anything I did."

He reached out a hand. "You have a point. Slow down and stop trying to walk away from me."

She whirled to face him, her face flushed. "I'm simply tired of always being criticized by you for being young once, and probably silly and stupid at times, like all teenagers. And of you always acting like you were some perfect little saint and a continual victim."

"Ouch."

She pushed at him. "Well, ouch back. You wrote about all of us here in Bryson City in your books, making fun of us before the whole world. And now, despite those books, does everyone here act mean to you about that or treat you with scorn over it? No, everyone has acted nice, attending your book signing, congratulating you on your success."

He frowned. "Very few of them have a clue they inspired those books. We talked about that before." He grabbed her arms and made her look at him. "You know I didn't set out to make fun of anyone in print."

"Yes, I know, but most people remember mainly the pleasant, happy times from their school years, Warner. And they forgive the negative memories of peer group problems, realizing they're simply a part of growing up."

He let her go, shaking his head. "I wish that was totally true. But many young people get scarred by their early years of being ostracized, ridiculed, or bullied. I know that more now than I did before, because of the streams of letters I get from kids, even the comments I receive from adults. It does matter, Olivia, maybe more than we think."

She walked on. "Even if you're right, we can't go back. No one can. We have to go on from today."

They strolled down Everett Street in silence, thinking about their words. Olivia followed Warner onto the bridge over the Tuckaseegee River.

He paused to prop his arms on the rail, looking down at the rippling water below, watching a bird peck at the mud along the bank. "I'm sorry I keep bringing up the past so much." His voice sounded soft.

"Maybe you need to talk it out and work through it." She leaned against the rail beside him. "I want you to know I'm sorry for anything I did in the past to hurt you. I never did it with malicious intent."

He grinned at her. "Those are big words."

She shifted away from him, irritated, but he moved to close the gap between them. "I'm sorry for anything I did in the past to hurt you, too. I know a lot of my problems were my own. I didn't know how to resolve them, how to fit in, how to make it better."

He tucked her arm in his and they walked across the bridge, past the barbershop, several stores, and the courthouse before coming to The Cork and Bean on the corner of Main and Everett. Warner pushed open the door to let her in. They ordered coffees, plain for Warner and a café latte for Olivia, plus homemade cinnamon rolls for a treat.

As if by unspoken agreement, their talk changed to more pleasant topics. Warner told humorous tales of his time on the road, of mishaps and funny times at signings and events he attended. Olivia caught him up on Bryson City gossip and goings on, relayed amusing stories of church, school, and town events.

Walking back they followed Island Street, curling along the river on quiet side streets, before heading back to the Fairgarden Florist. As they turned the corner by her father's clinic on Greenlee, Warner suddenly grabbed her arm, pulling her back.

"What?" She looked up at him.

He shook his head, putting a silencing finger to his mouth.

She looked around, feeling panicked, thinking of the vandals.

He nodded toward the side porch on the clinic. Olivia could see the outline of a couple there in the dim light.

She squinted to see better. "Oh, that's only Daddy."

Warner held her back again as she started to move forward. "Shhhh." He pulled her into the shadows off the street.

Olivia's eyes moved toward the clinic again, where she saw the couple move closer, talking. "Why are we skulking in the shadows?"

"Who's the woman?" Warner whispered.

"Helen Allmon." Olivia started to walk forward again. "Just an old friend of Daddy's. Her husband Bob was an anesthesiologist friend of Daddy's. He died three years ago, and Daddy takes Helen out to eat sometimes. Occasionally, they go places together. Daddy knows how it feels to lose a spouse."

Warner sent her a questioning look. "You think that's all there is to it?"

"Well, of course." She answered.

He chuckled. "Maybe you should look again."

Her eyes turned back to the couple, now locked in a close embrace and kissing. Her breath rushed out in a *whoosh*. She gripped Warner's arm. Frozen in place, Olivia watched the couple kiss once more, lingering in each other's arms before moving apart to walk down the clinic steps, arm in arm, to her daddy's car on the curb.

Only after they drove away did Warner speak. "I guess it's safe to walk on now." He turned an amused glance to Olivia. "Looks like your daddy has his own little agenda going on during choir practice nights."

Shocked, Olivia pulled away. "That is not a nice thing to say, Warner. Helen Allmon is a businesswoman here in Bryson City, owns the Unique Boutique, and lives in a nice home not far from her store. She has two grown daughters in Chicago about my age, goes to our church, and is a fine person. She and Daddy are only friends, and I'm sure there is a perfectly good explanation for why Daddy needed to comfort Helen tonight for some reason."

Warner laughed. "If you call that comforting someone … I'll be glad to offer you a little comfort before we go home."

Feeling her cheeks blotch with color, Olivia stomped up the street. "I see your car there by the curb. Mine is around the corner behind the shop. I can see myself home now. Thanks for the coffee."

"Whoa." He grabbed her arm to turn her to face him. "Why are you suddenly mad at me?"

She tried to pull away. "You tried to insinuate something unsavory about my father."

"No." He studied her face. "You're simply upset about what you saw and not wanting to acknowledge that your father might be a normal man with normal desires. It seems obvious to me he's *very* fond of Helen Allmon."

She turned her eyes away from his, near tears. "My daddy loved my mother very much. You don't understand."

His hand tightened on her arm. "You think I don't understand the loss of a spouse? I lost my own wife only two years ago. Your mother's been gone for years and years. Should your father lock up his emotions and never care about another woman again?"

"It's not the same." She sniffed, swiping at tears starting to slip down her cheeks. "You're young; you weren't married very long, but Daddy's old. He and my mother were married for twenty years."

His voice grew soft. "It doesn't take twenty years to love

someone. And you don't have to quit loving someone you've lost to love someone else."

"I don't want to talk about this." She tried to pull away from his hold. "Let me go, Warner."

"Sure." He dropped her arm. "I guess Daddy's girl needs to go home and boo-hoo because her daddy might have developed loving feelings for another girl besides her. Is that it, Olivia?"

"No." The tears fell faster now. "That is so mean, Warner. It's just that I'm surprised, shocked." She pulled herself upright. "And I'm sure there's a logical explanation we haven't considered."

Warner reached out a hand to wipe gently at her tears. He pulled her close against him. "Your daddy won't stop loving you, Olivia, even if he loves another woman, too. There is room in a person's heart for many loves."

Olivia jerked away from him, wiping her face. "I want to go home now."

"And what if Daddy's there and sees you come in crying. How will you handle that?"

Her eyes flew wide open.

He shook his head. "Go over to my place to calm down if you see his car there when you get home." He started up the street, leading her along. "However, if you hurry, you'll probably get home before him. He'll take Helen home before he heads back to the house."

Warner walked her back to her car and tucked her into it. "Olivia, don't confront him about this right now. Think about it first. You're too emotional tonight to talk to him about what you saw. Go slip into the house, get into your pajamas, turn out the lights, and feign sleep when you hear him come home."

She put a fist to her mouth, but Warner pulled it away to lean into the car and kiss her. "You've been the best of daughters, Olivia. Never think anything else."

CHAPTER 12

Several days passed, and Warner often thought about Olivia and wondered how she was processing the new information about her father and his girlfriend. Busy, he hadn't found a chance to connect with her. Thursday, he spoke for the Rotary Club luncheon at Calhoun's in Bryson City, and on Friday, by request from Imogene, he drove over to speak to several literature classes at the community college in Sylva followed by a presentation and book signing at seven at City Lights Bookstore. On Saturday, he met with Mac Olsen's Boy Scout troop and, later in the evening, joined his family for dinner at his brother Vance's home near Whittier. Warner watched for Olivia in the garden, but saw no sign of her.

Sunday, knowing Olivia would attend church to sing in the choir, he decided to attend service with his family. As he left the church, he ran into Olivia's father and Helen Allmon waiting for Olivia near the side door.

"Warner, nice to see you again," Ray Benton reached to pump Warner's hand. He turned to Helen. "I don't believe you've met Helen Allmon yet, Warner. The Allmons came to Bryson City shortly after you left. Her husband was an anesthesiologist at the hospital and a good friend of mine."

"How do you do?" Warner shook Helen's hand, his eyes gliding over the short, attractive, auburn-haired woman with brown eyes and a pleasant face. "I hear you own a nice gift shop downtown in Bryson City. I'll try to stop by one day."

"Oh, I'd love that. It's called the Unique Boutique and is a block off Mitchell Street." As she started to chat about the store, Warner caught sight of Olivia coming out the door.

"Olivia!" her father called. "Over here!" He gestured.

Olivia's face blanched at the sight of Helen. Collecting herself, she pasted on a gracious expression and walked over.

"Nice service," Warner said, smiling at her.

She nodded.

Ray Benton put a hand on his daughter's arm. "Helen invited us to come to her house for Sunday dinner. She claims she needs to pay me back for all the times I treated her to dinner." He sent a fond look Helen's way.

"I hope you'll come, Olivia." Helen tilted her head, the sun glinting off her auburn hair. "I don't think you've seen my house."

Seeing Olivia hesitate, Warner stepped in. "That's a nice invitation, Helen, but I think Olivia forgot to tell her father we already planned a picnic and hike in the mountains for after church today. It's why I was hanging around the door waiting for her. I planned to drop her by the house to change before we head to the park. I hope you don't mind if she takes a rain check."

Helen's face dropped. "Well, of course not. She can come another time, and it's a beautiful day to get outdoors. You two go and enjoy a good time."

Ray Benton linked an arm through Helen's. "With Olivia not coming, that leaves more of your good pot roast for me. Maybe I'll take you for a drive over to Fontana after lunch. We can walk across the dam and take a little stroll outdoors ourselves."

He turned to Olivia. "You two run along and enjoy the day. And, Olivia, don't forget we're hosting Helen and her girls for dinner next weekend when Barbara and Meredith come down from Chicago. We'll all have a nice visit then."

Ray and Helen turned away to greet some friends, and Warner led Olivia in the other direction toward the parking lot and his car.

"Thanks, Warner," she said in a small voice.

"No problem."

"You don't need to take me to the mountains, of course, but I appreciate you making up that fib to help me out. I guess I'm still not used to Daddy seeing someone." She sighed.

"I'd like to take you to the mountains. We can pick up some sandwiches at the deli on the way home, change clothes, and head out. Helen's right. It's a beautiful day, and you and I haven't hiked one of the trails out of the campground together in a long time."

"All right." Her gaze softened. "Let's walk up the Deep Creek Trail along the stream. It's one of my favorites. We can eat lunch at the picnic grounds before we start out."

Warner walked Olivia to the car and opened the door for her before sprinting around to drop into the driver's seat.

"About lunch," she said. "I stopped by the Stoltzfus Bread Basket yesterday—you know, that wonderful Amish bakery—and bought fresh-baked sourdough bread, deli meats and cheese, veggie chips, and apple turnovers. I planned to make a quick lunch for Daddy and myself after church today. Let me pack a lunch for us at the house instead of trying to stop somewhere to pick up something."

"Okay." Warner watched her fidgeting with her seat belt and helped her adjust it.

Heading out of the parking lot, he made idle chatter with Olivia as they drove toward their homes and the mountains. "It's nice to drive and see only green hills, quiet shops, rural homes, and barns again. Traffic around New York is always a killer."

"Did you like it there?"

"New York has its charm." He slowed for a curve. "I always forget you've never seen it. Beautiful old buildings, museums, fabulous restaurants and shops, lovely parks, the theatre, and a constant array of entertainments to choose from."

"I remember how much you talked about it after the summer you stayed with your grandparents."

"Being there that summer opened a whole new world to me."

Her voice grew wistful. "Like a siren calling."

He grinned at the words. "Yes, like a siren calling. I 'found myself' in New York that summer, Olivia."

"I know." She breathed out a sigh.

Warner decided to shift the subject. "Tell me how you got into the florist business." He eased the car around another curve. "You went to Western to major in business, if I remember."

"Yes, I helped Daddy in the clinic office my last years in high school and thought I might manage the clinic after graduation ..."

"But?" He glanced her way.

"But life took me in another direction." Her lips curled in a smile. "I started working in Verlie's florist, The Flower Shop, when she lost an employee. You probably recall she and Grandmother Lila being great friends."

"Yes, and an odd match, I thought, with Verlie easy-going, warm-hearted, and funny and your Grandmother so stuffy."

"Perhaps they balanced each other out. Friends sometimes do, you know."

"So Verlie needed you ..." He encouraged.

"Yes. Daddy hired a new office manager when I went to Western, and I found less and less to do in the clinic office when at home. I took the job at Verlie's, mostly to help her out, but ended up loving it." She turned a bright face toward his. "I worked there every summer after that, part-time around my school schedule and on school holidays. After graduation, Verlie offered me a full-time job, and I jumped on the offer. I attained my design certification and began to handle more and more of the ordering and administrative work for Verlie as her health declined."

Warner slowed to take the turn on Cemetery Road, not far from the park boundary, leading toward their homes.

"The rest I told you before. When Verlie died, I decided to buy her equipment and supplies and open my own florist shop." She brushed a strand of hair behind her ear. "I truly appreciated my business courses then and wished I'd applied myself more in my accounting classes." She laughed.

Warner thought over her story. "You said on the day we lunched at Island Park that I influenced your decision to open Fairgarden Florist."

She put a hand on her hip. "No. I said that reading about Flora

Fair in your Gilmore books, with her dreams of having a flower shop, reminded me of my girlhood dreams."

"Dreams you shared with me." He turned into his own driveway. "We did a lot of dreaming and wishing together when young."

"We did."

Warner stopped the car beside his garage apartment. "Come inside with me while I change clothes. It won't take long. You can look around and see how Mother changed the apartment."

"All right." She followed him up the stairs.

Warner shed his Sunday suit in the bedroom and pulled on shorts, a comfortable T-shirt, socks, hiking boots, and a ball cap. Rummaging through the closet, he found a backpack to stow their lunch in and tossed in a hiking map, pocket knife, small towel, and a few other needed items for the trail.

He found Olivia in his office, looking through a couple of magazines on a side table.

"Do you still work for *Kite Magazine*?"

Warner nodded. "I write regularly for them. I do stories, cartoons, puzzles, and drawings. I like doing short pieces and art around my other writing and it pays well."

She looked around. "Do you have an office in New York like this to work in?"

"Two of them. One at *Kite* and another at home in my new apartment." He frowned. "I moved after Nelle died. The memories of that neighborhood proved too hard … walking past the market where—" He stuffed his hands in his pockets, not adding more. "You ready to go?"

"Sure." She put a hand on his arm, patting it as she might a child's. "It's so difficult to lose someone you love."

Picking up his backpack, he headed to the door, glad she moved ahead of him to start down the steps without further comment.

They drove the short distance to Benton House, pulling into the driveway near the back entrance. Warner trailed Olivia through a side porch and into the sunny kitchen.

"You can wait here or in the living room while I run upstairs and change." She sent him a smile. "Make yourself at home."

A thousand memories swamped Warner as he wandered around the sunny, yellow kitchen and into the breakfast area where its wide windows opened onto a shaded patio offering views of the garden. Earlier, when he picked Olivia up for Barry's party, he'd followed Ray Benton into the formal living room, but today he wandered into the downstairs den, where he and Olivia usually settled as children to play games, watch favorite television shows, or sit and talk. He found the décor little changed in the high-ceilinged room.

Walking closer to the fireplace, he stopped to study the photos along the mantle—framed shots of Olivia at different ages, Margaret and Ray Benton in younger years, pictures of Olivia's grandparents Lila and her husband Sinclair Fairchild. He picked up the oldest photo, a formal, sepia-toned one of an unsmiling couple.

"Those are my great grandparents, Edward and Olivia Fairchild," Olivia said, slipping into the room. "I was named for Great-grandmother Olivia." She walked closer to look over Warner's shoulder. "I'm the fourth generation to live here at Benton House and the fourth woman in the family to tend the gardens my great-grandmother created."

Warner sat the picture back on the mantle. "And unless you marry and have children, there won't be a fifth generation."

She wrinkled her nose. "You sound like Daddy. He complained the other day about my still-unmarried state. Said he wanted a grandchild to dangle on his knee before he grew too old."

His eyes found hers. "Why haven't you married, Olivia—with all those offers?"

She turned toward the kitchen. "I suppose you'll tease me for a long time about Vickie Leigh's account of my past beaus."

Warner trailed Olivia into the kitchen, as she went to the refrigerator to pull out food to prepare their lunch. She wore navy shorts, showing off an expanse of trim but shapely legs, and a sky blue knit shirt that brought out the clear blue of her eyes. Her shoulder-length fair hair was pulled up in a ponytail and she, too, wore socks and hiking boots. Whether in her rose-pink church dress with its flirty skirt or in old, casual clothes ready to hit the trail, Olivia's classic beauty always drew eyes.

She turned to ask him a question, then paused as she caught his eyes moving over her. "What?" She looked down. "Do I have a hole in my shorts or something? They're old ones."

Warner smiled. "I don't think you often realize how beautiful you are, any more than some of those stunning roses in the arbor know how they steal the breath away from mere mortals."

"That's almost poetic." She clasped her hands self-consciously. "I suppose I should say thank you for the compliment."

"I guess you get tired of hearing compliments about your looks."

Olivia gave him a puzzled look. "I don't get that many."

"I doubt that." He moved across the room to give her a kiss on the forehead. "But let me say, in case there's any truth in that statement, that I think you're the most beautiful woman I ever met."

She blushed at his words. "That's kind of you, especially when you've traveled around so much and met so many sophisticated and fashionable women."

His voice dropped and he slid a hand down her arm. "None compared to you, Olivia."

She walked to the counter and opened a tin breadbox decorated with fruit motifs. "Do you want one sandwich or two?" She took out a loaf of bread.

Warner pulled out a kitchen chair and straddled it. "Two. My mouth is already watering, seeing that loaf of homemade bread."

She turned to smile at him as she took a knife out of the drawer. "David and Karen do make wonderful baked goods at Stoltzfus's. Yesterday, they'd just taken this loaf from the oven, along with apple turnovers. The smell in the shop was heavenly."

Olivia cut slices from the loaf and spread them with mayonnaise. "I bought deli turkey, roast beef, provolone cheese, and cheddar. What would you like on your sandwiches?"

"A little of everything. Do you have lettuce and tomato, too?"

"Sure." She pushed a bag toward him. "Taste these incredible veggie chips. They're much better than store-bought potato chips."

He munched a few. "Pretty good." Warner stood to walk to the sink to get a drink of water. "What can I do to help you?" He turned back to her.

"Start wrapping these sandwiches in aluminum foil. You'll find some on the shelf there." She pointed. "Then you can pack everything into that small picnic basket on the kitchen shelf."

He set to work, wrapping the sandwiches and stowing them, along with the chips, fruit, and turnovers she'd set out, into the basket. In the quiet space, while they worked, he realized Olivia had evaded his earlier question about why she'd never married. She also changed the subject and busied herself when he initiated a little intimacy. He recognized it as an old ploy of hers. She'd always been a master at keeping the direction of their conversations exactly where she wanted them. Warner smiled, realizing how little some things change in others' personalities throughout the years.

Olivia hunted up paper plates, plasticware, and a faded, red-checked tablecloth to add to the basket. Noticing he sat, simply watching her now, she said, "Warner, you'll find a small cooler in the pantry you can fill with a couple of canned colas and ice from the refrigerator."

She cleaned up the kitchen while he packed the cooler and then went into the pantry to bring out a bag of trail mix, two packets of peanut butter crackers, and two bottles of water. "When we get to the car, throw these into your backpack for a snack on the trail later if we want it."

A short time later, picnic and gear loaded, they headed out, following quiet Durham Branch to Cemetery Road, and then turning left on West Deep Creek toward the Great Smoky Mountains National Park. It was less than a mile to the park entrance.

"We used to bike over here when we were kids," he commented, as the familiar scenes of the Deep Creek picnic area and campground came into view. "I always thought it great that we lived so close to the mountains."

"We always stopped at the Miller's store at Deep Creek Campground on the way home, too, for an ice cream cone. Remember?"

"Yeah. Let's stop there on our way home today." He grinned at her.

She pointed ahead as they drove into the park. "Drive to the right and maybe we can find a table along the creek."

Warner kept his eyes peeled and pulled into a parking spot by a table right next to the creek under a shade tree. "How's this?"

"It's perfect. I'll go claim the table before someone else spots it." She jumped out of the car. "You bring the picnic stuff."

Eating along the streamside gave them opportunity to hear the sounds of the stream rushing over mountain boulders while they ate. Olivia, smiling, pointed out a group of tubers riding down the creek in the currents, laughing and shrieking as they bounced along. It amazed Warner how easily he and Olivia drifted back into friendship and familiar ways, as if only a year or two had passed instead of ten.

He knew so many of her ways. He knew, even before she did it, that she'd spread a nice tablecloth over their picnic table, even for an outdoor lunch, that she'd pour her diet soda into a cup over ice while he drank his straight from the can. He knew she'd cut their sandwiches on the diagonal rather than straight across and that she'd snack more on grapes than chips.

As if reading his thoughts, she said, "This feels so familiar, doesn't it? Even though it's been so long."

"Yeah, I guess the old saying about old friends being the easiest and best is true."

Her eyes moved to watch two small children wade into the cold mountain stream, waving their arms and laughing. "You seem to have fallen back into an easy friendship with Leonard and Barry."

"Yes." He watched the children, remembering the joy of wading in the cold water when younger. "Barry, Leonard, and I wrote and kept in touch over the years. Both came to New York a few times. Once all three of us met, along with my cousin, Miles, at a big dude ranch out west. Rode horses, herded cattle, did the macho cowboy, sleep-on-the-range thing."

Her eyes caught his. "I remember your cousin, Miles. You wrote each other letters and he came here one summer. I liked him." She wrinkled her nose. "But he didn't like me much."

He chuckled. "You met him the first time while with the girls at the drug store."

Warner watched her search her memory.

"I guess Roberta must have said something he didn't like."

"You might say." He finished off one sandwich and started on another.

She shifted the subject again. "What are you writing now, Warner?"

"A book about all the ways you always avoid questions you don't want to answer and evade subjects you don't wish to pursue." He grinned.

She sent him a scowl, then looked away. "I see you still like to tease me."

"And you still like to avoid touchy subjects."

Olivia put a hand on her hip. "You avoid touchy subjects, too. You've skirted the topic of your wife's death and several other subjects you didn't want to discuss." She paused. "Everyone does that. We all like to avoid painful or difficult topics."

He frowned. He didn't like Olivia mentioning Nelle, and he knew he avoided that subject.

They ate in silence, watching the tubers and the children playing in the creek.

"Look, I'm sorry I brought up the subject of Nelle," Olivia said at last.

He reached for an apple turnover. "It's all right. You spoke the truth. I do hate talking about the time when Nelle died." He paused. "She didn't only die, Olivia, she was murdered. Murdered in cold blood for no reason."

Warner hunched his shoulders, feeling suddenly chilled. "Nelle walked down to the small market near our apartment to pick up a few groceries after work one day. She needed something for a recipe she wanted to try. I found her recipe on the kitchen counter later and a scribbled list of ingredients on a scrap of paper in her purse. Two robbers came in the store while she was in line at the register, waiting to check out."

Olivia reached a hand across the table to grasp his. "You don't have to tell me about it."

"I know, but I need to get past avoiding the subject." He closed his eyes, remembering. "The police told me the two gunmen panicked when a clerk reached under the counter to push an alarm button. Already high on drugs, they simply started shooting. They killed the clerk, Olivia, and an older gentleman, the only people in the store. The gunmen then cleaned out the cash register and fled. They took three innocent lives for four-hundred seventy-eight dollars and thirty-five cents." He shook his head.

"I'm so sorry, Warner." Olivia's soft voice soothed his raw nerves.

His voice choked. "I went to all three funerals, each a nightmare of sorrow, filled with weeping, grief, and regrets. The sadness of unnecessary lives lost. The anger that it happened at all, that such cruelty can exist in the world."

"Were the perpetrators caught?"

"Yes. Both locked away in prison now. Two more wasted lives."

She came around the table, sat beside him, and wrapped him in her arms. He took in her strength, comforted by the familiar scent of her, the knowledge of her long-time friendship and love. A calm settled over him.

"Thanks," he said at last, feeling lighter. Better.

She stroked his hair. "This is what you did for me when my mother died and even when Grandmother Lila died." A smile tugged at her lips. "And there was little love lost between you and Grandmother Lila."

He smiled back at her. "I could never figure out why she didn't like me."

"Oh, Warner, she feared you would take me away. Didn't you ever discern that later?"

He pulled back, looking into her eyes. "Did she actually say that?"

Olivia shook her head. "No, and it took me some time to figure it out. I think it's one reason she made me promise, when she lay dying in the hospital, that I would stay and take care of Daddy and the garden."

"Are you serious?" Warner's eyes met hers. "She asked that of you when she was dying?"

"Yes." She grew thoughtful, remembering. "She knew I was getting ready to graduate, and I think she sensed you and I had started to develop feelings for each other. Grandmother also knew you planned to leave as soon as you graduated." She smiled at him. "You said so often enough, even in her presence."

"I'm stunned." Warner looked out across the creek with unseeing eyes. "Did she dislike me that much?"

"No, she loved the garden that much." Olivia sighed. "If I moved away, who would keep it, cherish it, and perpetuate it? Fairchild Gardens was Grandmother's deepest love."

"Even above you, her only granddaughter?" He barely disguised his shock.

Olivia looked away. "I think Grandmother thought a life here would be the happiest course for me. If her desires were self-serving, she didn't fully see that." She put a hand on his arm. "Don't be bitter and hate her. She knew how much I loved the garden. She felt I wouldn't be happy to go far away."

He scowled. "It wasn't her place to press her desires on you."

Her lips thinned, her eyes meeting his. "It wasn't your place to press your desires on me, either, but you did."

"I didn't—"

"Yes, you did." She shook her finger at him. "I had no interest in moving to New York. No interest in going to college there or in living in a big city so far from the mountains. But you pressured me to go. Told me if I loved you I would go with you. You said you hated Bryson City, never wanted to live here, wanted to get away and never come back. You put me in a horrible position. You basically said it was 'go with you' or 'lose you.'"

"I wanted you to come with me."

She shook her head. "I know, but like Grandmother, you weren't thinking at all about what might be best for me."

Warner didn't like the direction of this conversation. "When you look back, do you ever have regrets, Olivia?"

She paused, putting a hand to her forehead. "Yes, I'll admit I do … and I did more so when younger, after you first left. But Warner, I don't think I could be happy, even today, living in New York. This is my home. I love it here. And I do love the garden. It would be hard to walk away from Fairchild Gardens, even now. To leave my business. My friends and family." She patted his hand. "I'm different from you. I'm a rooted-to-one-place sort of person. I've never wanted to run away."

Olivia slid off the bench, stood, and stretched. "I'd still like to go hiking, though, if you would, too?" She sent an appealing glance his way.

"Yeah, let's do that." He stood, also. "I'll help you clean up, put everything in the car, and grab my backpack."

A short time later, they found the park sign for Deep Creek Trail at the back end of the picnic grounds and started up the wide, open trail, once an old settlers' road into the mountains.

CHAPTER 13

Olivia followed behind Warner, thinking about their conversation. She partially lied to Warner when he asked if she ever experienced regrets not going to New York with him. But how could she have told him the truth after he poured out that story about his wife's murder? Especially after seeing the anguish and love in his eyes for Nelle?

It was no moment to bare her soul, that's for sure. What could she have said anyway? She tried to imagine it. ... *Warner, I felt plagued with regrets for years. Wept myself to sleep many nights torn with conflicting desires. Missed you with every fiber of my being. Yearned to get on a plane every day, yet feared doing so. Felt angry at you for your harsh demands but angry at myself, too, for not tossing everything to the wind and following after you. For not realizing, until too late, the depth of my love for you.*

She kicked at a rock in the path. She'd have sounded like a ninny spewing all that out. And what difference would it make? Warner was here for a visit and then heading back to New York to live. She didn't want to move there with him even now, to leave her home and the garden. Best to simply enjoy him while she could, make some good memories to cherish.

She broke the silence. "Have you driven over to Cherokee or down to Nantahala yet?"

He slowed until they walked side by side along the wide roadbed. "I went rafting on the Nantahala with Barry and Leonard one day, but not to Cherokee yet."

She smiled at him. "My work schedule is flexible. Maybe I can take off to go ramble around Cherokee with you one day. We could go to the Oconaluftee Mountain Farm Museum by the Oconaluftee Visitor Center and maybe to Mingo Falls. Then walk around downtown and go to the Cherokee Indian museum."

He grinned. "And go rafting down at Nantahala another day?"

Olivia swatted at him, playfully. "You know I'm scared of whitewater rafting. You'll need to get Leonard or Barry to ride the rapids with you if you want to go again, but I'll drive down to share dinner with you at River's End Restaurant on the dock at Nantahala if you'd like. In summer, there's music many nights."

"Good idea." He shifted the backpack straps on his shoulders. "Maybe we can get Barry and Patti to drive down with us."

She laughed. "Playing matchmaker?"

"I confess I am. I like Barry and I like Patti. They seem a good fit to me." He slowed, pointing to the bluffs across the stream. "Look, Olivia."

"It's Tom Branch Falls." Olivia stopped to sit on the rough bench by the side of the trail to admire the long, cascading chute of water, dropping eighty feet before hitting the stream below.

Warner sat beside her. "I'd almost forgotten this little falls. It has pretty spillovers on the journey down." He pointed to a broad section in the cascade. "Like that one."

"That's the widest part of the falls. I read the water spreads out eight to ten feet across that rock ledge as the water spills over."

He pulled a water bottle out of his pack to take a swig, passing it to her next. "When we walked this trail years ago, I remember the whole falls barely a trickle on some days." He glanced back down the trail. "How far have we hiked before getting to this spot?"

"Only a half-mile."

"Isn't there another falls further up?" His eyes scanned the path ahead.

"Indian Creek Falls."

His eyes lit. "That's the one, but it's on Indian Creek Trail, isn't it?"

"Yes, but it's only a hundred yards from the trail intersection, maybe a half mile from this spot. We can cut up Indian Creek Trail to see the falls, if you'd like, and then walk back to hike further up Deep Creek." She stood, dusting off the back of her shorts. "The rains earlier in the week make all the waterfalls fuller. I'd say Indian Creek will be a show today, even more than Tom Branch."

"Cool. Let's do it." He started up the trail again, grinning and excited.

It gave Olivia a catch in her heart, seeing him happy and smiling after hearing his earlier sorrows. Picking up her pace, Olivia caught up with him. "Patti told me she and Richard have gone back to Barry's home a couple of times since Rich started a friendship with Cheryl and Reed DeMatteo's boy, Sam. It's too bad Sam doesn't attend the Swain County Middle School where Rich goes. They could see each other more once school starts if he did, but Sam goes to the new Mountain Discovery Charter School out on Jenkins Branch Road."

Warner picked up a leaf from the ground to study it as he walked along. "I haven't heard of that school."

"It's relatively new, focuses on an outdoor program mixed with a regular curriculum. The students take hikes and backcountry trips, learn outdoor skills."

"Boy, I'd have loved that as a kid."

"Cheryl says Sam likes it." She slowed to squat and examine a cluster of wildflowers along the path.

"Pretty." Warner stopped to look over her shoulder at the shiny yellow flowers, almost hidden amidst a cluster of tooth-edged leaves.

"It's jewelweed and it likes these moist woods." She pointed to the leaves. "See how the water droplets on the yellow flower petals reflect the light and shine? That's where the name jewelweed comes from. It makes the flowers look like jewels."

Eager to hike on, Warner started back up the trail.

"Patti's grandmother knows all sorts of stories about medicinal uses of plants." Olivia told him, catching up to him. "She said the juices from jewelweed will soothe skin irritations."

Warner punched at her with his elbow. "I always enjoy hiking with you because you know all kinds of cool stuff about nature and flowers."

Olivia sighed. "Most people find that boring."

"I never have."

"I know," she said. "It's one of the things I like about you."

Warner changed the subject. "Have you learned any more about Patti's background?"

"No. Like I told you, she's very secretive."

"So is Rich. The boy stopped himself several times from telling me about his past when I took him for a soda." He reached over to pick up an odd-shaped rock, studying it as he walked along. "Two boys picked on Rich the day we went to Soda Pops. I gathered from him that this happens a lot and makes him unhappy."

"I'm sorry to hear that. I know Rich didn't get along well socially at school last year, and Patti said he doesn't have many friends."

"Sounds like me at his age."

She frowned at him. "You had friends, and it's not the same."

Warner turned to toss the rock into the stream. "Maybe you're right. You know both Patti and Rich better than me, too."

"The situation does worry me. Rich had an accident on his skateboard the other day. He came in the shop with a bloody knee, a busted elbow, and scratched up hands. Patti was out to lunch, so I patched him up. I suggested he run over to Daddy's, to see if he needed a stitch on the knee." She looked across the stream, pointing out a lizard sunning on a rock. "Rich didn't want to go. He started acting nervous, spilled some information that made me think some guys pushed him, made him fall off the skateboard. I couldn't get him to tell me more."

Warner scrambled down the creek bank for a closer look at the lizard, but the creature slipped into a crevice in a rock. He started back up the trail and Olivia fell into stride with him.

"I think Rich worried I might tell Patti. He even said he didn't want her to know," Olivia continued.

"He's protective of Patti. I saw that, too," Warner said. "He told me he hated living in Bryson City, but that his mom loved it."

She shook her head. "Maybe gaining Sam as a friend will help Rich. I don't think it's healthy for a kid his age to harbor adult secrets. It's bad enough Patti carries secrets, but I think it's harder for a child to keep them."

"Have you told Patti that?"

"No, too cowardly, and I'm not sure it's my business to interfere."

"I felt the same way." Warner pointed ahead. "There's our first bridge. If I remember right, the intersection for Indian Creek Trail is only a short distance after the bridge."

She nodded, and they walked on, talking about trails and the mountains now, enjoying the day.

They hiked the short distance to Indian Creek Falls, where a broad cascade spilled forty-five feet over a rocky drop-off in the stream with an inviting green swimming hole at its base.

"My brothers and I came here to swim as kids." Warner skipped stones over the water as he talked. "We used to dare each other to slide down the falls."

Olivia's mouth dropped open. "Surely not! Look how rocky it is under that cascade. You could have been hurt."

He grinned. "The risk factor is what made it fun." He studied the wide cascade spewing over the rocks. "I wouldn't try it now though."

Returning to the Deep Creek Trail, they continued following the old roadbed by the stream as it rose gradually up the backside of the Smoky Mountains. The path, broad and shady, wove in and out over the creek, crossing five footbridges before reaching Campsite #60 three miles up the trail, their planned destination for this day's hike.

Warner and Olivia chatted about mundane things along the way, stopping often to study flowers or plants or to dabble in the creek. A few hours later on their way back, they rock-hopped to a large boulder in the stream below one of the bridges to take a rest break.

"One day I'd like to hike all the way to Campsite #57 again to see the millstone commemorating Horace Kephart's last permanent camp in that area," Warner said. "Kephart proved so instrumental in helping the Smokies become recognized through his writings."

"That hike to Kephart's marker isn't an easy one, climbing over that steep Bumgardner Ridge. Besides, if you're interested in Horace Kephart, you can see his gravesite in the Bryson City Cemetery or drive over to Western Carolina University to see memorabilia about him in their museum."

"Look." Warner pointed to a trout skimming through the water. "I should hike back to this spot with my fishing gear some day."

"A lot of people fish Deep Creek." Olivia unlaced her boots, pulled off her socks and shoes, and dropped her feet into the stream. "And others simply like to stick their feet in the cold water." She giggled.

Warner laughed, moving closer to her on the edge of the boulder to follow suit and remove his socks and shoes.

Barefooted now, they climbed into the shallow stream, wading in the cold water, laughing and flipping water at each other. A thousand memories crowded Olivia's mind, remembering other times she and Warner played in the mountain streams, tubed the creek, or hiked the winding trails in this backcountry. She and Warner shared such a legacy.

They settled on the sun-warmed rock again after wading, toweling off their feet and digging into Warner's backpack to find the crackers, trail mix, and water they'd packed.

Warner stretched his legs out across the big rock. "I was interested to see a woman minister at the church this morning," he said, tearing into a package of crackers. "Very progressive for Bryson City."

"It's more and more common for women to pastor churches today in many denominations. I like our minister very much."

"Me, too." Warner finished a peanut butter cracker and washed it down with water. "She gave a good message. I thought about it a lot as we hiked the trail today. She talked about Jesus not being a respecter of persons and refusing to let Himself be defined with any particular religious group of the day—Sadducees, Essenes,

Zealots, or whatever. How Jesus didn't avoid company with groups of people not like himself, either."

She smiled. "Yes, that shocked even Jesus's own disciples. Remember how horrified they acted when he fellowshipped with the Samaritan woman at the well?"

"Yes, but He changed her life."

"That's true," Olivia agreed. "And He changed the life of the tax collector Zacchaeus by going to lunch with him."

Warner nodded. "I like how she explained why it's natural for us to cling to the familiar and gravitate to those like ourselves, to often feel reluctant to step outside our comfort zone to friend those different from us." He glanced at Olivia. "That helped me. She even explained how sociologists have studied that tendency and found social beings naturally gravitate to others similar to themselves in looks and behavior and draw away from those too different. Opposites don't really attract. Like is drawn to like."

"That helped me, too." She finished off a handful of trail mix. "But she didn't justify the behavior, even through it's a natural tendency for people."

Warner looked out over the stream in thought. "That doesn't mean we should decide it's ungodly to never judge anything or recognize what is dark around us." He paused, considering his words. "I got the idea that the 'not being a respecter of persons' thing she talked about has more to do with outward social and material stuff which shouldn't matter to us as much as it does."

"Yeah, I got that, too." Olivia pulled her knees up and wrapped her arms around them. "I felt convicted by that message this morning."

He gave her a boyish grin. "We used to dissect the Sunday messages every week like this when we were younger. Do you remember?"

"I do." She smiled back. "You were one of the few people I knew who paid any real attention at church or thought much about the messages afterward."

He laughed. "We used to look up the pastor's scriptures back then to see if he got them right."

Olivia laughed, too, and then reached out a hand to touch his cheek. "Gosh, I've missed you, Warner."

"I missed you, too." Warner reached to take her hand. "You were my life. You can't know how hard it was to walk away."

"Why did you?" She searched his face for the answer.

"I had to. I knew something waited for me beyond this place. I needed to pursue it. I felt I'd die inside myself to stay here. Every day from middle school on, I dreamed and looked forward to leaving."

She tried to understand. "Why did you never come back to visit?"

He squeezed her hand, almost too tightly. "I felt afraid I could never leave again. Never leave you again."

She caught her breath. "Oh, Warner, sometimes I wanted to get on a plane or bus and come to New York so badly. Sometimes I felt like I'd die without you." A tear trickled down her face.

"What a mess we were back then. So torn." He leaned forward to brush away her tear. Their gaze locked for several moments and Warner's eyes darkened. He moved closer then to settle his mouth over hers. Gently at first, then less gently. He pulled her against him, sliding his hands into her hair and then down her back to draw her closer.

Olivia's heart soared. Throwing her pride out the window, she twined her arms around his neck. It felt like home to be with him again, to hold him and kiss him, to catch that citrusy scent of him once more.

"You taste like raisins and almonds." Warner pulled back to grin at her.

She smiled at him. "And you taste like peanut butter crackers."

He sighed. "It confuses me, feeling so at home with you, so right touching you and kissing you." He trailed a hand up her arm. "Especially because of Nelle."

Olivia studied his face. "Wasn't it only last week—when we saw Daddy with Helen outside the clinic—that you told me a person can cherish more than one love in their lifetime?"

He nodded, leaning in to brush his lips over hers again. "I did."

She traced her fingers over the familiar planes of his face. "I felt Daddy betrayed Mother's memory, kissing another woman, wanting intimacy with another woman besides Mother, but being with you has helped me better understand that people can love more than once in a lifetime."

He kissed her nose. "I know you dated others after I left, too. I remember when I learned you and Russell Simmons had become serious about each other." He scowled over those words. "Barry kept me in touch with everything. Did you love Russell?"

"No, not in that way. I think Russell was ready to get married and I was convenient and comfortable." She let a hand stray over his chest, feeling the new muscles there. "Russell's and Roberta's relationship had hit the rocks senior year with another fiery argument. I don't think either of them understood what to do with the intensity of their feelings for each other in those years. They often argued and broke up, and I dated Russell between their arguments."

Olivia laughed. "No major sparks ever went off between Russell and me, Warner. That summer after high school, with you gone, and Roberta away at her sister's fuming over her and Russell's latest quarrel, Russell and I drifted into another dating relationship. After the traumatic relationships we'd both experienced, we toyed with the idea of becoming a more permanent couple. I think Russell proposed to me simply to be nice."

"I doubt that." Warner snorted.

"Anyway, I said no. I knew marrying with only friendship wouldn't work. I think, deep inside, he did, too." She watched a squirrel skitter up a tree on the bank. "When Roberta came back, they made up—dramatically, I heard—got unofficially engaged, and Roberta enrolled at Vanderbilt so they could live near each other during college."

"Do they still quarrel?" Warner let his fingers roam over her arms.

"Of course." Olivia smiled. "But Russell has learned to hold his own with Roberta, and it is a love match."

"What about all those other men in your life?"

She swatted at him. "I liked them, but the more I got to know them the more I realized, as with Russell, that marrying any of them wouldn't be a love match."

"And that's important to you." He threaded his hands through her hair, letting them playfully pull on her ponytail, before sliding down her back.

"Yes. I want a love match." She tried to concentrate, but his touch made it difficult. "I also know I need someone I can share with, who understands the things I'm passionate about." She swallowed, looking into his eyes. "Someone I don't need to put on an act with, that I can be totally myself with. Someone who will encourage the things that matter most to me."

Someone like you, Warner.

As if sensing the direction of her thoughts, Warner pulled back, fishing out the other packet of peanut butter crackers from their backpack. "You want these?"

"No, you can have them." She found her water bottle and took a sip, trying to collect herself.

Warner threw leaves into the cascade in front of them, watching the rushing water catch and swirl them down over the rocks. "Tell me about Helen Allmon," he said, surprising her with the change in topic.

She capped her water bottle before beginning an answer. "Helen's husband, Bob, was an anesthesiologist. They met in Chicago where Helen grew up. The two married and Bob worked at a hospital in Chicago through the years they raised their girls." She stopped to think. "If I remember right, Bob Allmon grew up near here, outside of Franklin. The Allmons came to the mountains for summer and holiday vacations, and Bob yearned to move back. He wanted to get out of the big city, to work in a smaller hospital. When an opportunity opened at Bryson City, he and Helen moved here."

Olivia and Warner watched two young men hike across the

bridge above them.

"And?" Warner turned his eyes back to hers.

"Helen found adjusting to small town living and the ways of the South very difficult at first," she continued. "I remember Daddy talking about it. He always liked Bob Allmon and sometimes went to dinner at their house, socialized with Bob and Helen at medical events." She picked up a round rock to toy with it while she talked. "Daddy always said the day Helen started her business turned her unhappiness around and gave her something to do."

Warner finished off his crackers and stuffed the wrapper back in his backpack. "Olivia, none of that tells me what *you* think about Helen."

Olivia wrinkled her nose. "Helen's a nice person. I know that, but I'm not comfortable with her."

"Why not?"

She rubbed her neck, uncomfortable with the question. "Too many differences, I guess."

Warner lifted an eyebrow. "Helen runs a shop like you. I would think that would give you something in common."

She sighed. "Yes, and that's the only thing we share in common. Even in that, we're different. I capitalize on local artisan's work for the gift shop in my florist business, selling simple products I can find around the area. Helen looks down her nose at that type of thing, preferring high-end items she orders from up north. The Unique Boutique reflects exactly who Helen is. Drop by some day. You'll feel her character in the store—and even in the two women who work for her."

Uncomfortable with the topic of conversation, Olivia began to pack their water and papers into the backpack. "Are you ready to head back?"

Warner strapped on his backpack and gave her his hand to help her up. "Only if you'll finish this conversation as we hike."

They jumped the rocks across the stream and scrambled up the bank. Walking down the trail again, Olivia tried to find words to express her concerns about Helen.

"Helen likes fine things, Warner. She enjoys eating out, going to movies and shows, entertaining, and shopping. She often drives to Atlanta or Asheville to get away from the quiet of Bryson City. She takes frequent cruises. Goes to Chicago on buying trips or to stay at length with her daughters. In some ways, her heart still isn't really settled here, and that worries me with Daddy."

"You think she'll lure him into marriage and then back to Chicago?"

"Maybe, but ..." She hesitated.

"But what?"

Olivia plunged on. "What worries me most is that Helen doesn't care a thing for the garden. She has no interest in flowers or plants. She can't even keep a houseplant alive in her store. I've delivered enough to the boutique to know and later returned to find them dying from neglect." She kicked at a pinecone in the path. "Her interests and conversations seem shallow and superficial to me. I know that sounds judgmental and partial, like the message at church this morning cautions against doing, but I can't help how I feel. Daddy acts different when she is around her, too."

"How so?" Warner slowed to study a dark caterpillar inching along the trailside.

"Well, ..." Olivia considered her words. "Daddy doesn't contradict Helen when she makes little snide remarks about our house being old-fashioned or needing to be updated. He doesn't grow defensive when she comments about the gardens being a lot of trouble or when she suggests that maybe they should be reduced in size."

"And you *do* grow defensive?" He caught her eyes.

"Yes. I do." She managed a wan smile. "I have to bite my tongue not to retaliate."

"I think you're afraid your father will marry Helen and that she will come into your home and change everything. Maybe even influence your father to reduce the garden. Or maybe even sell the property."

Olivia hugged herself. "I hold no claim on the property, Warner.

I own the little cottage I renovated for the florist business, but Benton House and the Fairchild Gardens belong to my father. He could sell them both, and there would be nothing I could do about it."

He tugged on her arm to stop her. "I don't think your father would do that, Olivia. He respects all your great-grandmother, grandmother, and your mother did to create the gardens. I believe he is proud of them."

"Maybe." A regretful laugh escaped from her lips. "But Daddy has never loved the garden deeply himself. Grandmother Lila worked in the garden, Mother worked in the garden, and I work in the garden, but Daddy never does. He seldom even walks around the grounds. In fact, he takes little interest in Fairchild Gardens. It never troubled me much before, but now ...."

"Now it does trouble you." Warner leaned over to kiss her on the forehead. "You need to talk with your father about this."

"And say what? I don't even know how serious he is about Helen." Olivia twisted her hands. "Daddy and I live together, but in many ways we don't really talk about personal things."

Warner walked on, and Olivia fell into step beside him. "I heard your father say at church that Helen and her daughters plan to come to your house for dinner next weekend. Maybe that visit will tell you more. Give you a better reading of how things stand."

Olivia ran her hands through her hair. "I dread that dinner evening. I don't know why I didn't pick up on Daddy's growing interest in Helen when he first suggested it."

Warner chuckled. "We often don't see our parents as persons with romantic or passionate appeal. I guess we forget sometimes they must be passionate people on some level to have sired us."

"That's true." She shrugged, smiling. "Maybe it's why I felt so shocked to see my father kissing Helen."

"Grandfather Delacourt would ask you, 'What's the worst that could happen, Olivia?' He claims it's one of the best ways to dilute what he calls projective worries."

She paused, crossing her arms. "The worst that could happen is that Daddy would marry Helen, sell Benton House and Fairchild Gardens, and move away to Chicago."

"And if that happened, what would you do?"

Tears welled in her eyes. "I think I'd die, Warner."

"Are the garden and house who you are?"

"No, but I love them both—especially the garden. Surely you can understand that? You of all people?"

"I do, Olivia."

She waited for more, but he made no further comment. "So, what would your psychiatrist grandfather tell me to do?"

He smiled at her. "Take your worst fears to your father and consider what actions you'd take if your worst fears came to pass."

"Not the answer I wanted to hear." She flashed him a look of annoyance and then laughed. "But an honest one."

Warner's glance shifted toward the side of the trail. "Hey. What's that white stuff growing over there?"

Olivia followed his glance to the trailside where a clump of delicate white shoots grew beneath a large tree among the leaves. "That's Indian pipe," she told him. "Some people call it ghost plant since the whole plant is white. You often see it along the trail following soaking rains like we had this week. It's a parasitic plant, feeds off tree roots."

He leaned over to study it closer. "Like squawroot?"

"Similar, except Indian pipe puts out a white flower."

"You're a walking encyclopedia." He took a last look at the plant then started up the trail again.

"I'm not an encyclopedia about everything, only flowers and plants." She frowned.

"Don't get defensive. You know I love that about you."

"Yes, you said so before."

They walked along, listening to the sounds of the stream and the twittering of birds in the trees. The sunshine played through the lush foliage, dappling rays of light across the trail.

"Thanks for this day, Olivia," Warner said at last in a soft voice. "I worried how it would be, seeing you again. Wondered if we'd ever spend time together like we did in the past and what it would be like when we did."

His words touched her, and she liked the idea of him thinking about her as she'd thought of him so often. She sent him an impish grin. "The way we spent time together today would have been different if you'd visited when you were married."

"Yes." He swatted her playfully on the bottom. "And leave it to you to bring that up."

"Would Nelle have enjoyed it here?"

He considered her question. "I'm not totally sure. Nelle was a city girl, through and through, but she did enjoy outings to the park or over to Staten Island for walks on the beach. She appreciated beauty."

"I'm glad she helped you and loved you when you needed it."

He stopped, catching her gaze. "That's gracious of you to say. And I don't think Nelle would mind me seeing you again. She knew you were my first love and that I loved you long before her."

Olivia spotted the end of the trail ahead.

Following her glance, Warner said, "Let's not let the day end yet. Your father said he planned to take Helen to Fontana. Let's have dinner together. Maybe go to Cherokee to see a movie."

CHAPTER 14

Warner watched Olivia waver over his invitation. Their day on the trail had been sweet, and they'd talked out many things they needed to discuss. But he felt her hesitate at further close time together.

"Maybe we can get Barry and Patti to go with us." He could dilute the situation with another couple.

She brightened. "Oh, I'd like that. Do you think they'd say yes on the spur of the moment like this?"

"We could ask." He pulled out his cell phone.

After a couple of calls and callbacks, Warner finalized arrangements with Barry. "Barry got us a reservation for dinner at the Fryemont Inn for seven tonight," he told Olivia, dropping his phone back in his pocket. "I hope that's okay with you."

"I love the Fryemont." She smiled. "And we'll both have time to relax and shower after the trail before we need to head back to town."

Back at his apartment, Warner crashed for a short nap then showered and dressed in khaki slacks and a short-sleeved coffee-brown shirt for dinner. He lavished on a handful of Lacoste Essential cologne, too, remembering Olivia commented several times on liking the citrus scent.

Grinning, he remembered his publicist telling him the fragrance a man wears provides an indication of his personality, attitude, and style. *Who'd have thought I'd ever care about anything like that?* He laughed. It's a big change from the kid who used to smell like skateboard oil and wear baggy, wrinkled shorts, superhero T-shirts, and black high-topped sneakers with no socks.

Warner shook his head at the memory. He probably did make it difficult for many people to like him in the past, not only because of his disregard for appropriate fashion, but because of his equally oppositional attitude. Time and maturity had taught him the importance of a good impression. Even if you were the greatest person in the world, if you looked like a slob and acted like a jerk, it hardly helped anyone to want to know you better.

Looking through old family photos last week at his parents, Warner noticed so many shots of himself, sullen faced, making no effort to be agreeable or personable. What had Grandfather Delacourt told him so often in their conversations? That first impressions sometimes offer the only chance to get your foot in the door.

"Warner, haven't you ever heard of putting your best foot forward?" he'd say. "What's the point in ticking people off before they have a chance to get to know you?"

Warner laughed, remembering. It was the kind of straight talk he got in daily doses from his Delacourt grandparents.

Warner picked Olivia up shortly after six thirty, feeling his heartbeat pick up at the sight of her. She wore a flirty, flower-sprigged sundress.

"You look good," he said, walking to the car with her.

"So do you."

He watched her eyes slide over him. "Nice change for the better, don't you think?" He chuckled, as her eyebrows lifted in surprise.

Warner opened the door for her. "Being back in Bryson City has confronted me with my youthful past." He walked around the car and slid behind the driver's seat.

"And?" Olivia encouraged him to add more.

"And my afternoon spent poking around in old photo books and through a few youthful memory boxes showed me an awkward kid I'd rather like to forget."

Olivia reached over to put a hand on his knee. "I liked that boy. He was my very best friend."

Warner started the car, backing it out of the driveway. "Well, if I'd been smarter and less socially inept, maybe I wouldn't have lost the girl I loved."

"Is that how you see it?" She looked surprised.

He headed the Mercedes Benz down the road. "Well, let me ask you an honest question. Suppose I'd looked in those years more like I do today and acted more like I do now. Would you have gone to prom with me?"

A slow flush spread up her face and she turned to look out the window. "We can't go back in time, Warner, only forward."

"I guess I put you on the spot with that one." He slowed to drive the car over the low spot in the road that crossed through the shallow waters of Durham Branch. He wisely changed the subject then. "I didn't see your dad's car at the house."

"He called from Fontana. When I told him we planned to eat with Patti and Barry, he said he thought he'd take Helen to the Mountview Bistro at Fontana Village Resort before they headed back. He loves their grilled trout."

Warner glanced at her. "You doing okay about them spending so much time together?"

She shrugged. "I suppose. It's not like I have any choice in the matter." She picked at a silver earring. "But I admit it feels funny to think about Daddy seeing someone."

He chuckled. "To realize you're not Daddy's only girl any more?"

Olivia flashed an angry look his way. "That wasn't nice."

"Sorry." He pulled onto West Deep Creek Road. Glancing across the street at the Miller's store, he turned to her and smiled. "It was great to drop by Miller's earlier, to poke around the old campground and buy an ice cream cone from Darleen Miller. Nothing's changed at the old store."

"Yes, it's nice some things stay the same," she replied, her voice pinched and quiet.

The car glided silently down the road, past lush, green fields and hills, picturesque country farm homes and barns, and an occasional spot of commerce. Trying to lighten the mood, Warner caught

Olivia up on happenings with his family as they drove. Light chatter, nothing serious.

They soon wound into Bryson City, driving down Everett Street and over the river bridge, continuing across the intersection at the main highway to wind uphill on Rector Street to Fryemont. Warner pulled into the parking lot at the inn and found a space for the Benz near the door.

"I remember my dad telling me the Fryemont Inn was built as a hotel by the timber baron Amos Frye in the 1920s," Warner said, leading Olivia up the steps of the old building.

She smiled at him. "I'm glad the Browns, the new innkeepers, kept the rustic charm of the original hotel. It makes the Fryemont special—as does the resident cat." She reached down to pet a yellow tabby just inside the entry door.

Warner watched the cat rub against Olivia's leg. "This feline obviously knows you."

"His name is Punkin. He belongs to the Georges who own the Fryemont, and he meets and greets all the guests."

Following Olivia through the doorway, Warner saw Barry waving from across the room. The foursome soon settled into a table near the window in the beam-ceilinged dining area, a vast stone fireplace the focal point of the comfortable room. Paddle fans turned quietly near the ceiling and the hardwood floors gleamed in the fading sunlight.

They chit-chatted after ordering iced tea and studied their menus.

"What are you ordering, Olivia?" Patti asked.

Patti wore a summer sundress, too, hers in a deep green that complimented her olive complexion and black hair. She looked attractive, Warner thought, although her elfish looks could never compare to Olivia's blond, classic beauty.

Olivia lowered her menu. "I'm ordering the chicken tapenade with olive paste, feta cheese, and couscous. It's wonderful."

Barry pushed up his glasses, and sent her one of his sideways grins. "Sounds like a chick dish. I'm getting the braised lamb shanks with mashed potatoes."

"Why do men always seem to gravitate to meat and potatoes?" Patti wrinkled her nose. "I think I'll try the pecan-crusted trout."

Olivia laid her menu by her plate. "You won't regret that choice, Patti. It's one of the inn's specialties."

Warner chuckled as the waitress walked up. "Well, I'm going to stay male-traditional and order the prime rib with potatoes."

The girls laughed.

After placing their order, Patti caught Olivia up on happenings at the florist shop. Then Barry entertained them with witty stories about downtown happenings.

"The vandal struck again last night," he announced as the waitress brought the soup and salads that always came with every Fryemont meal.

"Oh, I hate to hear that." Olivia winced. "Was anyone hurt?"

"No." Barry scratched his head. "And I thought this episode a weird one."

"How so?" Warner asked, curious.

Barry grinned. "The vandal dressed the angel statue in the hillside cemetery in a black bra, pointy hat, and a sleazy black skirt. Even put lipstick and rouge on the angel's face. Disrespectful, but nothing that couldn't be fixed."

Warner couldn't help laughing at the image this conjured up.

"Who would do that?" Olivia's mouth dropped open. "That's Fanny Everett Clancy's gravesite."

"Who's Fanny Everett Clancy?" Patti asked.

Olivia stirred dressing into her salad while she answered. "Fanny was the young daughter of Epp Everett, one of the town's most influential citizens. In the late 1880s, Fanny died of tuberculosis shortly after her marriage to Ernest Clancy. I remember Grandmother Lila telling me the story, and I thought it sad."

"Several Clancy families still live in Bryson City, if I remember right," Barry said, spreading butter over a hot roll. "I expect they'll be incensed over this. I know Mabel Clancy has several grandkids in the school system, and she's a dramatic type. I bet she'll be on her bandwagon about this happening."

"This type of non-violent vandalism smacks more of pranking than real criminal activity." Warner finished off his soup and started in on his salad. "My granddad took me and my brothers to that old cemetery on the hill when we were kids. He pointed out to us that the tip of one of the angel's fingers was missing. Granddad said a group of naughty boys shot it off not long after the statue was erected. That sort of thing does happen."

Olivia propped an elbow on the table and leaned forward. "You forget, Warner, that these incidents have gone on for quite some time. It's not only one random act we're talking about."

"Did the vandals write a message with this prank?" Patti asked. "They left messages before."

"Yes, and the message seemed an odd one." Barry took a swig of his iced tea. "I remember the newspaper reported it: 'Just because a girl looks like an angel doesn't mean she can't be a witch.'"

Patti looked up, a small smile touching her lips. "Well, that explains the witch hat and black skirt."

"Good point," Barry said. "And the ratty broom the police found leaning beside the statue with the message taped on it."

"None of this makes any sense at all." Olivia sat back in her seat, picking up her fork to eat her salad.

"Random acts of vandalism don't need to make sense," Warner added.

"No." Barry tapped his fingers on his chin. "But I think when this group is caught that a link and connection between every act will be found."

Warner winked at him across the table. "I think you've read too many of those superheroes comics, seeing despotic acts in everyone's motives, plots behind every random action." He waved his hands dramatically as he talked.

"No." Barry toyed with his silverware on the table. "You're new to town, Warner. I've been watching this." He paused. "Besides, I've got a feeling about it."

Their entrees arrived and the conversation shifted to less serious topics. Warner enjoyed the evening more than he expected. The pace in Bryson City moved more slowly and sweetly than in the city. People from other tables stopped by to visit and chat as they came and left. No one seemed in a hurry. The casual dining room atmosphere seemed to encourage camaraderie and ease. Even the paddle fans overhead created a swishing soothing background to the conversation in the dining room. Warner found himself inwardly relaxing for the first time in months.

Hearing Patti talking about Rich, Warner decided to quiz her about her background. "Patti, tell me a little about yourself since I'm the new boy in the neighborhood."

She dropped her eyes and fidgeted with the napkin in her lap. "I grew up in Virginia, raised by my grandparents," she said at last. "They ran a small florist shop, and we lived in an apartment above it. That started my love for the floral business. I married, moved out west, and had Rich." Her face tightened. "The marriage proved unhappy. Rich's father had some serious problems too difficult for us to contend with. We moved back east, and I divorced."

"Why to Bryson City when you grew up in Virginia?" he probed.

Her gaze still didn't meet his. "I didn't want to go home and burden my grandparents after my divorce. Visits to the mountains here made me want to see if I could find work in this area." She looked at Olivia. "I met Olivia when she opened her shop."

"And that was a lucky day for me." Olivia rescued her, reaching across the table to take Patti's hand. "I don't know what I'd have done without Patti these years. She's wonderful in the store."

Patti smiled, relaxing with the compliment. "Thanks. I love working at Fairgarden Florist, and I like Bryson City."

She sent a shy glance Barry's way with her last words, and Warner decided not to push her any further for more details. It seemed obvious there was far more to Patti's story than she wished to reveal.

At dinner's end, Patti reminded them she'd left Rich alone and needed to get back home. She and Barry said good-byes, and Warner and Olivia prepared to leave, too.

"Do you mind if I slip into the girls' room a minute?" Olivia asked.

"No," he said, pushing in their chairs. "I'll wait for you in the lobby."

Warner wandered into the spacious lobby, a vast room enhanced by a huge stone fireplace and a comfortable seating area. As he waited, Brody Hanks and Logan Staley sauntered through the main door to head for the bar. The Fireside Bar at the Fryemont Inn was a popular spot with visitors and locals.

Brody nudged Logan as they headed Warner's way. "You still hanging around Bryson City, War-ner?" Brody created a singsong sound with Warner's name.

Warner bit back a sarcastic reply. "I plan to stay in town for several weeks visiting with my family."

Logan looked around. "What brings you over to the Fryemont tonight?"

It rankled Warner how these two always assumed it their right to know what others were doing and with whom. "I enjoyed dinner here with friends earlier."

"With some of your loser buddies?" Logan smirked.

Warner tensed but tried not to rise to the bait of their old taunting tactics. "These are not high school days anymore. All of us have moved on."

"Yeah, and some of us would like to see *you* move on again." Brody glared at him.

Olivia picked that moment to walk into the lobby looking for him. Not noticing Brody and Logan at first, she lifted a hand and waved at him.

Brody's face colored, his fists clenching at his side. "Is this the old friend you shared dinner with?" He leaned his face closer to Warner's. "I thought I made it clear Olivia and I were an item now."

Olivia breezed up before Warner could answer. "Oh, hi, you two." Her eyes roved over Brody and Logan. "What are you guys doing here at the Fryemont?"

"Stopping by for a drink at the bar and a game of billiards," Logan replied, acting more friendly now.

Less congenial, Brody moved closer to Olivia. "I called you after church, but couldn't get an answer. We held another impromptu meeting of the reunion planning committee this afternoon. You missed it."

Olivia's face fell. "Oh, I'm sorry. I wish I'd known you planned to meet. I went hiking and didn't carry my cell phone."

"Hiking by yourself?" Brody raised an eyebrow.

"No, Warner and I went." She glanced Warner's way with a smile.

"And then shared a nice, cozy dinner here at the Fryemont?" Brody frowned, stepping closer to Olivia to catch her eyes with his. "Since when did you start running around with Weird Warner?"

Logan snickered. "Probably since he came into a little money and tidied himself up."

Olivia put her hands on her hips. "That is *so* not nice, Logan." She turned to Brody. "And you don't need to act nasty because I missed one of our planning meetings. The group should schedule their sessions in advance so everyone can make plans to attend."

Deciding this altercation couldn't improve, Warner walked over and slipped Olivia's arm into his. "I think we'd better go now."

"Okay." She said good-byes to Logan and Brody and followed Warner onto the porch.

Outside the door, she put a hand on her hip and turned on him. "What happened with those two before I came out? Both of them were obviously upset."

Warner turned to her in surprise. "And you think I started something with them?"

She glared at him. "Well, something got them all whipped up. It's not like them to be rude to *me* like that."

Warner grabbed her arm. "And it's okay for them to be rude to me, is that what you're saying?" He snapped the words, his voice laced with sarcasm. "Brody and Logan walked in the door and started in on me before you came out of the restroom. I can't believe you always take up for them." His hand tightened on her upper arm in irritation.

"You're hurting me, Warner." Olivia glanced down at his hand

and tried to pull back from his grasp.

A soft sound alerted Warner to the presence of another closing in behind him.

"You heard the lady. Let her go." In a quick blur of movement, Brody broke Warner's hold on Olivia's arm, yanked him around, and leveled him with a sharp jab to the jaw.

Warner fell backward, tripping over a wooden rocker, and sprawled on the porch.

Brody stood over him, fists raised, while Logan kicked at him on the floor.

"Get up. This isn't over." Brody raised his fists, his face red with anger.

Olivia pushed at him. "Stop that, Brody Hanks. This is over *now*. I won't have you fighting about me. Whatever were you thinking to hit Warner like that?"

She squatted beside Warner. "Are you okay?"

Still stunned, Warner put a hand to his jaw in disbelief.

Logan shuffled his feet. "We saw him hurting you, Olivia," he explained. "Brody and I only meant to protect you."

"Well, you misinterpreted the situation." She glared at them. "Warner was simply holding my arm a little more tightly than I'd like—hardly a reason to start punching him on my behalf. Honestly!"

Brody moved toward Olivia. "I'll take you home, Olivia." He slid an arm protectively around her waist.

"No, you won't." She jerked away. "Warner will take me home. I came with him and I'm going home with him." She took Warner's arm as he got to his feet. "And I don't feel happy with you right now, Brody Hanks."

Rubbing his jaw, Warner found his fists clenching at the angry flush spreading over Brody's face at her words.

Seeing the movement, Olivia turned her eyes to his. "Don't even think about it, Warner. This situation is finished, and I want to go home right now. Do you hear me?" She pulled on his arm, drawing him down the steps with her.

Warner glanced back to where Brody and Logan still stood on the porch, glaring after them. "Maybe you should walk on ahead to the car and let me go back and deal with this."

She gave him an annoyed look, clamping down on his arm harder. "For a two-on-one fight? How would that help?"

He stiffened and scowled at her. "I don't like to appear a coward and my self-defense skills are more developed than when I was a skinny school-aged kid. I can hold my own."

Olivia continued walking toward the Benz, practically pulling him along. "I won't have the three of you fighting over me for something stupid."

Warner opened the door and helped her into the car, his eyes shifting to the inn again.

"Don't you even think about going back up on that porch, Warner." Her icy eyes met his. "I meant what I said about wanting to go home. If you head back to fight with them, I'll walk down this hillside and call my father to come get me."

Warner stalked around the car to slide into the driver's seat. "I don't like leaving things like this. It reminds me too much of past times when they bullied me and got away with it."

"This is hardly the same," she insisted.

"Maybe not to you, but it is to me." Backing up the car, he started out of the parking lot, trying to avoid glancing behind him. He lurched down the hill from the Fryemont a little too fast, taking the sharp curves with a squeal of his brakes. In silence they drove through town and then out West Deep Creek Road toward home.

Warner fumed silently the entire way, irritated that he'd allowed himself to be bullied by Brody and Logan one more time in his life.

Olivia sighed as they pulled into the driveway of her house. "I hate our evening ended so badly after we had such a nice day."

Warner, still angry, struggled to hold his tongue.

Olivia reached over to put a soft hand to his face. "Does your jaw hurt?" she asked. "I hope you won't have a bruise."

"If I do, I'll only feel bad I didn't give Brody Hanks a bruise or two to match." He turned cold eyes to Olivia. "I can't believe you let those two act that way around you, assuming they have a right to insult and attack your friends."

Olivia's eyes lifted in surprise. "I think Brody and Logan simply misinterpreted the situation. When they came out on the porch they thought you were hurting me."

"You actually believed that?" He snorted. "No. They were looking for an excuse to go at me. In the lobby before you came out of the restroom, they approached me aggressively, threw out several nasty insults and insinuated I should leave town. I imagine it really goaded them to see you walk into the lobby and realize I'd shared dinner with you."

Her lips formed a thin line. "I didn't hear any of that and, knowing you as I do, you probably read more into their comments than either of them intended. I think Brody and Logan felt annoyed I'd missed the reunion planning meeting, and I think they truly thought you were behaving aggressively toward me." Her blue eyes met his. "You were hurting me, Warner."

His hand tightened on the steering wheel. "You always take up for them."

"No, I try to keep things in perspective, which you seem unable to do." She lifted her chin.

Scowling, Warner leaned across her to open the car door. "If you don't mind, I don't think I'll walk you to the door."

"Fine," she said in irritation, swinging out of the car. "I hope when you cool down that you'll see this situation for the misunderstanding it was, rather than some personal attack against yourself. Obviously, you learned nothing from that sermon at church today."

He lifted his eyebrows at this final dig. "And you think you did, Olivia Benton, with your continual favoritism to the members of the Elite Eight no matter what they do?"

She slammed the car door and headed up the sidewalk, obviously still upset with him.

Warner watched her walk to the door, and then put the car in reverse. "Thanks for reminding me how things are, Olivia Benton," he muttered. "For a little while, I was beginning to think you'd really changed."

CHAPTER 15

Olivia didn't see Warner at all in the coming week. She did see Brody and Logan at another planning meeting with the reunion committee, but neither brought up the incident with Warner.

She found herself thinking back with mixed feelings about her times with Warner as she worked in the kitchen Friday night to get ready for the dinner party for Helen Allmon and her two daughters. Her cat Sybil sat on a cushion on the kitchen stool watching her.

"I dread this party," she told the cat. "It's mean of me, I know, but somehow Helen doesn't feel like she belongs here at Benton House. She isn't comfortable with the Country French interior—or what she calls the clutter of decorative items—and she constantly offers ideas about ways everything should be modernized and updated."

Olivia looked around at the sunny yellow and white kitchen, her eyes wandering over the hand-painted floral tiles above the counter and to the glass-fronted cabinets filled with floral-print dishes. Like most rooms in Benton House, the love of flowers echoed throughout the décor. Every room in the house held floral paintings, floral needlepoint pillows, floral upholstery or floral rugs.

She sighed. "Helen Allmon doesn't even know one flower from another. How could she fit in here as the lady of the house, Sybil?" She walked over to pet the cat. "She even claims she's allergic to cats, which doesn't bode well for you."

The cat meowed as if in protest.

Olivia glanced toward the menu posted on the refrigerator as the phone rang. It was Lulu.

"Hey, Olivia. I wanted to tell you Eva loved the book you brought her yesterday when you came to visit. She had me read it over and over to her last night, and she wants me to make all the animal sounds like you did." She giggled.

"I'm glad Eva liked it." It felt good to hear her friend's voice today.

"How are the preparations going for your big dinner tonight?" Lulu asked. "It feels funny to think about your daddy romantically involved with Helen Allmon."

"Tell me about it." Olivia sat on the kitchen stool by the phone, an old landline still mounted on the wall in the exact same place it had hung since Olivia's earliest remembrance.

"Do you think your daddy will marry her?"

Olivia twisted the phone cord. "I don't know. Maybe I'll be able to tell more when I see them together tonight."

Lulu changed the subject. "What did you decide to cook?"

Olivia glanced toward the menu on the refrigerator. "I felt afraid that any fancy fare I prepared would be compared to Chicago restaurant standards, so I went country on my choices." She giggled. "I baked a ham, and I'm serving homegrown vegetables from the garden—green beans, a squash casserole, succotash with fresh corn and lima beans, deviled eggs, homegrown tomatoes and cucumbers, and a peach cobbler with vanilla ice cream and whipped topping."

"Yum, that's my kind of meal. Can Rob and Eva and I come?"

"I wish you could. I feel so nervous about entertaining Helen's daughters. They've never lived anywhere except Chicago and only rarely visited in this area."

"How can they not love it? It's a tourist mecca and a charming town."

"I hope you're right."

Lulu cleared her throat. "Olivia, did Brody really punch Warner out on the porch of the Fryemont Inn?"

Olivia made a face. "How did you hear about that?"

"Vickie Leigh told me. Her friend Clayton Reese works at the Fryemont. He saw it out the window." She hesitated. "Vickie said Brody told her that he hit Warner because he was hurting you. That doesn't sound like Warner."

"No, and it wasn't like that either." Olivia got up for a minute to check on her cooking. "I had dinner on Sunday with Warner, Patti, and Barry. After Patti and Barry left, I went to the restroom, and Warner waited in the lobby for me. Brody and Logan came in to play pool in the bar, ran into Warner and, from what Warner told me, started picking on him."

"They always did like to tease Warner," said Lulu.

"Yes, and I wish they wouldn't anymore." Olivia sat back down on the stool. "It made Warner mad, and he and I argued about it on the porch of the Fryemont. Warner grabbed my arm while we were arguing. Brody came out and saw it, and he reacted by hitting Warner in the jaw. He knocked him down on the porch. Then Logan started kicking at him. I was so embarrassed."

"Oh, my gosh. What did you do?"

"I tried to keep them from fighting any more and that made all of them mad." She sighed, remembering it.

"Brody and Logan didn't say anything about this earlier this week at our meeting, so I guess they're over it." She paused. "How is Warner?"

"I haven't seen him," Olivia admitted. "He wouldn't walk me to the door when he brought me home Sunday. He was really angry."

"Oh, I'm sorry," Lulu commiserated. "It seemed lately as if Warner might be getting kind of sweet on you. The two of you were always friends growing up, so I thought maybe something might be starting …." Her voice dropped off. "You know."

"I doubt anything could come from any relationship starting between Warner and me." Olivia bit her lip. "Warner will be heading back to New York any day now. He's a big-name author. He won't want to stay around in Bryson City."

"Ron says most authors can live anywhere they want to."

"You've talked about this with Ron?" Her mouth dropped open at Louise's words.

"Well, sure. Ron and I like Warner—and we like you—and we thought it might be kind of nice if maybe ...." Her voice drifted off again.

"Well, don't start matchmaking for me, especially with Warner."

"If you say so." She sighed. "I probably need to go and check on Eva. She's napping, but it's about time for her to get up."

"Okay. I need to finish dinner and get dressed."

"Hope everything goes well."

"Me, too," Olivia said, hanging up.

Turning from the phone, she shook her head at the cat. "Great. Now the story of Brody socking Warner Zachery on my behalf will wander all over Bryson City, plus speculation that Warner and I are a couple." Irritated, she settled back to work, preparing her company's dinner.

Later that night, Olivia sat at her usual place at the dining room table at Benton House listening to the flow of conversation around the large table. Helen sat in her mother's old place at the end of the table and Helen's daughters, Barbara and Meredith, sat across the table from Olivia. They'd finished much of the dinner already, and the girls had remarked several times on how good the food tasted.

"I guess everyone in rural areas is very domestic," Meredith offered. "Gardening, cooking, crafting, and all ...." She let her words drift off as through it wasn't much of a compliment.

"Perhaps it's what you get used to." Barbara studied a perfectly manicured nail. "I have a gorgeous kitchen in my condominium, but I hardly ever use it. Working so many hours at the Merchandise Mart and traveling so much as a buyer, I seldom find time to boil an egg, much less devil one." She glanced toward the glass serving-dish of deviled eggs on the table and giggled at her own joke.

"Tell Olivia and Ray what you do, Barbara," Helen put in. "I know they'll be interested." She smiled with motherly pride. "I think Barbara and Meredith both have such glamorous jobs."

Barbara tucked a strand of red-highlighted hair behind one

ear. "I'm an events coordinator with the Merchandise Mart." She smiled around at them. "The Mart holds the largest collection of luxury boutiques in the world and covers three blocks. There is always some tradeshow or event to organize—Bridal Week, the Architectural Digest Design Show, the International Antiques Fair, holiday and gift shows …." She shrugged.

Helen leaned forward. "Barbara works with beautiful things all the time and very important people. I love it when I get a chance to go up to Chicago and attend some of the shows."

Olivia studied Barbara as Helen babbled on. She was tall and slim with short hair shaped in a perfect cut to frame her face, her eyes brown like her mother's, her makeup perfect and her outfit, although casual, probably costing more than Olivia made in a month. Meredith, also tall and slim, had red tones to her brown hair, a smattering of freckles, and blue eyes, her outfit obviously high fashion, too. They made Olivia feel drab in comparison in her blue summer sundress.

"Meredith works in a perfumery and is engaged now." Helen enthused. "I'm going to have the thrill of organizing a wonderful wedding."

Olivia smiled. "If the wedding is here, I'd love to do the flowers."

All three women raised their eyebrows in obvious shock.

"Oh, Meredith will marry in Evanston, Illinois, Olivia." Helen gave her an indulgent smile. "Evanston is about twelve miles above Chicago, very trendy and affluent with chic shops and a beautiful, historic Episcopal church where Bob and I married long ago. Meredith and Howard will marry at the same church, near where all the girls' friends and associates are."

Olivia's father gave Meredith a fond glance. "Tell me about this perfumery where you work."

She smiled at him. "It's called the Aroma Workshop. I help to create signature scent creations and I teach aromatherapy classes." She warmed to her subject. "Making perfume is like making music, with different notes combining to make different harmonies each time."

"That sounds almost poetic." Olivia's father reached for another helping of succotash.

Helen sent a sweet look toward her daughter. "Meredith studied at IFF—that's International Flavors & Fragrances in New York, the best known perfumery school in America. She learned her skills there and is one of the top employees at the workshop now. She created the fragrance I wear."

Meredith's eyes turned toward Olivia. "I noticed your floral fragrance when we met. It has notes like lily of the valley, doesn't it?"

Olivia smiled. "It's Muguet Du Bonheur, very similar to the Muguet des Bois scent my mother wore and that I wore as a girl. Sometimes I can still find Muguet des Bois, even though it's discontinued."

Meredith's eyes widened. "You mean that old scent by Coty?"

Olivia nodded.

Barbara stifled a giggle. "I think Meredith was ten years old the last time she bought a dime-store cologne. She'll go crazy now until she finds you a more sophisticated scent, Olivia."

The evening waxed on in much the same vein, with subtle comments tucked in here and there making Olivia feel colloquial for her tastes and lifestyle.

"Mother showed me your cute little shop," Barbara said at one point.

"I hope you liked it." Olivia pasted on another smile. On the surface, there was nothing wrong with Barbara's comment, but the tone came across patronizing, grating on Olivia's nerves.

Later, when Olivia toured Helen and her daughters through the garden, they worried about getting their shoes damp or snagging their dresses and expressed concern about walking on unpaved pathways.

"You know, if you paved these walkways, you might get people to pay to see these gardens," Meredith suggested. "The flowers are stunning."

Barbara laughed. "I doubt many people would come here, to the back of beyond, to see flowers, Meredith, when so many fantastic gardens can be found more readily in the city. Like the Chicago Botanic Gardens. I helped host an event there last year. It's one of the most famous gardens in America with three hundred eighty-five acres and twenty-three display gardens."

"Oh, I've visited there." Meredith gushed over her memories, as she walked by the pond and one of Fairchild's most beautiful beds of summer lilies with totally unseeing eyes.

When Sybil came to rub around Barbara's ankles in welcome, she shooed her away. "That cat shouldn't be allowed to roam around freely here." She frowned at Sybil where the cat now sat on a brick wall watching her. "I'm sure a lot of people visiting the gardens, besides me, have allergies to cat dander, Mother included."

"This is Sybil's home," Olivia answered, receiving a frown from her father for her words.

He tucked Helen's arm into his. "I'll ask Olivia to put Sybil up the next time you come, Helen."

"What breed is your cat?" Meredith asked. "Is she papered?"

"No, Sybil is only a mixed-breed cat," Olivia replied, weary with every aspect of their talk focusing on the monetary value and worth of everything.

Back in the house, Barbara declared Olivia's peach cobbler too rich after a big dinner and inquired if she had sorbet. When Olivia shook her head no, Barbara suppressed a little frown of displeasure before turning to Meredith.

"Do you remember that lovely strawberry sorbet we sampled in that marvelous little restaurant on the Loop we went to after the symphony in Chicago last month?" she asked.

"Oh, yes." Meredith's eyes brightened. The remembrance set them off again, describing the city's pleasures to Olivia and her father.

"You really must come to Chicago," Barbara told them. "There is so much to see and do. I know Mother would love to show you around. You can stay in my condo downtown. It has stunning views of the skyline at night. You'll love it."

Olivia felt worn out by the time they left. She stood on the porch, in the Benton's family tradition, to wave good-bye to them before her father drove them back to Helen's house. Somehow, Olivia managed to opt out on the trip to Asheville and Biltmore House they planned for the next day. Ideas she and her father offered for entertainment around Bryson City held no appeal for them.

As Barbara said, waving a hand. "Mother, once you've walked down the main street in Bryson City and looked in a few shops, you've seen it all—don't you think?"

Indeed, thought Olivia snidely.

Depressed, Olivia cleaned up the dining room and kitchen. Then she wandered through the house, growing more despondent as she remembered all the criticisms the girls and Helen made as they toured the rooms.

"Good heavens," Barbara said once. "I didn't know anyone actually used wallpaper in their homes anymore! How quaint. And wallpaper with such floral designs, too. Doesn't it jar your senses?"

Olivia hugged herself as the bad memories haunted her mind. "I feel almost sick over this evening," she told Sybil, slipping out the back door to seek solace in the gardens.

Olivia headed to the familiar White Garden, curled up in a ball on a bench in the gazebo, broke down, and wept.

"Rough time?" a voice said after a while.

Glancing up, Olivia saw Warner standing there in old cutoffs, a wrinkled plaid shirt, and scuffed loafers.

"You're a happy sight and you look good." She ran her eyes over him, seeing the boy she remembered so well in the man.

"I think your vision's failing you." He chuckled. "These are my bums. I was typing at the computer and looked out and saw you run into the garden not long after your father's car drove up the road."

He sat beside her on the bench. "I remembered then that this was the big night Helen and her daughters visited for dinner." He reached out a thumb to brush away a tear on her cheek. "I gather it didn't go well."

"It was a nightmare," Olivia said on a sob, the tears welling up again.

"Oh, come here." Warner invited her into his arms.

Shamelessly, Olivia let him gather her close to weep. "Oh, Warner, what am I going to do? It feels like my whole world is crumbling."

He patted her back while she wept on his shirtfront. "Come on. It can't be that bad."

She lifted puffy, red eyes to his. "No, it's worse. Helen Allmon seems almost a sweetheart compared to her snobby, city daughters. They made me feel like a country bumpkin."

He tweaked her nose. "You are a country bumpkin, Olivia."

She punched at him. "I'm serious, Warner."

He pulled back to look at her. "I'm serious, too. The world of Bryson City is a very small world in comparison to big cities like Chicago and New York. Many people who are used to city life can't imagine how anyone could be happy in a small town environment like this."

"Is that how you feel?"

He kissed her forehead. "We're not talking about me. I was raised here. This place is my home, with every corner filled with memories. I know the charms of Bryson City. But I gather Helen's daughters didn't have eyes to see them."

She blew out a deep breath. "That's an understatement."

"Tell me about what happened." He tucked her under his arm and leaned back against the gazebo bench.

She repeated the conversations to him, describing the tones and condescending looks. "Through it all, Daddy seemed oblivious to the subtle digs and criticisms. They simply slid over his head while he beamed affectionate glances at Helen and fawned over those awful girls."

Warner chuckled. "Sounds like he's got it bad."

"Oh, Warner, I don't know what I'm going to do if Daddy marries Helen. I can't see myself happy any longer at Benton House with her as the new mistress."

"You don't think it will work out with time?"

'No." She shook her head.

He stroked a hand down her arm. "Have you talked to your father yet about all this?"

"No, not yet." She closed her eyes. "I guess I'm in denial."

"It might be good to move out of that mindset so you can talk to him with honesty." He gave her a little hug. "It might be good, too, to rein in some of your criticisms of Helen and her girls. It might set your father off to hear your feelings of disapproval expressed too candidly."

Olivia considered this. "You're probably right."

She looked out into the darkness. "What will I do if Daddy marries Helen, sells Benton House and the gardens, and moves away to Chicago?"

"I assume one of your options isn't to go with them?"

"No. Never!" She turned to look at him in shock.

"Just checking," he kidded. He watched her head droop.

"Olivia, could you afford to buy the house and gardens from your father?" he asked. "Do you have any money of your own?"

Olivia shook her head. "Most of what I had I invested in the florist shop."

"Well, the shop is one thing you have that's all yours."

"Yes," she said in a small voice. "But my nightmare lately, waking me with the sweats, is of a bulldozer plowing through the gardens, taking everything down."

Warner tried not to smirk. "Olivia, I told you before I think your father values the gardens and their legacy. I can't imagine him allowing that."

She wrapped her arms around herself. "He may sell everything. New owners can do whatever they want with a property."

Warner turned Olivia around so she could see his eyes in the darkness. "I want you to stop tormenting yourself about this. First, if your father marries Helen and you don't want to live with them, you can build yourself a small home on the property and live independently. I'm sure Mother and Dad would let you live in the garage apartment at our place for a time if you wanted."

"Oh, I hadn't thought of that." A sweep of relief slid over her. "That's a good idea."

"Second, if your father does decide to sell the place, you call me. I'll buy it. Then we'll work out terms so you can buy it back from me." He put his hands on her face. "I want you to quit imagining some horrible scenario about these gardens that isn't realistic."

Her heart turned over. "Would you really do that for me? Buy the house and gardens? Do you have enough money to do that?"

"Yes to all three answers." He traced his hands over her face. "I get really angry at you sometimes, and half the time I don't understand you or how you see things, but I fell in love with you as a boy and apparently love isn't something I fall out of easily."

"You love me?" She felt incredulous to hear the words.

"It isn't as though I haven't said the words before." He smiled at her. "In some ways you're my oldest and dearest friend."

Her spirit dropped at those last words.

"We do go back a long way," she said quietly.

"That we do." He leaned over to pick a small white flower from a shrub beside their bench and handed it to her. "So I want you to quit tearing yourself apart about this situation with your father. He's fallen in love again, whether the woman is the choice you'd have made for him or not. Love can blind a man to many faults. So he sees everything with rose-colored glasses. Perhaps that's a good thing."

"Perhaps." She said the word, wanting to understand and accept it.

He shrugged. "Anyway, your life will go on—happily—even if you're not Daddy's *only* girl anymore. You have your work, your friends, your interests, and your talents. You might not solely hold all your father's affection anymore, but you will be okay. Places and things don't define us. Who we are, and the strength of who we are, is within."

She sat up, scrubbing at her face. "You've been kind to me tonight. I'm grateful." She put a hand on his arm. "I'm also grateful you came home when you did. Your friendship has helped see me through a difficult time."

"Do you think you'll sleep better tonight and not entertain nightmares of bulldozers hacking down the rose arbor and the White Garden?"

She smiled. "I hope so."

"Well, then, go get some sleep." He stood. "I'll head back to my place and see if I can finish that chapter I was working on."

"Warner?" She said his name as he started to leave.

He turned back. "What?"

"I'd like to come see you sometime when you go back to New York. Maybe you can show me the big city and the things you like about it."

A surprised expression crossed his face before he masked it. "I'll fly you up," he said, grinning. "Give you the grand tour."

"Okay." She smiled.

Olivia watched him walk out through the gate of the White Garden. She sat in the gazebo until the sound of his footsteps receded.

"He loves me as a friend," she said out loud. "Just as a friend. A person can go away and leave their friends. With regret, of course. But they can walk away and move on with their lives and leave their friends behind." She closed her eyes and sighed. "He's left me before, and now I know he'll leave me again."

She started back to the house, Sybil suddenly appearing out of the darkness to walk along beside her.

"I thought this night couldn't get any worse," she told the cat. "But it has. I might find a way to keep the house and gardens I love, but I'll lose both the men I love. That's been made clear enough tonight."

Starting down the gravel path through the rose garden, she stopped to take in the heady fragrance. She looked around at the draping bower of red and white blooms. "For the first time, Sybil, I wonder if this alone—all this legacy and beauty—is enough."

CHAPTER 16

Warner found the summer weeks slipping by. School supplies began to fill the shop windows, making him realize he needed to think about moving on. He could hardly make excuses to stay much longer with his parents and he needed to get back to work at Kite. They'd let him take a long break from the office in New York, allowing him to send in his illustrations, stories, cartoons, and puzzles for the monthly magazines, but he'd missed several important meetings now and left his apartment empty for months.

"A penny for your thoughts." Leonard's words intruded.

Leonard, Warner, and Barry had caught a bite to eat downtown—spaghetti carbonara at Pasqualino's—and then headed up to Leonard's place on the mountain to play a few games of pool. They sat outside on Leonard's rustic porch, drinking Bootleggers Red Table Wine that Barry had bought earlier at the Bootleggers Homemade Wine store in Gatlinburg on the Parkway. Leonard's wedding was coming up, and the three wanted to enjoy a last bachelor fling.

"I could ask the same of you, Len—about your thoughts before your upcoming wedding. You're the first of us to marry." Warner shifted the question back to his friend.

Leonard swirled the wine in his glass. "You know Imogene and I will be happy, and you're avoiding my question."

"Which was?" Warner raised an eyebrow.

Barry topped off their wineglasses from the bottle on the table.

"Which *was* to ask you what's weighing on your mind, Bro? Quit evading the inevitable and spit it out."

He shrugged in resignation. "I realized that after the wedding, I'll need to head back to New York."

"And?" Barry probed.

"And I'm not as excited about going back as I should be." Warner scowled.

"Did you think any more about my offer to write for the paper?" Leonard asked. "You know I could use you."

"I'm not a journalist, Len. That's your specialty." He propped his feet on the porch rail. "Besides, I have a writing job—more Gilmore sequels contracted to Whitehouse Press, another YA series in the talking stages—plus my work for Kite."

"All of which you've done from here this summer." Barry looked at him over the top of his glasses. "You could work out something to keep doing that if you wanted to. Hang around. Be a Bryson City boy again."

Warner laughed. "I'll never be that boy again."

"I hope you don't expect me to say 'more's the pity'?" Barry chuckled. "We've all grown up and moved on from those awkward years."

"Don't you ever feel the past haunts you here?" Warner asked.

"No." Leonard sat his wineglass on the table. "I was a kid then. I'm a man now. I see some of who I was in that long-ago kid, and I'm honest enough to realize events of those years helped to shape me for who I am now. I think those years molded what I think and believe, what I hold important, who I care about."

"Maybe," Warner acknowledged.

"There's another factor you're not mentioning." Barry's eyes focused on him. "Do you think you can walk away from Olivia Benton again without it ripping your heart out?"

"That's an exaggeration." Warner scowled. "We've gotten close again, but it's not like that."

"Isn't it?" Barry smirked at him.

"Warner, you do have that lovesick look about you whenever

Olivia is around." Leonard raised a glass to Barry in agreement.

Warner stiffened at their teasing. "So? It doesn't matter what I might feel. Olivia wouldn't leave her Daddy and the garden to go to New York with me the first time, and I doubt she would now." He sipped at his wine, morose. "Her store has a hold on her, too."

A small silence settled before Barry spoke again. "The first time you went to New York you needed to get away to find yourself, to make your way. Now you've done that. You have flexibility, Warner. Admit it. You can have the best of both worlds if you want to. Live here much of the year, fly to New York when you need to for meetings with Kite or your publisher." He paused, swirling wine in his glass. "I think both of them value you too much now to insist you live in New York full time. They simply want you to keep producing, to do what you do so well for them."

"I think Barry's right. If you wanted to stay, you could probably work something out. And maybe propose to sweet Flora Fair." Leonard grinned at Warner, knowing he used the character name from the Geeky Gilmore books based on Olivia.

"How would Imogene feel about your idea, Leonard?" Warner challenged. "She wouldn't even let Olivia do the flowers for her wedding."

Leonard shrugged. "Imogene had her little revenge. Besides, she made that decision *before* you came down here and started seeing Olivia. She's beginning to feel differently about Olivia now. She said so."

"High school was then. Now is now," Barry added. "We're all moving on."

"Well, Olivia and I still have a lot of unresolved issues." Warner ran a hand through his hair. "And what would I do in Bryson City when my writing didn't take all my time. I need to stay busy." He shifted restlessly in his chair. "You have the newspaper, Leonard, and, Barry, you have the shop. I could never fit in with the family pharmacy business."

Barry shrugged. "So buy a business. You have money."

Warner could practically see Leonard's business mind considering this. "You know," he said, "a dry cleaners is for sale out on the highway and a liquor store is available off the main street downtown."

Warner shook his head.

"All right, what about the Hartsell Graphics shop? I hear Dean and Maggie Hartsell want to sell."

Warner closed his eyes in disinterest.

Barry punched him. "The point is you could find something that appeals to you if you looked around."

"I can't run a business full time and write."

"But you can own a business, let someone else manage it, and write," Barry argued. "It's like insurance for a rainy day."

"You think my writing career will flop in time?" Warner opened his eyes, surprised.

"No, but I think you'd like to own a piece of Bryson City if you're going to live here much of the time. You were the one who always used to suggest we'd all own pieces of Bryson one day."

"I was joking around."

"Well, it stuck with me," Barry said.

Warner grinned at him finally. "Thanks for all this encouragement." He punched Leonard. "You, too, Len. I'll think about all you've said."

"Changing the subject," Leonard said, "what do you think is going to happen with these vandal incidents? Do you think they'll stop when all the kids go back to school?"

"You're assuming it's a kid or kids doing the pranks?" Barry asked.

"You have to admit, Barry, it seems like the sort of thing kids might do—breaking windows, defacing property, setting fires in trash cans, and leaving threatening notes around."

"Maybe." Barry pushed up his glasses. "But I can't help thinking there's something behind all this we're not seeing."

"You mean that the police aren't seeing," Warner put in. "Dad was saying they still don't have a single viable lead."

Leonard drummed his fingers on the table. "I wish I could see a link in the places targeted—the courthouse, the jail, a restaurant, the recreation center, the cemetery."

"I don't think there's a link in the places," Warner put in. "Didn't one of the notes say: 'The vandal strikes, you know not where?'"

"No." Leonard corrected him. "That note said: 'The vandal strikes, you know not when.'"

"That's basically the same difference." Warner considered this. "The point is the sites and times are not meant to be predictable."

Barry leaned forward. "I think the biggest clue was in the first message a long time back, the one found at the Courthouse: 'Be wary. A vandal stalks where no justice prevails.'"

Warner grinned. "Sound like a line from one of our superheroes comics, doesn't it?"

"So you think it might be a vigilante type, like a Robin Hood, trying to right wrongs in some way?" Leonard asked.

"I don't know." Barry scratched his head. "But like I've said before, I think we'll find there's a thread between it all when the vandal is uncovered."

Leonard scowled. "Well, I hope it's soon. These loony types are apt to go off the deep end and do harm to someone, or to themselves, if not found. I've seen it happen often enough working with the paper."

"Dad says it makes everybody in business around town nervous, too," Warner added. "He's worried they might break the windows at the pharmacy or cause some damage there. Olivia's been concerned about the same thing at her florist shop."

Barry glanced at his watch. "Speaking of Bryson businesses, I have to open mine at nine tomorrow morning. I'd better head home."

Leonard stood. "Yeah, it's getting late. But thanks for the bachelor evening, the dinner, the pool, and the good time."

Barry laughed. "You'd better remember to thank me for the wine. I know how you love it, and I drove all the way over to Gatlinburg to get it."

"And the wine." Leonard laughed, picking up the bottle. "I'm laying claim to the remainder and to the unopened bottle of Scuppernong in the kitchen. My night."

The men parted with good-humored hugs.

Back at the garage apartment of his parents a short time later, Warner headed to the computer to get some work done.

He finished up a story for *Kite Magazine*, due for an upcoming issue, and then stared out the window toward the Fairchild Gardens. "I need to come to some decisions," he said, thinking out loud.

"Do Olivia and I belong together or are we, as before, still too different? Do I belong here in Bryson City now, perhaps half-and-half as Barry suggested, or do I really belong in New York? And suppose I did move here, even half-time, where would I want to live? Certainly not with my folks, staying on in their garage apartment."

He got up to pace around the room, stopping in front of the photo of Nelle to pick it up. "I wish I could hear your practical advice now, Nelle. You always seemed to know what I needed to do to be happy even more than I did."

Dropping back into his chair at the computer, he laughed. Leave it to Leonard to suggest I buy a dry cleaners or a liquor store.

Without thinking much about it, he opened a search engine and began to look at potential businesses for sale around the area. *Would I want to buy a business even if I found one that interested me?*

He considered the idea. *And who would run it for me? I'd need someone I could trust, traveling as much as I do whenever a new book comes out.*

He stared out the window toward the gardens and then back to Nelle's photo. "Truthfully, everything depends on the situation with Olivia. I could never stay here if Olivia won't marry me this time—or if she's not ready to commit or to be flexible about the changes combining our two lives might bring. Barry's right that it's already going to rip my heart out again to go back to New York and leave her. My grandparents, school, work, and then having you in my life helped me survive the last time. But what about this time?"

Warner threaded his hands through his hair. "I don't even know if she really loves me. Or if she loves me enough to marry me."

He shook his head. "Her world is coming unraveled somewhat now, too. Her dad may marry and bring Helen to live at Benton House. Olivia may have to move if she feels like she and Helen can't get along." He swiveled in his chair. "Would she move in with me to another house if I found one? Would she want me to find it, surprise her with it, and then ask her to marry me? Or would she want to help locate it?"

Even in the dark, Warner could see some sort of flowering vine spreading in purple splendor over the wall of the garden. "It will kill Olivia to have to give up that garden, Nelle. I hope for her sake it doesn't happen."

He went back to searching businesses for sale in Bryson City, chuckling over some of the enterprises he found available. Eventually he headed for bed.

Maybe like Grandfather Delacourt says, I'll just let each day take care of itself.

Yet, even acknowledging this, Warner knew he couldn't continue living in his parents' garage with his future on hold much longer.

CHAPTER 17

It had been a long Friday at the florist. Olivia sat now making the bride's bouquet for the Fenton wedding that evening. Patti worked on the second of two large sprays of flowers to decorate the church altar, and Wanda wrapped and tied purple lisianthus for the bridesmaids' bouquets.

"You know, I like the colors Marjorie Fenton chose for her wedding—ivory and white mixed with lavender and this pretty deep purple." Olivia studied one of the lisianthus blooms with pleasure. "Most brides don't go for rich colors in a wedding, but they're real striking, don't you think?"

"I do," Patti agreed. "Marjorie showed me pictures of the silky, pale lavender dresses the bridesmaids and matron of honor are wearing and those lisianthus bouquets will be a stunning contrast."

Wanda glanced back to Olivia's workstation. "Looks like Marjorie is putting a little of everything in her bridal bouquet."

"Yes." Olivia studied the growing mound of flowers. "White and purple roses, white hydrangea, lavender freesia, carnations, and more of those purple lisianthus with lily grass mixed in."

"I think lily grass makes a pretty filler." Wanda added, glancing at the dark green strands of lily grass on Olivia's table.

The girls worked on, talking, and then Wanda stood to stretch. "I think we've about got this job done," she said. "Patti, if you'll help me load the van, I'll take everything over to the church and unload it."

Patti nodded. "Rich is coming to ride with you and to help you carry everything into the church. I called him a few minutes ago."

"Well, that's good news. He's a fine help." She paused, frowning. "I just wish he could lighten up and enjoy life a little more. Yesterday, I tried to get him to talk about starting back to school next week and you'd think I'd asked him to discuss heading to an open-casket funeral." She laughed.

"Rich didn't have a good year in school last year," Patti said, picking up one of the floral sprays to start toward the back room with it. "I'm hoping he'll make some new friends now and like it better."

A short time later, Patti came back into the front room and began helping Olivia clean up from the wedding preparation.

"We sure had a busy day today with all the call-ins for birthday and anniversary flowers and with the Fenton wedding to get ready for," Olivia said, as she swept up clippings, bits of ribbon, and a few stray flower petals from the floor.

"Yeah." Patti leaned against her workstation, where she'd been cleaning. "You know, I really am worried about Rich."

"Because of what Wanda said?" Olivia asked.

"No, but because she's right. Rich really dreads heading back to school next week." She sighed. "I hate that he's been so unhappy here."

Olivia propped a hip on her workbench stool. "Patti, do you think his feelings are altogether to do with our middle school or maybe related to other things in the past. I know you've wanted to keep that time in your life private, but if the two of you went through a difficult time, it might still be affecting Rich."

"We did go through a hard time, Olivia, but that shouldn't have anything to do with school here or why Rich isn't making friends."

"Rich enjoys his times with Sam DeMatteo, though, doesn't he?"

Patti brightened. "Meeting Sam at Barry's this summer was one of the best things that's happened to Rich since we moved here. I wish Sam and Rich could go to the same school this fall. The boys get along so well together. Whenever I go out to Barry's, Rich gets to play with Sam."

"And you get to play with Barry." Olivia smiled. "How is that relationship going?"

"Okay." Patti looked away. "I like Barry."

"Yeah, and I'd say that feeling is mutual." Olivia cleaned up her workbench while she talked. "Warner says he can't recall Barry ever having a serious girlfriend before now."

"I'm hardly a girl anymore." Patti laughed.

"You know what I mean."

"I do, but I don't know if I want to get serious about anyone again. So much can go wrong." She paused, a wistful look passing over her face. "You can think you know someone so well and find out you don't know them at all."

"I've known Barry since grammar school. What you see is exactly what you get with Barry."

Patti considered this, sweeping clippings off her desk in thought. "No one is really only what they seem, Olivia."

"Well, I don't want to overly interfere in your life, but I think you could safely trust your heart to a guy like Barry without a worry."

Patti lifted her eyes. "I think I could say the same to you about W. T. Zachery, and it seems obvious he cares about you."

"There are a lot of complications between Warner and me, not the least of which is that his work world of writing, his publishers, and his job are in New York, while mine is here."

"Is that difference what broke you up before?" Patti ran a hand through her short hair. "I don't mean to probe either, but it seems obvious your relationship isn't one that only began since W. T., or Warner's, recent visit here."

Olivia decided to be honest. "Warner and I fell in love in high school, but we kept that relationship hidden from others. Even then, we had big life differences, and the things that got in the way of our relationship now are the same ones that were in the way of our relationship then. I don't know if we can work our problems out."

"Well, I hope you can." Patti sent her a fond gaze. "You deserve to find someone who will make you happy."

Olivia thought about those words later as she drove to an early planning meeting for the school reunion at Louise's house after work. The committee alternated places for their meetings, and Louise had volunteered to host the get-together tonight. She and Rob were cooking a pot of their favorite chili, the Frazier's Funeral Home recipe that won the Chili Cook Off contest in Bryson City last fall. Olivia had made a grape salad the night before to bring and tucked it in the refrigerator in the shop until her workday finished. She'd also changed into a dress for the Fenton wedding later. She needed to run by and attend that event before heading home.

"Come in! Come in!" Rob opened the door in welcome as she walked up the back steps. He bussed her on the cheek before she headed into the kitchen. "Good to see you, Olivia."

"You, too, Rob." Her eyes roved over the friendly, familiar face of Rob Frazier, another friend since childhood years. She'd always been so glad he and Louise got together.

"Where's Eva?" She looked around for the dark-haired sprite that usually threw herself into Olivia's arms as soon as she entered the house.

"At her grandmother's," Louise answered. "I doubted any of us would get a thing done with that Energizer Bunny here!"

"Well, you tell her that Aunt Olivia missed seeing her." She pulled a small gift bag from her purse. "And give her this from me when you pick her up."

Louise took it and peeked. "Oh, how cute. It's a little pocketbook with a toddler lipstick inside. She'll love that." She gave Olivia a hug. "You don't need to bring her something every time you come. You'll spoil her."

"I only bring small things, "Olivia argued. "Besides, I enjoy having a little person to shop for."

"Well, that simply means it's time for you to marry and have children of your own," Roberta said, coming in the door behind them. "If you end up with two active boys like mine, you'll rejoice for a night out every now and then."

"Oh, you know you love your boys." Russell maneuvered his way into the door carrying a large cake tin.

Louise took the tin. "Is that for Brody's birthday?"

"Yes," Roberta answered. "His favorite—chocolate fudge cake."

The group of old friends soon arrived in force and settled around Louise's dining room table with bowls of thick chili, hot cornbread, plates of relishes, several side salads, and big glasses of iced tea. It was always comfortable to be with long-time friends, and Olivia wondered again how Warner could find it so easy to move away from friends and family he'd always known.

They talked about the upcoming reunion scheduled for the Labor Day weekend. This was their tenth class reunion, and they'd planned a dance Friday night with music from their era, a Saturday morning brunch, and a later dinner at the Hemlock Inn before the Saturday night football game. For the dinner they'd designed a short program, with a video of past school events, followed by awards and recognitions for individual accomplishments, some serious and some silly. Logan, their senior class president, would emcee the dinner event.

"I wonder if Weird Warner will hang around and come to the reunion dance or any of the other events after." Brody made a face. "If he comes, I guess we'll have to give him some recognition for writing those Geekly books."

Roberta rolled her eyes at him. "They are called the Geeky Gilmore books, and my boys love them, even at their young ages. The books are being made into a movie, too, Brody. Regardless of what Warner acted like in our high school years, you can't discount the fact that he's made a success of his life."

"Hey," Vickie Leigh interrupted. "Let's light the candles on Brody's cake so he can blow them out and open his gifts. I want to see what everyone got him."

Logan laughed. "Probably because you got him some gift appropriate only for adult audiences."

Vickie batted her eyes. "If you're nice, maybe he'll share it with you."

Bantering and laughter filled the room as they all wished Brody a happy birthday and laughed about the funny gifts they bought him.

"It will be like old times being back in the school gym for our reunion dance," Louise put in. "We haven't danced in that old gymnasium since our senior prom ten years ago."

"And this time, thank goodness, Logan isn't mad at me and he's taking *me* to the dance." Vickie Leigh leaned over to give Logan a kiss full on the mouth.

"Whoa! Looks like this relationship is blossoming!" Roberta fanned herself with one hand.

"So it appears. And now that you've married Russell, I get to take Olivia to the dance this time." Brody smiled across the table at Olivia. "Four couples of old friends."

A prickle of annoyance crept over Olivia. "Brody, we haven't talked about this," she said quietly.

"What's to talk about?" He laughed. "That doctor-guy you've been seeing wouldn't want to attend our reunion dance. Besides, Wanda told me you weren't going out with him anymore."

"Whoever I'm going out with is personal, and I don't like you probing my employees about who I'm dating behind my back."

"Youch!" Brody held up both hands in mock shock. "Sorry, sugar, if I took too much for granted." He got up to walk around the table to squat on one knee. "Olivia Benton, I hope you will do me the honor of going to the tenth reunion dance of the Swain County High graduating class with me." He grinned up at her. "Is that better? ... and maybe the next time I get down on one knee I'll have a ring in my back pocket."

They all laughed but quieted again as Olivia's face flushed.

"Brody," she replied, "except for the people who are married, there is no need to have dates for a class reunion dance. I plan to go to the dance, obviously, but I see no need to go with anyone as a couple." She straightened her shoulders. "There will be many past students coming into town from all over who will not be paired up. I don't want any of them to feel awkward that everyone seems to be in couples at our dance."

"Or maybe feel weird?" Brody stood up with a scowl. "Are you thinking about Weird Warner and how he won't have a date—if he even shows up?"

Olivia crossed her arms, more annoyed now. "I wasn't thinking of anyone in particular. And I'm getting a little tired of your continual nasty comments about Warner Zachery. We're not teenagers anymore, and we shouldn't act like petty teens."

He leaned toward her, his face growing angry. "Well, I'm getting a little tired of you running around with Weird Warner while he's hanging around town. You know he'll be heading back to the big city soon, girlie, but I'll still be here. You ought to keep that in mind and think about being nicer to me."

Olivia, upset and offended, pushed her chair back and stood.

"Settle down, you two." Roberta waved a hand. "Olivia's right that who goes with who to this reunion dance isn't a big issue. The point is for old classmates to all get together again."

She reached over to put a hand on Brody's arm. "It isn't as though you won't get to dance with Olivia at the reunion—or with me." She smiled at him. "And you shouldn't have put Olivia's back up by assuming she'd want to go with you without even asking her privately first. Women don't like that. For that alone, you deserve to have your invitation refused."

Olivia watched Brody make an effort to calm down.

"Well, maybe I did assume a little too much." He sent an apologetic glance toward Olivia.

"Please sit back down, Olivia, and overlook Brody's bad manners." Louise smiled at her. "We still have a few things to talk about."

Olivia sat reluctantly, knowing that to leave, as she yearned to do now, would only create more of a scene.

"All right," she said at last. "But let's make this quick. I put in a long day getting ready for the Fenton wedding, and I need to stop by the ceremony before heading home. The wedding starts at seven and it would look bad if I don't attend since Fairgarden did the flowers."

As she left later, Brody followed her out to the car. "I'm sorry

I made you mad. I guess I really thought you'd want to go to the dance with me." He moved closer. "We've been seeing each other and getting to be an item around town."

Olivia backed away. "Brody, we are *not* an item. We've gone out a few times as friends, and I want to make it clear that's all it was to me."

His face flushed again. "Oh, yeah? It seems to me you felt different about that before rich boy Warner Zachary showed up in town. It doesn't seem likely he'll give you more than a good time while visiting. Besides, underneath, he's still a weird guy. He hasn't changed that much."

Olivia slid into the car, tucking in the skirt of her dress, then closed the door and rolled down her window before responding. "Warner has always been my friend, Brody—ever since we were small children. I've known him much longer than I've known you. It's natural I'd want to spend some time with him while he's back home."

Brody scowled, making a fist.

She met his eyes. "I don't want you to pick any more fights with Warner Zachery or to act like you have a right to decide who I should see or not. Do I make myself clear?" She jammed her key in the ignition and started the car.

"Roberta always said she thought you had a secret crush on Weird Warner back in high school but didn't want us to know." He laughed. "There's no point in you getting up on your high horse with me about not being nice to Warner. You weren't nice to him in high school either. You turned him down as a date for the senior prom and at the dance, when he watched you like a sick puppy, you wouldn't even dance with him."

He paused for effect. "If anyone's a hypocrite in all this, sugar, it's you. I've never made any bones about not liking Warner Zachery. But it seems to me like you've been the one to play games about him. You think about that fact, huh?" Brody patted her car and walked away.

And heading to the Fenton wedding, Olivia did ... and she cried.

CHAPTER 18

On Monday, Warner sat by Leonard's desk at the Bryson City newspaper office waiting for him to finish some paperwork so they could go meet Barry for lunch downtown.

"Did you call Barry to let him know I'm running a little late?" Frowning, Leonard shuffled the pile of papers in front of him.

Warner nodded, glancing up from the e-mail he was answering on his iPhone.

"As soon as I get that callback, we can head out." He glared at the phone, willing it to ring.

Warner smiled as he sent the e-mail he'd just completed on to his publisher.

"I found out about another business for sale in town." Leonard pushed a slip of paper across to Warner.

Warner glanced at it. "Gil's Bookstore?"

Leonard shrugged. "Gil wants to retire. His wife retired from the school system this year, and they want to travel. He can't do that tied to the bookstore."

"So I should get tied to the bookstore so I can't travel?"

Leonard frowned. "It isn't the same thing. Like I said before, you could get a good manager. Maybe Gil would even stay on part-time."

The phone rang, interrupting them.

"I'll bet that's my call." Leonard snatched up the receiver, but then tensed, eyes widening, as he listened.

"Lunch is off." He dropped the phone back in place. "A kid

is holed up in the middle school, threatening to burn the place down."

"What?" Warner's eyes jerked to his. "Do they know who it is?"

Leonard made a quick call to get a camera crew alerted to follow him to the school before he answered. "Yeah, it's that kid of Patti's—you know, the one that works for Olivia over at her shop."

"Then I'm coming with you." Warner followed Leonard as he headed out the door. "I'm calling Barry to come, too. We both know that kid and some about his problems. Maybe we can help."

In the car, Leonard made another call on his cell while Warner called Barry. Dropping his phone back in his coat pocket, Leonard updated Warner. "Sheriff Colson says the janitor found the kid inside the school apparently getting ready to light a fire in a school trash can. The boy panicked when the janitor discovered him, brandished a gun, and told him to get out of the building."

Warner tensed. "The boy's name is Richard Headrick, nicknamed Rich, and I find it hard to believe that boy would own a gun, much less threaten anyone with it. He's only twelve years old and a nice kid."

"We don't always know people as well as we think," Leonard said. "I learned that quickly enough working with the paper and following the news." Driving fast, he roared over the bridge, crossed Main, and angled right to head up Arlington toward the Swain County Middle School.

Several police cars were already there, one officer talking on a megaphone to the boy inside, encouraging him to drop his weapon and come out.

Leonard found the sheriff. "Any luck on communicating with the kid?"

"No." The sheriff frowned. "I know he's scared, and I only hope he doesn't panic and start that fire he threatened—or try to shoot someone. It will go worse for him if he does."

Joel Harland from the newspaper arrived with his camera.

"You keep at a distance with that," the sheriff told him. "I don't want that kid spooked further with too much media hype."

Leonard conferred with Joel, who moved to an inconspicuous location with his camera, one that still offered a good view of the entrance of the school.

"Where is Richard in the school?" Warner studied the glass-fronted doors to the middle school that lay across a paved courtyard.

"He was in the main hall near the front office when Otis Tate, the school janitor, discovered him." The sheriff gestured to a grizzled, older man standing nearby.

The old man stepped forward. "I think the boy must have snuck in when I opened the doors in the back to carry out boxes to the trash bins." He shook his head. "I prop the doors open while going in and out with the trash loads. It's easier to push them big metal doors open with a shoulder when you're hauling a load versus setting everything down and unlocking every time. I haul out a lot of boxes before school opens every year with all the new supplies and books coming in."

"No one is faulting you," the sheriff said. "And I'm glad you came straight out when the boy panicked and didn't try to take him on."

"Yeah, that weren't smart of him, letting me loose." The man scratched his head. "You'd think even a kid his age would figure out I'd go call the police right off."

"Maybe he wanted to get caught," Warner said. He turned to Otis. "What was he wearing?"

"All black with a little mask tied over his eyes with two holes cut out, like a superhero in a comic book."

"Like Batman?" Leonard lifted an eyebrow.

"Yeah, I guess he looked something like that." Otis nodded. "But I recognized the boy anyway because he helped Wanda Baylor unload flowers for the Fenton wedding at the Methodist Church Friday evening. I help with the church's janitorial work there sometimes."

"Lucky break you recognized him." Leonard typed notes into his iPhone.

"The boy acted real polite and well-mannered that night helping

Wanda." Otis scratched his head. "Don't seem to me like he's the sort of kid to pull a prank like this."

An officer walked over to talk to the sheriff, telling him the boy wasn't responding to their requests to come out of the school and wanting to know what to do next.

"Let me go in and talk to him. I know the boy," Warner offered.

"Now, Warner," Sheriff Colson said, "I know you mean well, but you gotta remember this boy is armed. Otis saw his weapon."

Otis rubbed his chin, thinking. "I only saw the shadow of a gun when he hid it under one arm and threatened me with it. I don't know what sort of gun it were."

Warner turned to the Sheriff. "I don't believe this boy will hurt me. He idolizes me a little because of my books that he loves. Let me try going in to talk to him."

"You might well provide him with a hostage and make things worse." The sheriff frowned.

Barry walked up as these last words were spoken. "I know this boy, too, Sheriff. I don't really think he'd hurt anyone. He's just scared." Barry turned to Otis. "Did you see anything else when you found the boy? A note on a table, writing on a blackboard or a wall?"

"Yeah, funny you should mention that." Otis tapped his chin. "There was some sort of message written across the wall by the office—all in black marker pen, a big mess. I'd jest noticed the wall, thinking I'd have to clean it off, when I saw the boy."

"Did you see what it said?" Leonard moved closer to him.

Otis scratched his head again, trying to remember. "Something about there being no safety or justice here. It didn't make no sense to me."

"It does to me. Think about the words." Barry's eyes moved to Warner's and then to Leonard's.

"He's the vandal," said Leonard, his mouth dropping open in surprise.

"I told you it would all make sense when we finally located the vandal." Barry looked smug for a moment. Then he sighed. "An unhappy boy, being bullied by his peers, will try to find a way to strike back when he believes no one will listen to him or help him."

Warner winced. "Even more reason for me go in to talk to him, Sheriff. Rich is more unhappy and confused than dangerous."

"I don't know." The sheriff drew out the words, his eyes shifting toward the school. "Unhappy, scared kids are often dangerous."

"Give Warner a try at it," Barry encouraged. "I think he'd stand the best chance getting in. A kid, even a mixed up one, won't shoot his hero."

After several calls and consultations—and another try to get the boy to come out on his own—the sheriff agreed to let Warner go into the school.

Before entering, Warner used the portable megaphone to call out a message. "It's W. T. Zachery, Rich," he announced. "The janitor recognized you from the Fenton wedding on Friday. I'm coming in to talk to you. I know you're scared, but we need to talk. The sheriff is letting me come in by myself. I told him we were friends." He paused. "Rich, even a superhero doesn't act dumb when he gets cornered. I can help you figure out what's the best thing to do."

Barry borrowed the megaphone. "This is Barry, Rich. I helped talk the sheriff into letting Warner come in. Don't you let me down now and do something dumb, you hear? Your mom would be real mad at me."

Tense and nervous despite his brave words, Warner made his way slowly across the courtyard toward the glass doors of the school. He kept his hands out to his sides, as the sheriff suggested, so Rich could see he didn't carry a weapon.

Stopping at the set of doors by the plate glass windows at the front of the school, he paused, hoping for some sign that Rich had heard him and wouldn't panic when he heard someone walking in the hallway. "I'm opening the door now," he called out. "Can you let me know if that's all right? If you see me?"

A gun landed in the foyer from around a side hallway. Even from the door Warner could see it was a black pump water gun—a Super Soaker if he remembered right from his nephews' toys. Shaking his head at this sign that Rich felt ready to talk—and almost smirking over the gun—Warner let himself in the door, walking through the foyer and into the side hallway, looking for Rich.

Twenty minutes later, Warner exited the same door again, one arm around Rich, the water gun tucked under the other arm. Patti and Olivia had arrived, called by Barry—Warner learned later—and Patti, crying and upset, launched forward toward Rich as they came out. Rich let himself be hugged briefly by his mother before being led by an officer to a waiting police car.

Barry went with Patti, to follow Rich to the Sheriff's Office and juvenile detention center only a few blocks away on Brendle Street downtown.

Warner remained behind with Leonard and answered a few quick questions from the sheriff. Warner assured him Rich would tell him the rest at the Sheriff's Office.

"Good work." Sheriff Colson shook Warner's hand before starting toward his vehicle to follow.

"What will happen to Rich now?" he asked.

The sheriff paused, his eyes following the cruiser carrying Rich as it pulled out of the parking lot. "Did the boy admit to the other vandal incidents?"

Warner nodded.

"Any good reasons for doing those acts in your eyes?" he quizzed.

"Well, the boy's been bullied intensively in school and outside of school and felt no one came to his defense. I think his vandal acts were his way to speak back when he didn't think he had a voice."

"Anything else?"

"Some past family issues that need airing and that probably helped to build suppressed anger and frustration."

The sheriff patted Warner on the back. "We'll get them some counseling."

As the sheriff turned to leave again, Warner stopped him once more. "Will you detain him?"

"Assuming he is honest in confessing to the other vandal incidents, repentant of what has occurred, and cooperative in the investigation, he probably won't even be held overnight in detention. A cash bond will get him out until a court date is set in future. With no previous record, my guess is he'll get a prescribed number of community service hours and maybe court-ordered counseling or anger management help." He shrugged. "It goes a little different with each case."

Leonard grinned. "It will help that the weapon was a water pistol."

"Yep." The sheriff agreed, shaking his head. Looking at Leonard, he added, "Be nice in the media report in the newspaper. This family is going to experience a tough enough time dealing with this situation in a small town like Bryson City without it being blown out of proportion."

"I hear you," Leonard said, waving as the sheriff left to head for the office. He turned toward Warner. "You got a story for me?"

"Yeah, I guess." Warner ran a hand through his hair, tired now from the long ordeal. "I'll tell it to you over lunch. Let's pick up some sandwiches and go some place where we can have some privacy."

"I'm coming, too." Olivia moved toward them.

Warner blinked, realizing then that she still stood nearby.

"I came with Patti," she reminded him, coming to put an arm around his waist. "And you've had a hard day."

She gave him a kiss on the cheek, causing Leonard to raise an eyebrow.

"You know, I'd like to head somewhere private, but I've got a story to get out," Leonard told Warner. "Let's go sit at the picnic table and you spill it to me there. Then Olivia can take you home, pick up some food on the way, and give you a little TLC." He grinned. "I'll get a sandwich sent to the office when I get back. This story needs to get in the morning paper, and like the sheriff said, it needs to be written right. I'm doing it myself to guarantee that."

CHAPTER 19

Olivia had felt terrified as she drove Patti to the Swain County Middle School after Barry's call. How could Rich be in the school, threatening to burn down the building and brandishing a gun? It simply didn't make sense.

"I'm sure when we get there we'll learn more what's really going on," she said to Patti, trying to console her.

Almost choking on tears, Patti said, "I knew he was unhappy. I should have paid more attention to what he tried to say to me." She blew her nose. "I'll never forgive myself if something happens to him."

As they neared the school, they encountered a police roadblock. Olivia had to show identification and explain who they were to gain permission to drive closer to the scene. At the school, another officer motioned them to a parking area and then walked them carefully toward the main building to the sheriff.

Sheriff Colson urged quiet as they arrived, pointing to Warner, who was walking across the broad concrete entry toward the main door of the school, his arms held out from his sides.

"What is Warner doing here?" Patti asked in a strained whisper.

"He came with Leonard and the media earlier." The sheriff ran a hand through his shock of white hair. "When we had no luck getting Rich to come out on his own, Warner convinced me he wanted to go in the building to try and talk to your boy." He shook his head. "I hope I've done the right thing, but I hated to rush the building with a twelve-year-old inside."

Patti put a fist to her mouth, crying more now.

As the sheriff watched the scene and asked Patti quiet questions, Olivia stood with her heart in her throat watching Warner advance with caution across the concrete entry area toward the door. He paused at the wide glass-fronted entrance, one hand on the door, calling in muffled words to Rich. After a few moments, Warner opened the door and walked slowly inside, crossing the open foyer then disappearing down a side hallway.

Her knees feeling weak, Olivia sank onto a stone bench at the edge of the courtyard.

For twenty minutes that felt like hours, they waited. The sheriff had officers at all entrances to the building, preventing Rich from exiting at another location without being detained. As the sheriff explained, these officers would hear any gun reports or noise of an altercation in the building. Just the words gave Olivia chills.

Barry sat on a concrete bench with Patti, talking quietly with her. Leonard fielded calls from the media coming in to him, alternately talking and typing information into his iPhone. He paced, watching the door, his anxiety doing nothing to alleviate Olivia's fears.

Why would Warner do this? Was it because he empathized with Rich, knowing Rich was not well-liked at school? Or maybe because he carried a secret death wish after losing Nelle so tragically? She'd read about things like that. Olivia shivered at the idea.

She wished she'd arrived earlier. She'd have tried to talk Warner out of going into the school alone. He didn't really know Rich Headrick enough to take such a chance in confronting him. How did he know Rich didn't have mental problems?

Patti had kept unusually quiet about her past. Maybe the issues she wanted to conceal weren't only about her husband but about her son. Olivia found herself pacing as these thoughts filled her mind.

Listening to the conversation filtering around her, Olivia learned that it was Rich who'd been responsible for all the vandalism incidents around town. Why would he do such things? Defacing public property, setting fires in trash cans, frightening people as he had?

All these acts weren't simply random. He'd thought them out. Planned them. And now Warner was in that school, risking his life to talk to him.

Leonard came up and put an arm around Olivia. "I think he'll be all right," he said. "If Rich was reluctant to talk or angry enough to use a weapon, I think we'd have seen more action by now. I cover these things all the time."

"That doesn't comfort me, Leonard." She hugged her arms around herself. "Whatever possessed Warner to ask to go in there? I heard the sheriff say Rich had a gun. He threatened the janitor with it. If the boy is frightened or mentally unbalanced, Warner might be killed."

Leonard watched the doors, considering her words. "Warner wanted to go in, Olivia. He pushed for it, and Barry thought Warner would have a good chance of persuading Rich to give himself up and come out. Both thought Rich only scared, not really dangerous."

She twisted her hands. "Anyone who has a gun is dangerous, no matter what age."

Another call came in on his phone and Leonard walked a distance away from her to take it, leaving Olivia to watch the door anxiously again. *I'm still in love with him,* she realized. *I guess I've known it all along, but still the intensity of it has caught me off guard.*

Tears dribbled down her cheeks now. "Lord, please keep him safe," she muttered. "He always played superheroes when he was little, and I guess he couldn't resist doing it again."

Leonard chuckled to her right and grinned at her. "Good line for a news story, Olivia."

She rolled her eyes, but before she could give a reply, the officers closest to the school began to radio to the sheriff that they could see Warner and Rich coming out. Her eyes sweeping to the entrance, Olivia, too, could see the two of them coming slowly across the wide foyer just inside the middle school. Warner displayed the boy's weapon he held to assure the officers the situation was under control, but the sheriff and officers still watched with careful alertness as the two came outside.

Patti sprinted across the courtyard and gathered Rich into her arms, crying. Then the officers moved in to lead him away to a waiting police car.

Her knees weak, Olivia sat on the bench where Barry and Patti had sat before, trying to catch her breath. She wanted to run across the courtyard, to grab Warner into her arms, but she held herself back. He stood talking to the officers taking Rich into custody and to the sheriff, then to Barry and Patti and to Leonard. Olivia observed the scene with relief, her eyes following Warner, so grateful to see him walking around safe and well, talking, moving—not shot, not hurt. She struggled to quiet her ragged emotions.

As Warner spoke to the sheriff a final time, Olivia got up and walked toward them. Barry had taken Patti to the Sherriff's Office, and Sheriff Colson was preparing to head that way and follow them.

"Good work." Sheriff Colson shook Warner's hand before leaving.

"What will happen to Rich now?" Warner asked.

She listened to their conversation as Leonard walked over to join them.

Leonard grinned and slapped Warner on the back with affection. "It will help that the weapon was a water pistol."

A water pistol? Olivia hadn't known that. All she'd seen was Warner holding up a black gun.

Tuning back into the conversation, she heard the sheriff counseling Leonard to be kind in reporting the incident through the media.

He nodded and the sheriff left then, with only Leonard, Warner, and herself remaining at the scene.

As Warner talked about heading off with Leonard to fill him in about what had happened at the school, Olivia moved toward them. "I'm coming, too."

Warner blinked in surprise. He hadn't noticed her standing

quietly in the background.

As it turned out, since Leonard needed to get back to the paper quickly, he listened to Warner's story on the spot and suggested she drive him home afterward. She agreed, and a short time later, Olivia loaded Warner into her SUV and headed down Arlington away from the school.

Warner leaned his head back against the seat. "Man, what a day."

"You could have gotten yourself killed, Warner Zachery," she fussed.

He opened an eye to look at her. "And would that have troubled you, Olivia?"

"That is too ridiculous a question to even answer." Her hands gripped the steering wheel.

"Where are you taking me to lunch?" He leaned his head against the seat again.

"To my house," she said. "At any public place, you're likely to be mobbed and questioned as this story begins to circulate around town."

"And will you give me some TLC like Leonard suggested?"

She ignored his question. "Leonard was crazy to let you go in there. He and Barry both!"

"No, I did the right thing, going in," he insisted. "Rich has been bullied and tormented by a group of kids in school, in a worse way than anything I ever experienced. It needed to come out so something could be done."

"And what can you do?" Olivia tried to hold her annoyance in check.

"I don't know yet, but I'm going to do something."

"It's not your place." She frowned at the road ahead.

He turned serious blue eyes toward hers. "The reason these things continue without being stopped is because everyone decides it's not their place to intervene."

She didn't answer.

"I saw some boys ridicule Rich and then try to trip him downtown in Bryson City when I took him for a soda one day," he told her. "Later, at Soda Pops I got him to talk a little about it, and I learned kids in school made fun of him, called him names, and often gave him a hard time. He alluded to the fact that there'd been incidents at school and around town, and he told me no one ever did anything about it." Warner sighed. "If I'd listened then and tried to do something maybe all this wouldn't have happened. Maybe I could have gotten him help earlier."

Olivia thought about this as she headed the car out West Deep Creek Road toward the mountain and their street. "Warner, I remember us talking about that," she said at last. "Maybe I should have talked to Patti afterward, let her know things were more serious than she thought."

"That's the whole point," Warner said. "There are probably people all over town that saw incidents where kids teased and bullied Rich, but they never did anything, never felt they should interfere. Rich said as much to me, telling me about one incident after another where things happened and adults looked on, doing nothing to stop the problems."

"Is that what lay behind the vandal incidents? Rich's way of getting back?" She turned off the highway down the quiet back road leading to her house.

"As I told the sheriff, it was Rich's way of trying to get people's attention, to speak out that injustice and unfairness prevailed."

She pulled into her driveway then. "Let's go inside. You and I both need something to eat. It's after three now."

Olivia led Warner into the kitchen and dug into the refrigerator pulling out leftovers from dinner the night before to heat up.

"Mmmm. Meatloaf and mashed potatoes, one of my favorites." He lounged on a chair at the kitchen table, watching her.

She got out a plastic storage container. "I have green beans Wanda put up and a little corn salad left."

"What's in the salad?" he asked.

"Corn cut off the cob, chopped tomatoes, bell peppers, minced celery and onion, and a little ranch dressing. It's not a girly salad; Daddy likes it." She heated items in the microwave as she talked and soon put two plate lunches on the table, plus tall glasses of iced tea.

Warner dug in with pleasure as she sat down, putting a basket of warm cornbread sticks on the table, along with a stick of real butter.

His eyes moved to the cornbread sticks. "Your mother's recipe?"

She nodded.

"I remember her cornbread sticks. She made them in one of those black cast iron cornstick pans." He reached for one.

Olivia pushed the butter toward him as he did. "I still have her cast iron pan, and I use it when I make the sticks with her recipe."

He bit into one of the cornbread sticks. "Someone should have married you years ago just to get you to cook for them."

She attended to her plate, hungry herself.

Tucking in to lemon pie later and beginning to relax, Warner smiled at her. "Thanks, Olivia. A good lunch and some quiet time were just what I needed after today."

She looked up from the sliver of pie in front of her to smile back at him. "I like to cook. I always have."

"Mother used to say she wished she'd had a daughter like you to help in the kitchen. None of us boys were handy in that way, although Dad likes to grill."

She smiled at him, pleased she'd found something to do for him after all he'd been through with Rich earlier. "Do you want to take your tea to the sun porch out back? It's nice there."

"I'd rather walk in the garden," he said. "Let's go walk through the rose garden and down to the dock at Lily Lake. We can sit there and unwind by the water." He paused. "Unless you need to get back to work."

"Wanda's covering." She stood, cleaning up the table as she talked. "She can handle things by herself in a pinch."

They wandered outside behind the house, through the garden gate and under the rose arbor to the back pathway leading to the west end of the garden and the property around Lily Lake. More open than the walled garden, the property by the lake held a pavilion used for weddings and events, a quiet lake they called the Lily Lake behind it, and a winding hiking trail in the nearby woods named the Wildflower Walk.

On the rustic dock at the lake sat several Adirondack chairs looking out over the water. Tied up to the dock floated two old canoes.

"I remember taking those canoes out on the lake many times." Warner settled into one of the chairs.

"Me, too." Olivia sat on the edge of the dock, pulling off her flats and rolling up the hems of her capris to drop her feet into the water.

Warner pulled out his cell phone and made a call. Olivia could hear from his conversation that he talked to Barry, mostly listening for a long time and nodding. He occasionally made a comment, but said little more. "You take care of them, Barry," he said at last, before hanging up. Then he came to sit beside her on the dock, pulling off his own socks and shoes to drop his feet into the water beside hers.

Olivia sent a questioning gaze his way.

"Like Sheriff Colson said, they were able to post bail and take Rich home. A trial date is set, and the sheriff has already suggested a counselor for Rich and Patti." He blew out a breath of relief. "I'm glad they didn't put him in detention or ship him off to some juvenile detention center. I think that would have been the wrong thing for Rich."

"Are they back at Patti's?"

"No." He shook his head. "Barry took them by Patti's house to pack clothes and items they needed and then took them to his place outside of town where they won't receive ugly calls or harassment visits. Neither Patti or Rich need that right now."

"That's good of Barry."

He shook his head. "Not really. He's crazy in love with Patti. Haven't you figured that out? This is exactly the opportunity Barry needs to get past Patti's defenses and into her life. He loves Rich, too. He'll stand by them through this. Barry's a solid, reliable guy—

exactly what they need at a time like this."

"I'm sure you're right." Olivia turned to look at Warner, curling one leg under her to sit on it. "What else were you talking about? I could tell it was something about Patti's past—evidently some of it things Rich told you at the school."

"You might as well know. It's bound to get out now." Warner looked out across the lake. "Patti and Rich's last name, before Patti legally changed it, was Redman. She was Patricia Redman, R. D. Redman's wife."

Olivia struggled to place the name.

"Remember the big Ponzi scheme that R. D. Redman ran over in Asheville? Even in New York we read about it. It made the national news for weeks. The man embezzled millions out of his friends and business associates all over the Asheville area, including a large number of innocent investors from abroad as well."

Olivia shifted position, pulling her knees up to clasp her arms around them. "Oh, Warner! I do remember that now. Daddy read me the newspaper accounts over the breakfast table for days. He had a medical colleague that went to church with R. D. Redman and his wife. Daddy said they sat one pew in front of his family every Sunday morning. I remember Daddy going on and on about what a sly crook Redman was and how he even fleeced friends in the church out of their hard-earned savings, making them think he was investing their money for them."

"That's usually the way a Ponzi works."

A new thought hit Olivia. "Gracious! Did Patti know what her husband was doing? I can't believe she could have. It must have been simply awful for her—and for Rich—when all this happened." She paused, thinking. "R. D. Redman is in prison now, isn't he?"

"Yes. Caught and indicted after he tried to flee the country." Warner ran a hand through his hair. "And to the other question you asked—about whether Patti knew what he was doing, the answer is no. Patti told Barry she and Rich had no idea R. D.'s business was anything but what he told them it was, a secure investment company. Barry said they felt devastated when they learned all he'd done, the friends and associates of theirs he'd scammed."

"That must have been horrible for them." She studied the sun-kissed summer ripples on the lake, thinking about it.

"Barry said she cried telling the sheriff about it." Warner took her hand. "I guess it's easier to see why Patti came here the way she did, looking for a job, not offering formal references, staying to herself."

Olivia shook her head, trying to imagine all Patti and Rich had gone through.

"It makes more sense to me now why Rich didn't want to worry his mother about the ongoing bullying issues and why he kept his problems locked inside." He frowned. "It's also more understandable why Rich stayed to himself and didn't make many friends at school. He and Patti were afraid to get to know anyone too well, afraid they might slip and let people know who they really were."

"Oh, Warner, this is so sad." She stood and paced the dock, agitated about the situation.

He stood, too. "Let's walk back to the house before you pace off the edge of the dock." Warner grinned at her. "I need to get back home, too. The family will be hearing things and worrying about me."

After putting their shoes back on, they strolled back through the garden, still talking and trying to remember all they'd read about Redman's Ponzi scheme.

"Do you think I should drive over to Barry's to be with Patti?" Olivia asked. "I want to let her know nothing in her past makes any difference to me about her. I know people are going to give her a hard time, even here. And when the press gets hold of this, I imagine some of them will descend on Bryson City to try to get a story."

"I don't know if Patti is still newsworthy to the press after all this time, but you're right that it will set the locals talking." He stopped to look at her. "There are many who will question Patti's integrity. That could pose a problem. Hurt your business."

She stuck her chin up. "Well, let it! I don't care what a few ugly gossips say. Patti Headrick is my friend."

He smiled. "I'm glad to hear you say that. I'll pass the word along to Barry to give to Patti. Barry asked that everyone give Patti and Rich a couple of days to regroup from all this before phoning or dropping by. They've been through a lot, and Patti and Rich need some space."

"I don't want Patti to move. Do you think she'll move away again?"

Warner's lips twitched. "Not if Barry has anything to say about it she won't. Anyway, she can't leave until after Rich's court date—and probably not for a long time after if Rich is assigned community service."

Heading into the walled garden area, Warner gestured ahead. "I'll cut across the path here and through the side gate back to my place. When I have more news I'll let you know. Barry and Leonard will keep me in touch."

"Okay." Olivia stopped near the pool with the statue of the woman reading in the middle. She glanced toward the figure that looked so much like her grandmother and sighed.

Warner moved closer and pulled her into his arms. "Try not to worry too much, Livvy," he said, using her childhood pet name. "Everything will work out. In some ways it's best this all came out. Rich can get help now, and Patti can quit hiding behind her secrets."

"Maybe." She turned her face toward his. "I was so scared when I saw you heading into that school today, Warner Zachery. Don't ever do something like that again to me, you hear?"

He ran a hand down her cheek. "Did it make you realize you care a little?"

"You idiot." She pushed at him in aggravation. "Of course I care."

"Show me how much." He leaned in to kiss her. "I never did get that TLC you promised."

Forgetting her annoyance, she met his kiss eagerly, wrapping her arms around his back, sliding her hands up into his hair, enjoying the scent and feel of him.

"What are we going to do about us?" Warner whispered at last, his lips tracing up her neck.

Her thoughts following his, Olivia felt afraid to answer.

He cupped her face in his hands. "You do love me, don't you?"

"I always have," she answered honestly. "I never stopped."

"We'll figure something out," he said after another kiss. "We'll have to, even if I have to hog-tie you and carry you off to New York in the trunk of my car."

She knew he was joking, but the words were bittersweet.

His phone rang and he pulled it out to check the number. "It's my mother. I'd better head for home and reassure the family I'm okay." He kissed her on the nose. "I'll see you later. Thanks for the lunch."

He blew her a kiss as he started down the garden path, putting his cell phone to his ear to call his mother back.

CHAPTER 20

The town buzzed with the news of the events at Swain County Middle School for days. Leonard Goldstein wrote a compelling but honest piece about the event, playing up Warner's heroism in walking into the school totally unarmed to bring Rich Headrick safely out. The front page article highlighted Rich as more of a victim than a criminal, chiding the community for allowing bullying to exist in their town to the extent that a child needed to alert them by such drastic means to the dangers of injustice in their midst.

Wanda, her finger on the heartbeat of town gossip, read over the news reports in the shop every day. "I think the newspaper acted real nice, painting Rich as a victim instead of making him out to be a juvenile delinquent," she said, scanning the latest follow-up article. "Not that it stops people talking around town, of course, but it helped put an alternative spin on it."

Warner, who had dropped by to, hopefully, take Olivia to lunch, smiled at Wanda's honest observations.

"They sure did make you out a real hero, Warner." She grinned at him, laying the newspaper aside and starting to work on an arrangement. "Not that you weren't a hero, of course. But for those of us that know Rich, it's hard to imagine he'd have shot you, even if upset."

"You can never know what someone might do when they're upset and scared, Wanda," Olivia put in.

Warner agreed. Hindsight tended to diminish the intensity of a situation, but he still remembered the anxious thoughts rolling through his mind as he headed into the school that day.

Wanda blew out a breath. "You know, I still can't get over the fact that Patti is—or was—married to that scumbag R. D. Redman. Bless her heart. It must have been awful for her when she learned the scamming he'd been doing behind everyone's backs. I remember the way my friend Lucille talked about it. Everybody in Asheville was real upset over all that happened, I can tell you that. Can you imagine how Patti must have felt?" She jammed silk flowers into a foam wreath as she talked. "And how her little boy felt, knowing his daddy had done those wicked things? I'll bet everyone made their lives a real misery."

"Worse than a misery," Patti said, coming up the aisle from the back door.

"Lordy, girl, I didn't even see you come in." Wanda got up from her workstation, totally unashamed she'd been discussing Patti, to gather her friend into her arms to give her a massive hug.

She pulled back to look at Patti. "How are you doing, honey? I've been thinking about you nearly every minute, having to go through yet another trauma after what you already went through. How's Richard? Are you all doing okay?"

Warner grinned. There was nothing discreet about Wanda.

Olivia went to hug her, too. "What are you doing in here, Patti? I told you we could cover for a week or two until you felt like coming back."

"I was bored and restless at the house with Barry at work and Rich back in school."

Wanda's eyes widened. "You mean Rich went on back to school at Swain Middle after all that's happened? Is that wise? He threatened the school with what he wrote on that wall." She paused, shuffling through newspapers. "I just read again what he wrote: 'There's no safety and justice here. The vandal warns: don't open the school this week.'"

Patti sighed. "He didn't go to Swain Middle. He's going to Mountain Discovery Charter School on Jenkins Branch Road outside Bryson City. It's not far from Barry's home on Buckner's

Branch Road on the river and Rich's friend, Sam DeMatteo, goes to Mountain Discovery."

Wanda, ever candid, blurted out, "And you mean they let him in out there at Mountain after all this?"

At Olivia's shocked expression, Wanda put a hand on her hip. "Well, I just thought with all that occurred that any school might be reluctant to let Richard back in so soon."

Patti leaned against a workbench. "Wanda's right, but fortunately Mountain Discovery's administration felt sympathetic to all that happened to Rich and thought he deserved a second chance." She glanced toward Warner. "It helped that Warner, Barry, and Leonard visited the school and spoke to the director on Rich's behalf. So did Reed and Cheryl DeMatteo, Sam's parents. Sheriff Colson even put in a good word for him, as did the counselor that Rich and I have been seeing."

"Well, I'm glad Rich could get in Mountain Discovery," Warner said. "I hope he'll be happier there."

"So do I and he seems to like it so far." Patti sat on the bench at her workstation. "Like Wanda said, even if Swain Middle had let Rich back into school this week, it would have been awkward. Those kids that bullied him the worst are still there and Rich still hasn't been to court for the threats he made and the troubles he caused around town."

She straightened her workbench while she talked. "I know we're lucky he could get in Mountain Discovery. Barry thinks the hands-on course of study there and the emphasis on respect for self, others, and the environment will be good for Rich."

Warner grinned. "The middle school years are hard for a lot of kids. Barry told me some of the other boys at Mountain Discovery, who'd known bad middle school experiences at other schools, see Rich as sort of a hero or vigilante for justice against bullying."

Patti frowned. "Well, I can't say that's a good thing. I don't want what Rich did celebrated in any way or excused. It was wrong, no matter the motivation behind it."

"I know." Warner leaned against a shelf. "Rich knows that, too.

I'm only saying the kids at the new school aren't shying away from him because of what happened. They understand."

Wanda held up the wreath she'd been working on to examine it. "This wreath still needs a little something—maybe another pink peony on this right side." She worked the flower in before turning her eyes to Patti again. "Patti, can we assume you and Barry will be getting married now? After all, you are staying out at his place. People are talking."

Olivia gasped. "Honestly, Wanda Baylor, can you not bridle your tongue once in a while?"

Patti laughed. "Oh, leave her be, Olivia. With as much talk circulating around town about me already, what's a little more." She threw a scrap of greenery toward Wanda. "And Wanda, you're the one who's always encouraging us to get married and be happy like you and Harley."

"So does that mean you and Barry Jacobs *are* getting married?" Wanda's eyes lit up.

A small smile played over Patti's lips. "We're talking about it. I guess you might say we're officially engaged. And just so you know, Wanda Baylor, Barry is staying over here in town at my old place while Rich and I are staying at his place. If you'd snooped a little further and asked around more, you'd have learned that. Everybody's seen Barry walking to work every day from my house." She propped her chin on her hand. "However, as soon as Richard's case is heard and that matter settled, we're going to hold a quiet wedding ceremony on the river at Barry's."

"Not in the church?" Wanda looked shocked.

Patti shook her head. "No. With all that's happened, we wanted something small and less public. We're only inviting our close friends and family." She smiled. "You'll all get to meet some of my family from Abingdon, Virginia. I've hardly seen any of them since the problems with R. D. occurred. I didn't want to go back home and cause problems for anyone. The press tried to track Rich and me down for a long time, wanting pictures and interviews. They really hounded us."

Wanda tucked another flower into her wreath. "Did you really not have a clue what your husband was up to?"

"I feel stupid and gullible to say it, but I didn't." She sighed. "I married R. D. when barely eighteen, a young girl fresh out of high school. Raised with my grandparents in a small town florist, my life had been pretty sheltered. My grandparents, old-school Italians, raised me to be subservient in marriage. R. D. always talked in general about his investment business but never shared any specifics. I had Rich right away, and I kept house and raised Rich wherever we lived. We moved several times, first to Philadelphia, then suddenly to Vegas. Then after four years R. D. decided to relocate his business to Asheville. Looking back, I realize we always moved with little advance warning. Perhaps that should have alerted me to a problem, but it didn't."

She picked up a piece of greenery from her workbench to examine it. "I was stunned that day when federal authorities came to our door looking for R. D. He often traveled with his business around the U.S. and abroad and he'd gone on another of his trips. They searched our home, asked us a million questions, and then the media picked up on the ongoing investigation. That's when our nightmare really began."

Patti looked up with anguish in her eyes. "You can't imagine how betrayed Rich and I felt. R. D. was a true Jekyll and Hyde type of personality; no one imagined him anything but the charming, personable, charismatic, and outgoing man they saw, including Rich and me. We had no idea R. D. was a criminal."

Wanda shook her head. "Patti, I saw the pictures of that big, fine house you all lived in over in Asheville. Honey, you were rich, and that's a fact. On the Internet there's some photos of you back then with long, pretty hair and designer-like clothes, standing in big fancy rooms loaded with expensive furniture and art and stuff. Did the authorities take all that?"

She nodded. "Yes, to try to compensate all the people R. D. milked money out of, they confiscated everything, closed all our joint accounts, seized the assets. It was the most humiliating time of my entire life and, of course, a lot of people thought I was in on the Ponzi scheme. It took time for me to be completely cleared of all the charges. I cooperated in every way I could once I learned what R. D. had done."

"Did you come straight here after you left Asheville?" Warner asked.

Patti shook her head. "No, I wanted to go home to Arlington to help with the florist business again and to live with my grandparents. But even our initial visit there drew media attention to my grandparents, so I knew we couldn't stay. Fortunately, I had a small account in Virginia, from money saved before I married. I never needed that money with R. D.'s affluence so the account had grown. It gave me something I could live on for a time."

She managed a small smile. "Trying to distance myself from my grandparents to protect them, I rented a cabin in the mountains near Franklin for the summer. My Asheville attorney helped me find it. She also helped me attain a divorce and change our names legally so Rich and I could make a new beginning. I cut and darkened my hair and began to visit small towns in the area looking for a florist job. If needed, I knew my grandparents would give me a reference, but I hoped I might not need it. It seemed a lucky day when I looked down the road near the train depot here in Bryson City and saw your florist sign in the yard. Then I walked in the shop and found you getting ready to open the store."

"Maybe it was destiny." Olivia smiled at her. "Patti, I wish you'd told me everything earlier. It wouldn't have mattered to me."

"I couldn't be sure of that at the time. Most all of our friends in Asheville felt too embarrassed by the publicity to stand behind me—to stay friends—and I wanted to protect Rich. It's hard for a boy to know his father is a criminal and in prison."

"Barry will help him work through that," Warner put in. "And he'll be a good father to Rich."

Tears filled Patti's eyes. "I know, and I feel so undeserving of him."

"Pooh on that, you're a wonderful person." Wanda tossed the

words out with her usual candor. "Talented, smart, and nice. He's lucky to get you."

"I agree," said Olivia. "And I insist you let me do the flowers for your wedding—on the house."

"Oh, that'll be fun," Wanda agreed, grinning. She babbled on immediately with ideas.

In a pause, Olivia said, "You really don't need to work today, Patti. You've been through a lot."

"No, I want to work and be busy." She smiled. "It's kind of therapeutic, you know?" She glanced at the clock. "I came when I did so you could leave and go home. This is supposed to be your day off and I know you need to work in the garden. Wanda and I can handle things for the afternoon."

"We can," Wanda agreed. "And Warner already said he wanted to take you out to lunch. So you two go on. Patti and I will order in some sandwiches, and I'll catch Patti up on all the local gossip. It's not a very busy day here, and if anybody comes in the shop wanting to bother Patti or start trouble, they'll have me to deal with." She shook a fist aggressively.

Patti laughed. "There. You see? Nothing to worry about, Olivia."

"All right." Olivia agreed at last, laughing with them. She talked a little longer, going over orders to be filled before the day ended and then left with Warner out the back door.

"Will the Everett Street Diner be all right with you for lunch today?" Warner asked. "If so, we'll walk over. I heard the Daily Special was Charlene's fried chicken and mashed potatoes."

"Sure, Everett's is fine." She draped her purse over one shoulder. "I love their tomato dill soup."

Warner fell into step with Olivia as they started down the short, side streets leading to the diner on Everett Street. "If I'm extra lucky they'll have blackberry cobbler, too."

Later, seated at a table by the window and looking over a menu, Warner said, "I'm glad I was there when Patti came and shared her story. Barry's kept pretty closed-mouthed about Patti's past whenever Leonard and I quizzed him."

"He'll be good to Patti and Rich." Olivia stirred part of a packet of sweetener into a glass of iced tea. "I'm so happy that's worked out. I really feared Patti would bolt and leave Bryson City after all that happened with Rich, that she'd find it too embarrassing to stay."

"She ran once. I guess she felt it time to take a stand and stay this time. It helps that the business with R. D. Redman is so far in the past now. Leonard says he doubts any media will show up wanting to do any major write-ups. He says they might try to track Patti down in future if Redman gets paroled, but that's a long time ahead. Leonard told me he received a thirty-year sentence."

He paused to give the waitress his order, letting Olivia give hers as well before continuing. "Wanda Baylor is certainly an outspoken, upfront woman, but I kind of like that in her. She doesn't pussyfoot around any subject, that's for sure."

Olivia laughed. "No, and in a lot of ways I love Wanda for that. She's so direct and honest." She paused. "It was good of you to help Rich get into Mountain Discovery. I hope that school environment will work for him."

"Me, too. The boy deserves some good coming his way after all he's been through."

"Warner?" A voice interrupted them.

Warner looked up to see Sheriff Colson and the principal of the middle school getting ready to start out the door. The sheriff walked closer with the principal close behind. "We were talking at lunch about you speaking for the school's first PTA meeting Monday night," Sheriff Colson said. "You still planning to do that?"

Warner pulled out his iPhone and checked his event schedule. "It's still on my agenda, but I'm glad you reminded me of it today. I'd almost forgotten it."

The principal stepped forward. "We advertised the event and sent PTA invitations home with the students. It will really help our PTA membership drive to have you speak. I hope you'll still come."

"I will. What's the timeframe and the meeting agenda?"

"PTA starts at seven Monday evening," he answered. "I'll call the meeting to order, give a few announcements, encourage membership. We'll recognize the new PTA officers, hear a few short committee reports, talk about upcoming events, and then give you the floor. Refreshments are planned afterward, and we'll set up a signing table for you. A lot of kids and parents might want to meet you and buy books, especially those that didn't get to the signing at Gil's this summer."

"Is the talk still scheduled for about twenty to thirty minutes?"

"Yes," the principal said. "We try to let out by eight p.m. with school the next day."

Warner nodded.

The sheriff cleared his throat. "I'm posting a little extra security at the school on Monday after all that's happened. That's what we discussed over lunch today, plus a few other points." He shifted his weight. "Glad you're still planning to speak for the school, Warner. It will help them get past this. Move on."

The two left then, and Warner looked across the table to see Olivia giving him a questioning stare. "Won't it be upsetting for you to go back into that school on Monday after what happened there with Rich?"

"It's only another speech among hundreds I give." He made a note in his iPhone before putting it away. "Besides, I may have a few things to say at that meeting besides how a Bryson City boy started writing young adult books. Drop by if you want to and listen in."

She lifted a brow. "Warner, what are you up to?"

He shrugged as their food arrived and managed to avoid answering.

CHAPTER 21

With Labor Day weekend moving closer, Olivia found herself swamped every day with committee meetings and work sessions related to the class reunion. On Monday morning, four days before the reunion date, Olivia sat at Roberta's dining room table with Vickie Leigh and Louise, going over final plans for the weekend event.

"Okay, here's our program—printed and finalized." Roberta passed everyone a small booklet in the school colors of maroon and white. Swain High's logo and a color photo of the school decorated the front cover.

"Beautiful cover." Louise ran a finger over it in appreciation. "Everyone will love it."

"The Memory Books came in, too." Roberta gestured to several boxes stacked on the floor. "Our main task this morning is to pack all of the Maroon Devils tote bags. Remember, every graduate gets one when they check in Friday evening." She glanced down at her list. "We need to put the Memory Books, programs, and all the donated gift items from Bryson City merchants in them."

"Roberta, don't forget I brought three boxes of stuff from the Visitor's Center to put in those bags, too—brochures, maps, coupon books," Vickie Leigh put in. "I talked the Center into being real generous."

"Thanks for working so hard on that." Roberta gave her a genuine smile. "You did a lot helping to gather giveaway items from around town for us, too."

Vickie beamed at the compliment.

"I love, love, love our Memory Books," Louise enthused as she thumbed through one. "They turned out so nice with all the photos around the school and the wonderful now-and-then pictures of every graduate. There's information about where everyone lives now, what they're doing, the children they have. It's so interesting."

Olivia looked over Louise's shoulder. "Roberta, you really deserve a lot of appreciation for this. You did most of the work on the Memory Books, along with setting up and adding to the Class Reunion website."

"Well, we didn't get every past class member to send us info and a current photo, but most did." Roberta opened one of the spiral-bound Memory Books on the table beside her to flip through it. "We have more than a hundred planning to attend the reunion, that's half our graduating class. Some reunions only net twenty-five percent or less of their graduates."

Vickie Leigh wrinkled her nose. "Just promise me we'll only schedule these reunions every ten years. It's too much work to do it more often!"

Roberta propped an elbow on the table. "The guys said the same thing, so I guess we'll wait until twenty years for the next one."

"I hope everyone will have a good time this weekend." Louise straightened the headband in her short hair.

They sipped on coffee, looking through the weekend schedule.

"Let's go through this one last time." Roberta looked over the agenda. "We've got the Meet-and-Greet from six to seven on Friday at the gym, with the building open for people who want to walk around and see the school again. At seven, the Reunion Dance starts. Then Saturday morning, there's the Breakfast at the Hemlock Inn at nine, really convenient for the out-of-towners already staying there. Then our day options start, including events around town and the Great Smoky Mountain Railroad train trip from the Bryson City depot to Nantahala and back. Everyone will love that. A large crowd registered for the train trip, and we got a good group rate."

She scanned over the program. "Saturday night we're having the Awards Dinner, also at the Hemlock—but it's beautiful up there on the mountain."

Roberta snorted. "It's practically the only place large enough for a big event without using a church or school building in town, and everyone knows the family-style buffets at the Hemlock are incredible. People will remember the food fondly, if nothing else."

Olivia laughed. "They'll also remember the gorgeous flowers and decorations at the Hemlock for our dinner and at the dance, too."

"You've worked hard on the flowers and decorations," Roberta complimented her. "And I loved your idea of making small wrist corsages in maroon and white for all the women who come to the dance."

The three friends spent the rest of the morning loading tote bags and checking off last-minute items on their list, making sure everything was in readiness—photographer, caterers, needed transportation, sound equipment, and volunteers to man registration tables or to help with parking or direct tours.

"What's everyone wearing to the dance?" Vickie Leigh asked during a quiet interval, while loading yet another tote bag.

"Candy apple red, like I did at our senior prom." Roberta flashed them a smug look. "I can actually still wear my old prom dress, but I wanted something a little more spectacular this time so I bought a slinky new dress."

Louise sighed. "I couldn't zip up my old prom dress even if I'd kept it, but I bought a soft, floaty gown in baby pink that Rob loves."

Vicki leaned forward. "I'm wearing a chartreuse green gown with a purple cummerbund I ordered online."

Roberta raised her eyebrows.

"Oh, quit trying to rain on my parade, Roberta." Vickie slapped at her. "The dress is gorgeous, and it looks glorious with my green eyes and red hair. A pasty pastel would look awful on me. You know that."

Roberta shrugged. "What about you, Olivia?"

"In a cute shop in Asheville, I found a silky sapphire blue gown with cap sleeves, a drop back, and a long flared skirt."

"I've seen it. It's wonderful." Louise wiggled her eyebrows.

"Blue is good on you." Roberta finished the last empty tote bag from the stack on the table. "Girls, I think we're finally done here. And I need to go pick up the boys at my mother's. They wear her out after a couple of hours."

Vickie Leigh glanced at her watch. "I need to go to work, too. I'll catch a sandwich on the way in."

Louise stood and stretched. "Can we help you carry all these tote bags to your basement before we leave, Roberta?"

She shook her head. "No. Leave them. Russell, Logan, and Brody promised to haul everything to the basement later. They're meeting here tonight to go over a few things on their list." She glanced at Louise. "Rob's coming, too, if he doesn't get tied up with an unexpected death at the funeral home."

"So far, so good!" Louise walked out with Vickie while Olivia stacked and carried their coffee cups and dishes into the kitchen.

Roberta followed her, carrying the rest of the items from their earlier coffee hour. "Thanks for the help," Roberta said.

"Thanks for hosting us." Olivia turned to go.

"Listen." Roberta put a hand on her arm. "I know you've been seeing a lot of Warner Zachery while he's been in town." She hesitated. "And I know, despite the fact that you never mentioned it, a little something started stirring between you two back in high school days."

Olivia opened her mouth to protest, but Roberta stopped her.

"My point in bringing this up is because I'm worried about this situation for you." She pushed back a strand of dark hair. "Frankly, Warner acted odd and didn't fit in around Bryson City back then, and he still doesn't fit in now. I think he knows that, Olivia. Some people are meant to stay in a small town, and some aren't. It's simply the way it is. You're a small town girl, but Warner is a big city boy now. I don't want you pinning big hopes on the idea that W. T. Zachery will stick around. He left before, and I totally believe—

after our reunion and the end of his summer interlude—that he'll head right back to New York City."

Olivia tensed.

"Brody really likes you, Olivia, and the two of you have known each other for a long time. It wouldn't be a bad match for you." She studied a nail. "I wouldn't be too hasty to brush Brody off in favor of Warner."

Tempering her annoyance, Olivia considered what to say. "Roberta, I'd like to make it clear I think of Brody as a friend, and that's all. If I mistakenly encouraged him to believe our relationship was more than that, I regret it. I already told him the same."

Roberta raised a brow. "You seemed interested enough in Brody before Warner showed up."

"No, you're wrong. And if you'll remember, I was dating Martin Reese then, too, and that relationship showed more promise than my few dates with Brody—in my eyes."

"And in your father's eyes." Roberta gave Olivia an indulgent smile. "Too bad nothing came of that. Helen Allmon told me your father's eager to get you married off so he can pop the question to her. You've always been a Daddy's girl, Olivia, but don't you think it's time to let your father have a love life of his own again? If you married, he'd feel free to take a wife again. But as it is …." She gave an eloquent shrug. "Well, you know …."

Olivia forced a tight smile. "I'm well aware of Daddy's interest in Helen Allmon. She and her daughters came to dinner recently. Whether I'm married or single has no bearing on whether or not Daddy decides to remarry, despite what Helen says."

"If you say so." She trailed Olivia to the door.

Olivia managed a few pleasantries and then made her escape. "That cat," she said to herself as she headed down the road from the house, angry at Roberta's words. But then, of course, she cried about the conversation before she drove the rest of the way home. So many of Roberta's words always hurt.

Fixing dinner later, Olivia decided it was time to initiate that little chat with her father she'd avoided for so long. But he called and said a colleague passed on tickets to a musical show over at the Smoky Mountain Center for the Performing Arts in Franklin and that he'd decided to take Helen to the show and stop for dinner along the way. "You didn't go to a lot of trouble tonight, did you, Livvy?"

"No, of course not." She eyed the oven where a big Pyrex dish of lasagna baked. In the refrigerator sat a nice Caesar salad and a chocolate pie. "You and Helen go and have a good time."

She slumped at the table after his call, wondering if there was any truth to Roberta's earlier words. Was she holding her father back from commitment?

After putting dinner away and fixing herself a simple fruit and cheese plate, Olivia found her eyes straying to the clock. Warner was speaking at the middle school tonight. He'd said to drop by if she wanted to listen in. Maybe she would.

Using the excuse of bringing free flowers for the first PTA meeting of the year, Olivia slipped into the gymnasium at the middle school an hour later, chatting with people she knew. She arranged the big vase of multicolored dahlias she'd gathered from the Fairchild Gardens on the refreshment table, then settled into a seat at the back of the gym.

A crowd filled the room, eager to hear the visiting celebrity no doubt. PTA meetings weren't usually so well attended. The new officers, seated at a table by the door, took applications for new memberships, obviously delighted to start the new school year so well.

The meeting started at last with the principal saying a few words, new officers being recognized, and a spattering of announcements made. The crowd thundered applause when Warner strolled on stage to speak, and again Olivia marveled that this self-contained, confident man could possibly be the same awkward boy she played with in the garden as a girl.

Warner broke the ice telling a few stories to make everyone laugh and then reminisced in a fond way about Bryson City—winning over the locals. He talked about his books and about how he started writing stories for young adults. At a point in his speech, while talking about Geeky Gilmore, the nerdy boy in his popular young adult series, he paused, suddenly looking around, saying nothing.

The room quieted in the silence.

"You know," he said at last, leaning forward. "This is the second time I've been in this school this week. We've laughed together tonight about my awkward days in school, and I shared with you about Geeky's problems fitting into his middle school peer world. The concept makes for good stories, but it's a hurtful life to live in."

He ran a hand through his hair. "I make jokes about my past, but in all honesty I found it painful not fitting in with my peers. I wasn't a jock like my brothers, didn't look handsome then, and I'd have stumbled even walking up on a stage like this and been incapable of saying a word to a group this size. In the hallways at school and around my locker back then I got laughed at and poked at by my more popular peers. Cute girls mostly avoided me. I was Weird Warner then. Many of you remember that. Some of you felt sorry for me; some of you laughed at me. Many of you are surprised I amounted to anything. But here I am…" He grinned around the room.

People shifted in their chairs, not sure if they should laugh with Warner or look contrite.

"I was lucky, though." His eyes found the members of his family on one of the front rows. "I had a wonderful, supportive family that always thought I was the greatest."

One of his brothers made a sarcastic remark Olivia couldn't hear that made everyone laugh.

"I also had some great friends. I got lucky in that, too." His eyes found Barry and Leonard in the audience, along with others in his old group of high school and community friends.

"The boy I helped this week, Rich Headrick, who wrote threats on your middle school walls, wasn't so lucky." His eyes moved over the audience. "He and his mother fled another city after his father did some wrong things and ended up in prison. The FBI and the police searched their home, interrogated them, and wondered for a time if they'd been involved in the scandal. Rich was only nine years old then, an age when boys idolize their fathers."

Warner shook his head. "Can you imagine what that time was like for him? And then to have good people around them turn their backs on them, embarrassed and angry about their tragedy, no longer wanting to stand by them or be friends to them through a hard time."

He took a breath. "All their assets were seized, including their home and furnishings. When they tried to go to live with Rich's grandparents in Virginia, media sensationalists followed them— soon pushing Rich and his mother to move again. This time his mother changed her name and Rich's, lived in a rental cabin for a time near Franklin, and then came here—finding work at what she knew best, working in a florist shop for Olivia Benton."

Taking the microphone in hand, Warner moved away from the podium. "Can you imagine how much Rich wanted to fit in and find a place where he could have new friends? But he got bullied instead. A gang of boys, who I've learned enjoy bullying new boys and vulnerable kids, started in on him as soon as he entered middle school. The nicknames they created for him soon raced around the school, branding him and coloring all his chances of finding the kind of new life and friendships he yearned for here."

He pulled a chair around to sit on it backward, making eye contact with his audience. "Rich tried to talk to people about what was happening—to counselors, to teachers, to a few other adults. Often when the bullying happened at school and in the community—when Rich was called names, tripped in the hallway, or pushed against the wall—adults were nearby. But no one did anything. People told him, 'kids will be kids,' 'toughen up,' or 'don't pay any attention to that teasing.' But none of these things worked for Rich and the harassment continued. Week by tormenting week."

His eyes found Patti's in the audience. "He couldn't talk to his mother. She'd been through so much. He didn't want to cause more trouble for her. He wanted to protect her ... so he began to strike back in the only way he could. A person's anger, frustration, and hurt, if held in and held in and held in, finally has to find a way to come out. So Rich started writing his signs around town in the places where he got bullied—on the sites where his torments happened—but where no one intervened to stop them."

He stood to pace across the stage again. "One of the early writings was written right across the courthouse walls, complaining there was no justice here. It said: 'A vandal stalks where no justice prevails.' Another showed up at the public recreation center where Rich wasn't allowed to shoot basketball and was chased off the playground with catcalls. A little group of middle school girls decided it would be funny if one of them befriended Rich in jest and made him think she liked him. Then they could all laugh at him about it later. He retaliated by decorating her ancestor's statue as a witch." Warner shook his head, grinning. "It could almost be funny if it wasn't so tragic."

Warner walked back to the podium. "Friends, bullying or peer victimization is growing in our schools and society. It is especially problematic, prevalent, and damaging in the middle school grades— where children begin to define themselves, create self-schemas, establish self-esteem, and create life goals. Being targeted with peer victimization rather than support and acceptance in these years— or in any years—causes negative outcomes we can't afford in our kids: low self-esteem, low school engagement, school avoidance, low achievement, depression and retaliating aggression. National statistics reveal that seventy percent of youth are bullied by the time they reach ninth grade, many with emotional versus physical assaults that often leave the deepest scars behind." He paused. "Do you want this going on in your schools here in Bryson City? Do you want this happening to your kids or to your neighbor's kids?"

Olivia saw heads begin to shake around the room.

"I don't either. Things need to change here at Swain Middle, and throughout Bryson City, to protect children from being bullied and victimized. There are some good programs for bullying prevention. I've worked with them. They help schools and parents understand what bullying is, learn coping strategies, and realize the importance of treating others with respect." He took a deep breath. "Kids who are bullied need to know there is someone they can talk to in our schools and in our community, and that those people will listen and do something. I know your principal and sheriff are planning a series of meetings on this issue, some through your PTA. I hope every one of you will be here."

He let his eyes rove over the audience. "As for those of you whose children were involved in bullying Rich Headrick so that he had to reach out in desperation as he did to bring attention to the problem ... I hope you'll take those young people in hand and talk to them about their actions. Rich is receiving counseling to understand what he did that was wrong in response to bullying, but the children on the other end need the same help."

Warren closed the folder containing his speech notes. "I hadn't planned to talk about this issue at Swain Middle tonight, but I felt led to do so as I began to share about my past and to talk about Geeky—also a casualty of peer victimization. I know if Rich Headrick were in the audience tonight he'd stand right here with me to ask for something to be done to stop this problem in your school and in your city. On his behalf and mine I ...." Warner's voice dropped off as Rich walked up the school aisle.

Every head in the room turned to follow him, with whispers and muted conversation running around the audience.

Rich walked up on the stage and turned to stand beside Warner. He cleared his throat and spoke. "I came tonight to hear Warner but stayed outside the door, so I could listen but so no one could see me." His voice shook. "But I'm up here now and standing with Warner, like he said." He lifted his head as Warner slipped an arm around him.

"Who'll stand with us to help stop this problem?" Warner's voice broke with emotion.

People in the room began to stand one by one. Barry and Leonard walked up on the stage to stand with Warner and Rich. The principal soon joined them, encouraging applause, as more and more people stood to their feet. As the applause died out, the principal offered a few final words, closed the meeting, and invited everyone to enjoy refreshments and shake Warner's hand.

Olivia, from her spot in the back of the room, watched Barry, Patti, and Rich talk with warmth and affection to many in the audience before they slipped out a side door.

As the crowd trickled out at last, Olivia came over to find Warner loading books, bookmarks, and fliers into a box. "You did good," she told him.

"Thanks." His eyes found hers. "I thought I'd choke up when Rich walked down that aisle to stand with me."

She smiled at him. "It was a moment few will forget. I told Rich I was proud of him."

Warner busied himself loading the box. "I never got any refreshments." He grinned toward the now cleared table. "Working to hit a deadline earlier before I came, I didn't even find time to grab supper." He turned to her. "You wanna go grab a bite with me?"

She smiled. "Even better, why don't you come to the house and eat with me? Daddy skipped out on dinner earlier to take Helen to a musical over in Franklin. I still have a whole casserole dish of homemade lasagna, salad, French bread, and a chocolate pie in the refrigerator."

His grin was answer enough. "I'll follow you home as soon as I say my last good-byes and load these boxes in my car."

CHAPTER 22

Warner found it restful sitting at the kitchen table with Olivia after a full emotional day. He cut another square of lasagna and slid it onto his plate.

"This could become an addictive habit." He grinned at her. "Who knew Flora Fair would turn out to be such a good cook?"

"I'm sure Daddy would agree with you." She spoke the words with a tight voice.

"How's that situation going?"

She shrugged, picking at her salad. "I keep hoping to find a time to talk to him, but our schedules have both been really busy." She passed him the basket of French bread so he could snag another piece.

Warner delayed commenting, to see if she'd share more.

"Roberta said Helen told her Daddy hesitates to pop the question because I'm still unmarried and living at home. Do you think that's true?"

He looked at her, flushed and pretty with her blond hair drifting around her neck, her blue eyes as clear as a summer's sky. "I can't imagine your dad would hesitate to propose for only that reason." He gave her a sly look. "But just in case, you can marry me and move that potential obstacle right out of his path."

She barely disguised her shock. "I'm trying to be serious here."

He caught her eyes. "So am I."

She stood to get more tea from the refrigerator and walked behind him to refill his glass. "Warner, it's kind of you to make that offer in this situation … and you were nice before, too, saying you'd buy the garden from Daddy if he and Helen wanted to sell it." She paused, sighing as she sat the pitcher on the counter. "But I don't want you offering to marry me because you feel sorry for me."

Pushing back his chair, he crossed the room in three strides to wrap her in his arms before she could sit again. "Can you really believe I'd offer to marry you because I feel sorry for you?"

"Well, I don't know." She dropped her eyes. "It wasn't exactly a very romantic proposal, so I couldn't be sure."

He grinned. "Well, I'll give some thought to offering you a better one in a more romantic situation."

"Oh, silly." She pulled away. "Sit back down and finish your dinner before it gets cold."

Thinking over her words, Warner decided to comply for now. "You do make good lasagna, Olivia Benton. I could be tempted to offer for you based on your cooking alone."

She sat down and sent him a small smile. "So it's really my cooking you're interested in."

He ate a few more bites. "Well, it is nice you have so many domestic talents I admire. You cook, garden, sew, arrange flowers beautifully, create stunning table decorations …."

"Oh, stop teasing me. I really need your advice about Daddy."

"I told you before you need to talk with him." He forked up the last of his lasagna to finish it. "Olivia, all this talking about what you imagine your daddy might be feeling, what you think he might want, what Roberta thinks or says about it, or what she claims Helen told her isn't resolving anything. You need to talk to your father one-on-one."

Olivia got up to cut slices of chocolate pie. "But it's awkward. It's my father. How can I just come out and ask him if he's in love with Helen Allmon or if he plans to ask her to marry him? What if he thinks it isn't my place to pry into his private life?"

Warner laughed. "He certainly pries into your private life often enough."

"That's different." She put a dessert plate of pie in front of him, taking his plate away.

"Not really," he said, as she sat back down with her own dessert. "I think you're simply avoiding the confrontation."

Big blue eyes looked up at him. "Do you think it will be a confrontation?"

"I don't know. It might be, but I doubt it. I think the two of you will simply talk about this like two adults who love each other."

She swallowed. "I do love Daddy. I really do."

Mercy, Warner certainly knew that. "I know you do."

He decided to change the subject. "What else did the ever-wise Roberta say to you today."

She dropped her eyes. "She said that after the reunion you'd be going back to New York."

"She's right."

Olivia's eyes widened and looked to his in question.

"I have meetings I can't put off any longer. In fact, several are already set up for early next week. I'll probably start back on Sunday, stop over halfway, and roll back into the city Monday afternoon."

"I see." She picked at her pie.

"Olivia, I *have* to work. I've stayed here longer than I should without heading back already. Surely you understand that."

"Of course." Her voice sounded too soft. "I guess Roberta was right."

"If I remember correctly, Roberta is *always* right." He finished his pie and washed the last bite down with iced tea.

She stood, beginning to clear away the dinner dishes. He soaked up the sight of her moving around the kitchen, letting his eyes slide over her with appreciation. She wore one of her typical Olivia outfits, silky dark green slacks and a yellow knit top, layered with a short-sleeved, button-front cardigan in a fresh leaf green sprinkled with small yellow flowers.

"You always look like a beautiful fairy that might spring up out of your garden and dance down the pathways." He saw her blush at his words. "Speaking of dancing, what are you wearing to the dance on Friday?"

She dried off her hands. "A long sapphire blue dress."

"Sounds pretty. I'll look forward to seeing it." He stood. "Let's go walk in the garden."

"All right," she said, obviously pleased. "But let me change my shoes first." At the back door, she slipped out of her flats and pulled on an old pair of Keds. "Kind of spoils the look, doesn't it?" She glanced down at her feet, laughing.

Warner took in the sound, tucking it into his memory. He linked his arm through hers as they started down the main pathway under the fragrant arches of summer roses. "This is a beautiful place," he admitted.

"It is, and I think you're right that Daddy wouldn't sell it." She stopped to press her nose into a cluster of pink blossoms. "Even if Helen isn't overly fond of the garden, I doubt she would pressure Daddy to destroy it or mow it down. After all, we do have people who take care of the garden, me included. Helen won't need to do any work in it if she doesn't want to." She walked on as she talked.

"That's a good point." The mixed scents of the roses overhead and on either side, plus the soft scent of Olivia's cologne, drifted across his senses.

She paused at the pool, looking across it to the statue of the woman reading in the center. "I think I'll move into Patti's house next month when she and Barry get married. It's a small Cape Cod on the street right behind the store, and I can fix it up to be really cute."

Her words surprised him. Warner took her hand and turned her to face him. "You'd leave Benton house?" He glanced behind him toward the big two-storied white house he could glimpse beyond the garden gate.

"It wouldn't be the same with Helen in it." She sighed. "We're simply too different to live in the same home together." She reached over to swirl a hand through the water. "She'll probably change everything in the house, too, and I don't think I could stand to watch it."

"Are you sure you're not imagining that?"

Olivia lifted amused eyes to his. "Warner, she made it clear she doesn't like florals. So did her daughters. She also dislikes wallpaper, and she thinks the kitchen should be completely modernized. If I remember correctly, I think I heard the word gutted in one conversation."

"Ouch." He gave her a sympathetic look. He knew every room in Benton House celebrated florals in some capacity, either in upholstery, pillows, drapes, wallpaper, or bedspreads. Even the kitchen featured floral tiles.

He glanced across the pond, considering it. "Thinking about that even breaks *my* heart, Olivia. I love that house."

"Thanks." She leaned up to give him a kiss on the cheek. "That's a nice thing to hear right now."

With the sun dipping behind the trees, twilight was falling. Warner took Olivia's hand. "Let's go to the White Garden." It had always been their favorite place.

A short time later, they walked around the White Garden enjoying the evening—watching the white flowers glowing in the twilight—and settling on one of the benches in the gazebo as dark began stretching its fingers through the valley.

Warner turned to Olivia and, seeing her relaxed and looking across the garden with a smile, knew the moment was perfect. "Olivia Benton, I've loved you since we were children, and I've discovered my love for you hasn't diminished through the years. In fact it's grown stronger." He took her hand in his. "I don't think I can bear to leave you again. You thought I was teasing earlier when I told you I wanted to marry you, but I wasn't. I need you in my life, Olivia, in the same way these flowers need the sun and rain. I need you to tend me, look after me, snip at me when I try to grow incorrectly."

He smiled at her. "It's been sweet to come back home and be with you, to kiss you, and hold you in my arms. But I want more. I can bring a deeper, richer love to you than what we've shared before. I want that with you. I want to sleep with you, make love to you, wake up with you every day. I want to share breakfast and dinner with you, live in a house full of florals with you."

Warner saw a faint smile play over her lips at that.

He traced a finger down her cheek. "I want to have children with you—little boys who will romp through your garden with rowdy dogs and little girls with blond hair and blue eyes who will carry on the legacy of Fairchild Gardens."

She put a hand to her mouth, tears threatening her eyes now. "You know, those little girls might have dark hair like yours."

"I'll take the risk." He smiled at her, leaning over to kiss her. "What do you say, Olivia? Do you think you could handle the stigma of being married to Weird Warner?"

"Oh, you." She pushed at him and then leaned over to kiss him. Pulling back after a moment, she said, "But what will we do about our different jobs and lives?"

"How about a compromise?" He kept his arms wrapped around her, enjoying the feel of her close against him. "We'll live most of the time in your little house behind the florist shop—at least until we can build a better place—perhaps on the property to the west of the Lily Lake if your Daddy will sell some land to us or maybe across the street by the creek." He touched her face with fondness. "Some of the time, I'll want you to come to stay in New York with me. I think I can work it out with Kite and with my publisher to let me do much of my work from Bryson, but there will be times I need to be in New York—for meetings and business events. I'd like to have you there with me. I'd like you to *want* to share some of my world, too. To go on book tour with me sometimes, to come hear me speak, to accompany me to events I get asked to attend at ritzy places. It would be fun having you there with me."

"What about my florist business?" She dropped her eyes.

"I'd never want you to give it up," he assured her. "Anymore than I'd want you to give up the garden. But both could survive a few weeks without you once in a while, don't you think?"

Her eyes looked out across the garden. "I've hardly ever been anywhere, except to take a short vacation or two with mother and daddy long ago." She smiled. "Even then we usually traveled to some famous garden that Mother hungered to see."

"I remember." He grinned. "A lot of the places we might travel to also have gardens, but there are other interesting and beautiful things in the world. I'd like to broaden your experiences. I'd like to be the one you share new things with and make new discoveries with."

"I think I'd like to see more of the world." She gave him one of those smiles that lit her eyes and took his breath away. "And I'd love it to be you I share those things with."

"I hope that means you're saying yes to my proposal." He pulled her closer, looking into her eyes now. "And I hope you love me, too. I'd like to hear those words from you."

She met his gaze, her eyes soft. "Surely you know I love you, Warner Zachery. I have since we were children—since we first kissed and danced right here in this garden."

"We'll be happy, Olivia, I promise." Warner wrapped her in his arms again, finding her mouth and showing her with all his heart how much he loved her. He knew he possessed more confidence and skill now than in the younger years when he'd first kissed her. He wielded that skill with artistry and soon had Olivia offering him sweet moans and sighs in reward, hooking her arms around him and pulling him close against her with the discovery of heating desire. It felt wonderful.

"With your passion for flowers and growing things, I always figured you'd be an earthy, hands-on lover," he whispered in her ear.

She nuzzled her lips into his neck. "I want you to teach me everything, Warner."

"I look forward to it." He gathered her into his arms again. "And I will definitely talk to your father soon."

She gave him a small smile. "Perhaps he won't feel so reluctant to ask Helen to marry him now."

He smiled back at her. "And perhaps you won't feel so reluctant to leave him. That worried you before."

She nodded, remembering.

Reveling in this happy time, Warner asked, "What time can I pick you up for the dance on Friday? I know you probably need to go early, being on the committee, but I don't mind to go early with you. Perhaps I can help."

He watched a small frown move over her face. "I already told everyone I was coming to the dance without a date." She twisted her hands. "You see, Brody asked me—assuming I would go with him—and it was awkward because I didn't want to. So I told everyone I planned to come by myself, that I thought it would be good if not everyone came in couples." She refused to look at him directly. "You know, because others might come to the reunion alone—single, not married, or divorced."

Warner listened to her words, tensing as he heard her babble the words with nervousness. "Let me see if I understand this right." He stopped her. "Even though we're getting married and basically are engaged now, you still want to go to the dance on your own without me?"

She squirmed in her seat. "Well, we haven't actually announced to anyone that we're engaged yet, and no one really knows we've been seeing each other seriously. And since I told everyone I would come by myself I think I should still do that." She paused, thinking. "But, of course, we could dance together." She gave him a tentative smile over those last words.

He stood up. "I don't believe this, Olivia Benton. You've just accepted my proposal of marriage and, yet, you're still worrying more about what your peer group might think if you go to the reunion dance with me than what I might think."

"It's not that." She looked up at him. "Don't you understand? It's only that I already made a big point about how I intended to come by myself."

"So?" He backed up a step. "You weren't engaged to marry when you told them that. And who cares what they think anyway?"

Her mouth tightened. "I don't know why you're so upset. What difference does it make if we go to the dance together or separately?" She crossed her arms. "We'll both be going, and soon we'll be getting married and spending the rest of our lives together."

He lost his patience. "Actually, it makes a lot of difference." Warner backed up a few more steps, starting down the stairs out of the gazebo. "I'm not marrying anyone who is ashamed to stand up in front of her friends to say she loves me or who would deny me the privilege of taking her to our tenth year class reunion dance." Warner ran a hand through his hair. "How could you even think I could understand such a thing?"

She stood, twisting her hands again. "Well, if it's that important to you, I guess maybe I could try to explain to everyone why I changed my mind …."

He shook his head, furious now. "I can't believe I'm standing here having this conversation with you—listening to you give me excuses again about why you don't want to go to a dance with me. You did this same thing ten years ago. I actually let you convince me then that the nonsense you came up with about why you couldn't go to that dance with me was sensible."

"Warner, it's not the same—"

"Yes, it is, and that's sad." Warner grabbed both of her arms and locked eyes with her. "Well, here's my change in plans, Olivia Benton. You don't need to explain to all your friends why you changed your mind. I've changed mine. I'm going alone to the dance. Maybe I'll see you there."

Upset now, she moved closer to him, tears seeping out of her eyes.

Unmoved, he turned and stomped out of the gazebo.

"Warner!" She cried as he stalked away. "Don't leave like this. You're making too much of this. It's not like what you're saying, honestly …."

He stopped, turning back to glare at her. "No, Olivia, it's *exactly* like what I'm saying." He clenched his fists. "How do you think I'll feel Friday night, watching you dance with other men, keeping our love a secret once more? Knowing you're too ashamed to step forward and let people know how you feel about me?" He kicked at a rock on the path. "I'm sure, also, it will be much too embarrassing for you to find a way to tell your friends you've decided to marry Weird Warner. Isn't that really what this is all about?"

With that, he headed out of the garden, too angry to care that Olivia stood weeping on the steps of the gazebo behind him.

CHAPTER 23

Looking in the mirror on Friday evening, Olivia wondered how she'd made it through the week. She zipped up the sleek, sapphire dress and slipped into simple silver flats she'd found to wear with it. They shimmered with glitter, making a pretty match to the sparkling silver pendant and earrings she'd chosen to wear.

Yet all the joy about going to the dance had fled after she and Warner argued earlier in the week. She'd never imagined he would be so upset about not going to a reunion dance with her.

"Why should that matter so much to him?" she asked Sybil, who sat curled up on a side chair, watching her, seeming to sense that Olivia was upset. "To me it's only a school dance following six months of hard work, a time to welcome back our old graduating class."

Patti, going to the dance with Barry tonight, had chattered about the event all week, not helping Olivia feel any better. "I didn't attend many fancy dances growing up," she said apologetically at one point. "It probably doesn't seem like such a big deal to you like it does to me."

Wanda laughed. "You're right about that. Olivia's been going to gazillions of proms and dances since only a little girl. She's usually the reigning beauty queen at every event, too, wearing some sort of fancy crown and sash, riding down the streets of Bryson City in some parade Cadillac waving her little hand." She illustrated the wave as she talked, blowing kisses as to a crowd. "We both ought to hate her for it, but she's so nice it's hard to."

Wanda's words shocked her. Growing up, she'd despised being singled out so often for recognition. She'd known others resented her sometimes for winning so many awards, even for being pretty, but hearing Wanda teasing her about it hurt.

Remembering Wanda's words, she looked in the mirror at herself. "Is that the way it is with Warner?" she asked into the quiet of her room. "Is that how he feels about me? I hope not."

She closed her eyes on a small wave of pain, remembering again how he'd stalked away. "I've tried to get in touch with him all week to set things right, Sybil. To explain everything better. To say I'd go to the dance with him if it meant that much to him. To tell him I was sorry to ever suggest I wouldn't go. But he wouldn't answer my calls or any of the notes I left. He's avoided me all week. I don't know what else to do."

Olivia let her hand drift idly over the cat's soft back and then rose to pace the room. "It hasn't helped that I've hardly had three minutes to myself since that awful night. I've been so busy at work this week with two unexpected funerals to do, and I had to get together with the committee every day in order to finish up everything for the reunion. I couldn't simply drop my work or obligations." She looked out the window toward the gardens. "Yesterday, I was over at the Hemlock Inn nearly all day decorating—putting potted plants and ribbons on all the tables, hanging banners and tying silk flowers onto all the individual favors. Then today, I worked all day at the school decorating for the dance."

Even worse, of course, no one knew she had heart sorrows going on at all. With Warner so angry, she hardly wanted to tell anyone he'd proposed. She wasn't sure he even wanted to marry her now. The way he acted before he left, it didn't look good. Knowing it was expected, she'd smiled through her busy activities the whole week but felt sick on the inside.

Her dad hadn't helped things, either. He raced in after work to change clothes this afternoon, telling Olivia he and Helen planned to drive down to Franklin again for dinner. "Who's taking you to the dance?"

"I'm going by myself."

He looked stunned. "You mean no one asked you to go with them?"

"No, that's not it." She felt annoyed with him. "Brody asked me and Warner did later, but I thought it would be better if some of us didn't attend in couples. A lot of the class coming won't be paired up."

He snorted. "So you decided to be one of those not paired up? That doesn't make sense to me, Olivia. To be frank, I rather hoped you and Warner were beginning to develop some feelings for each other. He's shown a lot of interest in you while he's been in town."

She snapped back at him. "I thought you didn't like Warner, Daddy. You and Grandmother Lila always warned me away from him in the past."

Looking surprised, he answered, "That was when you were both kids. You've grown up since then." He rummaged in the refrigerator looking for a snack. "I never disliked Warner Zachary. I just worried about him. The boy didn't seem to have a clue who he was or what he wanted to be—always flaunting authority, going against the grain, causing problems for his parents. I worried he might have a negative influence on you."

"Is that so?" She knew her tone sounded sarcastic.

He turned to look at her. "What's the matter with you, girl? Are you wishing now you'd decided to accept a date for this dance?"

She saw a worry line forming in his forehead. "Perhaps I am, Daddy." She attempted a smile.

"Well, I doubt you'll lack for partners at the dance anyway, pretty girl like you." He patted her cheek. "You just set your mind to have a good time, and I'm sure you will."

He made it sound so simple. "I'll do that."

Checking her watch now and realizing it was time to go, Olivia felt sad her father wasn't here to see her off. He'd always been here in the past. In fact, when she'd been younger, he wouldn't have dreamed of missing a chance to watch her come down the stairs, dressed for a prom or a dance. He always took pictures, saw her off for the evening with hugs. He always wished her a good time and reminded her, or her date, what time she should be home.

Olivia sighed on the memory. "I guess I'm not Daddy's little girl anymore." Picking up her purse, she headed down the stairs.

At the gym, Olivia worked at the registration table, welcoming everyone to the reunion, helping, along with Vickie Leigh and Roberta, to ensure that everyone picked up a tote bag, that all the women received corsages, and that everyone felt welcome, especially those who now lived far from Bryson City.

When the band tuned up at seven, Olivia was still working at the registration table, checking in latecomers. Warner hadn't come and that saddened her. She hoped, even yet, to pull him off to herself and explain everything, to set things right with him, if possible.

Eventually, she closed the registration table, going in to the dance, already in full swing. Roberta, incredible in red, swirled around the dance floor with Russell, and Vickie Leigh, striking in her chartreuse and purple dress, laughed in Logan's arms, looking happy.

Louise ran over, in a swirl of pink, to give Olivia a hug as she came in the room. "Everything's going beautifully, don't you think? I checked the refreshment table again. Mrs. Belcher is doing a nice job taking care of everything. I'm going to dance with Rob now and have some fun."

Louise twirled away, laughing with Rob. Olivia stood by the dance floor a moment, enjoying her classmates dancing to a favorite song from their high school years. Soon, Carl Wheeler, an old school friend now living in Georgia, came to swing her onto the floor. Her father was right that she didn't lack for partners at the dance. She had fun catching up and talking with old friends she hadn't seen in many years.

Brody, still annoyed with her about refusing his invitation, had danced by her several times with other partners—making a point of letting her see how pleased they were to swing around the floor in his arms. At a pause between dance numbers, he came across the floor to find her. "About ready to dance?"

Seeing no reason to further annoy him, Olivia let him lead her out to the floor. An old fast song from their school days filled the room with its familiar words and sounds, and many of Olivia's classmates began singing along.

She was laughing over an old story Brody reminded her of when she glanced over to the gym doorway to see Warner leaning against the wall, watching her. She almost missed a step looking his way. He wore a formal tux, so different from anything she'd ever seen him in before, and he looked fabulous.

Seeing her attention shift away, Brody followed her eyes. "Well, well. Looks like our New York City slicker decided to drop in." He gave a mean laugh, and Olivia caught a little scent of alcohol on his breath. "Fancy clothes or not, to me he's still Weird Warner and always will be."

"No, you're wrong." Olivia scowled, tensing her hand in his. "He's not weird, and he never was. He simply walked to a different drummer. He had talents and gifts we weren't ready to see. High school is a narrow time with too much emphasis on fitting in and conforming. I'm not proud, looking back, to remember how little I understood that."

He sneered at her. "Be careful or you'll start getting weird, too." Brody gave her a mock bow as the dance ended. "I'll see you later."

As another dance began, Olivia hoped Warner would come and ask her to dance but, with disappointment, she watched him walk across the room to a tall brunette in a canary yellow dress. A few minutes later, Warner led her onto the dance floor, the two laughing and talking. Andrea Stapleton, now sleek and pretty, and a designer in Winston-Salem, North Carolina, had been one of the odd Goth girls in high school, always dressed in black, wearing combat boots to school and never really fitting in well with the high school culture.

"Who's that Warner Zachery is dancing with?" Vickie Leigh walked by with a cup of punch from the refreshment table. "Could that be Awful Andrea? The girl that always slumped in the back of the room in our algebra class?"

"Andrea Stapleton." Olivia clarified. "She runs her own design firm in Winston-Salem."

"Wow. Then she and Warner would make a good match—both so successful. She's turned out gorgeous, too, hasn't she?" Vickie giggled. "Some of our graduates make us small town girls look a little dowdy now, don't they?"

A prickle of jealousy ran up Olivia's spine at the words.

Logan walked up to grab Vickie's hand. "Come on. Put that punch cup down and let's dance, Vickie Leigh. This is one of my favorite songs."

They moved onto the dance floor, and another partner came to seek Olivia out.

The evening moved on like this, Olivia dancing consistently but never with Warner. Just like at senior prom, they acted as thought they hardly knew each other. Olivia felt sick over it.

"Okay, time for a pause." Roberta took the microphone, smiling at everyone from the small stage in front of the band. "I want to welcome everyone who came for the dance tonight and let you know how glad we are to see you—especially those of you from out of state we see too seldom." She began to give thanks to people who'd helped with the reunion and made a few announcements about upcoming events for the weekend.

"Now we're going to bring up our Senior Prom King and Senior Prom Queen from ten years ago." Amid applause and catcalls Russell Simmons and Olivia found their way to a spot below the front of the stage.

Roberta put up a hand for attention. "To start off our next waltz, we're going to let the Prom King and Prom Queen select the partner of their choice and then lead off the dance for a few special moments before the rest of us join in."

Olivia almost smiled, knowing this was Roberta's way of taking center stage with Russell in front of everyone, versus she and Russell—the Prom King and Prom Queen—dancing together as tradition. However, as Russell bowed before Roberta and took her hand, Olivia realized she needed to select a partner for the dance, too.

Frantic for a moment, her eyes scanned the room, and then she smiled, knowing exactly what she'd do. After all, the band was playing Whitney Houston's "I Will Always Love You." What could be more appropriate?

With the grace and poise learned over a lifetime, Olivia walked slowly across the room, the strobe ball glittering over her, spotlighting her, to stop in front of Warner.

He studied her, tense, his eyes locked onto hers.

Making a small curtsy, she held out her hand, smiling. "I've always loved you, Warner Zachery. Do you think I could have this dance?" Olivia offered the words softly, but they were spoken loudly enough for most everyone to hear and to start a buzz of speculation moving around the room.

Nodding, Warner put his hand in hers and waltzed her out onto the floor, gliding her with smooth steps around the old gym, circling Roberta and Russell, while all their classmates stood watching.

"You've done it now, Olivia Benton." Warner looked down at her with dreamy blue eyes, a small smile touching his lips.

"I hope so." She found his eyes with hers. "I'm sorry about the other night."

He glanced away.

"I tried to call; I came by several times …."

"I know," he said at last. "I wasn't ready to revisit the issue yet. I still felt angry."

"And now?" She leaned into him, tucking her head against his neck, letting her lips skim over his cheek.

"Now you're driving me crazy," he whispered.

She giggled a little. "We could ask them to play that song. Most bands know old classics like Patsy Cline's."

"I'll bribe them to play it if I have to." He whirled her around with practiced steps, others now joining the two couples on the dance floor.

"Well, it's about time," Barry said, as he swung by them with Patti, pretty in her rich magenta dress.

Olivia's eyes followed them. "It's good to see Patti smiling and happy."

"It's good to see you smiling and happy." Warner's arm tightened around her back, pulling her a little closer. "You look beautiful tonight. I thought I'd die of jealousy watching those other men dance with you."

"Hmmm." She offered him a look of wide-eyed innocence. "I couldn't tell from all the girls I saw you swinging around."

He grinned. "I wanted to make you jealous and show you what a good dancer I've become."

"It worked." She managed a teasing smile. "I especially saw green when you danced Andrea Stapleton out on the floor."

"Hasn't she become a stunner?" He glanced across the room to where she danced with another out-of-town classmate.

"Yes." She heaved a sigh.

Warner kissed her forehead. "But no one here is more dazzling than you, Olivia Benton. I remember watching you become more beautiful every year as we grew up and thinking you were like the flowers in your garden, blooming into greater and greater loveliness."

She leaned against his chest. "You'll turn my head with those romantic words."

"I hope so." He laughed. "I like flirting with you."

"This is wonderful, isn't it Warner?" She looked up at him with her heart in her eyes.

"Yes, it is," he said, sweeping her around in another turn.

They mingled with friends after the dance, with Warner's old friends and with many of Olivia's. It was a joyous time for Olivia.

She and Warner danced several sets and Warner did eventually lure the band to play "Crazy" just for them. Half the room sang along with the old classic as the words seduced them all. Even Roberta warmed up a little to the occasion.

"I might have been wrong about Warner," she said quietly to Olivia as Warner talked to Leonard and Barry. "He might be more of a Bryson City boy than I thought. Maybe you'd better keep an eye on him after all." She glanced around the room. "And keep a watchful eye on Brody, too. He isn't happy over this."

She swept away then, leaving Olivia to scan the room looking for Brody. However, she didn't see him.

Warner slid up to her, slipping an arm around her waist. "Want some punch? I'll go grab us a glass if you do before the next set starts."

She nodded and watched him work his way through the crowd toward the refreshment table. She shook hands and talked with a few old classmates while he was gone, and then stepped back from the dance floor as the band returned and struck up another number.

"That's one of my favorites," a voice said beside her. "Let's dance, Olivia. It's my turn now."

Brody pulled her onto the dance floor, swinging her into a sultry dance move to an old Eurythmics number "Sweet Dreams Are Made of This."

She tried to pull free of his hand as he moved closer, closer than she liked. "Brody, Warner went to get me some punch. He'll be looking for me."

"Let him look, the loser." His words slurred as he spoke.

Olivia, feeling worried, tried to redirect the conversation. "This evening's been fun, hasn't it, with everyone back together again for the dance?" She sidled a little away from him as she talked. "I'm sure everyone will make more good memories tomorrow, too."

He took her hand and jerked her closer again. "You should have come with me tonight, Olivia. I don't like seeing you make a fool of yourself with that Zachery nerd."

With his hand gripping her arm too tightly, she tried to pull away. "You're hurting me," she whispered, trying not to draw too much attention as she struggled to get free.

"I think you heard the lady." Warner appeared beside them, stepping closer to take her free hand. "And I *don't* think Olivia wants to dance with you anymore."

Brody scowled. "Oh, you don't do you? And what business is it of yours?" He swung at Warner then, slugging him in the jaw.

Even as a collected gasp moved around the room, Warner was quick to respond, belting Brody back this time with confident ease, knocking him to the gym floor and bloodying his eye.

"Warner, please!" Olivia cried in distress, seeing Brody sprawled on the gym floor, bleeding from both his nose and eye. "He was just being Brody. You know how he is …"

Fists still raised, Warner turned to her. "You're defending him, Olivia?"

The question echoed around the room, since the band had stopped playing when the fighting started.

She struggled to think what to say. "I don't want this evening ruined."

He shook his head, looking around. "Well, it's too late for that. But see if you can find a little more fun after I'm gone." He turned and walked out the back door.

Stunned, Olivia stood rooted to the spot for a few minutes trying to take the whole situation in.

"Dang, he's got a mean right," Brody grumbled, as Russell pulled him off the floor to his feet.

"Friend, you've been hitting the bottle too hard to start a fight like that at our reunion." Russell put an arm around him. "Let's go get you cleaned up and find you a cup of coffee in one of the vending machines."

Roberta waved the band back into action as Russell and Brody walked away, turning to the crowd with a laugh as she did. "Now, what would a school dance be like without a little fist fight among the boys?" She laughed again, shooing everyone back to the dance floor as a hip-hop tune started up.

Logan and Vicki Leigh helped to further smooth over the situation by prancing onto the dance floor in a series of outrageous moves that soon had the audience laughing and then following them around the floor in a conga line.

Walking by Olivia, Roberta lifted a brow. "Honey, you might want to go after that man that just chivalrously tried to defend your honor."

Her words woke Olivia from her stupor and she started in the direction she'd seen Warner go. She hurried through the hallway, looking for him. "Warner?"

Opening the main doorway to the parking lot, she saw with dismay the taillights of his Mercedes heading into the night.

Leaning against the door, she closed her eyes, trying to hold back her tears. "Oh, no. Not again. Couldn't one special moment go right just once?"

Barry found her. "Come back inside, Olivia. Let Warner cool down." He led her through the hallway. "You can call him later, or I will."

Slipping back into the gym, Olivia made an effort to be polite and help smooth over the earlier events. But the dance was spoiled for her.

Her mind only on Warner, she left as soon as she gracefully could, not staying until the end of the dance. Parking her car in the driveway at Benton House, she headed through the garden and across the yard to Warner's apartment. She found his car gone and the apartment dark with not even a light burning. Climbing the outside stairs anyway, she knocked on the door, but no one answered.

Panicked, she headed across the drive and up the front walk to Warner's parents' house.

His grandfather came to the door. "Olivia?"

"Is Warner here?" She twisted her hands, knowing it late to drop by. "He left the dance a little early, and I need to talk to him."

He gave Olivia a sympathetic look. "Warner's gone back to New York."

"What? ..." Olivia struggled to hold back her tears.

A frown creased the old man's brow. "Warner's Grandfather Delacourt had a stroke this evening. His mother and father flew out earlier, shortly after the word came. Warner packed and left as soon as he came home from the dance. He's driving back."

"Oh, I'm so sorry." She gave him a small smile. "Please tell everyone we'll be praying. I sincerely hope he recovers without any problems. Warner's always talked so fondly of him."

He nodded. "I'll tell the family you said that. Thank you."

She tried to think what else to say.

"I hope you both had a good time at the dance. I didn't really have time to get a report from Warner." He shrugged. "The boy had his cell phone off, and we couldn't reach him earlier when the bad news came, but as soon as he learned about his grandfather, he hit his apartment packing."

She smiled. "Thank you, Mr. Zachery. I'm sorry to knock on your door so late at night."

"Think nothing of it, dear. I was still up—what with all the excitement."

Giving him a little wave, she headed back down the sidewalk, cut across the side yard by the garage, and started toward her house. As she passed by Warner's apartment again, she looked up at the dark windows and started to cry.

"He'll never come back now." Her voice caught on the words. "Not after what happened tonight and not after this." She cried the whole way back to the house, cutting through the dark garden as she returned. But the beauty around her offered no comfort and the fragrance of the roses on the air only made her sadder.

CHAPTER 24

Over a month passed before Warner drove back into Bryson City. October's rich fall colors now bathed the mountain slopes in red, gold, and yellow, and along Everett Street straw-stuffed scarecrows, fat pumpkins, and harvest wreaths decorated the storefronts. Turning off Everett, Warner drove down a side street to Barry's shop, parking his car neatly by the curb. He'd missed Barry and Patti's dress rehearsal and dinner on Friday night, but at least he'd arrived in time for the wedding on Sunday afternoon.

Letting himself into the shop, Warner found Barry leaning over a dismantled computer on his desk. "Hey, Barry." He moved around the desk to hug his friend.

Barry looked up with his familiar sideways grin, pushing his glasses up his nose. "Warner, glad to see you got here."

"You know I wouldn't miss your wedding." He propped against the counter. "After all, I'm the best man."

Barry picked up a tool to probe into the computer. "Leonard said to tell you he was okay about that since I'd known you longer than him. He's consoled being a groomsman."

"Your older brother coming in?" he asked. "And your parents?"

"Yep." Barry tapped a few keys to see if the adjustment he'd made resolved the problem. "Everyone will be here by tonight."

"I'll be glad to see your folks. I've only seen them once or twice since your dad got transferred from the area after high school."

"They'll be glad to see you, too." Satisfied with his adjustments to the computer, Barry started to reassemble it.

Warner picked up a wire to twiddle with while he talked. "Sorry I couldn't get down for the rehearsal and the dinner afterward."

"It's all right. We knew you and your grandmother were moving your grandfather back home from the nursing home." He sorted through a pile of tools to find the one he needed. "How's he doing?"

"Restless with lying around so much, but glad to get out of the nursing home and out of therapy." Warner chuckled. "He gave them what-for over there."

Barry laughed. "I've always heard doctors are the worst patients."

"That's true, and psychiatrists try to analyze everyone on staff."

"I'm sure they loved that." Barry glanced up at Warner. "Did he do a little analysis on you while you hung around his bedside?"

"What else could he do with all that time?" Warner rubbed his neck.

"Hope it did you some good." Barry tightened a small screw.

"Maybe." Warner changed the subject. "How did the court visit with Rich go last week?"

This time Barry smiled. "Good. The judge was pleased with Rich's progress and with the positive reports from his school, his counselor, and the sheriff. The upcoming marriage between Patti and me—and what the judge called new stability for Rich—helped, too. He gave Rich community service, as expected, town clean-up projects to suit the crimes, and some strong warnings." His focus shifted back to the computer. "With no further problems, this will go off Rich's record at eighteen."

"Sounds like that went well." Warner handed Barry a tool just out of his reach. "I'm sure you're eager to settle in as a family. Are you and Patti still driving down to the Gulf Coast for a little honeymoon time?"

"Yeah. And thanks for working out that condo visit for us through your friend in the publishing company."

Warner shrugged. "Stanton hardly ever uses his condo there, and he gave me a good deal on it for a wedding gift for you." He shifted the subject again. "Who is Rich staying with while you're gone?"

"Olivia's staying over at Patti's house with him." He leaned closer to the computer to work with a small wire. "She's talking about renting the place after Patti moves out."

"She told me." He glanced out the window. "Has she told her dad about this move?"

Barry shook his head. "Patti says she's waiting until it's closer to the time for her to move in, in case she gets some argument from him. She seems purposed to move though and to clear the way for her father to propose to Helen."

"You like Helen?"

"She's a little fancy for my tastes, but a nice enough woman from all I can see. She seems to really care for Olivia's father." He swapped tools again. "You talked to Olivia yet?"

"I stopped here as soon as I got into town."

Barry raised an eyebrow. "That isn't what I asked? Have you phoned her?"

Warner turned away to study a display, uncomfortable with Barry's questions. "I felt like the things I need to say to her are better said in person."

"Hard man." Barry leaned back into the computer.

"Well, it was my call." Warner glanced at his watch. "I'd better go. I have several people to see before I head out to see the family." He pulled an envelope from his pocket. "The Delacourt family sent you and Patti a wedding gift—a little money to spend on your honeymoon."

Barry eyed the envelope. "I imagine the check is overly generous, especially from folks not my family."

Warner grinned. "They said they liked you when you visited in New York."

Pushing the envelope to the side, Barry picked up another tool. "Sorry to keep working while you dropped in, Warner, but I'm trying to get everything done so I can close the store next week."

"It's okay. I'll see you at the wedding tomorrow." He glanced toward the window. "Looks like good weather for an outdoor event."

"Yeah, and it was good of Olivia to let us hold the wedding at the Pavilion at the Fairchild Gardens. Nicer for Patti than a tent set up in my backyard." He rubbed at a kink in his neck. "Patti and Olivia have been out there all day today decorating and helping the caterer set things up. Pretty place. I drove out earlier at lunch. Even in October, there are flowers in bloom—roses in pathways near the pavilion, water lilies on the lake, azaleas in bloom in big groupings. I know Olivia will miss that place."

"Yeah." Warner frowned. "Well, I'd better go." He gave Barry a pat on the back and let himself out the door.

He climbed back in the car and then headed down a side road leading to Ray Benton's medical clinic. He had a few things he wanted to say to the man, and he hoped he'd find him in.

Later, at the end of a long day, Warner finally found an opportunity to check his e-mail, call Grandmother Delacourt to check on his grandfather, and jump in the shower. Pulling on a pair of jeans and a worn Henley shirt, he sat down at the computer again to work.

At nearly seven o'clock, he grabbed a hoodie to pull on over his shirt and headed across the yard to the gate into the Fairchild Gardens. If luck was with him, Olivia would be checking the pavilion a final time before dark fell to see that everything was as it should be for the wedding of her friend tomorrow.

Warner cut past the fountain, walked down a pathway between an array of October flowers—late roses, clumps of chrysanthemums, and daisy-like cosmos. Merging through the gateway on the west end of the garden, Warner followed a familiar winding path around the Lily Lake toward the pavilion. Rounding a corner, he spotted Olivia sitting on a rustic bench by the lake.

Hearing him on the path, she looked up, her eyes widening in surprise.

"Sitting here staring out over the lake and dreading seeing me tomorrow?" He stopped by the bench.

A smile twitched at her mouth. "Yes, in a way," she answered honestly. Remembering her manners, she asked then, "How's your grandfather?"

"Better." He sat down on the bench beside her, crossing an ankle over his knee. "Grandmother and I took him home from the nursing home Thursday afternoon. They'd scheduled him for release earlier, but the doctor didn't sign off." He scowled. "You know how those things go. It was dinner before we got him home, and I wanted to be sure he was settling in well before I headed out of New York. So I missed the rehearsal."

"At the wedding you walk out to stand by Barry and the minister in a tuxedo. I think you'll figure it out without the rehearsal run." A smile tugged at the corner of her mouth again, and then she sighed.

"I should have called you, Olivia."

"Yes." She twisted her hands. "I ran after you, but you'd already left. Then I came to your place after the dance, but you'd gone to New York."

"Granddad told me you came by and seemed upset."

She looked away from him, toward the shadows along the lake. "I didn't mean to champion Brody over you at the dance. I simply didn't want blood and fighting at the reunion—and especially over me."

"Yes, I know. You like everything to go nicely."

She turned to him in annoyance. "Is that so wrong?"

"No, but life doesn't always work out that way. Things don't always turn out nice, and people don't always act nice."

Her temper flared. "And this lecture coming from Mr. Nice who hasn't even bothered to call me in almost a month? The same man who walked out of the dance mad at me, creating a big spectacle?" She scooted further away from him on the bench, her breathing escalating with her words.

He watched her. "I heard the rest of the reunion, the breakfast and the awards dinner all went well. Leonard filled me in."

Olivia leaned her head back, closing her eyes. "Why are you here?"

"We have some unfinished business between us."

She sighed. "And what is that?"

"It seems to me we have a wedding to talk about for ourselves."

He heard her deep intake of breath, watched her turn her eyes to his. "Don't play games with me. I'm not in the mood."

Warner laced his hands in his lap. "I had a lot of time to think while sitting with my grandfather in the hospital and at the nursing home." He chuckled. "Grandfather Delacourt kept his patient analysis skills up to date giving me what-for during these last weeks. Showing me all the ways I wasn't letting go of things in the past I needed to let go of … and showing me all the ways I was goofing up my future by not embracing new opportunities life was presenting me."

She considered this. "And which one of these am I, Warner, one of those things you need to let go of or one of those new opportunities you need to embrace?"

"Nice word: embrace." He moved closer, grinning. "I always think about words like embracing and kissing and loving when I'm around you."

"You're toying with me." She eyed him warily.

"At the dance you called it flirting." He scooted closer.

Olivia edged away again. "You're going to push me off this bench."

"Then quit moving away from me." He scooped her into his arms and kissed her.

"Oh, what are you doing, Warner Zachery?" She sighed the words into his neck after they'd kissed until both of their hearts thrummed in their ears. "This only makes it worse when you leave again."

"I'm not leaving again without you, Olivia Benton."

She lifted shocked eyes to his. "Warner, I told you before I cannot move to live in New York City with you. I have roots here."

"So?" He leaned back, holding her loosely in his arms so he could look down at her. "I'm putting down some roots here, too. I've bought a business in the area, and I'm negotiating the sale of a big house with a garden in the back of it."

She put a hand on his chest and fixed her gaze on him, her eyes narrowing. "I've spent a long wretched month with you gone. Don't you dare play games with me about this."

He laughed and kissed her forehead. "I missed you too, and having to be away from you helped me to see that I had to come back—and that I need to stick around to have those babies with you we talked about."

"Oh, Warner, you crazy man. I hope you mean that, and if you don't kiss me right this minute after saying that, I'm kissing you."

Warner obliged, loving the feel of her in his arms, loving the scent of her mixed with the fragrance of flowers on the night breeze.

She snuggled against his chest afterward. "I'd so dreaded the wedding tomorrow and felt so guilty for doing so. I knew you planned to come, and I didn't know how I could get through the day, smiling and acting polite and pretending everything was all right when it wasn't."

He kissed her nose. "You've spent a lot of your life doing that, haven't you? Doing the right thing, doing what was expected of you? Being nice and polite—and often keeping your real feelings locked inside."

She raised her eyes at him in question.

"Some of Grandfather Delacourt's wise counsel." He hugged her against him. "He said both of us have allowed ourselves to care too much about other people's opinions, often suppressing our real selves."

Olivia smiled at him. "What else did Grandfather Delacourt say?"

"He said one of our problems was that we hadn't ever experienced a proper or normal courtship, that instead we'd shared this secret love only we knew about." Warner considered his next words. "Grandfather said none of our friends or family could respond to us in a genuine fashion because we weren't being genuine and upfront about our relationship before the world. He suggested we do a little normal courting before all our friends and associates here in Bryson City. Let them know we care about each other. Let them see us obviously in love and showing that love in public. He advised that we should let our friends and family enjoy watching us become a couple, rejoice with us in getting engaged, and then anticipate coming to our wedding."

She traced a hand softly down his cheek. "Remind me to give your grandfather a big hug the next time I see him."

"I'll do that." He kissed her fingers. "Will you be my Bryson City sweetheart, Olivia Benton? Will you go out with me to the movies, to dinner, to happenings around town? Will you walk the downtown streets holding hands with me? Let me steal a kiss sometimes, even when someone might see? Will you let me show you and Bryson City my romantic side?"

"I think I'm liking the sound of this." She leaned in to kiss him again. "I've been so scared I'd have to learn to live without you again. I cried myself to sleep so many times these last weeks, Warner, it's a wonder I don't have huge dark circles under my eyes."

Warner kissed her eyelids. "I see no dark circles. Just two beautiful eyes I love."

She giggled. "I think I'm going to like seeing this romantic side of you."

He sent her a steamy look. "Honey, you ain't seen nothin' yet."

Laughing, she moved into his arms again. Then after a few minutes, she pulled back, a question in her eyes. "Warner, what did you mean about buying a business here in Bryson City?"

He leaned back against the bench. "I bought Gil's Bookstore."

"You what?" Her eyes shot open.

"Leonard and Barry kept telling me I needed to buy a business in Bryson if I wanted to be a legitimate and respectable citizen. When I learned Gil wanted to retire, I decided a bookstore was just the thing for a writer. My accountant agreed. He drew up an offer, reviewed all the contracts, and helped to finalize the sale." Warner picked up a twig from the ground to play with it in his hands.

"Gil has agreed to continue working part-time at the store for a time, and two of the women working there now plan to stay on. Gil and I are talking to my brother Dean's wife Lisa about possibly coming on board to potentially manage the store. Dean's salary as a teacher and coach isn't that great and her education and background was in retail management. She even worked in a bookstore while in college. Her two children, Abigail and Kenton, are both in school now. Lisa's been itching for something to do."

Olivia thought about this. "I like Lisa. I think that will be a good choice." She clasped her hands together. "This is wonderful, Warner. Everyone worried Gil's might not remain a bookstore when sold, and it's the only bookstore we have in town. Will you keep the name?"

"For now." He ran a hand up her arm, enjoying the realization that he'd be able to touch her and hold her whenever he wanted. That she'd really be his.

She straightened his shirt, tucking a stray hair behind his ear, as if enjoying the same idea. Then a little scowl touched her forehead. "Warner, what did you mean about that other thing you said—you know, about negotiating the sale of a big house with a garden? Surely you wouldn't buy a house for the two of us without letting me look at it first. What if I don't like it? I want us to always make big decisions together if we're going to get married, especially ones that affect both of us. I think that's important."

He smoothed the scowl on her forehead with his finger. "Olivia, I talked to your father about buying Benton House today when I went to tell him I wanted to marry you."

She gave him an anguished look. "Oh, Warner, you shouldn't have suggested to Daddy that he give up his home. That isn't right!"

"Olivia, calm down. It was your father's idea."

"What?" She looked stunned.

"He told me the one thing he'd always loved about the house was your mother—and then you." Warner paused. "He said he'd always hoped you might marry so he could let you have the house and move out. He wants to live in town with Helen." He managed a teasing smile. "You were right that he wants to propose to her. But he knows Helen isn't really fond of Benton House and that she finds the gardens intimidating. The house also speaks too much of your mother Margaret in every nook and corner. Helen finds that difficult, too. Ray says he doesn't want Helen to feel she's always in Margaret's shadow or in the shadow of others who came before Margaret."

Warner looked around. "It's wise of him to see that. This is the home and gardens of the Fairchild women and their descendants. The garden is in their blood. It's not in Helen Allmon's blood."

"I don't know what to say."

Warner put her hand to his lips and kissed it. "Your father wanted to gift the house to you as a wedding gift, but I told him I wanted to share in making that happen. So he agreed to let me buy the house at a reduced cost. That way he and Helen can buy a condo at Hilton Head, something they've been dreaming about."

"What?" Her eyes jerked to his again.

"They'd like to go down to the beach for holidays and maybe partially retire there later on." He grinned at her. "They want their own life, Olivia. Your father told me—and you, if you remember—that he came to Bryson City because of your mother. He really wanted a more active city life, but he wanted your mother more."

She put a hand to her mouth. "I remember him talking about that the time you came to pick me up for Barry's party."

He nodded. "So you don't have to leave your home or your gardens to settle for me."

She slapped at him. "Don't you dare say that, Warner Zachery! You know I told you before, I'd be happy living with you in that little rental of Patti's behind the shop—and you and I both know that's a small house. I also told you I'd travel with you and go to stay in your New York apartment with you when you needed to go to the city for meetings and such."

"So you think maybe you love me more than the gardens?"

"Yes, you silly thing." She leaned forward to dust a kiss across his mouth. "I love you more than anything."

"I'm glad to hear it." He traced his hands through her hair. "I'll need to go to New York about once a month. Kite said I could do most of my work here, but I would need to fly up for monthly meetings related to upcoming publication plans, marketing strategies, and such. My book publisher, Whitehouse Press, said I could schedule my meetings and business with them at the same time." He looked out over the lake. "I wasn't sure I could work everything out, until I talked to them. I had to resolve that before I could make plans here."

"Where will you stay when you go up?"

"I've kept my apartment."

She bit her lip, thinking. "What is your apartment like in New York?"

He laughed. "Not very big compared to Benton House, but nice. It's near restaurants, parks, galleries, theatres, shops, and tourist attractions. I think you'll enjoy exploring New York with me, Olivia … and visiting the other cities and towns we'll travel to."

She turned to look at him with a wistful expression. "It looks like I'm going to have a whole new life."

"Mixed in with your old comfortable life." He stood, offering her his hand. "The most important thing is we'll be together."

She took his hand and stood.

He leaned over to kiss her forehead. "I love you, Olivia Benton."

"I love you, too, Warner Zachery."

Warner glanced toward the darkening sky. "Come on," he said. "Let's go walk to the White Garden. We can tell all the flowers we're getting married and then dance in the twilight."

"Oh, you. As if they would listen."

He turned to her. "Oh, Olivia, surely you, of all people, would agree that all the flowers of the garden, and all the fairies and elves, the birds and frogs, and the insects and butterflies will rejoice with us tonight that we're planning to stay here together as a couple, with them, to love and tend them, and to cherish them all as we will each other."

"Perhaps you're right." She smiled, her eyes dancing. "Will it be all right if we keep the name of the garden Fairchild Gardens for my grandmother who started them?"

"Of course." Holding her hand, they walked through the gate, heading down the pathway toward the White Garden. "But I think we might change the name of the house."

She sent him a teasing look. "To Zachery House?"

"No." He paused beside the pond, thinking. "To something that represents both of us. What about Green Manor?"

She giggled. "That's what we used to call the house and gardens when we played fairies and elves around the grounds when we were little."

"So, do you like it?"

"I love it."

"Oh, Olivia, we're going to be so happy." Warner picked her up and swung her around, laughing in joy with her, the night fragrance of the rose arbor behind them scenting the air like magic.

A Reading Group Guide

DADDY'S GIRL

Lin Stepp

About This Guide

The questions on the following pages are included
to enhance your group's reading of
Lin Stepp's *Daddy's Girl*

DISCUSSION QUESTIONS

1. This book is set in the small mountain town of Bryson City, North Carolina. Many of the places and businesses mentioned in this book are real. Have you ever visited Bryson City? Did you recognize place names in the city or hiking trails in the nearby Smoky Mountains? How do you think life in a small town of this size is different than life in a big city?

2. Olivia Benton and Warner Zachery both grew up in Bryson City. What happens when they meet at the downtown drugstore and what happens later that night in the Fairchild Gardens behind Olivia's home when they meet a second time? How do these encounters show they perceive their pasts differently, and how do they both seem torn between the past and the present?

3. Peer groups play a big role in the lives of all children and especially in the lives of teens. Olivia and Warner belonged to different peer groups. What were these and how were they unique? What are some of the peer groups you remember from your school years? Research findings show that the impacts of peer group definitions continue to follow into the adult years. Do you think this is true?

4. Olivia Benton owns a small town floral shop in downtown Bryson City called Fairgarden Florist. How did she get involved in working with flowers and opening her own business? In contrast, how did Warner become W. T. Zachery, a professional writer and author of the successful Geeky Gilmore books? Many people leave the town or area they grow up in while others stay. What are the advantages and disadvantages of staying in one place most of your life or in traveling and living in many different places?

5. Roberta Simmons toys with Warner's emotions in the drugstore early in the book and mentions Warner's wife's death in a somewhat offhand way. What happened to Warner's wife Nelle? What did you learn about Nelle as the book progressed? What traits in Nelle drew Warner to fall in love with her and to marry her? We never met Nelle, but do you think you would have liked her?

6. Olivia still lives at home with her father Ray Benton, a doctor in Bryson City, when this book begins. Most young people look forward to leaving home right after high school graduation, but Olivia has stayed. What factors and loyalties kept Olivia in Bryson City—and kept her at home with her father? Could you relate to Olivia's love for the Fairchild Gardens behind her home? Have you visited formal gardens like this one depicted in the story?

7. Warner and Olivia grew up next door to each other; Olivia was an only child, but Warner was one of three brothers in a more active and vibrant family. How was Warner different from his brothers Vance and Dean? Warner's artistic bent probably came from his mother, Rena Delacourt Zachery, who is a painter. How does she help Warner with his feelings and understandings as the book progresses? And how are Warner's Delacourt grandparents in New York a help? Family has impacted Olivia's and Warner's lives, as have peer interactions. In what ways do you think families can be both a positive and negative impact on our lives?

8. Patti Headrick and Wanda Baylor work for Olivia at the Fairgarden Florist, and she treasures strong friendships with both women. What did you like about each of these characters? How does Patti, early in the book as an outsider not from Bryson City, see Olivia's interactions with Warner and Olivia's friends in the shop as rude? How does Olivia respond to Patti's observations at the time and then think about them in a different way later? Do

you think friends can help to balance us in our viewpoints and relationships? ... It is obvious, too, from early in the story that Patti has a past she doesn't want to talk about. How do you gradually learn about her past as the book unfolds? How has Patti's past impacted her son Rich's life?

9. Warner has two old friends in Bryson City he has stayed close to—Leonard Goldstein and Barry Jacobs. What did you like about both of these characters? How were both good friends and counselors to Warner? Barry Jacobs reveals early in the book that he is interested in Patti Headrick at Olivia's floral shop. What hinders their relationship from developing? How is Barry a help to Patti and her son Rich as the book moves to a climax and after?

10. Bullying is one of the themes playing through this book. Bullying in schools and workplaces has always been a societal concern, but studies reveal that bullying has dramatically increased, creating serious and often fatal problems, especially among children. How is Richard Headrick a victim of bullying in this book? At what point did you realize that Rich was the vandal causing problems around Bryson City, defacing property and leaving messages like: "Be wary. A vandal stalks where no justice prevails." Why do you think so few interventions were made to help Richard Headrick? How does Warner identify with Rich and his problems and how does Warner help Rich in this story? What situations of bullying have you experienced or observed that have troubled you?

11. Olivia and Warner were first childhood friends and then became sweethearts. However, no one knew they'd fallen in love and that they talked of marriage together in their high school years. Why? What reasons did Olivia give for not making her love for Warner public? Did you feel these reasons were valid? Did Warner? How did Warner look back on his life at a later point and see how

he may have created many of his own problems or, at the least, not made them better by his actions? If Warner and Olivia had married right after high school, do you think they would have been happy?

12. At one point in the book, while sharing a picnic lunch downtown on Island Park by the river, Warner reveals to Olivia how he created the Geeky Gilmore books—his bestselling series of young adult stories about Geeky's struggles with a middle school peer group. When did Warner first begin to write about Geeky? Who encouraged him to turn his childhood stories into books? What character was most like Olivia in the books and which character was most like Warner? Are any other of Warner's friends aware that they might have inspired a character in his books? How do they feel about that?

13. Many of the individuals who inspired the characters in the Geeky Gilmore books pop up in different places throughout this novel. Readers meet the Elite Eight early and different members of Warner's old peer group along the way, including several at Barry's party, like Imogene Vogel, aka Imogenius Vogel—soon to be Leonard's wife—and Frances Rutherford, a prototype for Ella Phant in the Geeky books. How did Imogene and Frances turn the tables on Olivia at the party so that Olivia realized how she and the girls in the Elite Eight used to treat their less popular peers? How did being at that party help Olivia to see she might not have known many of her high school peers outside her own social circle very well? How does Warner tease her about this at the end of the evening?

14. As Olivia and Warner renew their love again, many of the same problems they experienced when they were young rear their heads. How are their problems revealed in the early scene in the Fairchild Gardens and in various scenes after? Why is Warner still harboring

anger at Olivia after all these years? And why is Olivia still angry at Warner? How are these problems resolved in the book? How is Olivia and Warner's hike on Deep Creek Trail, taken one Sunday after church, somewhat of a turning point in the story? What important things did they share with each other that day on the trail?

15. The book title *Daddy's Girl* comes from Olivia's close ties to her father. How is Olivia impacted when she realizes her father has a love interest? What did you think of Helen Allmon and her daughters when they visited at Olivia's family home? What are Olivia's deepest fears about her father possibly marrying Helen? How does Warner help her with these conflicting feelings? Do you think most people are anxious about major changes to their lives as Olivia is?

16. A critical scene occurs in this book when Leonard receives a call at the newspaper that the vandal is holed up in the middle school with a gun. Warner is with him at the time and insists on accompanying him to the scene as soon as he learns it is Richard Headrick at the school. What happens when they arrive? What does Warner do? How are things resolved after? Later, how does Warner address this issue at a PTA meeting at the middle school?

17. Brody Hanks has a crush on Olivia and he resents it when Warner comes back to town, sensing their mutual interest. How does Brody threaten Warner and try to warn him off from seeing Olivia? What happens later at the Fryemont Inn when Brody and Logan Stanley realize Warner and Olivia have been there on a dinner date? What occurs after their fight? At one of their high school reunion meetings toward the end of the book, Brody asks Olivia to go to the reunion dance with him. How does Olivia react to this invitation, and how does Brody respond? At the reunion

dance, how do things come to a head between Brody, Olivia, and Warner?

18. When Olivia runs after Warner, shortly after the fight at the reunion dance, she finds that he's gone home to New York. What caused him to leave so suddenly? Why does Olivia think he will never come back again? Why does Warner wait so long to return to Bryson City, and how do he and Olivia resolve their differences?

19. Discuss and share your favorite things about this novel. Who were your favorite characters? What scenes did you like best? Would this be a book you would recommend to others and why?

Meet the author:

Lin Stepp

CKatie Riley

Dr. Lin Stepp is a native Tennessean, a businesswoman, and an educator. She is an adjunct faculty member at Tusculum College where she teaches research and psychology. Her business background includes over 25 years in marketing, sales, production art, and regional publishing. She has editorial and writing experience in regional magazines and in the academic field. A *New York Times*, *USA Today*, and *Publishers Weekly* bestselling international author, Lin has ten published novels, each set in different locations around the Great Smoky Mountains. Her most recent novels, published by Kensington Publishing are *Welcome Back*, *Saving Laurel Springs*, *Makin' Miracles*, and *Down by the River*. In addition, a short novel "A Smoky Mountain Gift" was included in the Christmas anthology *When the Snow Falls* released by Kensington in 2014. Lin and her husband J.L. also published a Smoky Mountain hiking guide in 2014, distributed through The University of Tennessee Press, *The Afternoon Hiker*, which includes 110 trail descriptions and over 300 color photos. Lin has two grown children, two cats and loves to hike, paint, read, teach, speak and share about her writing. She enjoys keeping up with her readers on Facebook and Twitter and on her website at: *www.linstepp.com*